HERC'S MERCS: THE COLLECTION

VOLUME 3

ARI MCKAY

CONTENTS

NO PAIN, NO GAIN

ROOM FOR ONE MORE

NO PAIN, NO GAIN

HERC'S MERCS #7

Note: This book deals with someone suffering from PTSD.

The subject of PTSD is a serious one. We have known combat veterans who have suffered from their experiences in wartime, as well as other people who have survived traumatic situations such as physical, sexual, mental, and emotional abuse. For every person who has suffered trauma, the way back to themselves is different. Many are helped by counseling. Others need different kinds of therapy or medical intervention. Some find their own coping mechanisms, be they positive or negative. And, unfortunately, some never make it all.

We have tried to portray PTSD realistically. It is not our intent to in any way diminish what anyone has experienced or to claim BDSM is a solution for all cases. Obviously, it isn't. But for some, it is their way of dealing with their experiences and of finding a way through their pain. Just as everyone's pain is personal, so is their journey to healing.

Hunter's journey is fictional, but if you or anyone you know needs help dealing with the real effects of PTSD, we urge you to seek the help you need. There are many resources available, and you are not alone.

https://www.ptsd.va.gov/public/where-to-get-help.asp

PROLOGUE

"Hey Able, look at this!"

Hunter Callahan, also known as Able, looked across the tent to where his best friend, Mark "Stack" Hansen, held up his tablet, which was playing a video of a small blond boy: Stack's two-year-old son, Jake. Jake was throwing a ball to someone out of frame, laughing and squealing with delight as he caught the ball when it was tossed back to him.

"You've obviously got a starting pitcher on your hands," Hunter said, giving a snort of laughter at the proud expression on Stack's face. Stack had married late, believing no woman would be willing to take on a rough mercenary who blew things up for a living, but he'd been wrong. Jennifer Hansen was fifteen years younger than Stack, a tiny brunette who had fallen hard for the big, burly merc, and Hunter had been best man at their wedding three years before, then stood as godfather a year later when Jake was born. He was happy for Stack, but he was envious as well. Not that Hunter was looking for a wife and kids; no, he was hoping for the right man to come along.

"You just wait. My kid is going to take the world by storm someday," Stack said. "With my looks and Jen's smarts, he can't help but be a winner."

"Of course he is. He's my godkid, after all," Hunter said, returning his attention to his book as Stack lowered the tablet and continued to watch the video.

Hunter knew Stack cherished the videos Jen sent him, which were the only real contact Stack had had with his family for the last six months. But Stack had been with Lawson and Greer, the private military contractor they both worked for, for almost twenty years now, and he was set to muster out and collect a pension in less than four months. If he managed things carefully, Stack could be a stay-at-home dad and be there for Jake all the time, making up for his absences during Jake's first two years.

"Able! Stack! We have a situation out here!"

The deep voice of Blaze, their unit commander, sounded from outside. His tone was urgent, and Hunter tossed his tablet aside before crossing the tent in three long strides and slipping out between the flaps, with Stack hot on his heels.

"Where's the fire?" he asked, seeing Blaze a few feet away with his back to them.

Blaze didn't turn around, but he gave the hand gesture for them to approach slowly. As Hunter stepped forward, he saw Joker, their second-in-command, standing off to one side and speaking into a walkie, his face betraying his tension. Around them, men emerged from other tents in the billeting area, and Joker waved them away, indicating they should get the hell out of the area fast. As his cadre moved away, Hunter drew abreast of Blaze and saw the reason why.

The kid couldn't have been any more than seven or eight years old, and he was barefoot and dressed in ragged clothing. His face was smudged with dirt, but there were clean streaks down his cheeks from his tears, and as Hunter stepped closer, it wasn't hard to see why the kid was crying. If someone had strapped a bunch of bricks of C4 around *his* body, Hunter would be pretty fucking upset too.

"Ah, shit." Stack stepped up beside him, the anger in his voice echoing Hunter's feelings. "God *damn* these bastards! What sort of monster does that to a kid?"

"Let's leave the philosophical debate on the table for the

moment," Blaze snapped. "Why don't you tell me what the fuck we're going to do about this?"

Hunter had dealt with suicide bombers, or at least with the aftermath once the snipers got through with them. If their vests didn't have a dead man switch, Hunter and Stack were called in to disarm the unexploded ordinance. One had never gotten past the sentries and into camp before — but then, none of them had ever been a kid either.

"'*Ana la 'urid 'an 'amut!*'" The kid startled them all by calling out, and Hunter translated the Arabic in his head. *I don't want to die!*

"Smart kid," Blaze said. He looked at Hunter and Stack. "Can you two handle this?"

"I guess we have to, don't we?" Stack said, his brown eyes dark with anger.

"We have this," Hunter agreed. "Go on, boss man. Get everyone, including yourself, out of here." He looked at the kid and spoke rapidly in the same dialect the child had used. "We will help you, but you have to stay very still. Can you do that?"

The kid nodded, and Hunter looked at Stack. "Go get our tool bags. I'll make sure he doesn't go anywhere."

"Right." Stack took off, and Hunter stepped closer to the little boy.

"I need you to answer some questions, so I can be sure we'll get this off without hurting you," he said. He kept his voice calm as he asked about what the boy remembered what the men who had wired him up said as they put the vest on him. By the time Stack came back with their tools and an anti-ballistic box, wearing his disposal suit and carrying Hunter's, Hunter had gotten all the information out of the kid he could.

"They told him to keep his thumb on the trigger until he got to the middle of the camp," he relayed as he got into his suit. "It looks like two connections, one under each arm. The boy doesn't remember them saying anything about failsafes, but be careful."

"Got it," Stack said, his voice echoing hollowly within his helmet.

Hunter finished donning everything but his own helmet and

turned to the boy. "Don't be scared. These suits are just for protection, okay? Like spacemen."

The kid nodded jerkily, and Hunter could see he was on the verge of hyperventilating. "Hey, don't worry! Breathe slow and deep, right. In... out... in... out..."

Stack was already on his knees next to the boy, and once Hunter was sure the kid wasn't going to pass out, he moved to the other side. He wondered about the wisdom of taking the trigger from the kid, but it was a big risk. If they fumbled the transfer, it would be all over — even their state-of-the-art bomb suits wouldn't protect them from that much C4 going off in their faces.

They'd done this before, but on corpses, not a living person, and that made it a hell of a lot more dangerous. Hunter was already sweating inside his suit, and he knew they didn't have long to work before heat fatigue started to take its toll.

"Looks like basic stuff," Stack said, tracing the wiring path through the cloth of the "vest." It was no more than rough-cut fabric with pockets to hold the C4 and the shrapnel it would hurl in the detonation, acting like a massive shotgun blast going off in all directions. The wires sticking out revealed the job had been done quickly and sloppily — but that didn't mean it was any less deadly.

They started by removing as much as they could of the mess of ball-bearings, screws, and small pieces of metal scrap that made up the shrapnel, then started on the vest itself. After a moment, Stack held up his hand.

"Wait... aww, fuck. We can't remove it all at once. We're going to have to do it brick by brick." He pointed to a second circuit hidden in the pouches under the shrapnel.

Hunter resisted the urge to grind his teeth. Instead of being able to take the vest off the boy intact, they'd have to take each piece of C4 off by itself, then break the circuit connecting it to the mass of the vest. It was as though there were ten separate bombs instead of only one.

Grimly they set to work, removing each block of C4 one at a time and placing it in the protective box before going on to the next. By the third brick, Hunter was panting, but he'd learned to work through stress before, and he kept his focus on what he was doing, making each movement precise.

After the ninth brick had been removed, Stack looked at what was left, then drew in a deep breath. "Good. I think we took out all the redundancy," he said. "Now we can remove it like a regular one."

"Got it," Hunter said. They carefully loosened the last of the wires and lifted the vest off over the kid's head. As he was freed, the boy cried out in relief, and Hunter had to grab his hand. "Don't release it yet! We're not done."

The boy nodded, trembling where he stood, as Stack disabled the detonator circuit. Hunter took the trigger from the boy, and the boy dropped to the ground, sobbing as he wrapped his arms around his knees and pressed his forehead against them.

Stack put the vest on the ground, then popped open his helmet. "Hey, kid, it'll be okay," he said, patting the boy on the back.

Hunter opened his helmet as well, drawing in a deep breath of desert air that felt cool in comparison to the inside of his helmet. And that was when he heard it — a soft beeping. Coming from the vest.

"It's hot!" He cried out, instinctively pushing the kid back, as though an extra few inches would do anything to protect him from the live bomb in their midst. Then time slowed down, as Hunter was pushed, a hard hand ramming into the center of his chest and knocking him off-balance. He'd still been on his knees, and he twisted as he fell, unable to believe Stack had pushed him away. But Stack was turning away, too — in the direction of the bomb.

"No!" Hunter cried out, but he was too late. As Stack fell across the vest, the C4 detonated. A brilliant flash enveloped Hunter's world, a sharp, burning pain sliced along one side of his head, and then everything faded to black, as Hunter's soul screamed in horror that his last sight was his best friend being blown to bits right before his eyes.

1

"You wanted to see me, Herc?" Payne Gibson knocked on the door frame and poked his head into Cade Thornton's office after his PA, Lexy, waved him through.

Normally, he didn't stop by Hercules Security headquarters before his shift — overnight watch duty on a multimillionaire businessman who'd received death threats over a class action lawsuit he was embroiled in — but he'd woken up to find an email from Herc requesting a meeting with him.

Herc glanced up from his computer. "Thanks for coming so quickly," he said, gesturing to a seat in front of his desk. "You're just the man I need to see."

"Is this about the Peterson case?" Payne asked as he took a seat.

"Yes and no," Herc said, regarding Payne with a serious expression. "You're doing great work on it, by the way. But what I really wanted to know is if you'd be willing to take on a partner. A trainee, I suppose, at least in surveillance."

Payne's eyebrows climbed to his hairline, and he leaned forward in his chair, surprised by the question. He'd been with Hercules Security for five years, and this was the first time Herc had asked him to take on a trainee. It felt like a mark of honor, as if he'd finally arrived... or maybe it just meant he was now officially an old-timer in the company.

"Sure, I'm willing," he said, imagining a fresh-faced, eager newbie he could take under his wing and become a respected mentor for, as his mentors had been for him.

"Before you commit, I need to give you a complete briefing on the man in question," Herc said. He turned his computer monitor around to face Payne, and with a few key taps, he displayed two pictures. On the right was the face of a man who appeared to be in his mid-thirties, with short cropped brown hair and a close-cropped beard emphasizing his square jawline. He looked into the camera with a slight smirk on his lips, and there seemed to be amusement in his blue eyes.

The same man was pictured on the left, but the changes in him were striking. No longer smiling, he seemed to stare *through* the camera, almost as if he didn't know it was there and wouldn't have cared even if he had. He looked haggard, with dark circles under his eyes, and he seemed to have lost weight. But the biggest difference was a scar tracing a vivid red line along his right temple and back into his hair. The picture must have been taken a month or two after the injury which had caused it, for the hair growing back in the area stood out as a silver streak amid the brown.

"This is Hunter Callahan about five months ago," Herc said, pointing to the picture on the right. "And the other is of him three months later."

Payne recognized the thousand-yard stare, and he turned wide, round eyes on Herc. "That guy has seen some shit," he said. "You want to tell me what I'm getting into here?"

"Hunter was one-half of Lawson and Greer's best demolitions team," Herc said quietly. "He used to go by the nickname Able, but he is vehement about no one calling him that any longer. The other half of the team was Mark Hansen, known as Stack. You may recall the names if you read the after-action report on D-Day's little outing with the Eastern Light in Europe about a year ago. They're the guys we borrowed from L&G to deal with the nuke."

"I think everyone in the company read that report," Payne said, remembering how widely it had circulated after word got out about D-Day having tackled a truck with a live nuke in it. Despite the brevity of Herc's description, it didn't take many pieces for Payne to get the picture, especially given Herc's use of the past tense. "Let me guess. Something happened to Hansen."

"It did." Herc managed to convey a great deal of sorrow and regret in only two brief words. "I have the full after-action report for you to read, but those are just facts, and I wanted to tell you about the real men involved. I knew Stack well. He was already an old-timer when I went to work for John Lawson and Matthew Greer. He was one of their original team when they formed the company. Able — Hunter — came in two years after I did, a cocky little son-of-a-bitch out of Army Special Forces. He was kind of like D-Day, but with a little officer spit-and-polish. His special skills involved blowing the shit out of things, so he and Stack were teamed up. Mark was a no-nonsense kind of guy, and I think he kicked Hunter in the ass and made him grow up. They were a hell of a team. I was at Stack's wedding, where Hunter stood as his best man, and when Stack's son was born, he asked Hunter to be the godfather."

Herc paused and drew in a breath. "Three months ago, Lawson and Greer were on a deployment near Fallujah, guarding a group of American 'military advisors.' They'd run across some IEDs and the unit had even fragged a couple of would-be suicide bombers. But then the twisted bastards got the idea to send in someone no American soldier would shoot on sight. It was a seven-year-old kid, wearing enough C4 to blow the entire camp straight to hell. Able and Stack were called on to defuse the kid's vest while the camp was evacuated. The kid was petrified. He was told he had to do it or his mother and sister would be killed. He held onto the trigger, though, refusing to blow himself and everyone else up. But when they got the vest off the kid, a timer went off. They'd already detached most of the C4, but one block was enough. Stack threw himself over the vest to protect Hunter and the kid. They lived...He died."

Payne gazed at the more recent photo of Hunter Callahan with a sharp surge of sympathy. "Shit, that's rough. I'm guessing a bad case of survivor's guilt on top of PTSD?"

"I think that's likely," Herc said. "One problem when you deal with smart people, though, especially ones who know the drill, is that psychological tests and interviews don't give you the whole picture. Hunter is damned smart, and the psychologists said he seems to be fine now. Of course, they don't know him the way Matthew Greer, John Lawson, and I know him. He's hurting, but he's shut everyone out. The fact he refuses to answer to the nickname he's had for fifteen years is proof enough of that. Matt and John aren't about to send him back into the field, no matter how good he is or how much they need him, not with what he's carrying around inside. So they asked me to take him on as a 'temporary assignment.' We've told him we want him to have some time away from the battlefield. So when I said I'd help him out, I immediately thought of you."

"I take it this is less about me training him in surveillance and more about my background?" Payne asked dryly. He had a BA and a MA in psychology, and he'd been toying with the idea of pursuing a Ph.D.

"That's part of it," Herc admitted. "You don't have to do this if you don't want to, which is why I was asking, not ordering. It's definitely in the 'above and beyond' category, but you might be his last hope. He's not going to go for counseling, and we can't force him. But Ghost trained you in infiltration, and you're not only smart and have the training in psychology, you've been in combat before. You can understand what he's going through. Maybe you can't help him, and he'll end up washed out no matter what any of us do. But maybe you can get inside his head and show him the way back out."

It was a tall order, especially for someone who wasn't a licensed therapist, but Payne had always been driven to help people. He wasn't sure whether it was due to the example his father had set or his own basic nature — perhaps a little of both — but it was a fundamental element of who he was, one he couldn't change or ignore.

"I'll do my best," he said. "When do we get started?"

Herc grinned, obviously pleased. "I'll email you the after-action report and give you a couple of days to review everything. How about you come by here next Tuesday around four, and I'll have Hunter here. You can meet him, and I'll let the two of you work things out."

"Works for me." Payne gave Herc a questioning look. "Is there anything else I should know going in that isn't covered in the report?"

Herc's smile grew wicked. "Well, at the risk of giving you too big of an ego, I'd say using those big blue puppy eyes on him might help. Hunter walks on our side of the street, and as I recall, he's got a weakness for a pretty face."

Payne laughed and batted his lashes at Herc, although he knew Herc was immune to his charms. Herc's husband, Jude, was the one who held Herc enthralled. "Duly noted."

"All right, then, check your email later." Herc paused, his expression turning serious once again. "I do appreciate this, Payne. Hunter Callahan has saved hundreds, if not thousands, of lives by risking his own. If you can help him, you'll be doing a favor not only for me personally, but for everyone else he might save in the future. And if you can't help him, I don't think anyone can."

"Oh, good, no pressure," Payne said as he pushed back his chair and stood up.

Herc rolled his eyes. "Go on, get your smart mouth out of here," he growled, but there was no heat in it. "Before you make me wonder if I'm doing Hunter a favor after all!"

"Pfft!" Payne grinned unrepentantly at Herc. "I got my nickname for a reason," he said as he sashayed to the door. But despite his flippant demeanor, he was already thinking about Hunter and ways he could bring Hunter out of the dark place he was mired in.

Hunter Callahan needed Payne's help, and he was going to get it — whether he liked it or not.

2

Hunter stood just inside the gym doorway, frowning as he watched at least a dozen big, burly bodyguards working out.

It wasn't that the sight displeased him; if anything, he should have been enjoying the view of sweat-covered skin and flexing muscles, in a variety of shapes and sizes like a smorgasbord for his eyes and libido. Three months, ten days, and some-odd hours ago he would have been quite happy to have a ringside seat to the display of hunks, but not anymore. Maybe not ever again.

No, he was frowning because he didn't want to be here. Not that he wanted to be anywhere except back with his unit, to be honest, but life didn't give a good goddamn that Mark should be the one standing here, and Hunter should be the one taking an eternal dirt nap. Life was a bitch all right, a cold-teated bitch without mercy or conscience.

The psychiatrists told him over and over it wasn't his fault, which he knew and even accepted on an intellectual level. Shit happens, as the saying went, and Hunter had seen it enough to know it was true. Which meant there was nothing he could have done to alter what occurred and ripping himself up over it was a pointless exercise. Right? Right.

The only problem with accepting something based on logic was it did fuck-all to convince your gut.

Unfortunately, short of checking himself into a nice padded room somewhere so he could check out mentally, the only thing he could do was go on and hope someday something made sense again and that the diamond-hard knot inside of him loosened to where he could feel something other than a fury so deep and cold, it must have originated in the ninth circle of Hell. It was probably what people like Matthew Greer and Cade Thornton sensed within him, like a coiled serpent awaiting its opportunity to strike. Which was why they'd sent him here, and not back into the field.

He wasn't suicidal. There was a bad joke that had been around for years, about what do you call a suicidal merc? Dead already, of course. It was true, too. Men who were as good at killing as Hunter and his cadre were would be self-destructive for the entire second it took them from decision to action. No fuss, no mess, no big scenes or attention-getting drama, just oblivion between one breath and the next. He'd seen it happen, too, but it wasn't his way. His way was different. Very different.

"I'm glad you made it."

Cade Thornton spoke from beside him, and Hunter gave a start of surprise and annoyance. He'd found himself becoming far too absorbed in his own thoughts lately, which was neither good nor professional.

He looked at Cade, whom he'd known for years. Herc had been injured and had mustered out of L&G about five years after Hunter had joined. He hadn't been part of Herc's platoon of mercs, but he'd worked with them plenty of times in the field. Nor had he been tempted to leave L&G when Herc started his own company. As far as he knew, there wasn't much call for people who knew how to blow the shit out of things in the bodyguard business. He and Mark had been called on a time or two to help out in dicey situations — which still seemed to be Daryl "D-Day" Greer's bread-and-butter — but Hunter's skills were far more suited to the battlefield than the board-room. Which was another reason he felt out of place here.

"I didn't have much choice," Hunter said, giving a one-shouldered shrug. "Matthew and John won't approve me for the field until they're convinced I haven't hit the wall. Apparently, they don't trust the shrinks and think you've got a direct line to Christ or Professor X to see inside my head."

Herc raised a brow. "They don't trust the shrinks because the shrinks don't often deal with someone who can hide the fact he's five seconds away from going dinky dau."

Hunter shrugged again. Herc had used an old military slang term for going crazy, and he knew more than one guy had pulled one over on the shrinks, then gone back out into the field and fragged his entire platoon. "Not my way."

"You're a smartass, Hunter, but I've seen that busy brain of yours at work, and you and I both know you can probably convince the shrinks of anything."

Herc was right, but Hunter wasn't going to admit it. "So the plan is to set me up with a babysitter until you all can be sure I'm not going to throw sand at the other kids." Hunter said the words flatly, because it wasn't a question.

To his surprise, Herc put his hand on Hunter's shoulder. "Not quite. We're going to set you up with a babysitter until *you* are sure you're not going to throw sand at the other kids. And here comes your babysitter now."

Hunter frowned as he noticed someone approaching them. The guy had to be at least a half foot shorter than Hunter, and even if he moved with the grace of a martial artist, he looked like someone's geeky kid brother. Someone's *really* pretty geeky kid brother, maybe, with those big blue eyes set above high cheekbones and wavy chestnut brown hair, but he looked out of place among all the man-meat in the gym.

"*This* is my babysitter?" Hunter asked, looking the guy up and down in disbelief. "Christ, Herc, you need to throw him back. He's not finished growing yet."

The kid widened those big eyes at him. "Gosh! I'm supposed to train you? Gee, Herc, are you sure this is a good idea?"

Herc looked at the kid, his expression grave. "Hmmm... maybe not," he said. "If Hunter decided to do something rash, you might not be able to stop him."

Something in Herc's voice didn't sound right, but Hunter shrugged. "Probably not. I suppose it's a good thing I'm not going to do anything rash."

The kid's eyes somehow got even bigger as he blinked innocently at Herc. "I don't know, Herc. Maybe we should spar a little to be sure I'm not getting in over my head."

A couple of the nearby bodyguards made noises that sounded like stifled laughter, and Hunter noticed more of them seemed interested in the conversation than in their workouts. Probably because they thought he was some stupid boot who couldn't take on a little squirt. Hunter knew he'd lost weight in the last few months, and he'd let his workout routine slide, but he still had plenty of muscle. "Whatever," he said, shrugging in disinterest. He didn't have a damned thing to prove to anyone, not even Herc.

The kid beamed at him and practically bounced up and down. "Great! There's a free floor mat over here. Go easy on me, okay? You're so much bigger and buffer than me, and I bruise easy."

Hunter looked at Herc, who simply raised one eyebrow at him. With a long-suffering sigh, Hunter dropped his gear bag and shrugged out of his jacket, leaving it on top of the bag. He didn't look at the kid again, just walked over to the mat, turned, and waited. Maybe once this was over, he could get Herc to sign off clearing him to return to L&G where he belonged.

The kid trotted over to the mat and stood a short distance away from Hunter, cocking his head as he watched Hunter with bright-eyed anticipation. Some of the bodyguards gave up any pretense of disinterest and gathered closer to the mat, nudging each other and grinning.

Hunter looked at the kid, feeling nothing. He wasn't angry. He just didn't care about this or about much of anything that didn't lead to a plane ticket east. He waited for the kid to rush him, to do *something*, and finally, he grew bored and took a step in the kid's direction, intending to push him over and step off the mat.

But he hadn't even completed his first step when the kid *moved* faster than anyone Hunter had ever seen in his life. His feet were swept out from under him, and as he fell, twisting to the left instinctively to protect the injured right side of his head, the kid was behind him and climbing up his back like some kind of goddamned monkey. Hunter landed hard on his side, and the kid bore him over onto his stomach. Even as Hunter reached back to make a grab for the kid's hands, strong arms were wrapping around Hunter's neck in a classic sleeper hold. With the kid kneeling on his back and with his head yanked up and back, he couldn't get leverage to roll over to dislodge his attacker. He grabbed at the kid's arms, but they were as tight as iron vises around his neck, and as Hunter struggled, his vision began to gray out as the blood flow to his brain was cut off.

Being held by someone half his size was embarrassing, but it would be even worse to let the kid put him out. With what remained of his strength, Hunter slapped his palm against the mat, indicating his surrender. The kid instantly released him and hopped off his back while the men standing near the mat whistled and applauded. The kid held out his hand, offering to help Hunter up.

"Jeepers! I'm glad you took it easy on me," he said, giving Hunter a too-innocent smile.

It took a moment for Hunter's vision to clear, and the pounding in his temples warned he was going to have a bitch of a headache later. He ignored the kid's hand, rolling to one side and rising to his feet. He walked toward Herc.

"Fine, you slipped in a ringer. Very funny," he said coldly. "Cute little ninja tricks won't save him from a block of C4 in his gut." He bent to pick up his jacket, then glanced at the assembled bodyguards. "Next time you have a fucking nuke you want disarmed, call some other asshole."

Herc clamped his hand on Hunter's shoulder. "Did they blow up your sense of humor, too?" he asked, and Hunter felt a stab of fresh grief.

"Yeah, they did. They took everything that fucking mattered, all right?" He couldn't keep the bitterness out of his tone.

"I guess the question is, do you want any of it back?" The kid had joined them, his expression serious now as he gazed up at Hunter. "Or are you okay with feeling this way for the rest of your life?"

Hunter stared down at the kid in disbelief. "You don't know a damned thing about what I feel," he snapped. "You sure as hell don't care either. If you're supposed to be my babysitter, then you'd better understand up front I don't like fucking mind games. All I want is to go back where I belong as soon as I can."

"That's good, because I don't play fucking mind games," the kid said, dropping the "golly gee whiz" demeanor that made him seem even younger. "As for knowing how you feel, well, I was stationed at Camp Victory in June 2011, if that tells you anything."

Hunter narrowed his eyes, wondering if the kid was having him on, but without the wide-eyed look, it was easy to see he was older than he seemed at first. "Yeah? So you've seen people blown to shit too. Good for you. Welcome to the last fifteen years of my life."

"Welcome to the lives of pretty much every man in here," the kid said, encompassing the room with a sweep of his arm. "You're not special. So again, the question is do you want to spend the rest of your life feeling the way you do right now?"

Drawing himself up straight, Hunter glared at the kid. It was on the tip of his tongue to issue a scalding rebuke. The men in this room may have *been* mercs once, but Hunter was *still* one and probably would be until it killed him. It was all he knew and all he had left. They could take his life, but no one could ever make him not a merc.

But instead he focused on a vague curiosity. "What do you care anyway?"

"I care because we're going to be working together for a while," the kid said, still watching Hunter with an unwavering gaze. Although his posture appeared relaxed, he was alert and paying close attention to Hunter. "My current mission involves surveillance, and frankly, I don't want to be trapped in a van with fucking Eeyore for hours every night."

"Then complain to your boss, not to me," Hunter said, shrugging. His anger had faded back into a sense of weary resignation, and he looked at Herc. "That's the deal, right? If I can get through this little exercise of yours without going batshit crazy from Suzie Sunshine here, you'll tell Matthew and John I'm fine to return to duty?"

Herc glanced at Payne, then back at Hunter. "That's the general idea," he said. "If you don't want to do it, you could always resign from L&G and join another outfit."

Hunter made a disparaging sound. "I wouldn't work for any of those chickenshit outfits," he growled, and he meant it. He respected Matthew and John, and the men in his outfit were like brothers. He didn't want to work for anyone else. Not even Herc, but it seemed he didn't have any choice. "Fine."

"Welcome aboard, partner." The kid held out his hand again, giving Hunter a challenging look. "You can call me Payne or Pita. I answer to both."

Hunter could only stare at the kid in disbelief, and then he shook the kid's hand.

"That's not even funny," he said. "It's the story of my fucking life to get stuck with partner who's literally a pain in the ass."

A wicked gleam appeared in Payne's eyes, and a mischievous smile curved his lips. "Oh, honey. You have *no* idea," he drawled, and Hunter heard the Lowcountry in his voice.

"But I bet I'm going to find out, aren't I?" Hunter was tired, having had enough of strangers and demands and expectations he didn't want to face. "When do I start?" The sooner he began this farce, the sooner it would be over.

"Let's say Friday night," Payne said, his demeanor turning business-like. "That'll give you a couple of days to flip to the night shift. We'll meet here at seventeen hundred and proceed to the site."

"Fine." Hunter picked up his bag. "I'll be here."

He walked away, heading out of the gym. He'd originally considered working out before heading back to his hotel, but he no longer felt like it. This was only a temporary stop on his way back to the field, and he didn't care to get to know any of the bodyguards. He didn't want to make friends, and he didn't want to play nice.

What he wanted was his best friend back, and that was the one thing he could never have.

$\sim$

PAYNE WATCHED HUNTER GO, more concerned about this new mission now that he'd met his "trainee." He looked at Herc, his expression somber.

"I'd like to talk," he said.

"Of course," Herc said. "My office?"

"Yes, please."

Herc led the way to his office, and Payne walked with him in silence, not wanting to say anything until they were assured of privacy. It was bad enough how word of Hunter underestimating their resident PITA and paying the price was likely circulating already without Payne's assessment of the situation being overheard as well.

After they'd stepped into the office, Herc closed the door. Rather than taking a seat behind his desk, he gestured to a big leather sofa against the back wall. "Have a seat. We might as well be comfortable if this is going to get as deep as I think it is."

Payne went over to the sofa and sat down, and he absently ran his fingers through his hair as he thought about where to begin.

"It's going to get pretty deep," he said after Herc sat down as well. "I mean, *damn*, Herc — do you have any idea what you've dropped in my lap?"

Herc shook his head. "I didn't know he was that bad," he admitted. "But I can see why L&G wasn't about to send him back into the fray. He reminds me of some of the Vietnam vets I've worked with who had things so tightly bottled up, you knew when they finally exploded it was going to be messy."

"That's it exactly," Payne said. "He's got walls made of titanium reinforced with gun turrets and 'keep out' signs, but that's the easy part. The hard part is what's going on behind those walls. He's got some deep anger issues, but I'm willing to bet that under all the anger, he's as fragile as bone china."

For a long moment Herc said nothing. "If I'd known how bad it was, I never would have asked you to take him on," he said finally. "Look, Payne, you don't have to do this. I felt bad enough asking you when I thought it was a regular case of PTSD, but this is far more. He probably does need a professional."

"He does, but he's not going to trust a professional." Payne spread his hands. "He's fronting, and he's trying to do it well enough to get himself back on active duty. He's not looking for help."

"What should I do?" Herc asked. "L&G aren't going to send him back to the field, especially if you and I recommend against it. I'm relieved he said he didn't want to work for any other outfit. Some of them are so desperate for men to fulfill their contracts, they'd probably overlook certain irregularities. But that doesn't mean he might not do it anyway or decide to take off on his own, like some one-man demolitions force. He'd be pretty good at it, too, right up to the moment it killed him."

"I wouldn't put it past him," Payne said. "My guess is he's more interested in either working himself to death — perhaps literally — in an attempt to outrun his feelings or making someone pay for his partner's death. Either way, he doesn't seem to care about getting better at this point, which means we have limited options. The first option is to let him go and whatever happens, happens, but personally, I don't consider it to be much of an option."

"Agreed." Herc rubbed at his chin as he frowned. "What do you see as the other options? The only thing I can come up with is to call in D-Day, since the two of them get on pretty well. But I wouldn't be surprised if Hunter could talk D-Day into an impromptu visit to Iraq. Daryl is more the type of guy to enable Hunter's impulses than talk him out of them."

"Well, you could get one of our resident psychiatrists to go undercover," Payne said, ticking the points off on his slender fingers. "But the danger with that is one whiff of 'therapy is in session,' and Hunter is going to close up tighter than any clam."

"True enough," Herc agreed. "I could ask one of them, maybe Drake Matthews, but Hunter isn't dumb. He could look up any of them and find out who they were."

"Exactly, which leaves only one other option. Me," Payne said with a wry smile.

"I don't want you to feel like you're being railroaded." Herc shook his head. "If you don't want to do it, it's not a problem. I can take him on myself, since he knows he has to go through me to get back to L&G. I could take him out to the survival school in Utah and have us both dumped into the desert for a couple of weeks. Being naked and without food or water tends to put a lot of things in perspective."

"Ain't that the truth," Payne said, chuckling.

Herc offered the chance to go through the survival school to anyone who wanted it, and Payne had gone as a way to challenge himself and see if he could complete it. He had, but the experience ranked right up there as one of the most difficult things he'd ever done.

"I don't feel like I'm being railroaded," he continued. "I'm worried about what could happen if I fail. He needs help, and I want to give it, but I admit I'm at a loss for where to begin."

"If you fail, he's no worse off than he is now, right?" Herc asked wryly. "You could try talking to him. Hunter isn't normally a loner, you know, even though he appears shut off right now. He's always been a pretty social person, and he reads constantly. If you start out on some subject — art, movies, whatever you'd like — maybe you can draw him out into talking to you. You've already seen how he's underestimated you physically. Maybe by the time he figures out he's done the same thing about that devious mind of yours, you'll have wormed your way over those walls of his."

"I'm willing to give it a shot." Payne shook his head. "I can't walk away now that I've met him. Oh, the perils of being a caretaker! I knew it would bite me on the ass one of these days. Anyway, I'll see what I can do. If it seems like I'm making things worse instead of

better or not getting through to him at all, I'll let you know, and we
can formulate plan B."

"All right," Herc agreed. "And if you need anything — and I do
mean anything — all you have to do is ask for it. That includes if you
need to be relieved from the surveillance to take Hunter off somewhere as part of helping him. In fact, I'll have backup standing by,
just in case."

"That might not be a bad idea." Payne gave Herc a grateful smile,
relieved Herc understood how difficult the situation was. He wasn't
sure he would succeed in giving Hunter Callahan the help he needed
so badly, but if he failed, it wouldn't be for lack of trying. "Wish me
luck," he said as he stood up.

Herc stood as well. "Luck and everything else I can wish you," he
said. "And if it gets to be too much, don't hesitate to let me know. I
don't want you to go nuts trying to keep Hunter from going nuts. I like
Hunter, but ultimately, he's Matthew Greer's responsibility. *You* are
my responsibility."

"Understood," Payne said, and he meant it. He knew the dangers
of getting overly involved and driving himself to the edge of burn out
all too well, and he didn't intend to let it happen again. "I'll send you
reports on Hunter along with the regular mission reports."

"All right." Herc put a hand on Payne's shoulder. "I have faith in
you, but I don't expect miracles, so don't feel compelled to deliver
one. Unless, of course, one occurs." He grinned. "It can happen."

"I won't say no to a miracle or two in this situation," Payne said
dryly.

"I don't blame you." Herc stepped back. "You have my cell phone
number, so don't hesitate to call if you need me. Got it?"

"Got it. Thanks, Herc," Payne said, and then he headed for the
door, already losing himself in thought about how he could approach
Hunter to help him open up. With any luck, Hunter would continue
underestimating him until he burrowed under those thick walls —
and then the real work would begin.

B eing a bodyguard, as far as Hunter could tell, was the most boring job on planet Earth.

He glanced around the surveillance van, suppressing an urge to sigh. True, the vehicle looked like something from a James Bond movie, with monitors lining the inside so they could watch the view from the dozens of cameras on their client's estate. They could see almost every room in the house and around most of the grounds with cams, and there were other cameras equipped with motion detectors, which would rotate from time to time when an owl or fox triggered them. There were banks of lights to show the status of the alarm sensors on every door and window, and even sound detectors with waterfall displays so they would know if any window pane between here and the next county was broken. But none of the high-tech gadgets interested him in the slightest and staring at the unchanging displays was mind-numbing in the extreme.

His gaze fell on Payne, who was engrossed in some finicky adjustment of one of the displays, and he frowned thoughtfully. He didn't understand why Payne had agreed to train him, when Hunter had done his best to be as off-putting as possible. Despite Hunter giving monosyllabic answers to any questions and not saying anything

beyond that, Payne had acted friendly toward him, not just professional and polite. He was puzzled and a little unsettled, but there
didn't seem to be a damn thing Hunter could do to change it.

It was also hard to believe someone as short and lean as Payne
had managed to take Hunter down. Even though Hunter wasn't in
peak form — months of recovery had taken its toll — he was still big
and strong enough to handle most men in a fight. Payne must have
studied martial arts, and he had reflexes faster than anyone Hunter
had ever seen before. He also knew how to use those baby blue eyes
of his to devastating effect, and Hunter grudgingly admitted, if only
to himself, he wasn't as immune as he would have liked to be. Which
made the current situation all the more unbearable.

Still, this was something he would have to endure, as he'd
endured the heat of the desert and the fact they couldn't have booze
or chocolate or half a dozen other things he'd taken for granted
before his first deployment. He could get through this, and then he'd
be sent back where he belonged. After that... he cut off the thought
before it could even form, knowing he shouldn't get too far ahead of
himself. It was a hazard in his job, and one he'd learned to deal with.
If you started thinking too far ahead, you could lose focus on what
you needed to be doing at the moment, and that could get you dead
in a great big hurry.

The sigh escaped before he could stop it, and he growled in silent
annoyance. Maybe Herc and the folks at L&G thought doing this was
going to help Hunter get better, whatever that meant, but from where
he was sitting, he felt like he was being punished instead.

"Doing okay, big guy?" Payne swiveled his chair to face Hunter,
giving him a friendly smile.

Hunter kept his expression impassive. "Yes."

"No questions for me?" Payne asked, widening his eyes slightly.

At another time and another place, if Payne had looked at him
like that, Hunter would have been tempted to ask him out. He'd
always been a sucker for wide eyed, appealing looks, especially from
men as attractive as Payne. But it was out of the question, even if
Hunter had been tempted.

He crossed his arms over his chest, feeling a little irritated. "No. You explained the equipment, described the client, and made me aware of the threat. I can't think of anything else I need to know to sit here and stare at a bunch of screens."

Payne's lips quirked up as he leaned back and stretched as much as the confines of the van would allow. The hem of his tight black tee-shirt rode up enough to reveal a stripe of fair skin above the waist-band of his black and white camo pants.

"I get the impression you don't think much of surveillance work."

Hunter wanted to growl, but he bit down on the impulse, even though he wondered if Payne was being deliberately provocative. It seemed likely; the man was too damned smart and sure of himself.

"Oh, I think a lot of it," Hunter said, his tone dry as dust. "Just none of it positive."

"You don't think it has any value?" Payne didn't appear to be either surprised or defensive, merely curious.

Hunter was tempted to shrug and end the conversation, but he wasn't ready to be quite that rude — or at least not yet. "I didn't say that," he said. "I'm not stupid, you know. I realize it's necessary to maintain a secure perimeter at all times in a dangerous situation. But my talents are different. Maybe Herc thought since I can stare at wiring diagrams and spend hours tracing circuits to disarm a bomb that I'd be good at this, but I think I'd rather have my fingernails pulled out."

"Wiring diagrams and tracing circuits both take patience and attention to detail," Payne pointed out. "So how is it different from this?"

"Because the danger there is real and immediate. This kind of work, you're hoping nothing happens, right? You can even have that hope, because the threats to this guy could be someone just pissing up a rope. I'm used to being in the dirt. We can hope nothing happens, but it always does. Always."

"Is that what you want?" Payne cocked his head as he watched Hunter, still leaning back in a relaxed posture. "You'd rather have danger than hope?"

Giving Payne a narrow-eyed glance, Hunter chuckled, but the sound was bitter. "I've lived with danger so long, it's part of me now. If I'd wanted to do this kind of thing for a living, I would've mustered out with the others when Herc left Lawson and Greer. I know what I'm good at, and it's what I want to do."

"What happens when you can't do it anymore? Something like this could be a handy backup skill to keep you in the field even if age or an injury moves you out of demolitions," Payne said.

The question sent an icy finger down Hunter's spine. Stack had loved the work as much as Hunter did, but then he'd found something he loved even more, and Hunter had secretly envied him. Then the work had killed him, and none of it mattered anymore. Stack's death had blown a hole in a lot of lives, including Hunter's.

"I'll cross that bridge if and when I come to it," he said. Privately, he figured he'd end up going the way of Stack sooner or later, but at least when he did, he wouldn't leave a family behind to figure out how to get along without him.

"It happens to the best of us sooner or later," Payne said as he swiveled to check a monitor, but the movement turned out to be a cat running across the lawn. "But there are always other avenues. My mentor is former Mossad. Ghost tried retiring, but it didn't stick, so now he's the head of Herc's new training facility. D-Day is doing a lot more training than field work these days too. Priorities shift when they need to."

Hunter gave a snort. "D-Day's priorities shifted, but he's still D-Day. Once a merc, always a merc — at least for the ones who are real mercs to begin with." He gestured to the screens. "I can't see Daryl Greer sitting in front of these damned things for more than five minutes without putting a fist through one of them."

"I can't see it either," Payne said, chuckling. Then he turned a wide-eyed, curious look on Hunter again. "What's the difference between a real merc and — say — someone like me?"

"You?" Hunter asked, surprised at the question. "I don't know you, so how could I say?"

"Well, you know I never worked at Lawson and Greer," Payne

said. "But otherwise, you're right. You don't know me, and I don't know you. But we're going to be working together for a while, so maybe we should change that. Is there anything in particular you'd like to know?"

He should say "no" and end the conversation, since Hunter had no desire to give Payne hope he was going to reciprocate. But one thing had been bugging him, and since Payne had offered, he decided to take him up on it.

"Yeah." Hunter said sourly. "How old are you? I thought you were maybe eighteen, but you must be older, unless you started ninja lessons at two."

"Eighteen? I'm flattered!" Payne batted his lashes playfully and pressed his fingertips against his chest in a coquettish gesture. "But no, I'm thirty-two."

The revelation was a surprise, despite the fact Payne had admitted to being at the shitstorm in Iraq in 2011, when a base bombing had blown apart six soldiers even as the US was in the process of withdrawing. For all Hunter knew, Payne could have been a snot nose on his first deployment, but apparently that wasn't the case. "Enlisted or officer?"

"Enlisted." Payne stacked his hands behind his head and leaned back as he watched Hunter. "The Gibson men have a tradition of military service. My grandfather retired a colonel. My dad retired early and then taught at the Citadel, and I was a whiskey. E-6 by the time I mustered out."

Hunter raised a brow. "Combat medic?" He was surprised. 68Ws, or "Whiskeys", as the medics were known, were dedicated professionals, and if Payne had been one when Victory was bombed, then he would have been one of the people trying to put the bodies back together. Hunter couldn't help but respect medics, since they went into the worst situations in order to save others. They also had an old and rather risqué motto. "The louder I scream, the faster you come, huh?"

A wicked gleam appeared in Payne's eyes. "That's my motto for more reasons than one."

"Oh?" Hunter couldn't stop himself from asking, especially given Payne's expression.

"I like making my men scream," Payne said, an enigmatic smile curving his lips.

Apparently Payne was also a tease, and Hunter regretted giving in to his curiosity. He scowled. "So you were a healer, not a killer. Not a merc."

"Does it matter?" Payne asked, watching him intently. "Do you see me as somehow less than you because I'm not a 'real' merc?"

"Did I say that?" The surge of anger he felt surprised him, and he glared at Payne. "You asked, didn't you? All I said was a real merc is always a merc, and it's true. I'm a hired gun, a killer, someone who knows how to destroy with ruthless efficiency. That's what I do. It's what I'm good at. And if you don't like it, shut the fuck up."

"I'm not judging you, Hunter," Payne said in a gentle voice. "But it sounds like you may be judging yourself too harshly."

"So what? It's none of your business," Hunter snapped. A small internal voice tried to tell him maybe Payne had a point, but he didn't listen to it. "Fine, you answered my question. I don't need to know any more about you."

"Too bad, because I'm quite fascinating." Payne gave him the wide-eyed innocent look again. "But if you don't want to talk, we don't have to talk. There's always paperwork to fill out."

With that, he turned his full attention to the monitors and let silence fall in the close quarters of the van.

Perversely, Hunter was annoyed at letting Payne have the last word, but mostly he was relieved. Payne was too damned smart, too sharp, too prodding with his questions and statements, skating too close to things Hunter didn't want to consider. He could see why Payne had gotten his nickname, and it probably explained why he'd had to become so fast and sneaky. No doubt if he prodded other mercs, especially one with a notoriously short temper like D-Day, he'd have to be fast or he would've been dead by now.

Staring morosely at the monitor in front of him, he wondered if he'd be better off quitting L&G and going with some two-bit outfit who wouldn't care about either his past or his future. But Stack had once told him he believed the real measure of a man was his ability to keep going when it would be easier to quit. Hunter hadn't realized until Stack was gone just how hard he had always tried to live up to the standards Stack had set for himself, and now he couldn't seem to stop.

So he'd put up with Herc, and with Payne, and with the tediousness of staring at screens where nothing happened. He might die of boredom or frustration, but when he got to the afterlife, he'd be able to face Stack with pride.

It seemed the least Hunter could do when his best friend had sacrificed his life so Hunter could live.

4

Payne finished his set of deadlifts and peeked to see how Hunter was doing. Unsurprisingly, Hunter was off by himself on the other side of the gym, but his face was more relaxed than usual. Working out wasn't a cure-all, but it couldn't hurt, so Payne had convinced Hunter to meet him in the gym at headquarters for some exercise before they headed to the site for the night. Although Hunter still kept his distance from the other men, including Payne, he seemed to get a respite once he sank deep enough into his workout for the repetitions to take him out of himself, if only for a little while. That alone made it worthwhile for Payne.

He was glad *something* was working because he wasn't having much success with getting Hunter to talk to him. From what he could tell, Hunter was experiencing the typical mood cycles that followed in the aftermath of trauma. Sometimes, Hunter smiled a little at over-hearing some of the men's ribald teasing even if he didn't join in. Other times, his face was a stony mask. Sometimes, he seemed to pay attention to Payne's nattering about favorite books and movies, but then he'd withdraw into himself again, and Payne knew to stop talking.

Hunter had his good days and bad days, and there was no way to predict what kind of mood Hunter would be in from day to day. Payne took stock when he saw Hunter, looking for the subtle signs that would tell him whether to back off or take a chance at burrowing a little further under the walls. The process was slow and sometimes frustrating because Payne couldn't tell if he was helping or making any progress, but he kept trying because he felt like Hunter needed him, even if Hunter didn't want to admit it to himself, much less to Payne.

Payne was about to change the weights on his bar so he could move on to back squats when he noticed the other guys in the room abandoning their workout equipment and flocking to the door. Curious, he glanced over and saw Alec Davis and his partner, Jon Baldwin, standing just inside the room. Payne had gotten over being star struck — well, mostly over. He still had a damned hard time not getting fluttery in the stomach and blushing when Jon looked directly at him because Jon's default charisma setting seemed to be eleven. Still, he was used to being around Jon enough that he could be cool about it, so he sauntered over to see what was going on.

As he approached, he saw Jon was holding a bundle wrapped in a seafoam green blanket, and then he remembered hearing some time ago about Alec and Jon trying to have a baby with a surrogate mother. Excited by the prospect of a new addition to the family, he quickened his pace and used his size to worm his way past the bigger men surrounding the couple.

"Everyone, meet Alexandra Siobhan Baldwin-Davis," Alec announced, his smile so wide it looked as though it might split his face open. Alec had one arm around Jon's waist, and as he looked down at the baby, it was impossible to miss the love and pride in his gaze.

Apparently, Alec was one of those tough men who went gooey over babies, which wasn't a surprise. However, when Daryl Greer held out his arms to Jon, most of his fellow mercs looked stunned.

"Can I hold her?" D-Day asked. "I promise I know what I'm doing."

"Of course," Jon said, handing over Alexandra without hesitation. "I'm sure you've had plenty of practice with your nieces and nephews."

"You got that right," D-Day said, taking the baby with confidence and grinning down at her. "Look at you, pretty girl! With them big blue eyes, you're gonna have the boys all over you. Uncle D-Day's gonna teach you how to handle 'em, don't you worry. Ain't no boy gonna be good enough for our girl."

Herc had stepped into the room behind Alec and Jon. "You've done it, you know. You're not going to be able to pry her away from D-Day for an hour."

Alec nodded. "Yeah, I warned Jon about D-Day being a smooshball about kids."

The smooshball was totally ignoring the other mercs and the movie star in the room and was cooing to the baby about teaching her how to kick ass as soon as she could crawl. Alec rolled his eyes and gestured to the other mercs. "Jon, I'm sure you remember most of these guys. Hey, Finn, how's it going? And Mojo, and look, there's Pita. How's it going, Payne? When are you going to come out to California to become a stuntman? Jon is sure he can get you on with his studio."

"I've got a couple of things to wrap up here first," Payne said, chuckling. Sometimes he was tempted to give stunt work a try, but he wasn't sure he'd find it as satisfying as the work he did for Herc.

He peered over D-Day's arm at Alexandra, awed by how tiny she was. He had two nephews, but he'd been overseas when they were born, so he missed their infancy. "C'mon, D-Day, give the rest of us a chance," he said, poking D-Day's hard bicep.

Tearing his attention away from the baby, D-Day frowned down at Payne. "Oh, all right," he grumbled. "But if you drop her, I don't care how fast you are, I'm gonna kick your ass from here all the way to California." He carefully passed the tiny girl over to Payne. "Make sure to support her head."

For such a small person, she was surprisingly heavy, and Payne settled her against his chest, supporting her head as Daryl instructed. She stared up at him with owlish interest, and he stroked her soft cheek with his forefinger, his heart melting. He'd never thought about having kids before, but holding Alexandra showed him the appeal.

"She's gorgeous," he said, glancing up at Alec and Jon.

"We think so," Jon said, his smile every bit as proud and besotted as Alec's.

"Not that we're biased or anything, but she really is the most perfect child ever born on the planet," Alec said, his tone teasing. He glanced at the other mercs, and then looked beyond Payne, his eyes widening. "Hey, Hunter! I didn't realize you were here. Won't you come over to meet my husband and daughter?"

Payne glanced back over his shoulder, seeing that Hunter alone of all the mercs hadn't stopped his work out to come greet the new arrivals. As Alec spoke to him, however, Hunter put down the free weights he was holding and ducked his head, not meeting Alec's gaze. "Hey, Red," he said quietly, then looked at Jon, though he didn't make any move to come any closer. "Nice to meet you, Mr. Baldwin."

"It's nice to meet you too," Jon said, giving Hunter a friendly wave.

Hunter inclined his head in acknowledgement, then picked up his weights again, turning away from the others and resuming his workout. Alec frowned and looked at Herc, who shook his head slightly. Fortunately, no one else seemed to notice, but Payne saw the worry and sympathy in Alec's expression.

Hunter sounded polite enough, but Payne heard the remoteness in his voice. Hunter didn't want to get near the baby, and Payne had a pretty good idea why. He was tempted to carry Alexandra over to Hunter and show him it was okay, but Payne didn't want Hunter to feel cornered or damage what little camaraderie they had developed since working together. Instead, he handed her over to Mojo, who'd been hovering nearby, waiting his turn. Quietly excusing himself, Payne left the group and went over to join Hunter. He waited until Hunter finished his reps before speaking.

"You okay?"

Hunter put the weights back on the rack, then picked up his towel and wiped his face before glancing at Payne. "Sure. Why wouldn't I be?"

"I can think of several reasons," Payne said. "But mostly I wanted to make sure you know you're welcome to join us. The guys gave you a hard time the first day because it's a running gag around here to see which newbies will underestimate me, but they're good guys, not mean spirited."

"Yeah, I know." Hunter swiped the towel over his arms, then glanced at the group of men. "They know him better, so let them get it out of their systems. I'll say hello before they go."

Payne suspected Hunter would find a way to stall until Alec and Jon left, but he didn't want to push Hunter into something he wasn't ready for, so he nodded instead.

"She's a cute baby. She's safe," he said, leaving that for Hunter to interpret however he liked.

Hunter's head whipped around, and he frowned down at Payne. "Yeah, so what?"

"So nothing is going to happen to hurt her while she's surrounded by these guys, and nothing's going to happen to you if you get close to her," Payne said, meeting Hunter's gaze.

Hunter stared at Payne, his face pale. He swallowed hard, then looked away. "I know." Hunter's voice was ragged, and he cleared his throat. "It doesn't matter, anyway. How do you know I don't like kids?"

"We can call it intuition," Payne said gently. "I'm willing to bet you were good with kids before."

With a scowl, Hunter stuffed his towel into his gym bag. "It doesn't matter. I'm going to shower before we go on duty." He glanced back at the cluster of mercs, who were now passing the baby around and listening to Alec animatedly describing the joys of fatherhood. Hunter went still, an expression of intense grief and pain crossing his face, before his mask slipped back into place once again. He picked up his bag and headed toward the locker room. "I'll be ready in fifteen minutes."

"Sure, I'll do the same and meet you at the van," Payne said, recognizing the cue to stop prodding. For now, at least. Hunter needed to face whatever was haunting him, but this wasn't the time or place.

Hunter headed out of the room, not seeming to notice both Herc and Alec were also watching him leave. Payne rubbed the back of his neck, wishing he knew whether he was helping or hindering Hunter's progress. Maybe he ought to push Hunter a little harder, because Hunter didn't seem inclined to move forward on his own, but he worried that pushing would drive Hunter away. Payne didn't want Hunter to return to Lawson and Greer while he was still in this frame of mind or God forbid, join up with a group that wouldn't care about Hunter's mental stability as long as he could fire a gun.

But for now, they had a job to do, so Payne said goodbye to the others and headed off to clean up. Maybe tonight, he'd tell Hunter all about his favorite foods. If that didn't work, he could try favorite vacation spots, favorite album, and his bucket list plans. Surely one of those would coax a response out of Hunter, and if not, well, he had plenty of other ideas. If nothing else, Hunter would know far more than he probably wanted to about Payne by the end of their time together.

5

After three weeks in the surveillance van, Hunter had resigned himself to the tedium and to Payne's almost constant chatter. He'd even found, to his surprise, that Payne was as widely read as he was and had even found himself interested in Payne's opinions about books. And movies. And music. He told himself it was a defensive mechanism, because if he didn't reply to Payne, he'd have to choke the life out of him. Or try, at least — he'd learned his lesson about how strong and fast Payne was, and he wasn't at all certain that in a knock-down, drag-out fight he'd be able to get the best of his smaller partner.

There were still times when he didn't want to talk, where he found himself staring again into the pit of his own dark thoughts. At times like that he simply tuned Payne out, though he'd found that when Payne widened his big, blue eyes the way he did when he wanted something, Payne could sometimes pull him back from the brink. There were even times when he wanted to talk to Payne about what he was feeling; Payne was a good listener, and he'd made it quite obvious he was willing to listen. But Hunter always clamped down on the impulse, because he wasn't certain about Payne's real motives. Maybe he could understand Hunter's bitterness and anger, but maybe he was going to go running back to Herc and Matthew and tell them Hunter was a danger to himself and others, which would put an end to Hunter's career. He was a merc, and he had no idea what he could be if he wasn't a merc any longer.

He knew Payne had an uncanny knack for reading his thoughts, which was both intriguing and alarming. Somehow Payne had even guessed Hunter had felt an intense desire to run when Alec Davis had shown up with his husband and baby, though it wasn't for the reason Payne seemed to think. He knew the baby was in no danger and wasn't a danger to him or anyone else. Alec had looked at his tiny daughter as though the world rose and set on her. It was exactly the way Stack had always looked at his son Jake, and Hunter had felt a surge of anger and guilt that had been difficult to control. Alexandra Baldwin-Davis had her big, strong father to protect her, but Jake Hansen had no father any longer. Little Jake would never know the man his father had been, would never remember how Stack had loved his son with every breath in his body — and there wasn't a damn thing Hunter could do to change it.

That was what hurt, and why Hunter couldn't bring himself to go near Alec or the baby. He didn't want to face a reminder of his own helplessness to do anything about the way the world had shit on the people he cared about.

"I stayed up way too long watching Netflix," Payne said in the conversational tone that meant he was about to start nattering about something. Somehow, he seemed to know when Hunter was getting broody and he started talking, as if he was trying to distract Hunter. "I finally started watching a new superhero series they made. It's pretty good, although I only got a few episodes in before I conked out."

Hunter stared into the abyss of his thoughts, then with an effort pulled his attention back to the van and to Payne. It was like coming out of quicksand or trying to wake up from a nightmare, and he blinked hard. He started to glance away again, but then Payne widened his eyes, giving Hunter the puppy-dog look Hunter found hard to ignore. He was pretty sure Payne knew the effect that look had on people. Even with Hunter, it still worked.

"Which superhero?" he asked, wondering if Payne used the same look on people he wanted to take to bed. If so, Payne probably had more action than he knew what to do with.

"Daredevil. The guy who plays him is really hot, which is one reason why I kept watching instead of going to bed like I should have," Payne said, smiling mischievously. "But I found the story interesting too. He's a merc, basically."

Hunter hadn't seen the show, but perhaps he should check it out, if only to see how they portrayed a merc. And maybe, just out of curiosity, to see what kind of man Payne considered hot. "It's better than that stupid movie?"

"God, yes." Payne screwed up his face in dislike. "Although I suppose saying he's a merc is inaccurate, since he's not getting paid to be a vigilante hero. He does it because he wants to help people who are getting screwed over by a corrupt system. Still, he's working outside the law, and he's a badass fighter, so close enough."

One of the things Payne said caught Hunter's attention, and he frowned. "Do you consider us to be heroes?" he asked, genuinely curious.

"Well, yeah." Payne appeared surprised by the question. "I've read the report about the mission you guys collaborated with us on, the one where D-Day tackled a nuke. There's no telling how many lives you saved or how many international incidents you prevented, and that's only one mission."

"But we got hazard pay for it," Hunter pointed out, ignoring the sharp pain he felt when he remembered how excited Stack had been about that mission. "It was our job, and we were trained for it. I'm not going to say it wasn't dangerous, but it's not like we didn't know what we were up against going in."

Payne was silent for a moment, watching Hunter contemplatively. "I think we get in a bubble," he said at last, drawing a wide circle in the air with his forefinger. "In the army, at Lawson and Greer, at

Hercules Security — we're surrounded by men and women who are trained to put their lives on the line. Everyone we work with would take a bullet for their client because it's their job. But we forget not everyone is like us. Not everybody could even get through the training. I'd most people couldn't. So yes, I think you guys are heroes for putting yourselves out there despite the risks."

Hunter could see Payne's point. "So it's a matter of perspective," he said slowly. "I guess you're right." He paused, drawing in a deep breath, and when he spoke again, his voice was soft. "Stack was a hero. Probably the most heroic man I've ever known."

"He was very brave and selfless," Payne said, resting his hand lightly on Hunter's arm. "Definitely a hero."

The touch surprised Hunter. People didn't tend to touch him unless he initiated it, probably because he was so big and scary looking. The exceptions tended to be the people he was closest to, which these days was... no one. It was a sobering thought, one he didn't want to dwell on, so he nodded, deciding to change the subject because he felt like he'd revealed enough. "So this Daredevil series is good? I guess I'll check it out. If only to give my eyes a break from all the reading I've been doing."

Payne leaned back in his seat. "I'm only about four episodes in, but yeah, I'd recommend it. It's not art, but it's good TV," he said, taking the change of subject in stride.

The conversation drifted on to other television shows, while they watched the monitors. Suddenly Hunter whipped his head around, having caught movement on one display out of the corner of his eye. He frowned, leaning forward and watching a dark shadow skirting around the edge of the picture. It could have been an animal, but the stealthiness of the movement set off alarm bells in his head.

"We have an intruder," he said tersely. "North edge of the property. It's like they know where the cameras are, but I see the shadow moving. I don't think they counted on the moonlight."

"Good catch." Payne stood up, shifting into professional mode instantly. "I'll take care of him. You call in for backup."

"Right." Hunter picked up the van's phone, which was tied into a satellite network and didn't rely on cell towers and was much harder to jam. He heard Payne leave the van, but he kept his eyes on the monitor, watching the shadow creeping forward toward the house.

Hercules Security kept a night crew on call at all times, and Hunter described the situation and requested backup. If they were lucky, one of the mobile teams the company had in the field checking out facilities that didn't maintain 24-hour surveillance would be close by and able to respond. The night crew would also call the local police and report the situation, so Hunter didn't have to divert his attention from his monitors.

He watched Payne approaching the target on one of the other monitors, but before Payne reached the area, all hell broke loose on Hunter's panels. A sensor on the sliding door at the rear of the house flashed red, and an audible siren went off at the same time.

Hunter surged to his feet, weapon drawn, and jumped from the van. He crossed the lawn at a dead run, making it to the house in less than a minute. He could see the jagged glass where the sliding door had been broken with one of the metal lawn chairs, but he didn't stop to survey the damage. After a quick look to make sure there were no intruders still lurking outside, he entered the house.

The slider was part of the huge kitchen of the house, and it took only a moment to ascertain the intruder hadn't lingered in the empty room. The attack had been well-coordinated, and that meant whoever had pulled it off had an objective, one Hunter was pretty certain involved injuring or killing the client. He was familiar with the layout of the house, even though he'd only been inside it once. Weeks of watching every room on the monitors gave him the ability to move quickly and surely in the direction of the master bedroom.

As he'd expected, the door was open, and a masked man with a drawn gun stood staring down the Petersons as they clung to each other in their bed. Hunter didn't hesitate; the wailing of the siren covered any sound he made as he stepped into the room, raised his gun and slammed the unsuspecting intruder in the side of the head, knocking him unconscious. The man crumpled at his feet, and Hunter looked at the Petersons.

"Are you all right?" he asked, shouting to be heard over the alarm.

Steven Peterson nodded jerkily, but before he could say anything, Hunter heard a scream even over the siren. A child's scream.

"Stay here!" he shouted, then sprinted from the room, mounting the stairs toward the bedroom belonging to Adam Peterson. The door was open, and Hunter ran inside, weapon lifted, only to freeze as the situation became horrifyingly clear.

A large, masked man had picked up Adam Peterson, holding the five-year-old around the waist with one arm. In his other hand was a gun, which he pressed against Adam's head.

Hunter went rigid, unable to move, as he watched the intruder circled toward the door.

"That's it. Stay right there, and I won't splatter the little guy's brains all over the room," the intruder shouted.

All Hunter could do was watch in agony. He was a good enough shot to take the intruder out with a single round to the head, but he couldn't make his fingers move. He stared at Adam Peterson, who had stopped screaming and was looking at Hunter with wide, imploring eyes. The boy knew Hunter was supposed to save him, but Hunter saw another boy, one with darker hair and brown eyes who had watched Hunter the same way as Hunter and Stack had worked to remove the explosive vest the boy wore. In his mind, Hunter was screaming, wanting to do something, but his body was paralyzed, unable to act, waiting for the blast of the gun the way he'd heard the sound of the explosives which had ended Stack's life.

The intruder stepped backwards out into the hall, and through his mask, Hunter could see the way the man grinned, teeth bared fiercely in victory. Then time slowed, or at least it did for Hunter, and he watched what followed almost as though it had been a movie.

As the intruder moved into the hall, he didn't bother to look behind himself, but even if he had looked, he wouldn't have seen Payne, who had crouched low against the wall, hidden in the shadows. Payne stepped up behind the intruder, grabbing the man's right arm near the elbow in a vise-like grip. The move caused the gun to fall from the man's now nerveless hand, but before the weapon hit the carpet, Payne was in motion, adding a second hand to the man's arm and wrenching it violently backwards. Hunter heard the snap of breaking bone, and the shriek of pain the intruder gave as he dropped young Adam and instinctively turned toward his attacker.

Payne seemed to anticipate this move, and he stepped in to meet it, releasing the intruder's broken arm and grabbing him around the head. Payne yanked down on the intruder's head, raising his knee at the same time, and there was another snap as the intruder's jaw broke. Then Payne stepped back, and the intruder fell to the floor.

Payne knelt and picked up the little boy. "Are you okay?" he asked. "Does it hurt anywhere?"

The boy shook his head, then threw his arms around Payne's neck, clinging to him for dear life. Hunter still hadn't moved, and he stared at Payne, ice-cold fingers of dread running down his spine.

Holding Adam close, Payne approached Hunter slowly. "It's over, Hunter. All clear," he said, his voice quiet and steady.

Hunter blinked, coming back to himself and realizing he was still holding his gun out. He lowered it slowly, then holstered it, not meeting Payne's eyes. With an effort he made himself report. "I disabled an intruder in the master bedroom. I'll go turn off the alarm."

"Good work," Payne said. "Our backup should be here soon, but I'd like to get the intruders secured. Can you take care of it while I check in with the family?"

"Sure." Hunter made himself move. He was carrying plastic zip ties in one pocket of his cargo pants, and it took him only a moment to bind the feet and hands of the intruder in the hall. He continued on to the master bedroom, binding the intruder he'd knocked uncon-scious, before continuing back toward the kitchen. He disarmed the house alarm at the security panel, then headed outside, finding and restraining the intruder Payne had knocked out in the yard.

By the time he'd returned to the house, the cops had arrived, and he and Payne had to show their licenses and give statements as to what had occurred. The cops took the three intruders into custody, and Hunter nodded politely as the Petersons thanked both him and Payne for reacting so quickly and saving their lives. They didn't know Hunter had frozen in the middle of the confrontation, but Payne did, and Hunter had no doubt there would be a reckoning soon.

He sat numbly in the car while Payne drove them back to headquarters. They'd been relieved by the backup crew, but they had to make their reports before they'd be finished. Once at headquarters, Hunter gathered up the forms he needed to fill out, then made his way to one of the small conference rooms. Feeling disconnected, he described the events as best as he could.

"I'm not going to mention you froze," Payne said, glancing sidelong at Hunter from where they sat at an unadorned table. "I don't want you to mention it either. I don't think Herc needs to know about it right now, but we do need to talk about it."

"What?"

Unable to believe what Payne was saying, Hunter stared at him in shock. After a moment, he dropped his head into his hands, feeling defeated, knowing even Payne's upbeat philosophy wasn't going to do him a damned bit of good. "You can't mean that. You *know* what it means. I'm washed up. I froze in combat, so I'm no good to anyone anymore."

"No." Payne's voice held a hard edge Hunter hadn't heard before. "It means you were triggered by seeing a child in danger just like the situation with Stack. It means you need to get off your ass and face your shit. But it does not mean you're washed up."

Hunter knew a command tone when he heard it, and he looked at Payne again. "I face my shit every fucking day," he growled, suddenly angry — with himself, with Payne, with Stack, with the *world*. "Of course I'm washed up! Don't tell me you didn't know that from the minute you took me down in front of everyone. That's what all of this was about, right? Everyone knew I was finished. Everyone but me." He laughed bitterly. "Well, I finally faced it. I guess I should thank

Herc and Matthew for making sure I didn't get a bunch of my comrades killed."

Payne stood up and kicked back his chair, and he rounded on Hunter, his boyish face growing hard with anger. "You're only washed up if you want to be. You haven't been facing your shit. You've been wallowing in it and avoiding any kind of serious effort to heal. Do you think washing out is going to change anything or make you feel better? Is it what Stack would want for you?"

Hunter couldn't believe what Payne was saying. "Nothing is going to make me feel better," he said, slumping back in his seat. "You know what Stack would say? He'd tell me to suck it up and deal with it. But he's dead, he's not *here*, and he wouldn't know that being the one to live sometimes isn't all that great."

"No, it isn't," Payne said, folding his arms across his chest. "But you're still here, whether you like it or not, and you've got a choice. You can tell yourself and everyone else you're done and give up the job you love, or you can admit you need help — and *accept* it."

Hunter didn't answer. He looked at Payne, seeing the way Payne was so certain, so confident, and he wished he could believe Payne was right. "You mean talk to the shrinks, let them tell me everything's okay?" He gave a humorless chuckle. "I've read all those psych books, and I know what they all say, and you know what? It's all bullshit. Maybe it works for some people, but not for me. Maybe I do need help, but there isn't anything that will help me."

"If you're convinced conventional methods won't help, then no, they probably won't." Payne studied Hunter, his expression shuttered. "But unconventional methods might."

Hunter narrowed his eyes, looking at Payne intently. Payne's open and friendly gaze was gone, and against his will, Hunter shivered. "Unconventional? Like what? Some new age stuff about past life regression? Or maybe balancing my chakras?"

One corner of Payne's mouth quirked up. "No, nothing like that. What I have in mind is unusual, but it's helped other trauma victims. It might help you too."

Hunter shrugged. Hope wasn't a word in his vocabulary any

longer. He scrubbed at his face, suddenly as exhausted as if he had run a marathon. "So you want to help me? Why? Why not let me wash out? I'm no danger to anyone anymore, if that's what you were worried about." The thought of never going back into the field was painful, and he had no idea what he would do if he couldn't be a merc.

"Because I like you," Payne said, spreading his hands. "Because I don't believe you're washed up. Because I have the biggest caretaker streak of anyone you'll ever meet in your life."

Hunter knew he'd just about reached the end of the line. He didn't believe in himself anymore, so he had nothing to lose. He could accept Payne's help, or he could give up, go home and stare at the walls until he worked up the courage to walk in front of a train or went quietly nuts. Either Payne could help him, or he couldn't, and if Payne failed, the outcome would still be the same. Hunter was empty, and, in a perverse way, it made things simple.

"All right," he said quietly. He felt no real hope, just a hollow sort of nothing. "What do you want me to do?"

Payne pulled his chair close to Hunter and sat down again. "What do you know about BDSM?" he asked, watching Hunter somberly.

"BDSM?" Hunter thought for a moment, then it dawned on him. "Oh. *Oh.*" He raised a brow, looking at Payne in surprise. "I know what it stands for, and I know there's a lot of porn about it, but that's pretty much it."

"It's a facet of human sexuality," Payne said. "But it can have therapeutic benefits as well, mainly through helping you tap into your emotions, especially the deeper ones, and achieve catharsis."

Hunter wasn't certain what Payne had in mind, but he had to ask. "So... um, does that mean you want to tie me up and have sex with me?" The thought wasn't as alarming as it probably should have been.

For the first time ever, Hunter got to see Payne grow flustered. His cheeks flooded with color as he shook his head.

"If we're using it for therapeutic purposes, we should probably take the sexual component off the table," Payne said. "I mean, yes,

BDSM is sexy fun times for me, but that's not what we would be doing."

Hunter felt a sense of disappointment he had no right to feel. "If it's not sex, what is it for me? Or for you, for that matter."

"Like I said, it's about helping you reach a catharsis." Payne leaned forward, seeming to warm up to the subject. "Pain can be pleasurable. Maybe it isn't for you, and that's fine, but it *can* help you get out of your own head. Combined with the right kind of roleplay scenario, you could face your shit in a way that works for you."

Hunter thought about it. "I guess I don't have anything to lose," he said slowly. The thought of pain didn't frighten him; he'd been a merc for a long time, and he didn't think there was much of anything Payne could do to him that would be worse than what he'd already gone through. "So... what am I supposed to do?"

"Think about it, maybe do some research and make sure this is something you want to pursue," Payne said. "If it is, then we can talk more in-depth about what's involved, and I think a trial run would be a good idea too. It would give you an idea of what to expect, and it would give me an idea of what equipment works best with you."

"All right." Hunter looked back down at the forms. "Do you still want me to leave out the part about freezing? It seems wrong."

Payne rubbed his chin, seeming lost in thought for a minute. "Let's leave it out for now. I'll suggest to Herc we both need some time before we're given another assignment, and we'll use the time to try your new therapy regime. If it doesn't work and you don't show any signs of improvement, then we'll tell him. How about that?"

"I guess that works," Hunter said slowly. He grimaced as he looked at the forms. "I should get these done."

"We both should." Payne scooted his chair up to the table again. "Then I'll talk to Herc about time off."

"Okay." Hunter had to admit, he was just as happy to leave any discussion with Cade Thornton to Payne. Omitting something from paperwork was bad enough, but he didn't think he could handle trying to hide anything from Herc in person.

Turning his attention to the paperwork, Hunter made himself

concentrate on keeping things factual, leaving out anything he'd felt during the situation. After that, he'd go home and hope he didn't have nightmares about freezing. He was glad Payne had been there to save the boy, but Hunter knew he wouldn't forget how he'd been unable to react and how horrible the consequences might have been.

6

"This is my playroom," Payne said, opening the door and reaching in to turn on the light. He gestured for Hunter to go on in, and he hovered close behind, watching anxiously to see how Hunter would respond to what he saw.

The playroom was a sizeable interior room in the two-story house Payne had bought and renovated. The house sat on a couple of acres about forty minutes out from Hercules Security headquarters depending on traffic, but Payne considered the commute a fair tradeoff for the privacy.

The playroom didn't have any windows, but it was well lit, although he could dim the lights if necessary to create a certain ambiance. The opposite wall was dominated by a St. Andrew's cross secured in a heavy metal frame to make sure there was no danger of tipping over. It had restraint points for wrists, ankles, and waist, and it had wide footrests for extra stability.

To the left was his spanking bench, which also had a sturdy metal frame, and it was well padded with restraint points if they were wanted or needed. On one section of the wall hung his collection of canes, mounted so he could reach the one he wanted with ease. His floggers hung neatly on hooks next to the cane display, and his paddles were lined up on a shelf.

On the right, there were shelves with bottles of lube, a box of condoms, a box of latex gloves, a first aid kit, shears powerful enough to cut through rope, and an assortment of toys he often found useful. Next to the shelves was an antique loveseat he'd reupholstered with a stain-resistant fabric in a deep crimson that reminded him of something from a bordello. He also had a couple of comfortable chairs that were light enough to be moved around the room when he had observers.

There was also a mini fridge where he stored bottles of water and Gatorade, and a fire extinguisher just in case. The floors were laminate, made to look like hardwood but far easier to keep clean and unmarked. All in all, he didn't think it was as intimidating as some playrooms he'd seen, but Hunter was a complete novice, so even this might be more than he wanted to face.

"You can look around if you want," he said, tucking his hands in the back pockets of his jeans. "I'm sure you've got questions too, so fire away whenever you're ready."

Hunter prowled around, taking stock of the entire room. He lingered over the canes and paddles, as though curious, then continued on. After a few minutes, he returned to where Payne stood.

"It's not as weird as some of the ones I saw online," he said. "Which is good. I've seen the inside of a place where ISIS was torturing soldiers. I don't think I could be comfortable someplace that looked too similar."

"I wanted my playroom to be functional but comfortable," Payne said, taking a seat in one of the comfy chairs, which was currently grouped near the loveseat. "I know people who go for a more literal dungeon look, but that's not my style."

"Hm." The sound Hunter made could have meant anything, but he didn't run for the door and he didn't seem uncomfortable. If anything, he seemed neutral, as though reserving judgement for the time being. "I did some research online. From what I can tell, there's no rulebook for this, right? Just whatever you and I agree to?"

"Pretty much," Payne said. "Everyone likes different things, so it's up to the people involved to negotiate what they want and what they don't want. Since this is new to you, I thought this trial run would be a good time for you to start learning what you like and where your limits are."

"All right." Hunter continued to prowl around as though restless. Then he walked toward Payne. "I want to know something first, before we start. Have you ever done this for someone like me before? I mean, someone you aren't interested in having sex with."

Payne stalled for time by giving Hunter a wide-eyed look as he tried to figure out how to answer the question without embarrassing himself. "I don't recall saying I'm not interested in having sex with you," he said at last, taking refuge in plausible deniability.

Hunter waved a hand dismissively. "I'll rephrase the question. Have you done this with someone purely as therapy before? I'm serious. I'm trusting you with my well-being, right? I want to know that you know what you're doing. Since you can't exactly produce references, I'm going to have to take your word for it, but I'd like to know the truth."

"Have I done this purely as therapy? No." Payne spread his hands and shrugged. "But I've been an active part of the BDSM community for over ten years. For the most part, I'm a Dom, but I've subbed too because I think experiencing the other side of things is part of being a good Dom. I'm also familiar with the effect this can have — the release and relief it gives. The body stores emotion, you know? That's why some people start crying in the middle of a relaxing massage. But I don't think a good massage will cut it for you."

"If only," Hunter said, his tone dry. He looked at Payne intently for a long moment, then drew in a deep breath. "Okay, then. After everything I read, I think I understand the way this is supposed to work. Maybe it'll work for me, maybe it won't, but I'm willing to give it a try."

"Then have a seat, and we can discuss the specifics," Payne said, beckoning for Hunter to join him. "What did you think about what you read? Did anything in particular appeal to you?"

Hunter perched on the edge of one of the chairs. "I tried to keep my reading to the more clinical type studies," he said. "I understand about endorphins and the link between pain and pleasure, but if you're asking me if I'd rather you hit me with a cane or a paddle, I don't know. I do know what doesn't appeal at all, though."

"That's what the trial run is for, at least in part," Payne said, nodding to encourage Hunter. "We'll test out different toys and equipment to find out what you respond to best. What doesn't appeal to you? If there's anything that's a hard no, I need to know what it is so we can avoid it."

"All right." Hunter paused, watching Payne's expression. "I don't want to be degraded or humiliated. It wouldn't help me. It would only make me angry. I understand about the sub thing and giving you control, but I'm not compromising my self-respect."

Payne smiled wryly at Hunter's blunt assessment. He knew people who loved humiliation play, and he'd done it himself a few times as a Dom, but it didn't interest him as a sub either.

"That won't be a problem," he said. "Humiliation isn't all that high on my kink list either, although yes, I will be in control, and I will tell you what to do when we're in the scene. If you don't obey me, then there will be consequences you won't like. That's how it works. If you can handle that level of bossing around, we'll be fine."

Hunter frowned. "What if I get angry?" he asked. "What if you piss me off so much I try to slug you? God knows there were times when I was a plebe at the Point when I wanted to crush some asshole's head, and his rank didn't matter." His tone became rough. "After freezing the way I did, I realize I'm not fully in control of my actions any more. I can't guarantee that if you poke too hard, I might not go after you."

"Hunter, I've got thick leather cuffs secured with chains that say you can get as mad as you want with me, but you won't be able to do a damned thing about it," Payne said, matching Hunter's bluntness. "This is why I think BDSM will help, maybe even more than either of us realize. You aren't in control right now. Your fear, your anger, and your guilt are. But when you're in this room, *I'll* be in control, and you'll have a safe space where you can feel whatever you need to feel without worrying whether you're going to hurt me or yourself." He leaned forward, meeting Hunter's gaze intently. "Understand? You are safe in here, and whatever happens stays between you and me."

Again Hunter was silent, as though weighing Payne's words. "All right, I'll trust you. And trust you that if I use my safe word, you'll stop. I had to think about it a lot, you know. Trust isn't easy for me, and I haven't known you for long, so I'm taking as much of a chance on you as I've ever taken on anyone."

Payne felt a little flutter in his stomach, both pleased by and apprehensive about the level of trust Hunter was placing in him, and he hoped he could live up to it. He intended to try, because he felt more than ever like Hunter needed him.

"I appreciate it, and I don't take your trust lightly, believe me," Payne said. "I want to help you, Hunter. If I can do something to help ease your pain, I will."

"Thanks," Hunter said simply. "I guess the other things I'm not interested in are broken bones or stitches. I'm scarred enough already. I don't think more will improve my looks any."

Payne grinned, pleased that Hunter had relaxed enough to make a little joke. "Well, you're going to have bruises and possibly welts, especially if we use the canes," he said, gesturing to his collection, which contained several canes of varying lengths made from different materials from acrylic to rattan. "Those will leave a mark, and you won't sit comfortably for a few days. But I don't get off on causing damage more serious than that, so it shouldn't be a problem."

"Then I guess that's it." Hunter shrugged slightly. "Anything else will get sorted out during the process, right? And if it doesn't work for me, no hard feelings."

"Actually, there are a couple of other things I want to mention," Payne said, sitting back in his seat again. "First, I want you to have a true understanding of the dynamic that's going to be at work here. I'm going to be in control, yes, but you've got the power. We start, slow down, or even stop at your say-so. Everything I do will be your choice for your benefit. So if you don't like being caned? We won't do that.

I'm not going to force anything on you that you don't want – including myself."

Hunter frowned, obviously not understanding. "Yourself? What do you mean?"

Payne felt his face growing hot, but he forged ahead. "I mean BDSM is a pretty big part of my sexy fun times, so you shouldn't be surprised if I get turned on. You shouldn't be surprised or embarrassed if you do either, for that matter. But just because I get turned on doesn't mean I'll do anything about it. This is about healing, not sex, and I don't want you to worry I'll conflate the two."

"Yes, you already made that clear," Hunter said, his tone a trifle impatient. "I get it, okay? You aren't attracted to me, this isn't about sex, it's about healing. If you get turned on, I won't take it personally, since it's not about me."

"Whoa, whoa, whoa!" Payne held up both hands, startled by Hunter's response. "You're making a lot of assumptions, big guy. I believe we established earlier I never said I'm not interested in having sex with you. But if I need to spell it out, badass hunks with broad shoulders and biceps bigger than my head are my type, okay? And God help me, you're stomping all over my white knight hot buttons too. So let's dispel the notion that I'm not interested, because believe me, when you're naked and tied up right in front of me, and your ass is turning red as Santa's suit with every whack of my paddle, I'm going to be very fucking interested."

Hunter went still, eyes wide, as he stared at Payne in complete disbelief.

"Oh."

Payne blinked his big blue eyes at Hunter and smiled. "Are we clear?"

Hunter seemed to gather his scattered wits, and a flush crawled up his neck and into his cheeks. "Yeah. We're clear," he said, his tone more than a little hoarse, and the heat in his gaze as he looked at Payne was a clear indication he wasn't at all immune to Payne's words.

The look gave Payne a little hope that perhaps Hunter would

respond better to the BDSM therapy than he thought. His biggest concern was that the whole thing would leave Hunter cold, but perhaps not.

"Good, so we can move on to safe words," Payne said. "I'd like to suggest using a different system, one that will give you more agency. It's a color system — green, yellow, red. Green means you're fine, and red means everything needs to stop immediately. Yellow is like an early warning, and we can figure out what it means for you personally."

Hunter drew in a deep breath, seeming to pull himself back into focus. "All right. I assume getting angry or emotional isn't necessarily a reason to stop, nor is when something hurts. I suppose it's if I think it's getting to be too much?"

"I'll check in by asking what your color is," Payne said. "But you can be proactive and warn me if you feel like you're getting close to the edge, whether it's an emotional threshold or a pain threshold. It's to let me know we're heading into potentially difficult territory. We can pause and assess the situation. You can decide if you're good to keep going or if you want to call it red." He gave Hunter a stern look. "But ditch the 'suck it up, buttercup' mentality at the door. This isn't boot camp, and you aren't supposed to keep pushing through if it gets to be too much, whether it's physically, mentally, or emotionally. Continuing past your limits can do more harm than good, so *I'm* trusting *you* to be honest and not get mired in macho bullshit."

"I can understand that," Hunter said. "I work with explosives, remember? I know exactly what happens if you go too far too fast and make a mistake. I promise I'll stop, or at least pause and ask, all right?"

"That works," Payne said, satisfied with Hunter's response. "My style as a Dom is to work communication into the scene so I know what's going on with my sub. With you, communication is going to be vital, so I'll probably blindfold you, but I won't gag you."

Hunter tilted his head to one side. "Not that I'm averse, but out of curiosity... why blindfolded?"

"Less visual input means you'll feel everything more intensely, internally and externally," Payne said, then grinned mischievously. "Plus I like when my subs don't know what's coming. It lets me set the pace, and I enjoy making them get worked up with anticipation sometimes."

"Oh. All right." Hunter seemed to accept the answer without hesitation. "So... what's next?"

"Well, now I think we should test run some toys." Payne stood up and beckoned Hunter to follow him over to the paddle shelf. "We can also discuss ideas for the actual scene once we've figured out what you like and don't like."

Hunter followed along, hovering behind Payne as he looked over the paddles. "To be honest, I don't see what the difference is. Pain is pain, right? Does it matter if you're hitting me with a paddle or a switch or a flogger if it's all going to hurt?"

"Sure, it's going to hurt, but each type of toy provides a different kind of pain. A punch in the face doesn't hurt the same as a bullet," Payne explained. He picked up his favorite paddle, which was lined with leather on one side and fur on the other. "I think showing you will be more effective than trying to tell you, so why don't you go ahead and strip and get on the bench." He pointed to the spanking bench. "I won't restrain you or blindfold you this time, and I'll go easy so you don't have to wait to heal up before we schedule the real deal."

Hunter walked toward the bench. He sat down to remove his combat boots and socks, then stood and stripped his t-shirt over his head, revealing his broad shoulders and lightly furred chest, as well as tribal-style tattoos on each upper bicep. After stripping off his jeans and boxer-briefs with an apparent lack of self-consciousness, he folded his clothes and place them neatly to one side.

He didn't look at Payne before kneeling on the lower part of the bench, then draping his torso across the upper part. In that position, it was easy to see the intricate tattoo taking up almost the entirety of his back, from broad shoulders down to his tapered waist. In black ink, a stylized Meso-American sun spread jagged rays over Hunter's tanned skin. In the center was a face like a stone carving, wearing a fierce expression, teeth bared as if in defiance. Around the circle of the face were words in stark capital letters, spelling out a line from Nietzsche.

And if you look deep into the Abyss, the Abyss looks deep into you.

Payne twirled the paddle in one hand as he allowed himself a moment to admire the view. He'd had big, burly men in his playroom before, but the pleasure of seeing such badasses draped over his bench or tied to his cross never palled. He wanted to run his hands along Hunter's broad shoulders and explore those tattoos — preferably with his tongue — but he reminded himself that sex was off the table for more reasons than one.

"Paddles can either thud or sting, depending on the size of the paddle," Payne said as he went to stand beside the bench. "This one is going to be more thuddy. Normally, I'd warm you up a bit, but this is a quick demo, so we'll do that next time. Ready?"

Hunter raised his head to look at Payne. "Sure."

"I'm going to tell myself your lack of enthusiasm stems from not knowing how awesome this is," Payne said dryly — and then he landed a solid blow on Hunter's ass, one intended to provide a deep thudding pain.

Hunter drew in a sharp breath but didn't flinch. "I've been paddled before," he said. "Back when I went through the Point, you couldn't escape it when the upper classmen wanted to teach you a lesson."

"They were amateurs." Payne flipped the paddle and stroked Hunter's ass and thighs with the fur lined side. "Their goal was to teach you your place. My goal is to make my sub moan and beg for more," he said, teasing Hunter between his legs with the fur.

"Hey!" Hunter gasped, and then gave Payne a hard look. "I thought this wasn't about sex."

Payne widened his eyes innocently. "I want to make sure you understand the range of sensation, that's all," he said as he put the paddle aside on a nearby table. "Besides, I said you shouldn't be surprised if you get aroused."

"I didn't think you were going to do things actually meant to be arousing," Hunter said. "God knows I never felt the least bit of excitement over getting paddled before. Mostly I was hoping the assholes didn't hit in places that would leave me singing soprano."

"I've got years of practice, so you don't need to worry about your tender bits." Payne moved around to the front of the bench so Hunter could see him. "Sorry," he said, offering an apologetic smile. "The truth is, you look so damned hot, I couldn't resist. But if you don't want me to tease you that way, I won't. I don't want you to feel uncomfortable or like I'm taking advantage of your vulnerability."

Hunter frowned thoughtfully. "I don't know how to take it, to be honest. I'm used to a binary solution set. Either something is sexual, or it isn't. This is outside my experience. I assume you wouldn't tease me just to be frustrating, but then again, you do a lot of things meant to be frustrating, so I don't know."

Payne laughed, amused rather than offended by Hunter's blunt assessment. "You're right," he said with an unrepentant grin. "This can be sexual if you want it to be. I suggested taking sex off the table because you don't seem in the frame of mind for it, which is understandable," he added, hoping to reassure Hunter that his feelings were normal. "There are times when I'm not even sure you like me, much less want me touching you in the sexy fun times way, so it's totally up to you."

Hunter was silent, and it wasn't hard to see he was thinking it over. "I do like you," he said at last. "It's complicated. I'm used to directness. Remember, I told you when we met that I don't do mind games. Subtlety isn't something I'm used to, because in my line of work, you have to be direct and blunt or people could die. There isn't room for misunderstanding. So when I'm not certain what to say, I say nothing. I don't understand you completely, but I do like you."

This wasn't the strangest conversation Payne had ever had with a naked man before, so he didn't feel odd about pausing the demonstration to follow up with questions.

"I'm curious," he said, cocking his head to one side. "What don't you understand about me? I feel like I've been a pretty open book."

"An open book? You?" For the first time, Hunter laughed. It

started off as a chuckle, but it quickly progressed into a full throated, deep chested rumble of amusement.

Even as bewildered as he was by the response, Payne enjoyed the sound of Hunter's laughter. It sounded genuine, and Payne was glad to hear it even if it was at his expense since Hunter probably hadn't laughed since Stack's death.

Hunter took a few minutes to get himself back under control, and he wiped tears away from his eyes. "Sorry," he managed to get out, still chuckling, but then he drew in a deep breath and shook his head. "God. You're something, Payne. You look like this cherubic choir boy, and when I first saw you, I didn't think you were old enough to drink yet. Then you go all ninja on me, and *then* I find out that behind those big, blue, innocent eyes lurks the Marquis De Sade. An open book? Maybe, but if so it's in a language I never learned to read."

Payne couldn't help but smile at Hunter's description of him. No doubt he did seem somewhat opaque to someone as straightforward and blunt as Hunter.

"I'm an onion. I have layers," he said, sticking his nose in the air with a haughty sniff, but then he smiled to show he was teasing. "But I've been honest with you, and I'm not hiding anything. Not from you, at least. Most of the guys don't know about this, though," he added, gesturing to encompass the playroom.

Hunter's levity faded away. "I understand," he said softly. He went quiet again. "I do appreciate what you are trying to do for me. I don't know if it will work or not, but I wouldn't be here if I wasn't willing to try." He looked down, not meeting Payne's eyes. "Freezing the way I did was the second worst thing to ever happen to me. Only Stack's death was worse. Part of me hates feeling helpless, but what I read about BDSM makes me think it could be the only thing that would work for me because I won't really be helpless, despite how it looks. But I wouldn't even try this with anyone else. Only you. Because I trust you."

"That means a lot to me," Payne said quietly, warmed by Hunter's admission. He touched Hunter's cheek lightly with his forefinger, wanting to establish some kind of contact. "You may be tied up, but you won't be helpless. I hope this will be your chance to take back control."

"I know I can't control all situations, but I have to be in control of myself," Hunter said. He leaned into the touch. "I *am* attracted to you. That's why I was so annoyed when I thought you were belaboring the point about it not being about sex. The way you read me is sometimes a little scary, so I thought you'd picked up on it and wanted to send the message that you aren't attracted to me."

"No, I thought you considered me mouthy and annoying," Payne said, flattening his palm against Hunter's cheek and savoring the warmth against his skin. "All I wanted to do was make sure you didn't feel uncomfortable or pressured, especially given how intimate this is."

"Sometimes you are mouthy and annoying," Hunter said, but he smiled to show he didn't mean it in a bad way. "But you mean to be, don't you? You've been trying to shake me up since we met."

"Pretty much. I'm willing to do whatever it takes to help you, even if it means risking a punch in the face for talking too much."

"I appreciate it. I don't understand why you're so willing to help me, but I've finally gotten my head out of my own ass enough to realize I do need some kind of help. If this doesn't work, I lose everything that has mattered to me. My work has been my life, my identity... I don't know what I would do if I couldn't do it anymore."

"I don't want you to lose anything more than you already have," Payne said. Hunter had never been so open before, and Payne felt all the more determined to do what it took to get Hunter past his grief, anger, and fear now that he knew how much of Hunter's hope for the future was riding on their success.

"Thank you," Hunter said simply. Then he smiled slightly. "What now? I guess we've both had our assumptions corrected. Does that change anything about how this should go?"

"I think it circles back around to the question of whether you want me to do things like stroke your inner thigh with the fur side of my paddle or not." Payne did his best to look like the choir boy Hunter said he resembled. "We've established how hot I think you look, and that's even without the cuffs and blindfold on, so the final decision is yours."

"Now that I fully understand the situation, I'm willing to put myself in your hands completely," Hunter said, and there was no hesitation in his voice. "If you think doing those things will help me, then do them. And since I like to think I'm not completely self-ish, if you want to do it because you like to do it, that's fine, too. All right?"

Any deal allowing him to get his hands on a man as sexy as Hunter sounded pretty damned good to Payne. "If you're good with it, I am too."

"Then it's settled," Hunter said. "So... do we continue now?"

Payne glanced at Hunter's ass, pleased to see the redness from the paddle swat had faded. "Sure, it looks like our little respite has done your tender ass some good. You won't even have a bruise. Well, not from the paddle, at least. We can try a flogger next and leave the cane for last since that's what will hurt the most."

"All right." Hunter settled down across the bench again. "Let's do this."

Payne went to get two of his floggers and returned to Hunter, holding one in each hand. "So you know what a paddle feels like. I can make it sting, but mostly, it's going to be a deeper smack sensation. With floggers, it depends on the size of the strips. These are both leather, but this one has smaller strips." He lashed out and struck Hunter's right ass cheek, keeping the blow lighter than he normally would have. "Stings, doesn't it?"

"A bit," Hunter admitted. "But not too bad."

"That's because I pulled it, plus you only got one. Believe me, if I kept going, you'd feel the burn." Payne put the first flogger aside and switched the second one to his right hand. "Now this one has wider strips and more of them, so it's going to be less stingy and more thuddy."

This time, he struck Hunter's left cheek, wanting to give Hunter a clear basis of comparison.

"I see what you mean." For a moment Hunter considered. "I think the first one would feel like a sunburn. The second one is definitely harder."

"Yeah, the sensation goes deeper." Payne traded the flogger for the paddle and stroked Hunter's pinkened skin with the fur-lined side to soothe it. "If I was trying to get you wound up, I might use the fur flogger or maybe the horsehair one. Those can be used to tease through gentle stimulation, although the horsehair one can sting like a son of a bitch too."

Hunter drew in a breath. He seemed to find the pleasurable sensations more unnerving than the painful ones. "Which one is your favorite?" he asked, glancing back at Payne again. "When you've had this done to you, what do you like?"

"It depends on my mood and why I'm doing it," Payne said, trailing the paddle along the length of Hunter's broad back. "If I'm just playing for fun, then I prefer a paddle or a thuddy flogger. If I *need* it for whatever reason, then I want the cane. Hurts like hell, but I drop into sub space faster with it than anything else."

"I was reading about sub space." Hunter frowned thoughtfully. "I think that's one reason why I decided I could only do this with you, because of the trust thing. The thought that someone could do anything to me while I was out of it and I wouldn't object scares the hell out of me."

"Which is why it's important to have a conscientious Dom who understands how to take care of their sub," Payne said, still moving the paddle up and down Hunter's back in lazy strokes just because he could. "You lose the ability to think with clarity and rationality when you're in sub space. I get a bit loopy. I could have blood running down my legs from the caning, but if my Dom asked if I wanted more, I'd say yes because I'm blissed out on the pain and endorphin high. So the Dom needs to see I've reached that point and avoid phrasing their questions that way. But sometimes, I need to get out of my own head, you know? It's helped me come down off of tough missions."

Eyes wide with surprise, Hunter looked as though he'd never thought of Payne needing a such a release. "You've used this for therapy before? You never mentioned it."

Payne inclined his head slightly. "I guess because I never thought of it as therapy, but everyone needs a coping mechanism or two. This happens to be one of mine."

"That makes sense," Hunter said slowly. "It's what you know, after all. One of my coping mechanisms was to go out to the range with a fifty-cal and blow the fuck out of the targets. But it doesn't help anymore. Or at least it hasn't with this. It just seemed... pointless."

"There are some problems that even blowing shit up doesn't solve." Payne swatted Hunter's ass with his bare hand before heading over to where his canes were mounted. "Are you ready for this?"

Hunter looked at the canes, then drew in a deep breath. "As ready as I'll ever be."

Payne picked the rattan cane, partly because it was his favorite and partly because he thought it would give Hunter a good introduction to caning without the intensity of the fiberglass or derlin canes. He swished it through the air for dramatic effect, wanting to build up anticipation for the blow, and when he brought it down on Hunter's ass at last, he did so with more power than he had with the paddle or flogger.

Hunter let out a yelp, obviously surprised at the strength of the blow. He was breathing harder, but he didn't make a move to get up and punch Payne in the face, even though the gleam in his eyes let Payne know that if it had been anyone else who had hit him so hard, Hunter probably would have done his best to hurt them.

Payne surveyed the bright pink stripe on Hunter's ass with satisfaction. "You know, it probably says something about me that I just love leaving my mark on the pretty skin of big, badass men like you."

Hunter made a small sound almost like a growl, then bared his teeth in something not really a smile. "Some people might say you were compensating for something."

"Considering how often I got my ass kicked before I started learning martial arts, you're probably right." Payne stood in front of Hunter and rested the cane on his shoulder. "So when we're doing this for real, what do you want me to use? It can be one or a combination of them. Whatever you think will work best for you."

"The cane definitely had the most, um... impact," Hunter said. "Maybe start out with it, and if it's too much, I'll tell you? I guess we could start more slowly and work up, but what the hell... I might as well see if I can take it."

"I think you might need something a little high impact," Payne said. "If you think you need something for that last swat, I've got some salve. Otherwise, you can go ahead and get dressed if you want."

"I could be macho and say I don't need any salve," Hunter said, then gave a slightly sheepish smile. "But I learned long ago that 'toughing it out' was pretty stupid. I have to sit to drive back to my apartment, so I would appreciate the salve, please. Otherwise I might get a speeding ticket trying to escape the discomfort."

"You got it." Payne ran his hand along the back of Hunter's head in a comforting gesture, then went to get the salve he kept on hand for after care. "It's an antibiotic plus pain relief," he said when he returned.

"Sounds good," Hunter said. He paused, seeming hesitant. "Should I put it on myself?"

"No, I'll do it. It'll be less awkward, plus I can see where it needs to go." Payne unscrewed the cap, squeezed some out, and began smoothing the salve along the pink welt, applying it generously. "It's not too bad, so you should be fine in a couple of days. What do you think about scheduling the real session this weekend?"

"Sure. It's not like I'm doing anything else," Hunter said, giving a small huff of amusement. "Thanks. I appreciate it."

"After care is important, and I'm going to be here with you and for you through the whole process from start to finish." Payne screwed the cap back on and tossed the salve onto the table, and then he stood in front of Hunter again. "Pack an overnight bag. If things get as intense as I think they will, I want you to stay so I can keep an eye on you in case the drop hits hard. I've got a guest bedroom you can use." He paused, debating whether it was safe to flirt. He was tactile and flirtatious by nature, but he'd reined that side of himself in with

Hunter, assuming it would be unwelcome. "Unless you want to share," he added with an arch smile.

Hunter smiled slightly. "I think I could be convinced to share," he said, his voice low and husky. "I also don't snore and I make a mean cup of coffee."

"I don't snore, but I'm a blanket thief, probably because I'm cold natured. I do like coffee, especially if it's mean."

"I make the meanest," Hunter said. He moved off the bench and stood, looking down at Payne for a long moment. "You do look like a choirboy, you know. A badass choirboy."

Between the Army and practicing BDSM, Payne had no body modesty left, and nudity — his own or someone else's — didn't faze him. But he had his first unobstructed view of Hunter's big, buff body, and he didn't bother hiding his admiration as he looked Hunter over from head to foot.

"I know," he drawled. "I like it, actually. It's fun when people underestimate me."

Hunter snorted and shook his head. "It wasn't much fun for *me*," he said, then stepped closer. He ran his index finger down Payne's cheek; it was the first time Hunter had voluntarily touched him since the day they'd met. "But maybe it was what I needed."

A wide smile curved Payne's lips. "Good, I'm glad."

Hunter simply looked at Payne, then he gave a crooked smile and stepped back. "I'd better get dressed and get home," he said, picking up his neat pile of clothing.

"Okay." Payne watched as Hunter got dressed. He was tempted to invite Hunter to stay for dinner, but he wasn't sure if they were at that point yet. Besides, Hunter still seemed to need a lot of space, and Payne didn't want to push himself on Hunter. Well, not too much. "If you think of any questions or concerns between now and Friday night, you can call or text me. Otherwise, I'll see you then."

"All right." Hunter headed toward the door, then stopped with his hand on the knob. "Other than clothing, is there anything else I should bring?"

Payne followed Hunter, intending to see him out like the

gentleman his mama had raised him to be. "Any toiletries you want or need. I will paddle your ass until you can't sit for a week, but I will not share my toothbrush with you because even I have boundaries," he said, winking. "Other than that, I can't think of anything unless you sleep with a teddy bear."

Hunter wrinkled his nose. "Trust me, I have no desire to share anyone's toothbrush," he said.

After he showed Hunter out, Payne returned to his playroom to clean the toys and the bench, mulling over ideas for their scene. He had an idea he thought might work to help Hunter confront his anger and guilt and — hopefully — put him on the road to peace and healing. If his plan didn't give Hunter any help or release, he'd have to tell Herc he'd failed, and he didn't know what would happen then.

Being someone's last hope wasn't an easy or comfortable place to be in, but Payne had to try, even if he was the most unlikely white knight of all time.

7

Hunter hadn't known what to expect when he'd first seen Payne's "playroom," and he'd been glad the reality hadn't been quite as overwhelming as the picture his imagination had painted based on what he'd read online. If Payne had shown him something that had looked like an Iraqi torture chamber, Hunter would have run away as fast as he could, even if it cost him the career he loved. But as Payne led him back into the room two days after their trial run, Hunter felt a bit of trepidation that had little to do with the contents of the room.

When Hunter arrived, Payne had first shown him to the guest room, and Hunter had unpacked the things he'd brought, putting his toiletries into the bathroom with a wry smile as he remembered Payne's comment about sharing a toothbrush. Afterwards, he'd followed Payne back to the playroom, and now that the time had come, he felt a degree of nervousness he hadn't felt the first time. Maybe it was performance anxiety, to an extent, or worry he was putting himself through this and it wouldn't work. He also wasn't certain what kind of "scene" Payne had envisioned for them, though he felt he knew Payne well enough to be sure it wasn't going to be something over the top. Which was a good thing, and he told himself to stand down from alert and relax.

One thing he was quite glad about was that they'd cleared the air about the issue of sex. He wasn't at all averse to being with Payne, and if he was honest, part of his initial annoyance with Payne had stemmed from feeling attracted to him. He hadn't been happy about being forced to work for Herc, no matter how temporarily, and he'd resented finding the partner he'd been assigned to so appealing. Maybe they would end up having sex at some point or maybe they wouldn't, but at least he wouldn't feel embarrassed about being aroused.

He was also relieved to see Payne was dressed in much the same kind of thing he wore for work: black and white camo pants, a tight black t-shirt, and boots. The outfit looked good on him, since even though Payne was quite a bit shorter and far more slender than Hunter was himself, he had lots of lean muscle Hunter found attractive. Just as he found those big blue eyes appealing — yet he didn't think even the eyes would have helped him feel comfortable if Payne had dressed up like some of the Doms Hunter had seen online, in head-to-toe black leather with buckles and studs all over it. Not that Payne wouldn't look good in it, but that kind of outfit seemed more like a costume than something a person serious about the therapeutic aspects of what they were going to do would wear.

"So... this is it," Hunter said, taking in a deep breath. "What now?"

"Now we can discuss how our scene will go," Payne said, offering a reassuring smile as he reached out to squeeze Hunter's hand. "If you've got some ideas that appeal to you from your research, we can talk about them. I've got an idea too, if it works for you."

"I think I'd like to hear what you have in mind first," Hunter said, returning the pressure of Payne's hand. He was glad Payne was willing to touch him without it being part of the scenario they would act out. Maybe it was weak of him, but he found it comforting, a reassurance that whatever happened in the scene, Hunter wasn't just another body Payne was hitting. "Most of the stuff I found online either had me rolling my eyes or laughing."

"Most of what you saw online probably wouldn't apply to our situation anyway." Payne laced their fingers together and led Hunter over to the loveseat, and he kept hold of Hunter's hand even after they sat down. "I thought we could keep it simple with an interrogation scene. I'll tie you up to the St. Andrews cross," he said, pointing to the device, which looked to be sturdy and secure enough to handle even someone Hunter's size and strength. "I'll blindfold you, and I'll interrogate you. We'll start with what happened the day Stack died and go from there. How does that sound?"

Hunter couldn't help the shiver that ran down his spine. He'd had nightmares every night for months, and the memories were never far from his thoughts. After he'd started on the rounds of the shrinks Lawson and Greer had sent him to, he'd managed to learn to keep some distance from the events, but he still had dreams where he woke up screaming in denial as he watched Stack's death yet again. But he hadn't trusted the psychologists and psychiatrists, and he'd been smart enough to give them the answers which would convince them he was all right. But this was different. Payne wasn't one of those impersonal drones who had no real interest in him other than as a case study. Plus Hunter doubted he'd be able to hold back the truth when Payne was prepared to literally beat it out of him.

"I'm willing to try it," he said, licking his dry lips. "It seems like a reasonable place to start."

Payne squeezed Hunter's hand, then released it. "Then let's get to it, shall we? You get undressed, and I'll get my stuff together."

Hunter stood and went over to the St. Andrew's cross, looking it over more closely than he had before. Then he stripped, removing his clothing quickly and efficiently, folding everything neatly and placing it out of the way. He'd gotten over body modesty back at West Point, and so he stood patiently waiting for Payne, emptying his mind and telling himself this was going to work.

A few minutes later, Payne rolled a small metal table with wheels over to the cross. On it were a blindfold, the rattan cane, a bottle of water, the tube of antibiotic salve, a spray bottle, some cloths, and a little first aid box.

"I like having the things I might need within easy reach," he explained. He stood with his hands on his hips, one eyebrow raised, and for the moment, he looked like the same pain in the ass choirboy as he always had. "Any last questions before we get started? Once I restrain you, the scene will start, and there will be limits on what you'll be allowed to say."

Hunter looked everything over. The seriousness of what they were about to do seemed to press down upon him, but he shook his head. "I think I understand everything. And if it gets to be too much, I tell you 'red' and it stops, right?"

"Immediately," Payne said. "I'll also keep an eye out for warning signs, and if I think we need to end, I'll either check in with you or put a stop to the scene myself."

"Good." Hunter took a deep breath. "Okay. I'm ready."

"Step up on the footrests," Payne instructed. "I want your back to me. Keep your arms down for now. I'll secure your ankles first."

"Right." Hunter did as he was told, feeling his heartbeat suddenly speeding up.

Payne knelt on one side of the cross and fastened a thick black leather cuff around Hunter's right ankle, and he secured it to the cross with a sturdy D ring. "How does it feel? Too loose or too tight?"

Hunter looked down, then flexed his ankle. "It feels fine," he said, then looked at Payne as a question occurred to him. "Sorry, but I guess I should have asked... these are strong enough to hold me if I try to break free, right? So they'll hold me up if I pass out?"

"This cross has secured men as big as you many times," Payne assured him. "No one has broken free yet. I hope you won't pass out, but if you do, yes, the cuffs will keep you upright until I get you down. I can add thigh cuffs if you feel like you need some extra support."

"Can I tell you after you have me secured?" Hunter asked. "It'll probably be fine, but it occurred to me after the concussion I had, it might not be optimal to smack my head on the floor and knock out what's left of my brains."

"You're right, thanks for letting me know." Payne gave him a nod of approval. "We should probably add the thigh cuffs just in case. Go ahead and keep asking questions and giving me feedback. I'll let you know when we're starting."

He moved to the other side of the cross and secured Hunter's left ankle, and then he stood up and fastened a similar cuff around Hunter's wrist. "They're all fleece lined, so they shouldn't chafe your skin, but if you feel any pinching or loss of circulation, let me know."

Hunter tugged experimentally at the wrist cuff. "It seems right," he said.

Payne secured Hunter's other wrist, then stepped back and surveyed his work with a little smile of satisfaction. "*Damn*. You look even sexier than I thought you would, splayed up there like that."

Hunter couldn't help but feel a little smug at Payne's admiration, but he told himself not to get too excited about it. Or at least not yet. "Thanks," he murmured. "I'm glad you approve."

"Oh, I do." Payne walked behind Hunter, trailing his fingertips lightly across the warm expanse of Hunter's back. "You're a gorgeous canvas. Let me get the thigh cuffs so you'll have some extra support. They'll help if your wrists start getting tired too."

"All right," Hunter agreed. It was probably best to be safe, since he had no idea how he was going to react once they got started.

The thigh cuffs were also made of black leather, but they were wider and longer than the wrist and ankle restraints, and they weren't lined. Once they were fastened, however, they did help with both security and stability.

"Time for the blindfold." Payne approached with a black neoprene blindfold in his hand, and he dragged a low stool over to the cross with his foot. "Any last questions or comments? Once this goes on, we start."

Hunter looked at the blindfold, then at Payne. He saw the seriousness of Payne's expression, and yet there was something reassuring about it. Even though his heart was still beating faster than usual, and he knew Payne could do anything he liked and Hunter wouldn't be able to stop him now, Hunter nodded. "I trust you," he said, then closed his eyes.

Payne slid the blindfold over his head and settled it into place.

The elastic band allowed it to stretch to fit him, and the neoprene was soft enough that it didn't chafe.

"From this point on, you will not speak except to answer my questions." Payne's voice was deeper and harder, containing a note of authority. It was a voice accustomed to being obeyed. "The only exception to this rule is if your color goes yellow or red. You will tell me when that happens. Do you understand?" Payne asked, and Hunter heard as well as felt the swoosh of the rattan cane cutting the air somewhere close to his bare skin.

"Yes," Hunter said, sounding a bit breathless even to his own ears. The blindfold made things much darker than closing his eyes would have, feeling almost as though his vision had been severed. He couldn't even remove it if he'd wanted to, and the sensation of standing, bound, exposed, and with only his skin and ears to tell him what was happening was disorienting. He strained to hear where Payne was, trying to visualize Payne pacing behind him.

"Yes, what?" The words were punctuated with a sharp blow from the cane across his ass.

Even though they hadn't discussed this, Hunter had read enough to know what Payne was expecting, and he was annoyed with himself for forgetting. His skin stung from the contact of the cane, and he told himself not to forget again. "Yes, sir."

"Very good." Payne's warm hand caressed his stinging skin. "You're a quick learner. Now I'm going to ask you some questions, and you're going to answer me honestly. Do I need to explain what will happen if you aren't honest with me?"

Hunter swallowed hard. "No, sir," he said.

"Good." Payne rested the tip of the cane at the base of Hunter's skull and drew it slowly down the length of Hunter's spine as he spoke. "Tell me what happened the day your partner died. Start with explaining your mission. I want to know where you were and why you were there."

"Yes, sir." Hunter squirmed slightly at the slide of the cane down his back, not expecting non-painful contact. Fortunately, their mission hadn't been classified, so he didn't have to lie or talk around it. "I was part of a Lawson and Greer company deployed to guard some of the military advisors the government had sent to help out the Iraqi army," he said softly. With the blindfold cutting off sight, he found it easy to picture the expanse of desert where they'd been encamped with canvas tents for their billets, circled by the Hummers and Bradleys they'd used for transport. "We were near Fallujah, and the damned terrorists had IEDs seeded all over the desert. That was what Stack and I did. We ferreted out IEDs and disarmed them and dealt with any unexploded ordinance left after the snipers took out the suicide bombers they sent against us. Sir."

"Very good." Payne moved close enough Hunter could feel his presence, warm and close but not quite touching, and he rested his hand on Hunter's ass. "Tell me about your camp. Describe it for me," he said, kneading Hunter's ass firmly.

He found it difficult to concentrate on what had happened months before with Payne standing so close and touching him intimately. But part of Hunter's job required him to put aside distractions, so he made himself focus on the question.

"It was a typical temporary bivouac. We had ninety in our company, plus Blaze, our commander, and his XO Joker. Lawson and Greer doesn't stint, but we'd been on deployment so long, the tents were faded and patched. The grunts had three big tents sleeping twenty each, and the officers, like Stack and me, were billeted in twos. There was a mess tent, a shower tent, and one for the latrines. We'd been in that spot for about two weeks, waiting for the Iraqis to get around to staging the next big push. Water was trucked in every couple of days. You know how encampments are, sir. Some smartass had put up a biohazard sign over the door of the latrines, and Blaze had painted the canvas around his door flap with flames and the words 'Welcome to Hell'. There were probably a hundred or so civilians who had their own encampment nearby. We always had people following us, sometimes for protection, sometimes trying to earn money offering to sell us things. We kept them out of the perimeter as best we could, but they were always hanging around. That's pretty much it, sir."

"I can see it clearly," Payne said. "I want you to see it clearly too. Keep the image in your mind and tell me about the day Stack died. When did it happen? Morning, afternoon, or evening?"

Hunter's mind obediently conjured up the image Payne commanded him to see. Hunter felt like he was back in the military, reporting to his CO after a mission. "Early evening after chow, sir," he said. "We were in our bunk. I was reading a spy novel, and Stack was watching a video his wife had sent him of his son, Jake." Suddenly Hunter's throat felt tight. "He was so happy, sir."

"Why was he happy?" Payne asked. "Because of the video?"

"Yes, sir." Hunter swallowed hard, unable to get the picture of Stack's beaming face out of his mind. "He was proud to be a father. He hadn't seen Jake in six months, so every time Jen sent him a new video, he was like a kid at Christmas, sir."

"What happened next?"

"Blaze called for us," Hunter said slowly. His mind didn't want to move on from the memory of Stack's proud smile, but he forced himself to go forward. "We jumped up and ran out, and so did a bunch of the others. Joker was ordering people to get out, and I saw why when I got to Blaze, sir."

"What did you see?" Payne asked, pressing the cane lengthwise against Hunter's ass as a reminder.

Hunter didn't want to talk about it, and he knew what was coming: he had to relive the horror of Stack's death. The detachment he'd had when talking to the shrinks deserted him. Somehow standing naked, bound, and blindfolded was making him as vulnerable mentally as he was physically, and his mind rebelled at treading the path of his nightmares without his emotional armor.

"A kid, sir," he managed to grind out. "Just a kid, dirty and scared because someone had wired him up to enough fucking C4 to blow our whole camp to hell."

"What did you do when you saw the little boy?"

Hunter's heartbeat had sped up again, and he started to sweat. He closed his eyes despite the blindfold. "I told Blaze to get everyone out and sent Stack to get our gear, since he couldn't speak the local dialect and I could. The kid said he didn't want to die." Hunter drew in a ragged breath, anger flowing over him. He couldn't do anything to stop it. "He couldn't have been more than seven. Of course he didn't want to die!"

A blow landed on his ass, harder than the first one. "You're forgetting who you're talking to," Payne said sternly. "Focus. Tell me what happened next."

Hunter gasped at the blow, but the pain had the effect of helping him move past the anger. He realized he'd been in danger of getting lost in his fury, which was hotter now than it had been at the time. Payne's voice helped to ground him as well, and he stood still breathing hard, pulling his attention back as he'd been commanded.

"Yes, sir," he said, his voice hoarse. He forced himself to keep going. "I got the kid to tell me what he could remember about how they'd wired him up. When Stack got back, he was rigged up, and I put on my disposal suit. We started removing all the shit they'd loaded it with for anti-personnel effect. We were about to cut him out when Stack saw the fuckers had wired up the C4 in parallel rather than in series. The kid wasn't wearing one bomb made of ten bricks of C4. He was wearing ten bombs, each of one brick, and disarming one still left all the others. Not only were these assholes evil, they were smart. If Stack hadn't noticed what they'd done and we'd cut the wire, the whole thing would have blown me, Stack, and the kid all to hell. Sir."

"But Stack did notice." Payne tapped the backs of Hunter's thighs lightly with the cane. "What happened next?"

Hunter had fallen once again into the blackness of his memories, and it was a physical effort to get each word out. "We disarmed nine of the bombs and put the C4 in an anti-ballistic box so if something blew, at least those wouldn't go up too. When we were down to the last brick, it should have been just like a regular disarm. Cut the wire, remove the detonator, and there you go. We got the kid out of it, and he fell to the ground, bawling. Stack was trying to comfort him, but when I popped my helmet..."

He could hear it again, that beeping. The noise had become

anathema to him. He'd thrown his alarm clock across the room the first time the damned thing had gone off after he'd returned home.

Whack! Payne wasn't going easy on Hunter anymore, and when he spoke, his tone was stern and implacable. "Keep going. What happened when you took off your helmet?"

The pain of the blow seared across his skin, and Hunter cried out. "Beeping! I heard the goddamned thing beeping! I yelled a warning and pushed the kid back, but then Stack pushed me. I fell across the kid, and Stack... he did it on purpose! He fell on the damned bomb and covered it. His ballistic suit took most of the force, but his damned helmet was open! It blew his head off." Hunter went limp against the restraints, and he could barely speak past the sobs being ripped from his throat, almost as painful as the welts on his ass as he confronted the image that still haunted him, replaying before his eyes like a movie stuck in an endless loop. "It blew my best friend's head off and I couldn't do a fucking thing to stop it!"

Gentle hands pushed the blindfold up and off, bringing him out of the darkness. Then Payne knelt and unfastened the ankle restraints first, followed by the thigh cuffs.

"It's okay," he murmured, stroking Hunter's back. "You did great. I'm going to take the wrist cuffs off. If you don't feel like you can stand up, lean against the cross. It can take your weight. Then I'll help you once you're free."

Despite the return of light, Hunter could barely see. His vision was blurred by tears — the first tears he'd shed since Stack's death. His emotional armor was gone, and pain and guilt rolled over him. On some level, he heard Payne's words, and when his wrists were free, he leaned forward, resting his forehead against the cool wood of the cross as he bit back his sobs. He was beyond anything but his pain, not of his body but of his soul.

"Come on, let's get you to bed. You were so brave to face that, and I'm proud of you," Payne said as he tucked himself under Hunter's arm, helped him off the cross, and guided him to the door.

Hunter leaned on Payne, needing the support. His knees felt weak, and his breath came in shuddering gasps. He lifted his free hand to his face, squeezing his eyes shut and letting Payne guide him. Payne walked him to the guest bedroom and stopped next to the bed so he could yank back the covers with one hand.

"Climb on in," he said, gently coaxing Hunter into bed. "I'll take off my boots and join you."

It seemed an enormous effort, but Hunter did as he was hold, climbing into the big bed and collapsing on the mattress. He was no longer sobbing, but he couldn't seem to stop the flow of tears. As soon as his boots were off, Payne climbed in and drew the covers up around them.

"Let it out," Payne murmured as he wrapped his arms around Hunter and nestled against him, offering the comfort of his warm presence. "You're safe. I've got you."

Hunter had never considered himself a person who needed physical comfort; he'd been injured numerous times, had suffered the deaths of friends and come through without having to lean on anyone. He was a strong person, he knew it, but for once his strength had deserted him, and he wrapped his arms around Payne in turn as his tears soaked into Payne's shirt. The dam had burst, and everything he'd bottled up was flowing out, and he was unable to stop it.

Payne held him close and stroked his hair, occasionally murmuring words of comfort. He offered Hunter solace and let him grieve without judgment. Hunter wasn't certain how long they lay there, but eventually the tears stopped and Hunter was left feeling drained. Yet he felt relief as well, as though he'd finally released some of the pressure of grief that had been slowly crushing him from within.

His head was pillowed on Payne's chest, and he clung to Payne like he was a big stuffed teddy bear. Hunter could hear the strong, steady beat of Payne's heart, and his head rose and fell with the rhythm of Payne's breath. He'd been vaguely aware of it while he'd wept, and he realized Payne had been the solid, steady anchor that had kept him from being consumed by his own pain.

"Thank you," he said. The words seemed inadequate to express what Payne had done for him, but he had the feeling Payne would understand.

"You're welcome." Payne buried his fingers in Hunter's hair and massaged his scalp gently. "I hope you feel a little better."

Hunter closed his eyes and relaxed into the stroking, letting the comforting sensation help bring him back into himself. "I do. I feel some relief," he said slowly. He wasn't used to sharing his emotions with people other than Stack, but Payne had a right to know and also a need to know. If they were going to do this again, Hunter knew it was not only stupid but also potentially dangerous not to be completely honest with his Dom.

He sucked in a breath as he realized he thought of Payne that way. Hunter wasn't sure he was comfortable with the thought, but it was there, and he couldn't deny it.

"I'm glad." Payne continued the gentle massage for a minute or so longer, and then he slid his hands down so he could stroke Hunter's back. "It was a good first step. You were very brave."

"Was I?" Hunter arched slightly into the stroking, enjoying the contact. "I didn't feel brave. I felt... overwhelmed. Angry. Horrified." He paused for a moment, considering. "And sad. I hadn't been able to cry for him before. I don't know if I've ever cried for anyone, not like that. But I never lost anyone so close to me before either. Stack was closer to me than my own brother."

"You were brave for facing the anger, horror and sadness and letting yourself feel them for the first time," Payne said, smoothing his palms up and down Hunter's back as far as he could reach. "You were brave for being self-aware enough to realize you needed help and to try to find something that worked for you. You needed to grieve for him. There's nothing weak about it."

Hunter lay quietly for several long moments, enjoying the stroking. "Is it always this draining?" he asked. He started to feel the marks on his ass, and he wriggled slightly.

"Not always. But you're working through some heavy emotional shit, so it's going to be harder for you in the aftermath for now." Payne gave him a questioning look. "Are you ready for some salve now? I can go get it right quick."

"I would appreciate it." Hunter reluctantly pulled back and attempted a version of Payne's own wide-eyed look of appeal. "My bottom hurts."

Payne chuckled at the sight of Hunter's pitiful look. "The student is trying to become the master? You don't have the choirboy face to pull it off, but it's a good effort," he said as he pushed back the covers and got out of bed. "Would you like anything else while I'm up? A bottle of water or something to eat?"

"Water, please?" Hunter asked, realizing he probably did need the hydration. "I'm not hungry."

"Go ahead and roll onto your stomach," Payne said. "I'll be right back."

Hunter did as instructed, pillowing his head on his crossed arms. The bed felt oddly empty without Payne in it. But in a matter of minutes, Payne returned, and he sat down on the bed beside Hunter.

"We'll take care of your poor little bottom first," he said with a teasing smile.

"All right." Hunter closed his eyes. "It doesn't hurt as badly as I thought it might."

"You didn't get that many licks." Payne smoothed the cool salve on Hunter's stinging skin, coating the welts generously. "They do look pretty, though."

"Pretty?" Hunter raised his head, looking over his shoulder as best as he could, but he couldn't see the marks. "You actually like how they look?"

"Of course I do," Payne said in a tone that implied it should be obvious. "I put them there as decorations on your gorgeous ass. I hope you don't think those were random blows. I practiced on a pillow for weeks when I first started Domming so I could land the cane exactly where I wanted it. I can't draw for shit, but this is my artwork," he said, gesturing to the welts.

Hunter felt a little surge of something he was loathe to call jealousy. He had no right to feel possessive of Payne, and no doubt his feeling stemmed from gratitude. He dropped his head onto his arms again. "I don't mind being decorated. I suppose that's obvious."

"You're an amazing canvas," Payne said as he finished treating the welts. He put the salve aside and wiped off his hands, and then he picked up the bottle of water and opened it. "Here you go. There's plenty more if you need it."

"Thanks." Hunter took the bottle, lifting it to his lips and sipping slowly. Then his thirst made itself known, and he tilted his head back and drained the bottle in several long gulps. "I was thirstier than I thought."

"Do you want another? I've got some Gatorade too, if it would help," Payne said, smoothing his hand along the back of Hunter's head.

"Mm... no, I'm good for the moment," Hunter said. "That feels good."

"Is there anything else you want or need?" Payne continued stroking Hunter's head tenderly. "More cuddling is included in that offer, so don't feel awkward about asking if you feel the need for more contact. It's not unusual."

Part of Hunter wanted to refuse, to show he was strong enough to take care of himself. He could rebuild his walls, but the idea of cutting himself off from Payne didn't appeal to him at all. No one, not even his mother, had taken care of him the way Payne had, letting him cry himself out and treating him as though it wasn't a sign of weakness, but of strength. To be honest, he *wanted* the cuddling, perhaps even more than he needed it.

"Only if you want to," Hunter said somberly. "You've done so much for me, and I know you aren't getting anything out of it. I can manage on my own if you don't feel like doing it. I don't want you to feel like I'm going to be an emotional leech."

"Hunter, even if I didn't like you personally, I couldn't leave you hanging in the aftermath of a scene like that and call myself a responsible Dom," Payne said, moving his hand down to rub Hunter's neck soothingly. "But I do like you, and I want to be there for you through each step of the process. I *am* getting something out of it: the satisfaction of knowing I'm helping you."

Hunter looked up at Payne through his lashes. "Well, if you really want to, I'd like it." He felt his cheeks growing hot, which was unusual for him, and he blamed it on the aftermath of his emotional outburst.

In response, Payne crawled under the covers again and lay on his side, facing Hunter. Scooting close, he slid one arm across Hunter's waist. "Do you want to be the big spoon or the little spoon?"

"Big spoon, or the salve will get all over your clothes," Hunter said. He didn't have much of a preference usually, but it appealed to him to wrap himself around Payne as though he were a stuffed toy.

"I've had a lot worse than a little salve on my clothes," Payne teased, but he didn't hesitate to turn over and nestle back against Hunter. Hunter wrapped his arm around Payne's waist and pulled him close. He hadn't held anyone this way in a long time, and it was comforting.

"You feel good," Hunter murmured.

Payne wriggled closer and released a slow sigh, relaxing in Hunter's arms. "So do you."

"I'm glad." Hunter meant it, and despite the emotional turmoil he'd been through and the lingering sting of the welts, he felt more at peace than he had in months. He was surprised, but he wasn't going to question it; anything was better than the road he'd been headed down, and he could now see and admit, at least to himself, that the road had been leading him toward a bad end. But Payne had stepped in, and Hunter knew he was lucky Payne had been there and hadn't given up on him. He wasn't healed yet, but for the first time he thought that maybe, someday, he might get back to something approaching normal.

And he had Payne to thank for it.

Smiling slightly, Hunter closed his eyes and drifted off to sleep more easily than he had since his world had fallen apart.

8

Payne woke up before Hunter, slipped out of bed, and went down the hall to his bedroom to take a shower and get dressed. Since he didn't have plans to go anywhere, he put on gray sweatpants and a plain white t-shirt and didn't bother with shoes. Then he went downstairs and got a pot of coffee going and started planning his menu, although he held off on cooking anything until Hunter showed up.

By the time Hunter got up, Payne was putting together a nice brunch even though they were both still on night shift hours and it was well after noon. It always took a few days for Payne's internal clock to reset, and he wasn't worried about rushing it since Herc had given him an open-ended break to work with Hunter.

It wasn't long after the coffee finished brewing that Hunter entered the kitchen. He was dressed in soft, faded jeans that molded to his legs, and a black tank top that set off the ink of his tattoos. His hair was mussed, and he looked better rested than Payne could remember seeing him before, although he still yawned before giving Payne a somewhat sheepish smile.

"Hi," he said, seeming perhaps a little hesitant, as though he wasn't quite certain how he should greet Payne on this type of "morning after."

"Hey." Payne offered a reassuring smile as he handed over the mug he'd put aside for Hunter's use. "I've got sugar on the table," he said, pointing to the small, round dining table on the other side of the kitchen. The whole wall was covered in long windows looking out onto the backyard, which Payne kept landscaped. There were white shutters on the windows, but he had them open so they could enjoy the view. "There's some creamer in the fridge, if you want some. Are you hungry? I was thinking about making some egg sandwiches."

For an answer, Hunter's stomach growled, and he chuckled, seeming to relax. "That would be great, thank you." He carried the mug over to the table and spooned in sugar while he looked out the window.

"This is a nice place," he said. "Can you believe that at my age I've never owned a home of my own? I could afford anything I wanted, but it seemed kind of pointless, when I was always in the field."

"You've done what works for you," Payne said as he rummaged around in the fridge for bacon, eggs, and cheese. "Me, I tend to stick close to home, so I could afford to put down roots. Besides, I wanted someplace where I could have some privacy with enough room for a dedicated playroom."

"Makes sense," Hunter said. "I sure as hell wouldn't have wanted anyone overhearing me last night." He dropped his gaze, looking down into the mug. "I don't want it to go beyond you and me."

"It won't. You have my word," Payne said. He didn't even intend to tell Herc about their alternative therapy methods. All Herc needed to know was whether it worked or not. "I understand about being discreet. I don't flaunt what I do, because most people have preconceived ideas about BDSM and the people who practice it. Besides, it goes against the 'safe, sane, and consensual' motto to bring people into your scenes without their consent, which is why play is done in private, not in public."

Hunter pulled out one of the chairs and took a seat at the table, watching Payne as he fixed breakfast. "But what about those clubs? I read about them online, so I took it with a grain of salt. But they seemed to get off on being in public."

"The BDSM clubs? Those are safe public spaces. If you go to one of those, you know what you're getting into. Or if you don't, you figure it out right quick," Payne said, grinning at Hunter over his shoulder. "The point is, they're designated spaces where it's okay to play in public. But going to a regular bar or club and doing a scene? Not cool. You're pulling everyone else in the place into your game, and they didn't agree to it. There are people who don't know better or who don't care. We try to teach the ones who don't know, and the ones who don't care, well, they're assholes, and they're probably going to find themselves with a very small pool of play partners."

"Hm." Hunter hesitated. "Do you like to go to those kind of clubs?"

"I don't go on a regular basis, but I do enjoy it." Payne grabbed some tongs so he could put the bacon on a paper towel lined plate to drain. "Having someone watch while I play isn't one of my huge hot buttons. I prefer one-on-one scenarios, but clubs and private play parties are good ways to meet new people."

"I can't imagine wanting anyone to watch." Hunter made a face. "But then, I've never had exhibitionist tendencies. Sure, I don't have any real body modesty, but that's just in front of other mercs. This is all so new to me... It's like this different world I had no idea existed."

"I don't mind answering any questions you have," Payne said as he cracked a couple of eggs into his cast iron skillet. "I like keeping the lines of communication open."

"Thanks. I appreciate it." Hunter took a deep sip of his coffee before continuing. "How did you get into it? Was it something you'd always thought about?"

"The how I got into it part is easy. Internet!" Payne struck a dramatic pose and made jazz hands. "I didn't always think about it, at least not on a conscious level. First, there was the whole 'oh, hey, I'm gay' realization. Fine-tuning my sexuality after that took a while." He popped some bread into the toaster while he gathered his thoughts, trying to explain what had been a convoluted process. "During some of my teenage fumblings, I realized I *really* liked biting, hair pulling, and stuff like that, but I was like you. I had no idea BDSM was even a thing. Then I had a boyfriend who wanted to be spanked, and holy *shit*, did that go over well with my libido. I was a little scared, though, because I thought it might be weird, but Google showed me I wasn't alone."

Hunter chuckled. "The internet is for porn," he drawled, then paused thoughtfully. "The idea of being spanked doesn't bother me. I like playing rough myself. I can't say I'm really into pain on the receiving end, but you know what's funny? The thought of hitting someone else, even if they want it, gives me the willies. Outside of combat, I mean. I've beat the shit out of plenty of guys, but it isn't the same."

"It required a mental adjustment for me too," Payne said, inclining his head to acknowledge the point. "But I do get off on having someone tied up and at my mercy. I like knowing I can hit them just right and give them what they want too. If it's not your thing, though, you don't have to continue once it's no longer useful for you."

"I'll have to think about it," Hunter said slowly. "I suppose it depends on if the guy I'm with is into it."

All kinds of questions rose up in Payne's mind. "What if the guy you're with is me?" "Are you interested in dating me?" "Are we going our separate ways once you're feeling better?" But he didn't ask, partly because he wasn't sure Hunter was in the frame of mind to think about such things and partly because he was hesitant to put himself quite so far out on a limb. Hunter was letting him in slowly, but it didn't mean Hunter was interested in him as anything more than a friend.

"It's something you'll have to work out if you end up with someone like me," he said at last. "Speaking personally, I wouldn't want you to do things you aren't into just for my sake, but at the same time, this kind of play is important to me, and I wouldn't want to give it up completely."

Hunter looked at him intently. "I'm sure you don't lack for accommodating partners. Not with your looks and personality. How many men have been your willing slaves after one of those wide-eyed looks you give?"

"Enough to keep me happy in the short term," Payne said, deciding it was time for some reciprocal honesty. Hunter had laid himself bare in the playroom, and Payne thought it might help ease any awkwardness if he opened up as well. "But I haven't found anyone I'd like to be with for the long term. That's what I've been looking for lately. Someone I can settle down and build a future with."

The answer seemed to take Hunter by surprise. "I got the feeling from the stuff I read that Doms sort of got around, if you know what I mean. But you know how the internet is — all the most lurid stuff seems to turn up first in the searches."

Payne got a couple of plates and assembled the sandwiches, and then he carried them over to the table, pausing long enough to snag some napkins along the way.

"Like anything else, it depends on the person," he said as he set down the plates and then took a seat. "Sure, there are Doms — and some subs — who want to play the field, and there are Doms who have long term monogamous relationships with their sub. I played around when I was younger, and it was fun, but I'm at a point in my life where I want something different." He gazed at Hunter steadily. "I want to fall in love. I want to make a commitment to someone, maybe even marry them if it's what they want, too."

Again Hunter gave him an intent look, then picked up his sandwich. "I can see that. You seem to be the marrying kind. Like Stack was..." Sadness flitted across Hunter's face. "He liked to take care of people, like you do. Especially his son."

Apparently not wanting to get bogged down in memories that were still painful, Hunter took a bite of his sandwich, falling silent while he chewed.

Payne debated whether to follow up on that line of conversation, but Hunter was probably still processing what happened, and they had plenty of time to discuss the next step. Instead, he decided to ask something he was curious about.

"What about you? Are you interested in the white picket fence scenario, or do you prefer not to get tied down?"

Hunter spoke almost hesitantly. "I'd never considered it before, but I've had a lot of time to think over the last few months. My job has always been my life, and I've never met anyone who meant enough to me to give it up. After what happened to Stack... I'd have to give it up. I think my line of work is too risky when you have someone to go home to."

"I suppose the question you have to answer is if you'd be willing to give it up for the right person. You said you didn't know what you would do if you couldn't do your job anymore," Payne said. "That's a pretty big compromise to make."

Hunter was quiet for several long moments, obviously considering his answer. "On Thursday, I got a call from D-Day. He wanted to see how I was doing, and we've always had a lot in common. I asked him how he could give up the risky jobs, when he'd always been one to thrive on the danger, even live for the rush. He said it was easier than he'd thought it would be. He said his partner gave him more of a thrill than tackling a nuke any day. That says a lot."

"He's seemed much happier and more settled in his own skin since he's been with Emerson," Payne said, thinking about the changes he'd noticed in his colleague. He wondered if Hunter would respond in a similar way if he found the right person. "They don't seem like they belong together on the surface, but from what I can tell, they have some fundamental similarities that make them a good match."

"D-Day said the same thing," Hunter agreed. "Sometimes I think if that crazy son of a bitch can do it, maybe I could, too. But I don't know, and it's not like men are beating down my door. I don't have to work... one advantage of being single, homeless except for my job, and working in such a dangerous field is that I've been socking away money for years. I could be a man of leisure, except I'd die of boredom in a week."

"Yeah, I can't see you being content without something to do." Payne picked at a slice of bacon poking out the end of his sandwich. So many of his colleagues had found their partner recently, and he was still looking for someone who could accept his job and the long, erratic hours it sometimes entailed *and* his kink. Unfortunately, the two together created a pretty small dating pool for him. "I'm not sure I would do well without a job either. I want to help people and be useful for as long as I can."

"So do I. And I realize that no matter what, I can't keep doing it forever anyway." Hunter shook his head, his expression pensive. "Once the vision starts to go and the reflexes slow down, it's too risky. I'm pushing forty, so it's not like I have much longer before I'd have to step aside for someone younger. Someone less aware of their own mortality."

"Maybe now is a good time for you to start thinking about future options. I'm sure Matthew and Herc would both have suggestions," Payne said. "They've probably got connections in just about any field you might want to go into too."

Hunter shrugged. "Probably. But before I can even think about it, I have to deal with my problems." He smiled slightly. "Someone told me I have to face my shit, right?"

"Right, and we're still not done," Payne said, pushing his plate aside. He wasn't hungry anymore, and he was glad to focus on Hunter's therapy again. "You've got a few days to process the first round and let the welts go down, but then we'll need to think about round two."

"Yeah, I didn't figure it was one and done," Hunter said. "It helped more than I thought it would, though." Suddenly Hunter reached across the table, placing his hand over Payne's. "I'm sorry for the way I treated you when we were first working together. I was a dick to you, and you didn't deserve it."

"Well, you had a reason for being a dick," Payne said, offering a reassuring smile. "You were already hurting, and then you probably felt like Matthew and Herc were backing you into a corner, so you lashed out at the nearest convenient target, which happened to be me. I understand why you behaved the way you did, and I didn't take it personally."

"That's generous of you, but it doesn't make it right." Hunter made a face. "I'm not normally such a jerk, and you still wanting to help me after all I put you through must be one of your more masochistic tendencies." He tightened his fingers on Payne's hand, pulling it toward him across the small table. Then he lifted Payne's hand to his lips and pressed a kiss to Payne's palm. "Thank you."

The warmth of Hunter's lips against his skin sent a pleasurable shiver through Payne. "You're welcome," he said huskily.

"So... where do you think we should go from here?" Hunter squeezed Payne's hand and then released it to reach for his coffee cup, shifting a bit in his seat. "Given how my ass feels, I'm inclined to agree about waiting for a few days."

"Your ass needs time to recover, and you need time to process what happened," Payne said. "If anything starts bubbling up and you need to talk, I want you to call me, even if it's the middle of the night."

Hunter gave him a searching look. "Okay. I still have nightmares sometimes. Not every night, like at first, but a couple of times a week."

Payne debated whether to voice his first thought, which was to offer to stay with Hunter or let Hunter stay with him. He didn't want to push too hard when it seemed Hunter was willing to open up to him at last, but the caretaker in him couldn't help but hover.

"Would it help to have company?" he asked. "If nothing else, having someone around in the aftermath might help you connect to reality quicker."

Hunter hesitated. "Would you think I was weak if I said yes?" He grimaced. "I didn't have any last night. I don't know if it was the scene, or having you with me, or maybe both. But after reliving everything all over again, I wouldn't be surprised if they got bad again."

"I'd never think you're weak for needing help after what you've been through," Payne said, reaching across the table to squeeze Hunter's forearm. "Besides, you're right. The nightmares might flare up again, and if they do, I'd like to be there for you. I can go to your hotel, or you can stay here, whichever you're more comfortable with."

"I'd prefer to stay here, if that's okay," Hunter said, giving Payne a crooked smile. "It's quieter than the hotel, and if it gets as bad as it was in the beginning, I... well. I've woken people up from screaming."

"You won't disturb anyone out here, except maybe some deer or rabbits," Payne said, offering a reassuring smile. "If you want, you could go ahead and get your stuff from the hotel and check out this morning. My house is your house for as long as you need it."

"Are you sure? I don't want to intrude on your space." While Hunter seemed hesitant, Payne could see the way the tension line between Hunter's eyes relaxed when he made the offer. "I insist on helping with housework and cooking and any other chores. Plus paying for meals."

"That's fair," Payne said. If it were up to him, he wouldn't have asked Hunter to help out, but he understood Hunter well enough to know refusing the offer would do more harm than good to Hunter's independent nature. "This house is plenty big enough for both of us to have private time and space when we need it, so don't worry."

"All right, then. Thank you — I appreciate it. I won't make a nuisance of myself. I mean, I *hope* I won't. I haven't stayed in anyone's house since... well. Stack." He grimaced as though it was still hard to say his friend's name.

What Payne wanted to do was wrap his arms around Hunter and hold him until all his pain faded away, but they weren't at that point yet. They might never reach that point. For now, it was enough that Hunter would be close by so Payne could provide a safe place and take care of him while he healed.

"If there's a problem, I'll tell you," Payne said, drawing an X over his heart. "I want you to do the same. Good communication solves most problems."

"I can do that," Hunter said. "After I wash the dishes, I'll go back to the hotel to get my things, if it's okay. If you want to decide what chores you want me to do, I'm fine with that. I'm not a messy person by nature."

Payne leaned back in his chair and flipped his hand toward the sink. "Okay, roomie, time to start earning your keep," he said, deciding to lighten the mood a little. "I want those dishes sparkling."

"Yes, sir!" Hunter stood up, then picked up their plates and carried them to the sink. "I guess all the time I did on KP duty in the Army will come in handy." He glanced back over his shoulder at Payne. "Would you be shocked to learn my smart mouth got me in trouble?"

"Probably about as surprised as you'd be to learn the same thing about mine," Payne said with a mischievous grin. "I got my nickname early."

"Then we'll either get along great or kill each other in a week," Hunter said, mirroring Payne's grin. "Any bets on which it will be?"

"I'm an optimist, so I'll put my money on the two of us getting along fine," Payne said.

And maybe if things went well enough, Hunter would never want to leave.

9

"Am I ready for this? I've been in combat on four continents, I've disarmed everything from land mines to a live nuke... but am I *really* ready for this?"

Hunter's reflection in the mirror didn't reply, which was probably for the best, all things considered. But the question remained, and Hunter suspected he wouldn't have an answer until it was too late to back down. Walking into a nest of snipers was one thing, but who would have known Hunter would be intimidated at the thought of going to a BDSM club?

Hunter didn't think the idea seemed so bad when Payne had first suggested it. Two days after their scene, Payne thought Hunter needed a bit longer to heal before they went any further in his therapy. Since Payne had offered to answer any questions Hunter had about his lifestyle, Hunter had taken him up on it, finding himself curious about the kinds of people who participated and what needs had drawn them to it. He was also surprised at the wide range of kinks the lifestyle encompassed, and when Hunter had said he wasn't sure he trusted much of anything he read about it on the internet, Payne had suggested they visit a local club so Hunter could see for himself.

That was why Hunter was now standing in front of his mirror, wondering if he was going to be completely out of his depth. When he'd asked Payne what to wear to the club, Payne had given him a wicked grin and suggested something tight that would show off his muscles. Then Payne had gone off to get himself ready, while Hunter went through his clothes, wondering what he had that would be appropriate. He had a leather jacket, but otherwise most of his wardrobe consisted of jeans or uniforms. He finally settled on combat fatigue pants in black, white, and gray digital camo tucked into his combat boots, and a sheer black mesh tank top that was part of his hot weather gear for the Middle East. The tank was not only form fitting, but it also revealed far more than it covered, leaving all the tattoos on his upper body visible. He wouldn't have worn the shirt to a regular club, but if it was too over-the-top for where Payne was taking him, he could always keep his jacket zipped up. Hunter had never backed down from a challenge in his life, and he sure wasn't about to start now.

Taking a deep breath, he left his room and went downstairs to wait for Payne in the foyer. A few minutes later, Payne appeared at the top of the stairs, and the choirboy was gone, replaced by a leather clad Dom. Payne wore black leather pants that clung like a second skin to his hard thighs, and his sleeveless black leather vest revealed the strong arms that had once locked Hunter in a sleeper hold. His black boots added an inch or so to his height, and eyeliner made his blue eyes appear even more vivid and intense.

When he reached the bottom of the steps, Payne gave Hunter an appreciative onceover. "Good choice," he said, giving Hunter a thumbs up. "The mesh tank is hot."

"Thanks." Hunter couldn't take his eyes off Payne. He'd always thought the whole leather thing was over the top, but on Payne, the look worked. For the first time Payne looked as dangerous as Hunter knew he could be, and it was sexy as hell. He motioned with one hand, encompassing Payne's entire outfit. "You look amazing. Like some kind of leather ninja."

A slow, sensual smile curved Payne's mouth. "Thanks," he said. "If you think the front looks good, wait until you get a look at the back."

Hunter raised one eyebrow, then twirled his finger. "Let's see."

Payne turned around and cocked one hip, and Hunter stared at the absolutely gorgeous ass revealed by the tight leather.

"Whoa..." Hunter swallowed against the surge of pure lust he felt looking at Payne's perfect rear. "If I didn't know you can take care of yourself, I'd feel like I need to protect you from being dragged off and molested."

Payne gave Hunter a coy look over his shoulder, then ruined the effect by laughing. "I'm glad you like the view."

Hunter drew in a deep breath, wondering if he was going to need a cold shower before they even walked out the door. "I have to ask if you're a diehard top. Because with an ass like that..."

Payne faced Hunter, and a sensual smile curved his lips as he trailed his fingertips down the length of Hunter's arm. "I am primarily, but not exclusively a top, just like I'm primarily, but not exclusively a Dom. I believe in flexibility — in more ways than one."

"Good to know," Hunter said. His mouth was dry, and the slide of Payne's fingers on his arm raised goosebumps. It had been a long time since he'd had sex with anyone, and he hadn't had any interest in it in months. But his libido seemed to have come roaring back to life at the sight of Payne's perfect ass. "I think I need a drink."

"Maybe after we get home," Payne said, clasping Hunter's hand. "Club Twist doesn't serve alcohol or allow it on the premises. There are a few other rules, but we can go over them and any questions you have on the way. Ready to go?"

"As ready as I'm going to be, I suppose. Let's go before I come to my senses."

Within minutes, they were in Payne's SUV and headed for Club Twist.

"What are the rules?" Hunter asked. "I feel like I'm going into combat and need a situation report."

"No alcohol or drug use allowed on the premises, for obvious reasons," Payne said. "Consent issues aside, you don't want someone in an altered state of consciousness wielding a cane or having one used on them. It's grounds for a ban from the club. Tonight, you'll be my guest, but if you want to go back, you'll need a membership. No phones or cameras are allowed beyond the locker area. You'll probably see people in various states of undress, but sex and masturbation aren't allowed in the public areas." He paused and glanced at Hunter. "Any questions so far?"

"So if there's no alcohol, no phones and cameras... what do people do? Just hang out and talk? Hook up? Discuss sports scores?" Hunter wanted to have some idea what he was getting himself into.

Payne laughed. "Actually, yes. I've had some rather mundane conversations with my fellow Doms while our subs sat at our feet. There's a stage for demonstrations and shows, and there are private rooms available, but mostly it's a place where someone like me can be with like-minded people without fear of being outed or ridiculed or called a pervert. We can relax and be ourselves, and sometimes, it means sitting around with our water or orange juice and rehashing last night's football game while decked out in fetish gear."

Hunter mulled over what Payne had said, not sure how he felt about some parts. "Um... am I going to have to sit at your feet?"

"Not if you don't want to," Payne said. "In fact, you don't have to identify as a sub at all if you'd rather not. You can be a guest who's interested in learning more about BDSM but who isn't ready to participate. No one will force you to do anything you don't want to do. Our motto is 'safe, sane, and consensual,' which means you'll always have agency. If someone approaches you tonight, you can say no, and they'll leave you alone. Pressuring someone is against the rules. You get a warning first. After that, a temporary ban. After that, a permanent ban. Consent is a big fucking deal."

"Good." Hunter was glad to know there were rules as far as consent. He'd been to more than one bar where guys had gotten handsy and hadn't wanted to take no for an answer. Not that Hunter, at his size, had to fend off many advances, but he'd seen plenty of men who were no bigger than Payne get groped and handed around like they were pieces of meat. "Sounds more civilized than some of the places I've been to in the past. The last time I went to a club, it was in Thailand. I was with D-Day, and we rescued this kid who couldn't have been more than sixteen from an Afrikaner squad who seemed to think one boy for six mercs sounded like an equitable arrangement."

Payne tightened his grip on the steering wheel until his knuckles turned white, and his features grew hard. "I'm glad you rescued him."

"Yeah, no one fucks with a kid with D-Day or me around." Hunter frowned. "Are you okay? Oh..." Realization dawned, and Hunter felt something inside himself twist in sympathy. "Shit. I'm sorry. You've had to fight off scumbags more than once, haven't you?"

"More than once, yeah," Payne said dryly. He drew in a deep breath and released it slowly, and some of the tension left his body. "It was bad enough that when I mustered out, I grew a thick beard and let my hair grow down to here." He tapped just below his shoulder with the side of his hand. "I thought it would make me look older, but instead, people started calling me Jesus, so I shaved and got a haircut."

Hunter grimaced in sympathy. "I'm sorry you had to go through so much shit. The worst things I've ever had to deal with are people thinking that because I'm so big, I must be a total idiot, or because I'm a merc I'm a sociopath waiting to gun down a shopping center full of civilians for the hell of it. Though I've been groped more than once — but usually by women, if you can believe it."

"I can, actually," Payne said. "But no one will grope you tonight unless you've given them permission."

It was on the tip of Hunter's tongue to say he certainly wouldn't mind Payne groping him at all, but he wasn't sure if it was appropriate. Their relationship had changed in the last week or so, and it was still changing. Hunter wasn't certain where it was going to end up, but he wanted to find out. What he didn't know was if Payne's interest in him could become something more — something worth leaving the field for.

"Good to know," he said, giving Payne a warm smile. "If you have any interest in groping me, let me know. I suspect if you give me that wide-eyed look, I won't be able to tell you no."

Payne gave him a sidelong smile. "I'll keep that in mind. Do you have any other questions?"

"Not that I can think of," Hunter said. "Though I wonder if we should work out some kind of signal so you can tell me if I'm doing something wrong. I don't want to embarrass you in front of your friends, even by accident."

"If you're going in as a visiting observer, no one is going to expect you to behave like a sub. They'll probably assume you're a Dom anyway," Payne said with a little snort. "So basically, don't touch anyone without asking, don't stare at anyone unless they're on stage, and if you're unsure about something, ask. Most people will be more than happy to help out a newbie because we were all new once, and we know how it feels."

"Okay." Hunter drew in a deep breath. "I can do this. What's so hard? There won't be any explosions, no one will be shooting at me, and I don't have to kill anyone. Piece of cake."

"That's the spirit!" Payne grinned and clapped Hunter on the shoulder.

Within a few minutes, Payne pulled the SUV into a parking lot in front of what looked like a row of warehouses. Hunter wondered if they'd come to the right place. Even though he'd read the BDSM community liked to keep things low key, he'd expected something to indicate there was a social club inside. But the building was quite plain on the outside, indistinguishable from the other warehouses surrounding it, and the only sign was a small brass plaque below the building number with the name on it. If it weren't for the smattering of cars in the mostly-empty parking lot and the faint, bass beat of music he could hear when Payne switched off the engine, he'd have thought the place was deserted.

"They obviously aren't looking for much foot traffic," Hunter commented as he unfastened his seat belt.

"No, definitely not," Payne said. "You don't want people stumbling into a place like this unawares."

"I can imagine."

They got out of the SUV and Payne locked it, then Hunter followed him to the club entrance. Once they stepped inside, there was a small foyer area with a guard who asked for their ID. Payne produced a membership card, explaining that Hunter was his guest, and Hunter showed his driver's license. Hunter was used to far stricter security checks, and he was surprised they weren't sent through a metal detector or patted down for contraband. Instead they were waved toward a set of double doors, and as Hunter stepped through, he looked around, unable to keep from scanning his surroundings for possible threats. Having been in the field for so long, he still hadn't fully adjusted to civilian life.

They entered a sort of ante chamber. There were lockers on the right, and a shop displaying bondage gear and accessories on the left. Straight ahead, Hunter could see the main club area.

"I guess we need to put our phones in the lockers?" he asked.

"I leave my wallet, phone, and keys," Payne said, patting the seat of his leather pants. "I don't want my lines ruined or the view obscured. We can share a locker, and you can leave your jacket unless you're more comfortable wearing it."

"Definitely don't want to ruin those lines," Hunter said, eying Payne's ass again. He needed to stop thinking about Payne's ass so much, and he was grateful his own pants weren't skin tight. "I'll leave the jacket for now. I was worried about feeling under-dressed, but I guess it's not going to be an issue." He'd already noticed some of the people walking by were wearing a lot less than he was.

"Definitely not," Payne said, laughing.

They stashed their belongings in a locker, and then Payne led Hunter into the main area of the club. Several circular booths to the left offered more privacy for intimate conversation than the numerous tables and chairs scattered in the middle of the room, and off to the right was a long bar, where two young men in tight pants and fishnet shirts served the patrons perched on tall stools. The back wall was dominated by a wide stage with lush crimson velvet curtains.

"Want something to drink?" Payne asked. "They've got water, sports drinks, and all kinds of juice. They can make smoothies too."

Hunter wasn't thirsty, but a drink would give him something to do with his hands to help hide his nervousness. "Sure. Water would be good."

Payne beckoned for Hunter to follow him, and as he approached the bar, one of the young men offered an enthusiastic greeting.

"Master Payne!" The young man smiled and leaned forward on the bar. "Welcome back. What can I get you?"

"Two bottles of water, please," Payne said.

"Sure thing." The young man retrieved two chilled bottles of water and handed them over, and his gaze lingered on Payne's ass as Payne approached Hunter.

"Here you go." Payne held out one of the bottles.

Hunter normally prided himself on his control. Working with dangerous explosives meant he couldn't afford to lose his cool in difficult circumstances, and he was damned good at it, normally. He wasn't certain if it was because his emotions were running a bit closer to the surface these days, or if he was developing too much of an attachment to Payne, but he wanted to lunge at the man behind the bar and punch him for looking at Payne. He was able to confine his reaction to a glare that made the guy flinch, but as Payne held out the bottle, Hunter also realized he was growling.

"Thanks." He cleared his throat, hoping Payne hadn't noticed his reaction, and he reached out to take the bottle.

Payne's eyebrows climbed as he stared at Hunter, and then he glanced back at the bar. "Were you growling?"

It probably wasn't a good thing to admit feeling possessive of Payne, not when their relationship wasn't at that stage yet — and might never get there. "I was clearing my throat."

"Uh-huh." Payne's expression was dubious, but he didn't argue. Instead, he tucked his arm through Hunter's and guided Hunter away from the bar, a pleased little smirk playing at the corner of his mouth.

Hunter decided it was better to let the subject drop for the moment. "You seem to be, uh, well known here."

"This is where I've come to play since I started working for Herc five years ago," Payne said, stroking Hunter's bicep casually. He seemed about to say more, but he was interrupted by someone calling his name, and his face lit up when he spotted an older man waving at him from a nearby booth. "This is great! Come on, I'd like you to meet someone," he said, tugging Hunter toward the booth.

Hunter went along, but he was distracted by the way Payne had caressed his arm. The casual touch was far more arousing than it should have been, and he wondered if Payne had even realized he was doing it.

Forcing his attention back to matters at hand, Hunter found himself looking at a man for whom the phrase "Silver Fox" must have been invented. His hair was black with striking patches of pure silver at his temples, and his jaw looked sharp enough to cut paper. Hunter remembered an older drill sergeant from his days at the Point who had radiated the same air of total confidence, something Hunter had always thought was sexy as hell.

Payne released Hunter's arm so he could shake hands with the silver fox, who was seated next to a younger man, who was beaming at Payne, but didn't say anything. The younger man was shirtless, but unlike most of the other patrons, the silver fox wasn't wearing leather or fetish gear. Instead, he was dressed in a charcoal gray three-piece suit that appeared tailor made.

"Payne! It's so good to see you. It's been too long." The silver fox looked Hunter up and down with an appreciative eye. "And you brought a friend!"

"James, this is Hunter," Payne said. "He's interested in learning about BDSM. Hunter, this is Master James, one of the best Doms in the state."

James made a scoffing noise, but he seemed pleased by the compliment. "Won't you join us? You know Tyler, of course. I've got him under a vow of silence right now."

"I figured," Payne said as he slid into the booth across from the couple, and he patted the seat beside him, watching Hunter expectantly.

"Nice to meet you," Hunter said, taking the seat beside Payne. He looked at the much younger man with James, a cherubic-faced blond with guileless blue eyes and a head of curly ringlets. Hunter was surprised to see Tyler was wearing a black leather collar with an attached leash, the end of which James held in one hand. "A vow of silence?"

"It means he may not speak unless I give him permission," James said, smoothing his hand along the back of Tyler's head, and Tyler leaned into the touch. "Tyler is a bit of a chatterbox, but I've promised him a special reward when we get home if he obeys."

"I see." Hunter had to suppress a smile, though he shot an amused look at Payne, remembering how much Payne had talked back when they'd first met, trying to draw Hunter out. "It sounds efficient."

"If I was only trying to make him hush for a couple of hours, I suppose it could be called efficient," James said. "But this is a lesson in obedience, something meant to challenge Tyler and make him earn his reward. That makes it fun for both of us."

"Ah. A game. I see." Being in the military probably gave Hunter a different take on obedience, reward, and punishment than most people had, but he thought if anyone would understand him, Payne would.

"Yes, that's it exactly." James gave him a look of approval, then gestured to the rest of the room. "This is a playground, and we're here to play."

A very *adult* playground, Hunter thought, but he got the analogy. "A well-mannered playground, though," he said. "No one is allowed to be a bully or throw sand at the other kids. Or to take their toys? Or is that considered one of the games?"

"Only if it's agreed upon by all parties involved," James said. "I assume Payne told you about our playtime being safe, sane, and consensual?" He raised a questioning eyebrow at Payne, who nodded.

"I've explained the basics, but I thought he'd learn more from seeing for himself," Payne said.

"I'm no stranger to discipline, punishment, and consequences."

Hunter tried to keep his tone light, but a sudden mental image of Mark's mangled body caught him unawares. He closed his eyes and took a deep breath, then opened them again when he heard a crunch, and he realized he'd crumpled the water bottle in his hand. "Sorry."

James and Tyler appeared alarmed by the unexpected destruction of the bottle, but Payne immediately clasped Hunter's upper arm in a firm, warm grip.

"It's okay," Payne said, his voice low and soothing. "You're in a club in Raleigh with me. Whatever you saw isn't real. I am."

Hunter glanced at Payne, letting Payne's touch help ground him, as it had the night before, when Hunter had experienced one of his nightmares and Payne had come into the room to comfort him. "Thanks."

He could feel James and Tyler's curious gazes, and he knew he had to offer an explanation. He glanced at James, shrugging slightly. "Sorry. I'm dealing with something... complicated. It hits me out of the blue sometimes."

"It's all right," James said, his expression turning sympathetic.

Payne leaned close and pitched his voice for Hunter's ears alone. "Would you be okay with telling James what we're doing? He's been a Dom for almost thirty years. He might have some insights."

Hunter's automatic, knee-jerk reaction was to say no, but he knew that kind of response was a part of what had kept him in denial for so long. Instead of answering immediately, he looked at Payne. "Do you trust him?"

"I do," Payne said simply. "Master James is the one who's helped me after some rough missions."

Hunter remembered Payne saying he'd used BDSM as a way to deal with some issues. If James was the man who had helped Payne come to terms with things that bothered him, maybe James could help Hunter too.

"All right." Hunter said softly. "Could you start?"

Payne squeezed Hunter's arm gently before releasing it, and he rested his hand on Hunter's leg beneath the table instead. "Hunter has PTSD," he said, turning his attention back to James, who leaned forward and listened with an attentive frown. "Conventional therapy hasn't been helpful, so we're trying something unconventional. We're trying to help him process through BDSM, but this is a new experience for him and new territory for me."

Hunter swallowed against a lump in his throat. "I didn't want to admit I had a problem, and I don't trust shrinks. After... after I froze on a mission, I realized I'm in trouble. I don't particularly care if I die on a mission, but I don't want to get anyone else killed."

"Of course," James said softly, and while there was still sympathy in his expression, he didn't show any trace of pity or disgust. "What you're doing may seem unorthodox to most people, but it's more common than you might think. Have you tried anything yet or are you still in the planning stage?"

"We've, uh...done one scene," Hunter said. He glanced at Payne. "It's okay to talk about it? I mean...you're okay with me telling him?" He was still feeling his way around the protocols, but he figured "consensual" meant he didn't talk about what went on between them without Payne's agreement.

"I'm good with it if you are," Payne said with a reassuring smile, and he patted Hunter's leg.

Hunter placed his own hand over Payne's, taking comfort from the contact. He looked at James again, and for some reason James's resemblance to that long-ago sergeant helped. "I didn't want to relive what happened, but Payne tied me to a St. Andrew's cross and made me tell him about it. If I hesitated, he used a cane to...um...encourage me. I got through it, and it helped me to..." He dropped his gaze. "My best friend died saving my life, you see, and I hadn't been able to cry about it. Not until then."

"I'm sorry for your loss," James said, and beside him, Tyler gazed at Hunter with tears swimming in his eyes, but he didn't speak. "What I'm hearing is that the scene helped you achieve a catharsis you couldn't reach on your own. Am I right?"

"Yes." Hunter could hear how ragged he sounded, so he cleared his throat. "It's the first thing that helped in any way. I know I'm still fucked up, but I'm hoping maybe this can do for me what all the shrinks in the world can't."

James nodded, appearing lost in thought for a moment, and then he focused on Payne. "How did you approach the scene?"

"It was like an interrogation," Payne said. "I guided him with questions and kept him focused with the cane."

"And what's your goal moving forward?" James asked.

"Facing his grief was a good first step, but there's still a lot to deal with." Payne glanced at Hunter before adding, "Survivor's guilt, for one thing. The trauma of what he witnessed. Grief, loss, depression."

Hunter winced, but he couldn't fault what Payne was saying. Now that he'd decided he couldn't run away from his problems, he had to face them. All of them. "My work has been my life, and I can't do it being fucked up, because people would die. I've lost everything that ever mattered to me. I have nothing left to lose, I guess." He didn't mention the darkest times, when he wondered if he wanted to go on at all.

"I think Payne has the right idea with the interrogation approach," James said, his words measured and slow. He steepled his fingers as he studied Hunter, his brow furrowed. "He'll be your facilitator, but all the hard work falls to you, and I can tell you right now what the two most difficult things will be."

Hunter felt a lump of anxiety form in his stomach. He wasn't certain he wanted to hear James's answer, but he had to ask anyway. "What are those?"

"You've got a start on the first thing already," James said. "And that is putting complete trust in Payne. It means knowing, understanding, and accepting he's going to be there with you throughout this process, that anything he does to you in the context of a scene is for your benefit, and he'll take care of you physically and emotionally afterward. So do you trust Master Payne?"

"Yes." Hunter could say it without any hesitation. Payne had done for him what no one else had been able to do, and in refusing to report Hunter's failure to Herc, he might have saved Hunter's career and his self-respect. "I trust him completely."

"Don't tell me." James flipped his hand in Payne's direction, a note of authority entering his voice. "Tell him."

"Yes, sir," Hunter said, then turned to Payne. "I trust you. Even if it doesn't work, I know you'll try your damnedest for me. I trust you, Payne. And you know I don't trust easily."

Payne's expression softened, but before he could respond, James waved him silent.

"'I trust you, Master Payne,'" James said. "Use his title."

Hunter frowned slightly, but then nodded. "I trust you, Master Payne."

"Good." James smiled in approval, and beneath the table, Payne squeezed Hunter's leg hard enough to almost hurt. "Now here's the second thing, and I believe this is what will trip you up the most. For this to work, you have to surrender to the experience. You say you trust Payne, and that means you must trust him and yourself enough to give up control. Only then will you be free to face and process your trauma. If you fight or resist or put up walls, you're wasting your time and his."

"I thought that's what I was doing. Giving him control, I mean." Hunter raised one eyebrow. "I didn't like having to relive that day, but I could have ended it and I didn't. I knew if I told him to stop, he would. Wasn't that the point?"

"I'm not just talking about seeing the scene through," James said. "I mean you can't have any walls up in here," he added, tapping his temple. "You're new to all this, which I assume means you haven't experienced sub space, so this may be difficult for you to relate to. But I think if you want to defeat your demons, you need to stop fighting them. Let go of your body, your mind, your feelings — put all of it in Payne's hands and just be."

Hunter had read about sub space, and while he thought he understood, at least to an extent, what James meant, it was true he didn't have a frame of reference for something he'd never experienced. He chuckled. "Stare into the abyss, and let it stare into me."

"Yes." Payne answered this time, and he touched Hunter's back lightly where the tattoo was. "That's pretty much it."

Hunter looked at James. "I think I understand better than you might believe."

"Good." James cocked his head and gave Hunter a questioning look. "Now the question is, can you do it?"

"That is the question." Hunter returned James's gaze steadily, then focused his attention to Payne. "Do you think I can do it, Master Payne? Are you willing to help me try?"

"I'm willing to do anything to help you, Hunter," Payne said, flattening his palm against Hunter's back over the tattoo. "I want to be here for you until the end."

What Hunter wanted more than anything else at the moment was to pull Payne into his arms and kiss him breathless. Payne's words were like a lifeline tossed to Hunter when he felt like he was drowning, all the more precious because Hunter knew Payne meant them. But they weren't alone, and Hunter had to remind himself that Payne was a natural caretaker, and his words would have been said with equal sincerity to anyone who needed him. Hunter couldn't do something incredibly stupid like falling for Payne just because Payne was the only one who understood. Especially since Payne didn't need Hunter in return.

Unfortunately, it was probably already too late.

He became aware he'd been staring into Payne's eyes for longer than he should have, and Payne had an uncanny knack for reading him. He glanced away. "Thank you."

"You're welcome." Payne leaned his cheek briefly on Hunter's shoulder before sitting up straight.

James watched the two of them with a knowing smile while Tyler beamed proudly. "I think this will work," James said. "As long as the two of you work together, I think you'll be fine."

"I hope you're right," Hunter said. "Thank you for listening. Um... sir."

Chuckling, James leaned across the table and patted Hunter's hand. "You're a fast learner!" He grew serious again as he pulled a pen out of the pocket of his suit jacket, and he wrote something on a cocktail napkin. "If there's anything I can do to help either of you along the way, let me know."

He started to slide the napkin across the table, but Tyler stopped him with a hand on his arm, and at James's questioning look, Tyler made a beckoning motion toward the pen. James handed over the pen, and Tyler scribbled something on the napkin as well and then pushed it over to Hunter.

"You have our numbers," James said, giving Tyler a proud smile as he caressed the back of Tyler's head, and Tyler leaned into the stroking with apparent bliss. "Feel free to give either of us a call. Tyler isn't always under a vow of silence, and I'm sure he'd have plenty to say if you ever want to hear from a sub's perspective."

Tyler flashed a mischievous grin and nodded vehemently.

"Thank you." Hunter hadn't paid as much attention to the sub as he probably should have, but he hadn't wanted to cause him any difficulties. Now, however, he smiled at Tyler. "I appreciate it. I might need some advice in figuring all this out. It's not exactly like there's a home study course I can take."

Tyler gave him a double thumbs up and then leaned against James, who slid his arm around Tyler's shoulders again.

"You're in good hands," James said. "Our Payne is quite the caretaker."

"I noticed," Hunter said. He looked at Payne. "What shall we do now, Master Payne?" His lips twitched in amusement.

"Smartass." Payne shouldered him hard enough to budge him a little. "Are there any demos scheduled for tonight?" he asked James.

James glanced at his watch. "There's one featuring caning in about ten minutes. After that, it's going to be sensation play, then rope bondage, and I believe the last one is spanking."

"Would you like to stick around and watch the demonstrations?" Payne gave Hunter a questioning look. "You might see something you'd like to try."

Hunter was interested in seeing how other Doms and subs interacted, since he wasn't certain if most of the things he'd seen on the internet were real examples or simply porn. "Yes. I'd like to."

"Great!" Payne's wide smile showed how pleased he was.

"You're welcome to sit with us," James said. "Unless you'd rather move to a table closer to the front."

"I'd like to be a little closer, since I have no idea what I'll be looking at," Hunter said. "You've been helpful, sir, and I appreciate it."

"Anytime, darling. You two run along and have a good time," James said, and Tyler waved goodbye.

Hunter waved at Tyler, then slid out of the booth, stepping back and waiting for Payne, who exited the booth right behind him.

"Go ahead and pick a table," Payne said. "It looks like there are a few still open near the stage."

As he wove through the tables, Hunter used his training to make note of the different people he passed. There were several subs who sat or knelt at their Dom's feet, and even a couple who were curled up in laps. There were a few tables that had groups that appeared to be one Dom and several subs. Hunter found an empty table off to the right of the stage.

"Is this all right?"

"This is fine," Payne said with a reassuring smile. "Have a seat."

Hunter sat down and angled his chair so he could be close to Payne. "I might ask dumb questions. It's one reason I wanted it to be just you and me. I didn't want to look like a complete idiot in front of your friends."

"You're new to this." Payne rested his hand on Hunter's bare shoulder and rubbed it gently. "They wouldn't think you're an idiot for asking questions."

Hunter had noticed Payne was touching him more than usual. He liked it — probably more than he should — but he thought Payne probably wanted to reassure him through touch as well as words. "Well, my questions might include things like 'how in the hell does he get off on *that*?' Different strokes, I know, but some things I saw online seemed really strange."

Payne blinked and cocked his head as he watched Hunter. "What kind of things?"

"Things like borderline torture. Electric shocks, being suspended upside down in a way that would cause unconsciousness. Some stuff reminded me of crap the CIA got chewed out for as 'interrogation methods.' I'm sure some of it was intended more for shock value, but it did make me wonder if there are people who actually do go that extreme looking for the endorphin rush."

"There are, but more dangerous types of play — electric shocks, branding, breath play — are supposed to be done under very careful and controlled circumstances," Payne said. "That's not to say there aren't people who aren't careful, but they're outliers. Most people who want to play that way are stringent about safety."

"I'd certainly hope so." Hunter shook his head, then fell silent as the curtains opened.

On the stage, a man almost as tall and broad as Hunter was bound naked to a St. Andrews cross with thick leather cuffs around his wrists and ankles.

A woman in black leather pants and a black leather overbust corset studded with chains and metal buckles stood behind him, wielding a cane similar to Payne's. Hunter's eyes skimmed over the woman, but he was more interested in the sub. The Domme launched into a spiel about caning, going over the basics and demonstrating on the sub until his ass was practically glowing red, and bruises were already forming. The marks he sported were far more painful looking than Hunter's own welts, and he realized Payne had been holding back. Payne could have dealt Hunter an incredible amount of damage, and Hunter realized how much trust he was placing in Payne. The idea didn't bother him, which was good, and it also gave him an idea of how much control a Dom had to exercise over himself as well. Going into a scene angry or upset would probably be a bad thing.

"If you want more, you'd better get your ass where I can reach it," the Domme said, and the sub pushed his ass out as best he could, giving what sounded like a happy moan. "Five more. Count them off."

She delivered five more stinging blows while the sub called out the numbers, wriggling helplessly on the cross. But his face was suffused with bliss despite the pain, and after the Domme untied him and helped him down, he clung to her.

Hunter had read about the endorphins released during a session, but he'd had to admit to a little skepticism. But seeing the look on the sub's face demonstrated the truth of it in a way Hunter couldn't doubt. The marks on the sub's ass looked painful, and no doubt if he weren't on a hormonal high, they would have hurt enough to make the guy cry, no matter how tough he looked.

"What did you think?" Payne asked. Although his voice sounded casual, his cheeks were flushed, and there was a heated glitter in his eyes.

Hunter hesitated. "The stuff about endorphins must be true," he said slowly. "You weren't anywhere near that hard with me."

"No, we didn't reach that point," Payne said. "I might have if you'd been more resistant, but you didn't need it."

"I hope I don't ever need it," Hunter admitted. "Where do you draw the line on 'safe' and 'sane?' Having bloody welts you can't sit on for days seems to be pushing a boundary, at least to me."

"It's not pushing a boundary if it's what the Dom and sub have agreed on," Payne said. "What you saw in the demo was negotiated ahead of time. The sub knew what the results would be. He *wanted* them. That's how it works in any scene."

Hunter inclined his head to acknowledge the point. "Understood. Would it bother you if I said I'm not sure I'd like it that hard? Maybe it's because I'm aware being impaired in any way makes it harder to do my job."

"No, it wouldn't bother me." Payne ran his hand along Hunter's forearm in a soothing caress. "What we're doing is for you. Pushing you past your boundaries might cause more harm than good, and that's not what I want to do."

"Oh, I think I have your number, Master Payne," Hunter said, leaning closer and lowering his voice. "Daddy likes causing just enough pain that he can kiss it and make it better, right?"

Payne sucked in a breath, and the flush in his cheeks deepened. "Yes, he does," he said huskily. "But that's not all he likes."

Hunter couldn't resist the obvious set up. Their relationship seemed to be changing, and Hunter couldn't help but look at Payne a bit differently. "What else does Daddy like?"

A wicked smirk curved Payne's lips as he picked up his water bottle and pressed the still-chilly bottom against Hunter's warm neck. "Sensation play."

Hunter drew in a breath. He wasn't quite sure if it was the cold plastic or Payne's smile raising the goosebumps on his arms, but whichever it was, he liked it. A lot.

"Now that might be something I would like," he murmured. "I live by my senses, after all. They're highly developed."

"Then we could have a lot of fun." Payne trailed the bottle along the curve of Hunter's shoulder, leaving beads of condensation in its wake. "Imagine what it might be like if I had you tied up and blindfolded, and I used ice or fur on your bare skin."

All the air seemed to have been sucked out of the room, and Hunter stared at Payne, his eyes wide as arousal flowed over him in a heated wave. It took him several moments to find his voice, and when he did, it was rough with need. "I can imagine it."

The mischievous gleam in Payne's eyes was the only warning Hunter got before Payne leaned over and dragged his tongue along Hunter's skin to lap up the water. "You don't have to imagine it," he said. "I'd do it if you want me to."

Hunter shivered. He hadn't had sex or even pleasured himself in a long time. The specter that had haunted him since Stack's death rose up, trying to tell him he didn't deserve to feel good or to enjoy any life affirmation in the face of his loss. But the warmth of Payne's body and the seductive words drowned out that specter. "Trying to get me to stare into the abyss, Master Payne?"

Payne met and held Hunter's gaze. "I would love to make you stare into the abyss," he said, his voice low and beguiling. "I would love to witness the moment you surrender to sub space and set yourself free."

"I want it, too." Hunter reached for Payne's hand, grasping it and clinging to it like a lifeline. "I want it more than you can imagine."

Payne tightened his fingers around Hunter's. "Then let's go home, and I'll give it to you."

Hunter rose to his feet, not wanting to let go of Payne's hand. He was afraid if he did, the spell would somehow be broken, and his demons would rise up to torment him until he couldn't fight them any longer. But he thought he *needed* this just as much as he wanted it. He needed to feel things could go on, and that there was hope he could one day be the man he thought he was.

"Please... don't let go," he said to Payne. "Please."

"I won't." Payne squeezed Hunter's hand as he stood up. "I'm right here. I'm not going anywhere. I've got you."

"Yes, you do," Hunter said. Payne didn't know how many levels of truth there were in his statement.

They left the stage area, and Hunter nodded to James and Tyler as they passed their booth. It took only a few moments to collect their belongings from the locker, then they stepped out of the club into the warmth of the Raleigh evening.

Holding Payne's hand while Payne drove wasn't going to work, but Hunter kept one hand on Payne's leg. He'd never needed contact with anyone the way he did now, but he wasn't going to question it, since Payne didn't mind.

"This is going to be the longest drive home ever," Payne said wryly as he pulled out of the parking lot. "But if you change your mind between now and then, it's okay."

"I won't change my mind," Hunter said. "Just... talk to me. I don't want to be in my own head right now."

Payne clasped Hunter's hand and brought it to his lips for a swift kiss before replacing it on his leg. "I can do that. Want to hear about the first time I met James?"

"Yes, tell me about it," Hunter said, tightening his hand on Payne's thigh. "I like him. Tyler, too, even if he didn't say a word."

Payne began to talk, his voice smooth and calming. He kept the story light and amusing at first, but it became more serious as it unfolded, Hunter realized Payne was sharing the aftermath of a mission that had gone south and revealing the fears and guilt he'd wrestled with and how James had helped him cope. The story flowed into another, this one much less somber, and Payne kept the narrative going until they reached home at last.

"Thank you," Hunter said as Payne switched off the engine. "For sharing that with me. It makes me feel like I can come back."

Payne unfastened his seatbelt and slid closer to Hunter. "You can," he said, cupping Hunter's cheek in his palm. "You *will*."

Hunter clung to the certainty in Payne's voice. "Yes, Master Payne," he said.

"I had no idea hearing you call me that would be such a turn on," Payne murmured, his gaze flicking to Hunter's lips. "Before we go inside, there's something I have to do." Then he leaned in and captured Hunter's lips in a warm, gentle kiss.

The press of Payne's lips to his was as potent as an electric shock, and Hunter moaned softly and rested his hand on the back of Payne's neck. He kissed Payne back, feeling a sense of rightness he'd never felt from any other kiss in his life. With a hungry little growl, Payne coaxed Hunter's lips apart with his tongue and deepened the kiss, turning it into a possessive claim.

The growl made Hunter shiver, making him want more. He parted his lips and gave himself over to the kiss, losing himself in it, his world narrowing down to the two of them and the rising heat between them. Only after a leisurely exploration of Hunter's mouth did Payne draw back, his breathing already ragged.

"I've been wanting to do that all night," he said, touching his forehead to Hunter's.

Hunter was also breathing hard, but he felt more alive than he had in a long time. "I have too. Especially when you licked me."

Payne laughed softly. "It was a risky impulse, so I'm glad you didn't mind."

"Were you afraid I'd slug you, or clutch my pearls and call for James to expel you for not asking permission?" Hunter couldn't help smiling. "Tyler might have beaten you up, you know."

"I was afraid I might have read the signals wrong or I might be oversteppping or worse, you'd shut down," Payne said, sliding his hand around to stroke the back of Hunter's neck.

"Part of me wanted to shut down," Hunter admitted. He closed his eyes, relaxing at the gentle caress of Payne's hand. "A part I've listened to too much. But the part that wants you was louder."

"Good, because I want you too," Payne said, continuing to stroke Hunter's neck. "Now the question is, do you want to go to the playroom or the bedroom?"

"You said you'd show me the abyss," Hunter said. "I want to please you, sir. I want to show you how much I trust you."

Payne drew back enough to study Hunter's face, and he must have been satisfied by whatever he saw, because a slow smile bloomed on his lips. "Then let's go inside so you can get started."

"Yes, sir." Hunter was more eager than he could remember being in years. He unfastened his seat belt. "Should I go up to the playroom?"

"Yes, and once you're there, I want you to strip," Payne said as he scooted back to the driver's side and opened his door.

Hunter got out of the car, then waited for Payne to unlock the door. Once they were inside the house, he immediately headed up to the playroom. It only took him a couple of minutes to strip naked and fold up his clothing, and then he hesitated, wondering how he should wait.

He remembered the behavior of the subs in the club, and he decided emulating them shouldn't be too off base. Sinking to his knees in the middle of the room, he rested his hands on his thighs and waited for Payne.

Payne entered the room a few minutes later. He'd taken off the leather pants and vest, and while he hadn't scrubbed off the eyeliner, he looked far more casual in a pair of gray sweatpants, a black t-shirt, and bare feet. His eyebrows climbed when he saw Hunter kneeling, and a pleased smile curved his mouth.

"Someone's been paying attention," he said as he sauntered closer. "I like it."

Hunter smirked, which probably wasn't something a "proper" sub should do. "I'm glad, sir. I can't promise to be a textbook submissive, but I can try — especially if you like it."

"I don't want a textbook sub," Payne said, running his thumb across the lingering remains of Hunter's smirk. "I want you to be yourself and enjoy what we do together. Well, outside of our therapy sessions, at least," he added wryly. "Those won't be fun."

"I understand. But this isn't a therapy session, right? This is... us."

"This is us." Payne's pale eyes were warm and full of affection as he sifted his fingers through Hunter's hair. "I want to give you pleasure tonight, not pain. Well, maybe a little pain," he said with a mischievous smile.

Tilting his head to one side, Hunter grinned wickedly. "Actually, I was hoping for one big, hard Payne at some point tonight."

Laughing, Payne buried his fingers in Hunter's long, dark hair, tightened his fist, and tugged Hunter's head back just hard enough for Hunter to feel it without it being outright painful. "If you're good, that can be your reward," he said, leaning down until his lips hovered over Hunter's, almost but not quite touching.

Hunter felt breathless, Payne's display of forcefulness affecting him in a way he'd never felt before with anyone else. Staring up at Payne, he licked his lips. "If it will get you to fuck me, I'm prepared to be very, very good. Sir."

"Good to know." Payne smirked and gave Hunter's hair another tug before releasing him. "I'm going to get set up. You sit here and watch. If you have any questions, you may ask. If you have any concerns, use your colors. Got it?"

"Got it, sir," Hunter said, disappointed Payne hadn't kissed him again. But they had all evening, so he told himself to be patient and wait.

The gray sweatpants were tight enough to give Hunter enticing glimpses of Payne's ass as he moved around the playroom. Sometimes he seemed to be putting himself on display as he bent over to rummage in a cabinet.

Hunter's anticipation was building as he watched Payne walking around, but he was also curious. "What are you planning to do to me?"

Payne flashed a wicked smile. "I'm going to let you choose."

Payne didn't take long to set up the room and gather his equipment. He placed a large cushion made of forest green velvet on the floor near Hunter, and then he brought over his rolling cart, on which he'd placed several items.

"For now, I want to reserve the cross for our therapy sessions," he said. "Putting you on the spanking bench means I couldn't reach your nipples, so you're going to kneel on the cushion instead."

Hunter drew in a breath, his imagination more than able to supply him with images of Payne playing with his nipples. "Do you want me to kneel on it now, sir?" He hoped he didn't sound quite as eager as he felt.

"Not yet. First, you have to choose what you want me to use on you," Payne said, an anticipatory gleam in his eyes. He picked up a small bowl from the cart and showed Hunter it was full of ice cubes from the mini fridge. In his other hand, he held out a candle. "Ice or hot wax. This is a special candle made just for this kind of play, so the wax won't damage your skin."

He put down the bowl and candle and picked up a black handled flogger that was a mix of thin black leather strips and red faux fur. "This would be used to stimulate your skin. I wouldn't strike you with it. This time," he added with a little smirk as he put the flogger back on the cart. "One last thing," he said, holding up a black glove. It looked like any other heavy winter glove — until Hunter noticed the thumbtack sized spikes covering the palm side. "The vampire glove. Pick two."

"Ice," Hunter said without hesitation. "I spent so long in the desert, dreaming of ice." He looked at the three remaining items, wondering which would complement the ice best. "How about the vampire glove? I assume you'd use it lightly, not turn me into a human pincushion?"

"I'm not into drawing blood." Payne picked up a piece of ice and tapped it against his lips, and then he darted out his tongue and licked it. "So you want ice and the glove?"

Payne's actions were an erotic enough sight to make Hunter's body tighten. "Yes, sir. Unless you wanted to use your tongue instead. I'm good with that."

Payne widened his eyes in the way Hunter knew meant trouble. "Sure, I can use my tongue."

Holding the piece of ice against his tongue, Payne moved to stand in front of Hunter, and then he dropped into a squat and flattened his cold tongue against Hunter's nipple.

Hunter gasped at the intensity of the sensation, and he reached out instinctively to grasp Payne's shoulders. "Oh, God," he groaned. "That feels so good."

"We're just getting started," Payne said as he sat back on his heels. "But maybe I need to bind your wrists first, hm? We don't want you getting too grabby."

"There's such a thing as too grabby?" Hunter asked, trying to look innocent.

"Under other circumstances, no," Payne said, chuckling. "Under these circumstances, yes. Considering I plan to use new and different sensations on sensitive parts of your body, I'd rather not risk getting punched in the face thanks to your reflexes."

"I can see your point," Hunter chuckled. "Too bad you don't have a bed in here you can tie me down on."

"That's an excellent idea." Payne stood up and went to retrieve a set of sturdy leather wrist cuffs connected by a short chain. "If things go well, maybe you and I can customize one together."

Hunter went still, surprise freezing him in place. Was it possible Payne might be considering their relationship continuing past the time of Hunter's "therapy?" He didn't want to get his hopes up too much, but he liked the idea. A lot.

"I'd enjoy that," he said, trying to keep his tone casual.

Payne's face lit up, and when he returned to Hunter, he bent to brush a light but lingering kiss against Hunter's lips. "So would I."

"Good." Hunter grinned. "Do I get a blindfold too?"

"Oh yes," Payne said. "I want you to wait and wonder when the next touch is coming, and I want you to feel the full intensity when it does." He pointed to the cushion. "Go kneel and put your hands behind your back."

Hunter moved to the cushion, settling himself comfortably on it. It was definitely easier on his knees than the floor had been, and he obediently put his hands behind himself. "I'm ready, sir."

Payne knelt behind Hunter and fastened the cuffs around his wrists. "How does that feel?"

Hunter tested the cuffs, which bound him securely, but didn't chafe because of the fleece lining. "Feels fine, sir."

"Good," Payne said, his voice soft as he smoothed his hands down Hunter's arms from shoulder to wrist, conforming his palms to the curve of hard muscle along the way. He brushed a kiss against Hunter's neck and then stood up and returned to the cart. "Now for your blindfold."

Hunter watched Payne, letting his gaze linger on the curve of Payne's ass. "I lied, you know," he admitted. "I did growl."

Payne raised one eyebrow, but he didn't say anything. Instead, he knelt in front of Hunter, holding the blindfold in both hands.

"You scared the shit out of Kevin," he said.

Hunter bared his teeth. "Good. If he's scared, I won't have to gouge his eyes out and hand them back to him."

"What did he do?"

"He was staring at your ass," Hunter said. "Hungrily."

Payne dropped the blindfold and slid his arms around Hunter's shoulders, giving him a coy look from beneath his lashes. "Feeling possessive, are you?"

"Yes," Hunter admitted, hoping he hadn't overstepped Payne's boundaries. He leaned forward and grazed Payne's cheek with his lips. "You don't mind, do you?"

"No." Payne gave Hunter a speculative look. "Would it help if I promised I won't have sex or play with anyone but you while we're together? I don't need novelty. I want stability."

Hunter was glad Payne didn't mind him feeling territorial, but he hadn't expected Payne to be willing to be exclusive. Not that he minded at all. While he'd had friends-with-benefits arrangements with some of his fellow mercs over the years, Payne was different. What Hunter felt for him was different, even if Hunter wasn't sure where they were going to end up.

"Are you really good with it?" he asked quietly. "I admit, I'd prefer it that way, but I can't be sure I can fulfill all your needs." He smiled crookedly. "When it comes to stability, I'm sure Herc and Matthew still feel like I'm a loose cannon, ready to blow at any moment."

"You aren't a loose cannon anymore," Payne said, framing Hunter's face between his hands and meeting his gaze steadily. "You were, but I think starting the grieving process has helped you move past it. And yes, I'm good with being exclusive. Given the choice between you and any sub at Twist, I'd pick you."

Hunter drew in a startled breath, and his heart seemed to pound in his chest almost painfully. "I'm still fucked up, I know it, and I don't know if I'll ever be the man I was before."

"Don't care." Payne placed a gentle kiss at the corner of Hunter's mouth. "I'm not the man I was before Camp Victory. It doesn't mean I have to cut myself off. Neither do you."

Hunter wished his hands were free, because he wanted to wrap his arms around Payne and hold on to him. "Thank you. It means a lot to me."

Payne nuzzled Hunter's cheek, and then he drew back with an arch look. "Of course, exclusivity goes both ways. Don't make me have to take down some big, badass merc for going after you. You know I can do it."

Chuckling, Hunter shook his head. "You don't have to worry, I promise. I'm all yours." Hunter meant it on more levels than Payne suspected, but he didn't elaborate.

"Damned right you're mine." Payne picked up the blindfold and settled it in place. Then Hunter felt Payne's warm breath brushing across his ear as Payne whispered, "And I'm yours."

Hunter shivered, but Payne's words filled him with warmth. Even if Payne only meant it for now, Hunter wanted it to be true. "Yes, sir," he murmured.

The loss of Payne's body heat plus the movement of air when Payne moved away made Hunter's skin prickle, and he strained to hear footsteps to give him a clue about where Payne was and what he was doing, but he didn't hear anything. He wasn't sure how long he knelt there in utter silence; seconds felt like minutes as his anticipation built — and then he felt the wet chill of an ice cube on the back of his neck.

Hunter gasped, instinctively flinching, but then he relaxed and moaned as he bowed his head, offering Payne better access to his neck. The ice made his skin feel hot by comparison, while being blindfolded allowed him to concentrate on the sensation without distraction. It felt far more intense than he would have imagined, and Hunter gave himself over to the experience, focusing on the small area where the ice touched his skin.

Payne slid the ice down the length of Hunter's back slowly, pausing at each bump along his spine to circle the cube in one spot for several seconds. The cold numbed his skin, but that only made it more intense when Payne moved downward. Cool droplets trickled down his spine, and Hunter shivered, not from the cold, but from the sensation.

Payne lifted the cube away from Hunter's back and pressed it into the slight bend of Hunter's inner elbow, and he held it there.

"Oh..." Hunter hadn't anticipated the change, and it make the cold feel all the more acute.

"How does it feel?" Payne asked as he slid the cube down the sensitive underside of Hunter's arm. "Do you like it? Not like it? Feel indifferent to it?"

"I like it," Hunter said. "It feels good."

Only the stirring of air around him alerted Hunter that Payne had moved away, and he couldn't hear anything to give him a clue about where Payne was until he caught the faint clink of ice against ice. Whoever had trained Payne in stealth had done an excellent job.

And then without warning, Payne began circling a thick cube of ice around Hunter's nipple.

Hunter gave a start of surprise, as much from the fact he hadn't detected Payne as from the cold against his sensitive skin. "Remind me never to play hide and seek with you," he said, then gave himself over to just feeling what Payne was doing to him.

"Anticipation is part of my game," Payne said, trailing the cube down to Hunter's stomach and making his abdominal muscles quiver.

"Mm." Hunter closed his eyes, even though he was blindfolded, the better to concentrate on the movement of the ice. His line of work gave him the ability to narrow his attention down to a minute focus, and he used it now, not thinking about where they were or what Payne was going to do next, living in the moment as though he were in the field.

Payne drew a line with the ice from Hunter's navel to his chin, and then he traced the shell of Hunter's ear lightly and let the ice come to rest over Hunter's pulse point.

Hunter became aware of the beating of his heart, slow and steady where the ice drew his attention to it. He felt as though he was drifting, a different experience than when he was in the field and focused on a task. In that situation, he was always aware of what he had to *do*, while now he only had to be. He sank inside the moment, feeling a peace he'd never experienced before.

"That's it," Payne murmured, his voice low and soothing as he continued to trace patterns on Hunter's skin with the ice. "You're doing so well."

Forming words seemed like too much effort, but Hunter gave a hum of acknowledgement, a small smile curving his lips at the praise. His whole body felt warm and weightless except for where the ice touched it. If this was staring into the abyss, then Hunter liked it, and he didn't want it to end.

Payne began massaging Hunter's back and shoulders with cold, damp hands, and he smoothed his palms tenderly over Hunter's skin.

Every so often, he removed his hands, and when he touched Hunter again, they were colder than before.

The massage felt good, and it was different from the ice, allowing Hunter to expand his awareness back outward. Payne's hands were cold, but Hunter could feel the heat radiating from Payne's body, reminding him how close Payne was to him. Payne wrapped his arms around Hunter's broad chest and pressed against his back, and he teased Hunter's nipples with his chilly fingers.

As Payne's body touched his, Hunter's feeling of weightlessness went away, but it was replaced with awareness. As Payne teased his nipples, Hunter moaned softly, his cock beginning to harden again as his arousal grew. Payne trailed his fingertips lightly along Hunter's inner thigh, coming close to, but not touching his cock.

"Feels good," Hunter murmured, the teasing touch sending his arousal even higher. "I need more…"

Payne flicked Hunter's thigh hard enough to sting. "I need more what?"

For a moment Hunter was confused, before he remembered where he was. "I need more, sir," he moaned. He'd say anything at this point, if it meant Payne would touch him.

"Good." Payne pressed a kiss on Hunter's shoulder, and then he slid his hand up Hunter's thigh to cup his balls, kneading gently. "More like this?"

Hunter gasped, the intensity of the sensation fanning the spark of desire into a roaring blaze. It had been so long, and his cock suddenly felt so hard, it was almost painful. "Yes, sir! Like that!"

Payne mouthed kisses along the side of Hunter's neck and then bit his earlobe. "Are you ready for me to fuck you?"

"Yes, sir! Please!" Hunter arched back against Payne, wanting more contact. He ached with a need only Payne could satisfy. "I need you to fuck me."

Payne unfastened the cuffs binding Hunter's wrists, and then he eased off the blindfold. "Then come with me to bed," he said as he rose to his feet and moved to stand in front of Hunter, offering a steadying hand.

Hunter blinked at the return of sight, but then he smiled as he gazed up at Payne. He accepted Payne's hand, rising to his feet, surprised to find he felt a bit wobbly. "Whoa..."

Snaking his free arm around Hunter's waist, Payne pushed himself under Hunter's arm to help him stabilize. "That's normal," he said. "You started going under, so you might be a little unsteady at first. We'll take it slow."

"Sounds like a good idea," Hunter said, gratefully wrapping one arm around Payne, letting Payne steady him. "It was more intense than I expected."

"And we didn't even get to the glove," Payne said, chuckling.

Keeping his arm securely around Hunter's waist, he led Hunter to the master bedroom, which had a king size sleigh bed with a plain navy-blue comforter and pillow shams. The dresser and nightstands on either side of the bed were mahogany like the bed, and the floors were hardwood with a couple of thick blue throw rugs. On the dresser were a couple of framed photos and a few knick-knacks that looked like items Payne had picked up during his travels.

Payne guided Hunter to the bed and then released him. "Sit down," he said as he moved to turn on a lamp.

Hunter pulled back the comforter, then sank down on the edge of the mattress. His balance was getting better, but the bed was where he wanted to be for entirely different reasons. "I'm surprised you have a bed like this," he said, gesturing at the headboard.

"Why?" Payne asked as he moved to stand between Hunter's knees and rested his hands on Hunter's shoulders.

Hunter grinned as he wrapped his arms around Payne's waist. "No place for ropes or handcuffs," he said, then pulled Payne close, nuzzling his cheek against the soft fabric of Payne's shirt and inhaling his scent.

"That's what the playroom is for," Payne said, sliding his arms around Hunter in return. "This is my sanctum. I don't bring play partners in here." He bent to kiss the top of Hunter's head and added softly, "Just you."

Hunter was surprised by Payne's admission, but he was pleased on a level he didn't want to look at too closely. He could scarcely believe only a few weeks ago, Payne had been the biggest annoyance in Hunter's life, but now, he wanted Payne with a hunger bordering on desperation.

"I'm glad," he said, then pulled back to look up at Payne. "Should I still call you sir? Or can I beg you to fuck me before I die of the want?"

"In here, you can call me whatever you want," Payne said, giving Hunter a playfully coy look. "But if you want me to fuck you, you'd better undress me first."

"Sir, yes sir!" Hunter released Payne, then slid his hands under the black t-shirt, caressing Payne's warm skin beneath the fabric. He couldn't resist tweaking Payne's nipples before he tugged the t-shirt up and off.

Payne let out a gasping laugh and clutched Hunter's shoulders. "Naughty!"

"I wanted to see if you liked it," Hunter said, giving Payne a heated smile. He slipped his thumbs under the waistband of Payne's sweatpants, then tugged them down, careful to ease them over Payne's cock. He let the fabric drop to the floor, not at all surprised to find Payne was bare under the sweats. "My, my, sir... is that all for me?"

Payne stepped out of his sweatpants and kicked them aside. "Depends on how badly you want it. You mentioned begging?"

The sight of Payne's cock – big, hard, and flushed – was enough to make Hunter want to go to his knees, so begging wasn't hard. "Yes, sir. I want you to fuck me. Please, I *need* it. I need you, only you."

Capturing Hunter's face between his hands, Payne drew him into a deep, hungry kiss. "You've got me," he murmured against Hunter's lips when he drew back at last.

The kiss left Hunter breathless, but he knew what he wanted, and he wanted it *now*. He wrapped his arms around Payne's waist again, pulling Payne on top as he fell back on the mattress. "Please, Payne," he said, resting his hand against Payne's cheek. "I've been cold for so long. I need you to make me warm again."

"I'll do my best," Payne said, leaning against Hunter's palm briefly before sitting up and straddling Hunter's hips. He leaned over and rummaged in the drawer of the nightstand, and he pulled out a bottle of lube and a condom packet. He dropped the packet next to Hunter and then popped open the cap on the bottle of lube. "It's been a while for you, right?"

Hunter grasped Payne's hips and squeezed as he watched. "Yeah. Close to a year." He'd been with a couple of the guys in his unit with L&G during his last deployment, but the heat and the constant movement of their camp had put a damper on everyone's sex drive.

"Then we'll get you good and prepped," Payne said as he shifted to kneel between Hunter's legs. He squeezed out a generous dollop of lube and coated his fingers. Watching Hunter's face, he circled the tight ring of muscle before easing one finger inside.

Hunter drew in a deep breath and made himself relax. He wanted to feel Payne buried in him, to feel connected to him in the most primal way possible. The faint burn of being stretched wasn't unpleasant, especially since he knew the pleasure which would follow. "Yeah, real mercs don't use just spit or motor oil, despite the stories you might have heard."

Payne laughed softly as he drew his hand back and squeezed out more lube. "Good to know," he said as he eased two fingers into Hunter and scissored them slowly.

The burn was stronger now, but Hunter liked it, fisting his hands in the sheets to keep himself from moving and demanding more. "Blaze, my old CO, once tried to get L&G to pay for a bunch of dildoes by putting them down on the requisition sheet as 'Field Expedient Rectal Enlargers.' The only reason he didn't eat a reprimand for it was that John Lawson thought it was the funniest thing he'd seen in a year."

Payne threw his head back, peals of delighted laughter escaping him. "Please tell me he got the dildoes."

"Well, the dildoes were shipped, but they never made it to camp," Hunter said, grinning at Payne's amusement. "We figured the Iraqis swiped the crate, no doubt because they were even harder up than we were."

"Too bad!" Payne moved his fingers in and out slowly a few more times before adding more lube and a third finger. "How's that?"

Hunter growled, anticipation making him impatient. "It's good. It'll be even better when it's you instead of your fingers."

Payne's expression turned wicked as he pushed his fingers deep and twisted them. "Is that what you want? My cock buried balls deep in your tight ass?"

"Yes!" Hunter arched his back, fingers digging into the sheets as an electric jolt of pleasure zinged along his spine. "I want it!"

"That's what I want too." Payne eased his fingers out and grabbed a tissue from a box on the nightstand to wipe off his hands. Then he snatched up the packet and tore it open, and he rolled on the condom with shaky fingers. He poured out more lube and coated himself before tossing the bottle aside. "Now," he said, a growling undercurrent in his voice as he positioned himself.

"Now," Hunter agreed. He felt almost dizzy with anticipation, and he looked up at Payne not holding back any of his desire or need. "Please, sir. Fuck me now. I need you so much!"

Groaning, Payne eased into Hunter slowly, and once he was fully seated, he braced himself over Hunter and rocked his hips in a shallow, leisurely rhythm, enough to tease but not satisfy. "God, you feel good. So good…"

The sensation of being claimed and taken was almost overwhelming. It had been so long, and Hunter hadn't realized how empty and disconnected he'd been until Payne filled him, all the cold, empty spaces overflowing with the heat of Payne's presence. It was more than sex, more than having a lover again. Payne was *there*, giving Hunter everything he needed, not holding back anything. Hunter knew he was lost, knew that no one else would ever be able to give him what Payne did, and he'd never feel for anyone else the depth of love he felt for Payne.

Hunter grasped Payne's shoulders, holding on to Payne like the lifeline he'd become, Hunter's anchor, his safe place. "My Payne," he said, moving his hips, catching Payne's rhythm. "All mine."

Payne kissed Hunter's cheeks and chin before claiming his lips. "Yes, I'm yours, and I'm here. I've got you."

Hunter returned the kiss, parting his lips and moaning, wanting to drown himself in Payne's taste and touch. When they'd been in the playroom, Hunter had focused on where the ice had been, but now he wanted to feel every inch of his body where Payne touched him. Payne splayed one hand on Hunter's chest over his heart, and then he slid it down slowly until he could curl his fingers around Hunter's cock. He kept his thrusts slow and shallow as he stroked Hunter's cock with a quicker rhythm.

Groaning, Hunter threw his head back on the pillow, the coil of desire within him growing tighter and tighter. The feeling of Payne in him, of Payne's hand on him, pushed him closer and closer to the shining edge. For a moment he hovered there, and then he cried out Payne's name as he hurtled over it, shattering as he was overcome by pure, heated ecstasy.

"Yes, that's it..." Payne watched Hunter's face avidly as he stroked Hunter through his release.

It seemed to go on forever, but finally Hunter came down from the heights, his body wrung out and sated. He smiled at Payne, then reached up to caress his cheek. "Wow."

Smiling tenderly, Payne leaned into the touch. "Definitely wow. You're gorgeous."

"So are you," Hunter said. He moved his hips. "Now it's your turn. I want to see you lose yourself in me."

"Gladly," Payne said as he braced himself over Hunter again. He bent to nip at Hunter's bottom lip and began to thrust anew, harder this time.

Hunter let his knees fall open, and he ran his fingers down Payne's back, using his nails to increase the sensation. "Yes! Like that!" he gasped. Even though his body was sated, it still felt good to have Payne claiming him. "Be as rough as you want. I can take it."

Payne gasped and arched against the scrape of Hunter's nails, and the rhythm of his hips grew erratic as his need built. His demeanor of calm control faded as he let go and surrendered to the pleasure offered by Hunter's welcoming body.

"Mine, mine…" he chanted like a litany as he claimed Hunter with rough, pounding thrusts, and then with a cry, he buried himself deep and shattered.

"Yours," Hunter murmured. He caressed Payne's damp back, pressing open-mouthed kisses to Payne's neck, enjoying the feeling of Payne's heart pounding, and the sight of Payne lost in ecstasy.

Panting, Payne slumped on Hunter's chest and pressed his nose beneath Hunter's ear. "Mm… Yes."

Hunter chuckled, wrapping his arms around Payne and holding him close. "Did I finally discover the way to shut you up?"

"One of them," Payne said with a little snort. He tangled his legs with Hunter's and caressed Hunter's side gently.

"At least now I have one weapon at my disposal." Hunter sighed, closing his eyes and enjoying having Payne close. He felt more at peace than he could remember being in a very long time, the hurt and guilt he'd been carrying around temporarily, at least, banished in the warmth of Payne's embrace.

"But you already fired it," Payne said, a mischievous note in his voice. "How long before you can reload?"

Hunter groaned and smacked Payne's ass. "You're the one who looks like a teenager. I'll probably need at least half an hour."

"Then I guess we've got thirty minutes to kill." Payne nuzzled Hunter's throat with his lips and nose. "Would you like a nap? Cuddling? Shared shower?"

"Mm… hot shower, once I can move," Hunter said. "And maybe, if you're nice to me, I'll show you a few tricks I've learned over the years about getting someone off in a shower stall."

There were a lot of things they could teach each other, Hunter thought. But the most important thing Payne had taught him was that even though he was damaged and probably always would be, he still had enough of a heart to be able to love.

10

Payne hummed as he tackled the bowl of cooked and sliced potatoes with a masher. He could have used his mixer, but he preferred making mashed potatoes this way; he found it more therapeutic. Not that he had any aggression or frustrations to work out at the moment. He and Hunter had gone to the gym at Hercules Security earlier, and Payne was still pleasantly sore from the pounding Hunter had given him the night before.

Things had changed for the better between them since their visit to Club Twist almost a week ago, and while Payne knew any objectivity he might have had about Hunter was long gone, he didn't want to suggest finding another Dom. Maybe one who hadn't fallen in love with him.

Instead, he'd dropped hints about another therapy session and let Hunter get away with avoiding it because he'd been enjoying their new dynamic too much. He'd cleared room in his closet and dresser so Hunter could move into the master bedroom with him, and he'd encouraged Hunter to display any personal photos or items around the house to help him feel more at home.

Tonight, Payne was even preparing one of Hunter's favorite meals — chicken fried steak, mashed potatoes and gravy, and turnip greens

— as yet another way of enticing Hunter to stay with him. Usually, he preferred to use his words, but he wasn't sure how Hunter would react if Payne spelled out how he wanted a future with Hunter, and so he was showing his love through fluffy and lumpless mashed potatoes instead.

Hunter walked into the kitchen, a towel around his shoulders, smelling of soap and shampoo. He'd combed his hair, but it was still damp, the long strands clinging to his neck. When they'd returned from the gym, Hunter had mentioned getting a haircut, but he had dropped the subject when Payne had given him a mournful look.

"Smells good," Hunter said, moving behind Payne and pressing a kiss to the nape of his neck. He reached past Payne, dipping a finger into the bowl to steal a taste of the potatoes. "Mm... tastes good, too. Almost as good as you."

The kiss sent a little ripple of pleasure along Payne's spine, and he smiled at the casual show of affection.

"I'm glad it's only almost as good," he said, glancing up at Hunter with a flirty look. "I'd hate to compete with my own mashed potatoes and gravy."

Hunter grinned, then bent his head to kiss Payne with leisurely thoroughness. When he pulled back, there was a glimmer of heat in his eyes. "No competition at all. You're even better than chocolate."

"That's what I like to hear," Payne said, a little breathless from the kiss. As tempted as he was to instigate a vigorous round of sex on or against his kitchen cabinets, he didn't want the food to burn, so he gave Hunter a little hip bump. "Dinner will be ready in about five minutes. Will you set the table, please?"

"Yes, Master Payne." Hunter bowed his head submissively, but then spoiled the effect by giving Payne a wicked smile. He moved to the appropriate cabinets, taking out plates and glasses, then retrieving silverware from a drawer. "What do you want to drink? Sweet tea or juice?"

"Sweet tea, please," Payne said as he poured the gravy into a bowl.

Hunter crossed to the refrigerator, pulling out the pitcher of sweet tea. "You're spoiling me rotten, you realize," he said as he carried the tea to the table. "L&G didn't stint on the food, but they were limited as to what the chow hall could provide, since we had to keep mobile. Lots of times we went weeks on MREs. Having home cooked food is wonderful, especially since you're a fantastic cook."

"That's the idea," Payne said, giving Hunter an arch look as he carried the potatoes and gravy to the kitchen table. "Why would you want to go back to MREs when you could have this?" He cocked his hip and struck a provocative pose. "And this?"

"I'd rather eat you than MREs any day," Hunter said. He put the tea pitcher down, giving Payne a hungry look. "Maybe after dinner, I can have you for dessert."

"For you, I'm always on the menu." Payne put an extra sway in his hips to put his ass on display as he returned to the stove to get the chicken fried steak and turnip greens.

"How could I resist my own all-you-can-eat buffet?" Hunter asked. "Is there anything else you need me to do?"

"I need you to sit down and eat well so you'll be fueled up for the midnight buffet," Payne said, giving Hunter a heated look of his own as he took his place at the table.

"Yes, sir," Hunter said as he took his own seat, then began to fill his plate. Hunter had been eating better in the last week or so, and his face was beginning to fill out and lose its gauntness. "This looks so good. Thanks for making my favorites."

"You're welcome." Payne couldn't resist stroking Hunter's back briefly before loading up his own plate. He was tactile by nature, and Hunter brought out all his touchy-feely instincts. "It was my pleasure."

Hunter gave him a closed-lip smile, his mouth already full of food. Once he'd swallowed and taken a drink of tea, he chuckled. "I'm beginning to think there isn't anything you can't do. Stealthy ninja Dom who can take down bad guys, cook better than my mama, patch up any wounds, and is insatiable in bed. I might have to..." he stopped, then flushed slightly and looked down at his plate. "I have to find something to do for you in return."

"I hope you don't think there are any strings attached to what I'm doing," Payne said, leaning over to rest his hand on Hunter's arm. "You don't owe me anything." He squeezed Hunter's arm and offered a sultry smile. "But if you want to pay me back in orgasms, I might be persuaded to accept."

Hunter gave Payne a crooked smile. "I'm more than happy to do that," he said. "I know there are no strings attached. You... you're a good man, Payne. One of the best men I've ever known."

"You're a good man too, Hunter," Payne said. "I don't want you to doubt that. Not now, not ever."

"Thanks." Hunter said the right words, but he wouldn't meet Payne's eyes. "It means a lot to me."

Payne wanted to follow up, but before he could, the phone rang, and it was his landline, not his cell, which was a rare occurrence. "Hang on, I'll be right back."

There was a cordless extension in the kitchen, and he picked it up. "Hello?"

"Um... hi..." The speaker on the other end was a young woman, and her tone was hesitant. "Is this Payne Gibson? My name is Jennifer Hansen."

Hansen? Payne's eyes widened at the familiar name. "Yes, this is Payne Gibson," he said, careful not to repeat her name in case hearing it made Hunter bolt from the room. "What can I do for you?"

"I hope you don't mind, but Cade Thornton gave me your number," she said. "I wanted to speak to Able... I mean, Hunter. I was afraid if I called his cell phone, he'd see it was me and not answer. But I need to talk to him."

Payne's first instinct was to protect Hunter and say no, because he wasn't sure how Hunter would react. Hearing from Stack's wife might cause a setback, and Payne wasn't sure he wanted to risk it.

Then again, he knew he'd been too lenient with Hunter lately. Hunter was better, but he couldn't keep coasting along indefinitely, and talking to Jennifer might give him a kick in the ass he needed.

"Hang on a sec," Payne said, and then he carried the phone over to Hunter and held it out. "It's for you. It's Jennifer," he added so Hunter wouldn't think he was being blindsided.

The color drained from Hunter's face, and he stared at the handset as though Payne was holding out a poisonous snake. He shook his head in violent negation, then glanced up at Payne. Payne knew Hunter was a brave man, his field record vouching for the fact, but there was something close to terror in Hunter's eyes. "No..."

Payne straightened his spine and squared his shoulders as he shifted into Dom mode. "You need to talk to her," he said, an edge of command in his voice. "You can do this. I'll be right here the whole time."

Hunter looked as if he might push back from the table and flee, but then he drew in a breath, seeming torn between his fear and his desire to obey Payne. For several long moments, he didn't say anything, and then he closed his eyes, his shoulders slumping in defeat.

"Put it on speaker," he said, his voice so low Payne could barely hear him.

Payne hit the speaker button on the handset and placed the phone on the table. "Jennifer, Hunter is here, and he's listening," he said as he shifted to stand as close to Hunter's chair as he could and rested his hand on Hunter's shoulder. Hunter was trembling, but he stayed in the chair.

"Hunter?" Jennifer's voice was hesitant, and Payne could hear the sadness in it. "Please, Hunter, speak to me. I know you hurt, because I hurt, too, but please, say something."

"Jen." Hunter got her name out, his voice thick and raspy. He put his elbows on the table and buried his face in his hands.

There was a soft sigh from Jen. "Hunter, you're still blaming yourself, aren't you? Because if you weren't, you would have returned my calls by now. Mark wouldn't want you to beat yourself up this way."

Hunter's shoulders were shaking. "My fault," he said raggedly. "Jen, just... I'm sorry. I can't do this..."

"Yes, you can." Jen's voice held a sharp edge. "Look, you don't owe me anything, even though you were my friend too. I'm coping. I have my family here, so I'll be okay. For what it's worth, I don't blame you. I never have. I would help you if you'd let me, but I know you won't.

But damn you, Hunter, you can't ignore Jake! He's your godson, and you promised Mark you'd be there for Jake if he couldn't be! He misses you. He's lost his father, and he doesn't understand why his Uncle Hunter won't come and see him. It's his birthday next week, remember? And he told me what he wants more than anything is to see his Uncle Hunter."

The sound Hunter made was more like a wounded animal than a man. Hunter was shaking his head, and Payne wasn't sure Hunter could say anything even if he wanted to.

"Jennifer, would you mind if I come with him for support?" Payne asked as he stroked Hunter's back gently.

"He can bring an entire damned company of mercs, as long as he comes," Jennifer said. Her voice sounded thick, as though she, too, was crying. "Hunter, you know it wasn't your fault. I love you, Jake loves you, and Mark loved you like a brother. We're your family too. Please come. You don't have to say anything, just come see Jake. *Please.*"

"We'll be there," Payne said. Having Jennifer and Jake's love and support would help Hunter's healing process, and Payne was determined to get him to the party even if he had to hogtie Hunter and drag him there.

"Thank you." He heard Jennifer sniffle. "Hunter knows where we live. A week from Saturday, two PM. Hunter... it'll be okay. You'll see. Mark would want you to go on, the way he wanted me and Jake to go on. I'll see you. Take care." With that, the line went dead.

Payne left the phone where it was for the moment and slid both arms around Hunter's shoulders. "You need to do this."

Hunter turned in the chair, wrapping his arms around Payne and clinging to him like a drowning man to a life raft. Payne could feel Hunter's tears soaking into his shirt. "Can't."

Payne leaned his cheek on the top of Hunter's head and rubbed his back with slow, soothing strokes. "Yes, you can. You're a strong, brave man, and I'll be with you."

Hunter didn't reply, but slowly the storm of emotion seemed to pass, and Hunter let out a shuddering breath. "I'm not brave," he said, his tone raw. "I'm petrified to face Jen and Jake. I'd rather face a firing squad."

"That's normal and understandable," Payne said. He wished he could banish Hunter's fear and guilt with words, but Hunter had to wrestle those demons himself. "But bravery isn't the absence of fear. It's doing what you must in spite of the fear."

Hunter raised his head, looking up at Payne. His eyes were red, his face haggard. "I still don't think I can do it. I'll freeze again, or maybe I'll freak out. And... it hurts. Like a knife in my gut." He dropped his gaze. "It would have been easier if I'd died instead. I wish I had."

Payne stroked Hunter's cheek, aching for the turmoil Hunter was feeling. "We need to resume your therapy," he said. Letting Hunter slide would be easier, but it wouldn't be helpful. "Not tonight because you've been through enough, but tomorrow, we're going to have another session. You need to deal with your guilt."

Hunter seemed to sag. "I don't know if it will help. I don't know if anything will."

"We won't know until we try," Payne said, injecting an authoritative edge into his voice. "And we're going to try. I'm not going to let you be eaten alive by fear and guilt if I can do anything about it."

"I don't know why you put up with me." Hunter pulled back, then rose from his chair as though the very act of moving hurt. "Sorry. I... I need to be alone for a little while."

"Of course." Payne stepped back to give Hunter room to pass by. He wanted to wrap his arms around Hunter and hold him tight. He wanted to promise everything would be fine even though he didn't know for sure it would be. He wanted to confess that he loved Hunter and would always be there for him.

But he couldn't do any of that, and so he let Hunter go instead.

11

Sleep was elusive, and after tossing and turning for several hours — and dozing, only to awaken to nightmares — Hunter gave up the effort.

Beside him, Payne murmured a protest when Hunter moved, but Hunter smoothed Payne's hair back gently. "It's okay, go back to sleep," he murmured, then waited until Payne's eyes closed again before getting out of bed. He picked up the jeans and shirt he'd had on the previous night, then went into the bathroom to dress.

It was still a couple of hours before dawn, but Hunter left the house, welcoming the darkness. There was nothing to fear in the area where Payne lived, the widely separated residences each tucked onto several acres of land, most of them well set-back from the road. The few houses he passed were dark, the inhabitants finding the rest Hunter couldn't. As he walked aimlessly along the winding road, Hunter's thoughts stayed on the same mental gerbil wheel they'd occupied since Jen's phone call — a call that had shattered the first peace he'd found since Mark's death.

He was caught between reason and emotion, between logic and guilt. He knew Jen didn't blame him for Mark's death, and she truly meant it when she said she loved him and wanted him to see Jake.

For that matter, Hunter was sure Mark would kick his ass for feeling guilty for something he neither caused nor could have changed, but it didn't make it any easier for Hunter not to *feel* the guilt. To feel that *he* should have been the one to die, because, unlike Mark, he'd had nothing much to live for in the grand scheme of things. Sure, his buddies would have missed him, and his parents, whom he wasn't particularly close to, would have grieved, but they would all have gone on with their lives after a few days or weeks. Jen and Jake would never completely recover from Mark's death, which had left a hole in them nothing would ever fill.

In a way, the guilt was so much worse now because he thought he had a chance to experience what Mark had with Jen. Even though Jen had no way of knowing it, her call was a reminder that he had stolen the life Mark should have had. His mind told him it was bullshit, but it did nothing to ease the weight in Hunter's stomach. A weight that grew so much heavier when he realized if he *had* died and Mark hadn't, he never would have met Payne.

He walked until the sun rose, then headed back toward Payne's house, not having found any relief from his tormented thoughts. The scabs on his wounds had all been stripped away, and he knew, no matter what Payne had promised, there was no way he could face Jen and Jake, because seeing their pain would destroy him.

He hadn't taken his phone or watch, so he had no idea what time it was when he finally reached Payne's house again. He realized he'd locked the door when he'd left — too many years of security procedures had been drilled into him to have ignored something so basic — and he hadn't taken his keys or his wallet either. Payne was probably awake by now, so Hunter rang the doorbell and waited, feeling as hopeless as he had right after Mark's death.

Only a few seconds passed before the door opened, and Payne stood there with a cup of coffee in one hand and his cellphone in the other.

"Welcome back," he said, moving aside to let Hunter in.

"Sorry. I should have left a note. I... I didn't know I'd be gone so long." Seeing Payne made Hunter's heart lurch painfully, and once again he felt the horrible guilt of knowing he'd never have met Payne if Mark hadn't died.

"It's okay." Payne held up his phone and waggled it back and forth. "I put a GPS tracker in all your shoes, and since there aren't any drugs you could OD on in the house and you don't know the code to my gun safe, I figured you would be okay."

Hunter scrubbed his face with one hand. "Probably a good idea," he said. He knew why Payne had done it, and he wasn't upset. But he was reminded that just because he had feelings for Payne didn't mean Payne had feelings for him. Payne might be attracted enough to sleep with him, but Hunter couldn't imagine Payne wanted a relationship with someone as fucked up as Hunter.

"Herc's paranoia rubs off on all of us to some degree," Payne said, smiling wryly as he tucked his phone in the back pocket of his jeans. He clasped Hunter's hand and tugged him toward the kitchen. "Come on, I'll make you some coffee and breakfast if you want it."

The thought of food made Hunter grimace. "Coffee is fine, thanks," he said. Part of him wanted to pull his hand back, because having Payne touch him, even in such a small way, felt so good and right, and he didn't deserve it. But a bigger part of him needed simple human contact to keep him from becoming mired in a swamp of guilt and grief the way he'd been for months.

Once they were in the kitchen, Payne shooed him into a chair at the table and prepared a cup of coffee the way Hunter liked it.

"Here you go." Payne set the mug in front of Hunter and kissed the top of his head before dropping into the chair adjacent to him.

The simple kiss made Hunter's eyes sting, and he had to clear his throat before he could speak. "Thanks," he murmured, focusing his attention on the coffee cup. He didn't want the coffee either, but he knew he had to keep himself going somehow, so he took a sip of the hot liquid.

Payne leaned forward and rested his hand on Hunter's arm. "Is there anything you'd like to talk about?"

Hunter couldn't meet Payne's gaze. He knew Payne was doing everything possible to help him, but Hunter had to give to get anything in return. It was so hard to open up, to admit his despair to anyone, even Payne.

"I... don't know if I can," he said finally. "Part of me wants to run away from all this. I thought I was doing better, but I was wrong."

"You *are* doing better," Payne said, squeezing his arm tightly. "When we first met, you were completely shut down. But you still have a lot of shit to face, and I want to get back to it starting today."

Hunter shuddered. He didn't want to face it again, but what choice did he have? He could face it or run, but running meant leaving Payne. He didn't think he could do that, not yet. No matter how guilty he felt.

"I can't stop thinking about it anyway," he admitted dully. "Whatever you think is best."

"In that case, finish your coffee if you want it," Payne said, the familiar edge of authority creeping into his voice as he sat up straight. "Leave the mug on the table when you're done. Take a bathroom break if you need it, and then go straight to the playroom and strip."

"Yes, sir," he said, keeping his eyes on the coffee mug. He tried to empty himself of everything, doubt and fear and hope. Better to feel nothing than to dread what was coming.

Payne pushed back his chair and stood up, but he didn't move away from the table. Instead, he stood next to Hunter for a moment, and then he hooked his fingers beneath Hunter's chin and lifted it. He bent and captured Hunter's lips in a kiss that was lingering but not deep, seeming infused with warm affection.

The kiss surprised Hunter, so much so he had no defense against it, and he groaned softly, kissing Payne back, needing the connection. Instead of feeling empty, he felt warm. He shouldn't, but he couldn't help it, as Payne's touch anchored him, made him feel real again. Payne drew back slowly and stroked Hunter's cheek, and then he left the kitchen and headed upstairs.

Hunter drew in a deep breath, then gulped down the rest of the coffee. He left the mug on the table as Payne had instructed, then pushed back his chair and headed for the stairs. Obeying Payne was easier than thinking for himself at the moment, so he did as he'd been told, stopping in the bathroom, then going to the playroom. He stripped, folded his clothes neatly, and then knelt on the floor as he had before, bowing his head and waiting for Payne.

It wasn't long before he heard footsteps entering the room behind him, no doubt because Payne wanted him to hear them. He knew how quietly Payne could move, even in boots. Payne walked past Hunter and stopped beside the St. Andrew's cross. He was wearing the black and white camo pants and a tight black t-shirt again.

"I won't be surprised if you spend most of this session in the yellow zone because we're going to be pushing harder this time," he said, his expression somber. "If it gets to be too much, tell me you've gone red, and everything stops, but I don't want you to use the red zone as an evasive maneuver either."

"Yes, sir," Hunter said. At least he knew going in that Payne intended to be rough on him, but he was honest enough to know he needed it. This wasn't going to be pleasant, and part of him knew he deserved whatever Payne did to him. He wasn't even sure he could stop what was happening even if he wanted to, but he knew Payne would put a stop to things even if Hunter didn't.

"Then get up on the cross," Payne said, beckoning to Hunter.

Hunter rose and moved to the cross, taking up the position he had the last time. "I might need the thigh straps, sir," he said.

"I've got them right here." Payne gestured to the cart, which was already positioned next to the cross, and Hunter could see the thicker thigh straps and the blindfold on the cart along with Payne's usual supplies, which meant Payne must have set up the playroom while Hunter was out.

Payne fastened the wrist and ankle cuffs with swift efficiency, checking in with Hunter to make sure they weren't too loose or too tight along the way. Then he strapped on the thigh cuffs before stepping back.

"Do you feel secure?" he asked.

Hunter let his body go limp, testing the straps to make sure they would support his whole weight. They did. "Yes, sir," he said, closing his eyes. He didn't know how to even begin preparing himself for what was to come, either physically or mentally.

He heard the footstool being dragged across the floor, and then Payne eased the blindfold over his head and settled it in place.

"I'm going to use a cane, just like the first time," Payne said, smoothing his hand up and down Hunter's back. "You can do this, Hunter. Whatever you feel, let it happen. I've got you."

The caress of Payne's hand would have been comforting, but Hunter couldn't give in to it or he'd beg Payne to let him go, to not make him face any of this. So instead he gripped the chains holding the wrist straps to the cross, feeling the cold metal in his palms. "Yes, sir."

Payne moved away, and to Hunter, it felt like an eternity of silent waiting before the blunt end of a cane being pressed between his shoulder blades alerted Hunter to Payne's return.

"Go back to that day," Payne said, drawing the cane down the length of Hunter's spine. "You've heard Blaze yelling. You go outside. Tell me what you see."

Hunter didn't understand why Payne was going back to the day Mark died, since they'd already been over it, but he didn't protest. "I saw Blaze standing with his back to us, looking at something. When I moved forward, I saw Joker talking on a walkie and waving for the other guys to get away. When I reached Blaze, I saw he was looking at the kid with the suicide vest." Hunter had replayed the scene so often in his mind, he didn't even have to see it again this time, just repeat the facts.

"Tell me about the little boy," Payne said. The press of the cane disappeared, replaced by Payne kneading Hunter's ass in preparation for the inevitable blows from the cane. "What did he look like? What did he say?"

The way Payne was touching him distracted Hunter from the question, but he forced his attention back. "He was dirty and barefoot and dressed in rags like most of the kids who hung around camp. Just a little kid, maybe seven, but he could have been younger. He... he was crying. There were clean streaks down his face from the tears.

And he said..." Hunter stopped, squeezing his eyes tightly closed, wishing he could cover his ears as the kid's voice seemed to ring in his ears again, the tone of fear and desperation that should never have been in the voice of a child so young.

The first blow came swiftly, and the sting was enough to make Hunter's body jerk instinctively, but he had nowhere to go to escape.

"What did he say?" Payne's voice was quiet but held a note of command.

"*Ana la 'urid 'an 'amut!*" Hunter gasped out. The line of fire across his ass helped him focus. "It means 'I don't want to die,' sir."

"How did you feel when you heard that?" Payne asked.

"Like I wanted to throw up." Hunter's voice was thick with remembered anger. "Like I wanted to find the miserable bastards who'd strapped a bunch of C4 to a kid and give them a nitroglycerin enema. I was pissed off enough to have killed with my bare hands. Sir."

"Tell me what happened next," Payne said. "Focus on the boy. I want to know what he looked like when you and Stack helped him."

Hunter didn't want to remember the kid. He didn't want to relive this again. Tightening his hands on the chains, he shook his head. "I can't..."

Another blow landed on his ass, harder this time. "You can and you will," Payne said, a hard edge in his voice. "Tell me what the little boy looked like when you helped him. Tell me anything he said."

Hunter growled, cursing himself for letting Payne strap him up here, cursing Payne for making him remember, cursing the monsters who'd wired up the kid and sent him out to die. He cursed the L&G and the U.S. military fucking advisors, and Stack for being a goddamned hero and getting himself blown away.

"How the fuck do you think he looked? He was fucking scared! And he had a right to be! I was scared, too, because if we fucked up it would mean a *kid* died! How would you like to have that on your conscience, *sir*?"

Whack! This was the hardest blow yet, and Hunter couldn't hold back a cry of pain.

"Focus," Payne said sternly. "This isn't about me. I wasn't there. You were. Why are you angry right now, Hunter?"

Hunter was breathing hard, his ass burning. "I'm angry because they stole my life," he said bitterly. "I didn't die, but they might as well have killed me. Better than being left like this."

"Like what?" Payne tapped the cane lightly against one of the welts on Hunter's ass, exacerbating the sting. "How was your life stolen?"

"I can't do my job because I froze!" Hunter rattled the chains, feeling a violent rage rising up, worse than anything he'd ever felt before. "I can't face my best friend's wife because I'm ashamed I lived instead of him. I can't even look at my godson because I failed him. I lost everything I loved. I even lost my fucking self-respect, because I couldn't stop what happened, and no matter how many times I relive it, I can't fucking change it!"

WHACK!

"Why are you ashamed?" Payne's voice was implacable now. "How did you fail Jake? What did you do wrong?"

"I didn't save his father," Hunter ground out. He felt like he was in his own personal hell. "I should have known there would be a failsafe. I should have told Mark to keep his fucking helmet closed until we *knew* it was totally safe."

Another whack of the cane, this one escalating the sting to a burn. "How would you have known there was a failsafe? Who was responsible for keeping Stack's helmet closed?"

Hunter hissed at the pain. He was tempted to tell Payne he was red and end this, but pride wouldn't let him. "I should have known there was a failsafe because those sick, twisted bastards wouldn't waste all that C4 without some way to make sure they killed someone! I should have told Stack to close his fucking helmet because I was his partner and I was supposed to have his back!"

WHACK!

"Tell me the truth," Payne said. "How could you have known there was a failsafe? Who was responsible for Stack's helmet?"

"I should have known!" Hunter insisted. "I should have warned him!"

"How?" Payne struck him again, and this time, he couldn't hold back a sharp yelp at the pain.

"I just should have!" The pain seemed to radiate from Hunter's ass over his whole body. "I should have been more paranoid. I should have read tea leaves or the horoscope to see if there was some kind of sign it was all going to go in the crapper."

"Why are you bullshitting me, Able?" Payne struck him again, clearly no longer pulling the blows.

Hearing the name he'd been known by among his mercenary cadre for years hurt worse than the cane. He'd once been proud of his nickname, having earned it because he'd never lost a challenge, never failed on a mission. Mark had joked that he *had* to be Able, because it wasn't enough to be only ready and willing.

"Don't call me that," he said hoarsely. "I don't deserve it. Not anymore."

"Why not?" Another merciless whack of the cane. "What did you do wrong? Tell me the truth, Able. I don't want to hear your bullshit anymore."

"It's not bullshit!" Hunter shouted. "It's my fault. If I'd been better at my job, Mark wouldn't have died! What the fuck do you want me to do, blame Mark?"

WHACK!

"What did you do wrong?" Payne's voice was as hard as the blunt force of the cane. "How are you the only one responsible for what happened?"

"Because I lived." Hunter slumped against the bonds. "It has to be my fault, because I lived."

"Mercs and soldiers live and die every day," Payne said, although the words weren't accompanied by a blow from the cane this time. "How are you different, Able? Why does living make you solely responsible?"

Hunter's throat was tight with grief. He didn't want to say the words, didn't want to say what shamed him more than anything. But now he was facing the core of his torment, and he couldn't back down. "Because I can't blame Mark. It's easier to hate myself than to hate him for saving my life."

"I know," Payne said softly, and instead of striking Hunter, he rested his hand on Hunter's back. "Now tell me the truth. What did you do wrong? Are you solely responsible for what happened? What could you actually have done differently?"

Hunter let his head drop down. "Nothing, I guess," he said hoarsely. "I wish I could have. I want to believe I could have, so I could believe there was a chance I could have saved him."

"But you couldn't," Payne said, stroking Hunter's back. "Tell me the truth. Did you fail Jen and Jake?"

It felt like defeat, hearing Payne say it, but in a way, it was also liberating, and Hunter shook his head. "I don't know. I feel like I did. I feel like *they'll* feel I did."

A clattering noise on the floor told Hunter that Payne had dropped the cane, and then Payne stroked Hunter's back with both hands, soothing him.

"Do you think Jen was lying when she said she loves you and doesn't blame you for Mark's death?" he asked. "Do you think Jake would miss you and ask to see you if he felt like you'd failed him?"

Hunter leaned against his bonds, somehow feeling more exhausted than he could ever remember feeling. "I guess not," he admitted dully. "I feel like such a failure. Like I have nothing left. I don't even like myself anymore, so I don't see how anyone could love me."

The silence dragged out for so long Hunter began to wonder if Payne had left the room. Then he heard the familiar scrape of the footstool across the floor, and Payne removed the blindfold. Payne's eyes were red-rimmed, and there were dried tear tracks on his cheeks that said the scene had been difficult for him as well.

"Jen and Jake love you, and they aren't the only ones," he said, cradling Hunter's cheek in his palm. "I love you too."

Hunter's heart leapt, but then he reminded himself that Payne was a caretaker. Obviously Payne meant he loved Hunter as a friend, the same way Jen did. Which was still more than Hunter felt he deserved.

But it helped to know Payne cared about him. Payne had seen the worst of him, and if Payne still could regard Hunter with any kind of affection, it was a miracle.

He looked into Payne's beautiful blue eyes, eyes which had never regarded Hunter with contempt or loathing. Payne's acceptance had been unquestioning, and as awful as Hunter felt at the moment — and he felt like total shit— for the first time Hunter thought that maybe, just maybe, there was a way through his torment.

Since he knew Payne meant the words in friendship and acceptance, Hunter thought he could take a risk he wouldn't normally even consider. Emotional vulnerability had never appealed to Hunter, but in this one moment, he was safe — and Payne never had to know Hunter meant the words with all his heart.

"I love you, too. Sir."

A soft sound, half-moan and half-sob, escaped Payne's throat as he captured Hunter's lips in a deep, demanding kiss. Hunter was surprised by the kiss, but he closed his eyes, shutting out everything, ignoring the pain of the welts and the pain in his heart, kissing Payne back, parting his lips in silent invitation. It was a connection he needed, a reason to keep going, and Payne offered it as unstintingly as he'd always offered Hunter everything. Payne buried his fingers in Hunter's hair while he lingered over the kiss, and when he drew back at last, his eyes glowed with affection.

"Let's get you down," he said as he unfastened the wrist cuffs.

Hunter waited while Payne released the restraints. When he stepped down from the cross, he stumbled and nearly fell, and he grabbed for Payne. "Feel a little weak," he admitted. In fact, his head was swimming, and he wanted to lie down right there on the floor and curl into a ball.

"That's understandable." Payne held him securely around the waist and helped him remain upright. "All you have to do is make it as far as our bedroom. I've got some water and Gatorade and the salve waiting for you."

"Yes, sir," Hunter murmured. Somehow Payne got him to the bedroom, and Hunter stumbled to the bed, falling down face first on the mattress. It was soft and warm and smelled of Payne, and Hunter closed his eyes, breathing in deeply. Payne helped him get stretched out more comfortably with a pillow under his head.

"Do you want something to drink?" Payne sat down on the edge of the bed and stroked Hunter's hair tenderly.

"No." Hunter fumbled for Payne's free hand and grabbed it. "Don't leave me."

Payne brought Hunter's hand to his lips. "I'm not going anywhere," he said. "Let me take care of these welts, and then I'll get in bed with you, and we'll stay here for as long as you want."

"Okay." Hunter felt like he was drifting, but he didn't mind. It was getting harder to think, but Payne was here. Payne would take care of him. He was vaguely aware of Payne's hands on his ass, of the relief of the cool salve on the welts. Then Payne was lying next to him, warm and solid, and Hunter reached out, pulling Payne closer, curling around him, before he slipped away into an exhausted slumber.

12

The bedroom door was ajar, and Payne nudged it open wider with his foot and peeked in to see if Hunter was awake. Hunter had spent most of the two days since their therapy session asleep, and Payne hadn't tried to coax him out of bed. Hunter had a lot to process, and so Payne had let him rest, brought him meals and books, and snuggled with him when asked.

Hunter was awake, propped up against the pillows with a book in his hands, and Payne approached the bed carrying a tray which had a bowl of homemade tomato soup and a grilled cheese sandwich so warm the butter still bubbled on the sourdough bread, and the cheddar cheese gleamed as it melted over the crust.

"Lunch is served," he said, settling the bed tray over Hunter's lap.

Hunter smiled slightly and set the book aside. "Thanks. You're spoiling me, you know. I could have come down to the table."

"I like spoiling you," Payne said, smoothing Hunter's hair back from his face. "Besides, I figured you'll come downstairs when you're ready. There's no rush."

Hunter closed his eyes and leaned into the caress. While Hunter had been subdued since their session, he seemed to want to touch

Payne or have Payne touch him more than he had before. "I appreciate it. I don't know why I feel so tired."

"Because you went through an emotionally draining process." Payne climbed onto the bed and stretched out beside Hunter, nestling against his side. "You faced a lot of shit that you've been suppressing. It was very brave, but it was also understandably exhausting."

"I guess." Hunter picked up the sandwich and took a bite, then held it to Payne's lips. "Share."

Payne took a bite and then guided the sandwich back to Hunter. "You need this more than I do. How does your ass feel? Do you need any pain relievers?"

"I'm okay." Hunter hadn't said much about the session up until now, answering Payne's questions only briefly, obviously not ready to talk about it. He put the sandwich back down on the plate. "Just not hungry."

"Try some of the soup for me." Payne sat up and smacked Hunter's shoulder. "And if it hurts, tell me. Don't try to be macho about it. You took some hard licks, and I don't want you to neglect caring for your poor bruised ass. I also don't want you using the pain as penance," he added sternly.

Hunter picked up the spoon and dipped it in the soup, but he only stared into the bowl as he moved the spoon around. "Why not? You thought I deserved the blows at the time, right? I thought so too, or I would have said I was red and made it stop. Why is the pain unacceptable now when it was acceptable then?"

"No, I didn't think you deserved the blows," Payne said, smoothing his hand along the back of Hunter's head. Pushing Hunter so hard had been one of the most difficult things he'd ever done, and he'd found it far more difficult to hurt Hunter than he expected, even though he knew it was for Hunter's own good. "I thought they were necessary to motivate you. I didn't enjoy inflicting that much pain on you, and I don't like the thought of you being in pain now."

Hunter released the spoon. "What if I need it, though? To help me... focus. To help remind me. I remember when I was a kid and my father spanked me, he said part of the point of the punishment was not relieving the pain, so I'd remember not to do it again. Maybe I should still feel this so I don't forget."

"If that's what you want." Payne rubbed his cheek against Hunter's bare shoulder. "But I still want to check it regularly to make sure it's healing well."

"Okay." Hunter picked up the spoon again and ate a mouthful of soup. He swallowed before speaking again. "It helped, I think. I didn't want to admit some of those things, not even to myself. I didn't want to be angry at Mark. But I was. I guess a part of me still is."

"Anger is part of the grieving process," Payne said. "It's not healthy to suppress it. You have to deal with it if you want to heal. There's nothing wrong with being angry with Mark."

Hunter shrugged, his expression pained. "But it seems wrong. He saved my life. How ungrateful is it to be angry with him? Even..." He stopped, then bit his lip. "I even hated him. For saving me. For *dying* and leaving me behind. It's not like he wanted to die or planned it. I'm not even sure it crossed his mind that he *could* die. He just... acted. But there have been moments where I've hated him for doing it. And hated myself for not doing it first."

"Of course you did." Payne slid his arms around Hunter's waist and rested his cheek on Hunter's shoulder, wishing he could take away all the pain, guilt, and turmoil Hunter was wrestling with. "You love him, and you would have given your life for him. If you'd died and Mark had lived, he'd probably feel the same way about you. It's normal."

Hunter tilted his head to one side, resting his cheek against Payne's hair. "I guess. But he left people behind who needed him. I wouldn't have. It seems so much worse to lose him."

Payne's heart wrenched at Hunter's words, and he squeezed Hunter tightly. "What about your parents? Your friends? Or Stack? He would have lost his brother. Jake would have lost his uncle. And what about me? If you'd died, we never would have met, and I do need you."

"They would have been sad, sure." Hunter pressed a kiss against

Payne's hair. "You wouldn't have missed me because you wouldn't have known me, right? I'm sure you would have lured in some other brawny merc with those big blue eyes."

Tears stung Payne's eyes at the thought of missing his chance to know Hunter, and he clung to Hunter. He felt a little foolish for getting so emotional over a hypothetical situation, but part of it was the ache he felt for the implied lack of self-worth Hunter's words revealed.

"I don't want another merc. I want you," he said. "You may not want to admit it, but your death would leave a hole in the world too. There are people who love you and whose lives would be emptier if you weren't here. Just because Stack had a wife and child doesn't make his life more valuable than yours."

"It does to me," Hunter said quietly. He moved the tray off his lap, setting it aside so he could wrap his arms around Payne and hold him close. "I'm glad you want me. God knows why you do, but I'm grateful. You may have saved me from myself. It still hurts, and I know now that going back into the field would be tantamount to suicide. I... I don't know what to do with myself. For the first time in my life, I'm not who I thought I was."

"You're not the same as you were before Stack died," Payne said, still holding on tight as much for his own comfort and reassurance as for Hunter. "You couldn't be after experiencing such a trauma. But different doesn't mean worse. The good thing is, you don't have to rush to figure out who you are and what you want to do. You can afford to take your time."

"I suppose." Hunter rubbed his cheek against the top of Payne's head. "You probably saved my life too, you know. If you hadn't taken me in hand, I think I would have left L&G and gone back into the field with any outfit that would take me. And I'd probably have frozen and gotten my sorry ass blown up. So... thank you."

"You're welcome," Payne said softly, giving Hunter a little squeeze. "I'm glad your sorry ass was here to be spanked instead."

Hunter gave a little snort, the closest thing to a chuckle he'd made since Jen's phone call. "I guess I'll be glad about it too someday. I mean, glad without second thoughts or regrets." He was quiet for several moments. "Do you think I should see Jen and Jake? What if I freak out or freeze up? I don't want to cause Jen more problems than she's already got."

Payne had been thinking about the visit with Jen Hansen and her son, and he decided to propose an idea since Hunter had brought up his concerns. "I think you should see them, but it might be a good idea if you meet with them privately first. That way, if you do freeze, you won't disrupt Jake's birthday party. If it would help, we could invite them here."

Hunter lifted his head. "That might be better," he said. "I would hate to mess things up at a party, and with other people around, it would be more stressful. Thanks for thinking of it. It seems a little less terrifying that way."

"Then that's what we'll do," Payne said. "We could see if they're free to come over for dinner tonight if you're up to it."

"Tonight?" Hunter sucked in a startled breath, and Payne felt the tension in his body. "Isn't this sort of sudden?"

"Why would that be a problem?" Payne drew back so he could see Hunter's face. He suspected Hunter's objection was based on knee-jerk fear, and he didn't intend to let Hunter get away with stalling.

"She might not be available on such short notice," Hunter said. "Wouldn't we need to, uh, plan a meal or something? I don't know what Jake is eating these days."

"Then we'll call and ask," Payne said. "If she's not available, we can work out a time when she is, and we'll ask what Jake prefers. Maybe we can grill burgers or hotdogs."

Hunter was still tense. "If that's what you think is best," he said finally. "I can't claim to be thrilled, but I think we both know I'm not able to be objective about it."

"Definitely not," Payne said dryly, and then he leaned in to kiss Hunter's cheek. "I know you don't want to do this, but I think we need to rip the bandage off. Putting it off will only give you more time to fret."

"Okay." Hunter grumbled, but there wasn't any heat in it. "I can call Jen. Can you hand me my cell? I suppose I should get this over with."

Payne drew back from Hunter long enough to grab Hunter's phone off the nightstand and handed it over. "Would you like me to stay here or would you like some privacy?"

"Stay." Hunter was looking at his cell phone, but Payne could see the way his jaw clenched, as though he was waging an internal battle. Then he unlocked the phone, poking at the screen awkwardly. When he finally raised the phone to his ear, his hands were trembling.

"Jen? Uh... hi. Yes, it's me. Um... fine. Look, Payne suggested maybe you and Jake could come over for dinner this evening, so that... well. The party might not be the best place for me to see you for the first time." He listened, and he swallowed hard. "You will? Uh..." He glanced at Payne. "Six o'clock?"

Payne gave him two thumbs up and offered an encouraging smile. "Yeah, that works. No, just informal. Like burgers and hotdogs, okay? Yeah... See you then. Bye."

Hunter ended the call, then drew in a shuddering breath. "I need a drink. And a shower. Then another drink."

"Tell me what kind of drink you want, and I'll make it for you, and then I'll scrub your back in the shower if you like." Payne slid his arms around Hunter's shoulders and hugged him tightly. "I'm so proud of you. You're a brave man, Hunter."

"I don't feel brave," Hunter said, but he leaned into the embrace. "I'd rather face a firing squad than a boy who isn't yet three. How brave is that? Shit. I should skip the alcohol, shouldn't I?"

"One drink won't hurt," Payne said, rubbing Hunter's back soothingly. "What would you like?"

"I'll take whiskey," Hunter said. "I've never been a heavy drinker, and I can't even remember the last time I had anything more than a beer, but if you think it wouldn't hurt, then I could use it."

"Done." Payne leaned in for a lingering kiss before rolling off the bed. "Up to you whether you're still in bed or in the shower when I get back, but I can promise it'll be more interesting if I bring the drink to you in the shower," he said with a playful grin.

Hunter smiled, but Payne could see he was preoccupied, probably with thoughts about seeing Jen and Jake again. "Thanks," he murmured. "After the shower maybe I should take that salve after all. I'll probably have enough to deal with. Having my ass hurting would be overkill."

"I'll get something to help numb it," Payne said.

He wanted to wrap his arms around Hunter and promise everything would be okay, but he knew Hunter wouldn't believe him. But he felt hopeful about the dinner. Jen and Jake cared about Hunter and wanted him in their lives, and maybe this visit would help Hunter accept it.

In the meantime, he'd do whatever he could to help Hunter prepare for the visit, and if it meant he was a little more hovery than usual, well, Hunter would simply have to deal with it.

13

Hunter wasn't accustomed to being nervous. He was almost a legend among his cadre for being steady in a crisis, for not letting anything from automatic weapons fire to an airstrike thundering around him damage his calm. Which made it all the more appalling that he couldn't sit still, as every tick of the clock toward eighteen hundred hours seemed to twist his stomach into a tighter knot. The drink Payne had given him hadn't helped at all, and he thought it was probably a good thing he hadn't eaten more than a couple of bites of his lunch, because otherwise he'd probably be riding the porcelain pony like a plebe after a three-day bender in Bangkok.

Instead of praying at the altar of St. Crapper, he was attempting to wear holes in Payne's carpet. He paced a restless circuit from the living room, through the kitchen, up and down the stairs, then back to the living room. Despite the air conditioning, he was sweating, though his mouth was as dry as the desert, and he had to consciously stop himself from the desire to clench his jaw and grind his teeth. Instead he glanced at his watch every few minutes, torn between frustration that the hand was crawling with maddening slowness and horror at how little time there was before he would have to face the encounter he'd been dreading for months.

Some big, tough merc he was. He considered pouring himself another drink, but he figured he'd end up spilling it on himself or gagging.

"Can I get you anything?" Payne asked when Hunter entered the kitchen. He had several thick raw hamburger patties on a plate waiting on the counter, and he was in the middle of slicing some tomatoes.

"No, thanks," Hunter said. He stood behind Payne, feeling the overwhelming need for contact. Wrapping his arms around Payne, he closed his eyes and rested his cheek against the top of Payne's head. "Yes. You."

Payne put down the knife and grabbed a dish towel to wipe off his hands. "You've got me," he said, stroking Hunter's forearms gently. "I'm here, and I'm not going anywhere."

"You'd better not," Hunter growled. "You got me into this, and you have to be here to save me if I go into a meltdown. Or save Jen and Jake, maybe."

"I will." Payne leaned against Hunter. "I'll always be here for you, I promise."

Hunter would have liked to believe Payne meant the "always" literally rather than as a platitude, but the here and now was what mattered for the moment. "Thanks. Just... promise me if I start to lose it, you'll think of them first, not me, okay? I can't bear the thought of hurting them worse than they already have been."

"I'll assess the situation and take whatever action I think is best for all involved," Payne said.

Hunter frowned as he pulled away. "Come on, Payne. Please. Them first. You can scrape me up off the pavement later."

Payne turned around in Hunter's arms and tilted his head back so he could look up at Hunter. "As much as I'd love to be a completely objective third party, I'm not," he said, sliding his arms around Hunter's waist. "You're my priority. But okay, if it turns into a shitshow, I'll take care of them first, especially Jake."

"Thanks." Hunter was puzzled why Payne, as protective as he was of those who needed it, seemed to put his welfare above Jen's and Jake's, but at least he'd promised. Then the doorbell rang, and Hunter froze, his heart beginning to pound so hard he was afraid it would burst. "No..."

"I know you're scared, babe, but they love you, and they don't want to hurt you anymore than you want to hurt them." Payne stroked Hunter's back soothingly. "Just take a deep breath in through your nose and out through your mouth a few times for me."

Breathing was difficult, but Hunter did what Payne asked, willing his heartbeat to slow down. He felt the surge of panic subside into mere anxiety. "Okay. What should I do? Where should I go?"

"Do you want me to open the door?" Payne asked, still rubbing Hunter's back. "If so, you could go out on the deck, and we'll join you. If you'd like to talk to Jen privately, I can bring Jake back inside to watch cartoons."

"Sure, the deck is good," Hunter said. He appreciated what Payne was doing to try to soothe him, but short of hitting him with a massive dose of Valium, he doubted anything would help much. At least there was plenty of air outside, and if he needed to escape, he could run. "Thank you."

Payne gave him a squeeze and an encouraging smile. "You've got this. Just keep breathing, and we'll be along in a minute."

With that, he disengaged from the embrace and headed to the front door. Hunter watched him go, then went out onto the deck, moving to the railing and leaning back against it, crossing his arms over his chest. He knew it was a defensive stance, but he couldn't help it. All he could do now was wait.

A few minutes later, Payne walked outside with Jen, a petite brunette who made him look tall in comparison, and Jake, who was blond like Stack. As soon as she saw Hunter, Jen stopped and stared at him with tears in her eyes and a wobbly smile.

"Hey, Hunter," she said quietly.

The tears made a knife twist in Hunter's gut, and before he even knew what he was going to do, he was stepping toward her. But a tiny missile intercepted him, as Jake fearlessly threw himself at Hunter, and Hunter instinctively caught him and lifted him up.

"Unca Hunter!" Jake's small arms were around Hunter's neck in a choke hold, but Hunter didn't mind. The warm weight of Jake in his arms was both painful and precious.

Hunter continued to Jen, wrapping his free arm around her. "Don't cry," he said, pulling her close. "I hate it when you cry, and you'll make me start, too."

Jen wrapped her arms around his waist and squeezed him tight enough to hurt, a hiccuping sob escaping her. "I'm happy to see you, so I'll cry if I want to."

Hunter closed his eyes, holding them both close, his own eyes stinging and his throat closing up with emotion. He'd feared this, but now they were here, he realized he'd been terrified for nothing. Jen and Jake were all he had left of Mark, and he needed them as much as they needed him.

"Okay, fine, cry," he murmured. "It's okay. I'm happy to see you, too."

Sniffling, Jen buried her face against his chest and clung to him, her shoulders shaking. When she drew back at last, her cheeks were tear-stained, but she smiled up at him.

"You look like crap," she said.

Hunter knew he was thinner and paler than when she'd last seen him, and he smiled crookedly. "Yeah, well, you know what a terrible cook I am," he said. He lifted his hand to brush her dark hair back from her face. She was only twenty-eight, and she had lost weight too, and there were shadows under her eyes. "I know it's been rougher on you."

Jake tugged at Hunter's chin, and Hunter turned to face him. "Unca Hunter, Mama says Daddy is in heaven," Jake said with a frown. "Can you go get him and bring him home?"

Hunter felt like he'd been punched in the gut. "Oh, Jake. I wish I could, buddy," he said, his voice rough. "I'd bring him home to you and your mama. But I can't. No one can.QIIaZ" Words failed him, and Hunter looked around for Payne, feeling a rising sense of panic.

Payne was beside him almost instantly, and he patted Hunter's back gently even as he focused his attention on Jake. "Hey, buddy, I think your mom and Uncle Hunter want to have a grown-up talk. Want to watch some cartoons with me?"

"Mickey Mouse?" Jake asked hopefully.

"Definitely," Payne said. "I like Mickey Mouse too."

Jake smiled shyly, then held out his arms to Payne. Apparently liking Mickey Mouse was enough to put Payne high up on Jake's list of favorite people, and Hunter passed Jake over. The boy's question had almost been enough to break Hunter, and he gave Payne a look of gratitude for the distraction.

Payne nodded an acknowledgment as he settled Jake securely in his arms. "Take as long as you need. We'll be in the den with the Disney channel."

"Thanks." Jen caressed Jake's back and then gave Payne's arm a little pat as he walked by her into the house. Once they were out of earshot, she took a seat in one of the deck chairs and beckoned to Hunter. "So how are you? And if you say fine, I'll punch you in the balls."

Hunter winced, because he knew she meant it. Jen was no shrinking violet; no woman who took on a merc, especially one who worked with explosives, could afford to be delicate. In fact, her strength was the thing Hunter had always admired most about her.

He moved to take the seat next to her, knowing he couldn't dissemble. "I'm surviving," he said, then glanced toward the house. "Payne is helping me deal with... things. But I'm more concerned about you. Is there anything I can do to help?"

"Yes, you can visit me and Jake once in a while," she said bluntly. "Mark wasn't the only one who loved you. You're Jake's uncle just as much as if you were related by blood, and you're like a big brother to me too. We could be helping each other through this."

Hunter winced. "I'm sorry," he said, then scrubbed his face with his hands. "I couldn't before. I wasn't ready to face you. I was afraid."

"Afraid of what?" Jen asked softly, leaning toward him.

"That you'd blame me." Hunter looked at her, forcing himself to face her judgment, whatever it might be. "I blamed myself, so I was sure you'd blame me, too, and I knew if you did, it would destroy what was left of me."

Jen's features softened with sympathy, and she shook her head. "I don't blame you. Why would I? You weren't the one who strapped C4 to a little boy. You and Mark saved his life." Her lips twisted in a wry smile. "If I'm mad at anyone, it's Mark for being such a fucking hero. But that's who he was. Right now, I love him and I hate him for it."

Hearing Jen sum up his own feelings was a shock, and Hunter drew in a sharp breath. "That's how I feel, too," he admitted. He swallowed against the lump in his throat. "He saved my life, Jen. But sometimes I do hate him for it, because it left us to go on without him. It's hard to go on, when I feel like I should have saved him instead."

"It's easy to say that with the benefit of hindsight, but what could you have done in the moment?" Jen spread her hands and shrugged. "I'm sure it all went down in a blink. I know you, Hunter. I know you reacted as quickly and strategically as you could under the circumstances. You weren't standing there with your thumb up your ass. But Mark reacted and made decisions too. He chose to trade his life for a little boy's, and as pissed off as I am with him, I can't fault him for it either." She gave a shaky laugh. "It's made my therapy sessions interesting."

"Yeah, I bet." Hunter ached for her pain, knowing hers was so much deeper than his in many ways — deeper, but different because she didn't have the weight of guilt Hunter had been carrying around. "I thought you might hate me because he saved me. Because he did it without thinking of you and Jake. I hated myself for that, and I hated him for it, too. I felt guilty for being alive. Sometimes I still do."

"It's easy for me to say you shouldn't feel guilty," Jen said. "But it's something you're going to have to work through on your own. What I *can* say is I don't hate you. I still want you in my life. Maybe it's selfish, because you're a connection to Mark, but I don't want you to keep avoiding us. Jake still needs his Uncle Hunter too."

Hunter clasped Jen's hand in both of his. "Thank you," he said. His eyes were stinging again, but he felt as though a weight he'd been carrying for months had been lifted from his chest. "I'm sorry I haven't been there for you and Jake, but I will be from now on, I promise. Are you still going to therapy? L&G had better be paying for anything you or Jake need, or I'll raise holy hell with them."

"I'm still in therapy," Jen said. "Jake has been seeing a child psychiatrist too. I know he's young, but I want him to come out of this with as little damage as possible. Don't worry, I'm being well taken care of."

"Good. I'm glad you're going, both of you. And I'm glad it's helping," Hunter said. "I want you both to be able to be happy again."

"I want you to be happy again too," Jen said, squeezing his fingers hard. "Are you going to therapy?"

Strangely enough, Hunter hadn't been prepared for her to ask, and he felt himself blushing with embarrassment. "I... well. Conventional therapy doesn't work for me," he said. "But I finally found something that's helped."

"Good, I'm glad you found something that works," Jen said, seeming satisfied. "I was worried you'd been avoiding getting any help."

Hunter felt compelled to be honest. Maybe he felt bad for having neglected her and Jake, but he wanted her to understand. "I did avoid it for months," he admitted. "I was in denial and fixated on getting back to the field. I was able to fool the psychologists into thinking I was okay, but Matthew Greer knew better. Cade Thornton put me with Payne, and he... he understands me. He wouldn't let me lie to him or to myself."

"*Good*," Jen said with a fierce scowl at him. "That's what you need. He seems nice from what little I've seen so far. So he's a Hercules Security guy, not a merc?"

"He was an Army medic, and then he joined Hercules Security."

Hunter smiled slightly, remembering his doubts about Payne being a "real" merc. "Payne is a law unto himself. He may never have been in the field as a merc, but he's definitely one in spirit."

Jen studied him speculatively, her eyebrows climbing. "Am I sensing a vibe here?"

Hunter wasn't sure how to answer her, but now that Mark was gone, Jen probably knew him better than anyone else. Except maybe Payne. "It's complicated. Until I've managed to work through my issues, I'm not sure I'm a good bet for anyone. Payne knows I'm still screwed up, and he's a natural caretaker. I'm not going to read more into it than that."

"Uh-huh." Jen gave him a knowing look. "Well, I'll vet him over dinner tonight. If he passes, you have my permission to complicate your life." She squeezed his fingers again, her expression becoming serious. "Don't use what happened as an excuse to cut yourself off. You deserve to be happy and loved. Mark would want that for you."

Hunter bit his lip, as his vision blurred. It meant a lot to him for her to say it, but it was still painful, because it was a reminder Jen no longer had the man who'd made *her* feel happy and loved. Jen was unbelievably generous, and Hunter cleared his throat because he had to tell her.

"Thank you," he murmured. "I love you too, you know that, right? You and Jake are more important to me than anyone. It's one reason I was so afraid of you being angry at me. I wish... I wish I could make it all better for you. It kills me because I can't."

Tears welled in her eyes again. "I know. But nothing is going to make it better other than time and lots of therapy. I'll be happy one day, and maybe I'll find love again. Mark would want that for me too."

"Yes, he would." It was true. Mark was generous to a fault, and he always wanted the ones he loved to be happy. "I hope you do, Jen. You deserve to be loved. And we'll make sure Jake never forgets his daddy."

Jen's watery, lopsided smile returned, and one or two tears fell, but she seemed comforted by Hunter's words. "Yes, we will."

Hunter disengaged one hand from hers, then reached out to wipe the tears away with this thumb. "Okay, enough tears from both of us. Shall we go inside and see which of our blue-eyed boys has charmed the other? Normally I'd put my money on Jake, but Payne can work you over with those eyes in a way that will have you crawling on the floor."

Jen chuckled as she squeezed his hand and then released it. "I take it you know from experience?"

"Yeah." Hunter smiled crookedly. Jen knew him well enough that she could see how he felt about Payne, but he needed to make sure she understood their relationship. "Just... don't let on you know how I feel about him, okay? It really is complicated."

She raised both eyebrows, but she didn't question him. "Okay, I won't."

"Thanks." Hunter stood, then held out a hand to help her up. "You'll like him."

She clasped his hand and smiled wickedly up at him. "If Mark was here, he'd give you so much shit. I feel it's my duty to follow in his footsteps."

"As long as you don't do it in front of Payne!" Hunter groaned. He knew he was owed a bit of payback for the way he'd tormented Mark about Jen, but he didn't want Payne to pick up on it. Payne was too observant by half, so there was no way he would miss Jen's meaning if she teased Hunter in front of him.

They went into the house and headed toward the den. The TV was on, playing cartoons from one of the many kid-friendly networks available on cable, but Payne and Jake weren't on the couch. Instead, they were kneeling on the floor by the coffee table with the crayons and construction paper Payne had picked up when he went to buy groceries for dinner. They were bent toward each other in a silent show of comfort and trust, and Jake was giggling as they worked on their respective pictures.

Hunter stopped in the doorway, feeling a strange warm tenderness as he watched them together. He should have known Payne would be good with kids, and to see him with Jake, making Jake laugh, made Hunter's eyes sting again. Of course it had been an emotional day, so maybe he wasn't turning into a complete wuss.

"What are you drawing?" he asked. He had the feeling he looked completely besotted, from the way Jen gave a small snort of amusement.

"I'm drawing a house on a sunny day because I'm a terrible artist," Payne said, holding up a piece of construction paper depicting a house that leaned to the right with some stick figures in front of it.

Hunter laughed. "Did we finally discover something you can't do?"

Payne made a scoffing noise. "Would you like to keep this as proof?" he asked, holding out the drawing to Hunter.

"Yes." Hunter reached out to take the drawing, as Jake jumped up and ran toward him, waving his own picture.

"I drawded you and Daddy," he said, holding out the drawing to Hunter.

Hunter took it, looking down at two stick men with their arms around each other and what might have been helmets on their heads. "This is great. Can I have it, buddy?" he asked, his voice rough. "I want to keep it so I can look at it every day."

"Yes!" Jake jumped up and down, obviously pleased Hunter liked the picture. "Are we gonna eat soon? I'm hungry."

"Ask Uncle Hunter to get started on those hamburgers and hot dogs," Payne said. "He's the grill master around here."

They did a fair amount of grilling, since it was the one form of cooking Hunter was decent at. Hunter held out his arms to Jake, and Jake didn't hesitate to let Hunter pick him up. "Come on, you can help me flip the burgers."

As he carried Jake toward the kitchen — with Jake chattering a mile a minute about wanting a hamburger *and* a hot dog — Hunter found himself relaxing in a way he hadn't expected. As much as he'd dreaded this meeting, it had turned out fine. No doubt there would be painful moments ahead when Jake had questions about Mark or when he was old enough to ask Hunter exactly how his father had died. But for the moment, he was grateful to Payne for pushing him to do this, especially since he probably wouldn't have ever gotten around to it on his own.

It was one more thing he owed Payne for, as well as for saving his sanity and keeping him from getting himself killed in the field. At this rate, Payne was going to own Hunter completely — but for the life of him, Hunter couldn't bring himself to mind.

14

Payne slid into one of the circular booths at Club Twist and patted the space beside him. He'd picked a booth with a good view of both the stage and the tables so Hunter could people watch before the show began.

"Sit close. I don't want any unattached subs trying to seduce you away from me," he teased.

Hunter smirked. "You don't think I look subby enough for another Dom to try to seduce me away?"

Hunter looked far more relaxed than he had a few hours earlier. They'd spent most of the afternoon at Jake's birthday party, and while Hunter had held up well, being around so many kids had been a stressful reminder that even though he'd made a lot of progress lately, he still wasn't over his trauma. But at least Hunter hadn't taken one look at the room full of kids and gone running for the hills.

Coming to the club was part of Hunter's reward for having stuck out three hours at the party. Jake had been thrilled, introducing his "Unca Hunter" to all his preschool friends, then insisting Hunter be the one to hold him up to blow out the candles on his cake. That had been the worst part for Hunter, if his haunted expression and pained smile were anything to go by. Given there was a prominent photo in the living room of Jake being held up by his father to blow out the candles on his previous birthday cake — with Hunter standing in the background, laughing — Payne had a pretty good idea why.

"As open-minded as we try to be, we're still guilty of stereotyping at times," Payne said, resting his hand on Hunter's thigh beneath the table. "I've been mistaken for a sweet submissive, and a lot of people probably assume you're a Dom. The only way you could signal you're a sub is to wear my collar."

"I read about that," Hunter said. "Collars, I mean." He placed his hand over Payne's. "I bet you're one of those Doms who's waiting to collar the perfect sub. Are you looking for someone like Tyler? No one would ever mistake him for a Dom, I'm sure."

Hunter looked a bit sour, which amused Payne. Apparently Hunter still wasn't convinced Payne didn't care about being with a docile, obedient sub.

"I've been waiting to collar the perfect sub *for me*," he said, squeezing Hunter's thigh. "The good news is I've already found him."

Hunter drew in a breath, then looked at Payne rather pensively before glancing away. "Well, anyone who would mistake me for a Dom would be pretty disappointed anyway. I couldn't do what you do."

Payne hadn't expected that response, so he leaned closer, trying to see Hunter's expression. "You know I meant you, right?" he asked softly.

Hunter glanced at him, his eyes dark. "But how can you be sure? I mean... I still don't know what I'm doing. What if it's different when I'm recovered?"

"We've been playing together outside of the therapy sessions," Payne said. "How do you think it might be different after you've recovered?"

"I honestly don't know," Hunter said. "You've only known me like... this. What if you feel differently when I'm more like my regular self?"

"Are we talking Jekyll and Hyde differences?" Payne shouldered Hunter playfully to show he was teasing.

Hunter smiled crookedly. "I don't think that extreme, no. But I'm not normally the terse, moody bastard I was when we met, so if he's who you want..."

"You haven't been a fulltime terse, moody bastard for a while," Payne said. He turned his hand over beneath Hunter's and laced their fingers together. "If I wanted a perfect textbook sub, I'd find one, all right? But I don't. I enjoy how we play together, and it's what I want. I love who you are now, and I'll love whoever you become as you heal."

Payne found his hand being gripped tightly, and then Hunter leaned toward him, pressing his mouth to Payne's and kissing him hard. Payne parted his lips and returned the kiss, sliding his free hand into Hunter's thick hair.

Hunter gave a soft moan, and then he pulled back slowly and stroked Payne's cheek. "You really mean it. When you said you loved me, I thought you meant like a friend."

"What? No!" Payne stared at Hunter, wide-eyed. "I meant I'm in love with you. I want you to be my partner and my sub, and I want you to consider my house your home from now on. Or we could buy a house together. I don't care. I just want to be with you."

Hunter smiled, his expression tender. "I'm in love with you, too. I was afraid to assume you felt the same way, given how fucked up I am."

Payne chuckled and shook his head. "Meanwhile, I blithely assumed you understood what I meant and took it at face value when you said you loved me too. I've been thinking we were on the same page this whole time."

"Sorry." Hunter's voice was soft, and he caressed Payne's cheekbone with his thumb. "But I want to be with you too. I want to be your sub, even if I'm not perfect at it. Live in your house or wherever you want to live. I haven't had a place to call home in twenty years, so wherever you are is home now, whether it's a house or a hut or a tent in the middle of nowhere."

"Then it's settled," Payne said softly as he leaned into the touch, smiling. He wished he'd realized sooner that Hunter still harbored doubts about him — about them — but he was glad everything was out in the open now. "I'm your home, and you're my home."

"Sounds like a good deal to me." Hunter said. His lips curved in a wicked smile. "Too bad there's no sex allowed out here. I'd be tempted to get on my knees under this table and suck your cock."

"Well, there *are* private rooms for that, darling."

Payne was jolted out of the romantic bubble by the sound of James's voice, and he glanced over to see James and Tyler standing in front of their booth. James was smirking, of course, and Tyler was stifling laughter behind his hand.

"Maybe later," Payne said. "Good to see you both. Will you join us?" He made the offer mostly to be polite but also because he would be far less tempted to break the club's rules with Hunter if he was distracted by other people.

"Yes, please join us," Hunter said, scooting closer to Payne to make more room. "It's good to see you both."

"It's good to see you as well," James said as he and Tyler slid into the booth. "I was wondering if you'd be back, Hunter. How are you doing?"

Hunter looked at Payne, an almost goofy smile on his face. "A lot better than the last time you saw us. Or at least *I* am. Payne is the one everyone will think needs his head examined for taking me on."

James made a scoffing noise and waved his hand dismissively. "Nonsense! I could tell you two were a good match when I met you."

"Me too," Tyler said, smiling at them warmly. "You've got good vibes."

Hunter chuckled, tightening his grip on Payne's hand. "Considering how screwed up I was when you last saw me, I'm surprised."

"It doesn't matter what was going on up here," Tyler said. He tapped his temple, and then he flattened his hand on his chest. "You've got a good heart."

"That he does," Payne said, leaning against Hunter. He was prouder than he could possibly express of how hard Hunter had worked to face his issues and how much progress he'd made. But

Hunter was a fighter, and a few whacks from a cane had convinced Hunter to fight for himself at last.

Hunter leaned his cheek against Payne's hair. "Thanks. Both of you. I appreciate it. Especially since there have been plenty of times lately when I've doubted it myself."

"Sometimes all it takes to help us see things clearly is to put our fears, doubts, and control into someone else's hands for a while," James said.

"Or get our ass paddled until we finally get out of our own head," Tyler said with a playful smile.

Hunter laughed. "I think Tyler's closer to what works for me. But it took quite a lot more than a paddle. I'm a hard ass, after all."

James's face lit up with interest, and he leaned toward Payne. "Flogger or cane?"

"Cane," Payne said. "He responded better to the firm impact."

"I'll bet." Tyler gazed at Hunter with respect in his eyes, and he squirmed a little as if he could imagine the kind of firm impact Hunter had experienced.

"I've been trained to tolerate a lot of pain," Hunter explained. He was looking at Tyler, as if not wanting Tyler to feel bad. "I'm also big and muscular, so I can take it. It's a good thing it was on my ass. If he'd been hitting me on the head, I never would have felt it at all. Too much rock." He winked, and Tyler laughed.

"I never would've gotten through to him if I hadn't whacked his ass," Payne said, pleased to see Hunter felt relaxed enough to joke. "At least that way, I knew I was having some effect."

"I can't honestly say I'm crazy about it, but I *needed* it." Hunter snorted. "If I'm honest, I hope I never need it again. It was bad enough in the moment, but afterward... it fucking *hurt*."

James and Tyler burst out laughing, and Payne couldn't help but join in at Hunter's heartfelt understatement.

"Yes," James said with a grin, although not a mocking one. "Yes, it does."

"I don't want it either," Tyler said with another wriggle. "I'm more of a paddle and soft flogger guy myself."

"I hope you don't need it again," Payne said, squeezing Hunter's hand. The last session had been almost as difficult for him as it had been for Hunter. He'd hated having to push Hunter so hard and cause him pain, physically and emotionally, and the more Hunter unraveled, the more Payne had ached with sympathy for what he'd suffered since his partner's death.

Hunter lifted their joined hands so he could press a kiss to the back of Payne's hand. "I appreciate you doing it. I know it wasn't easy on you, either." When he spoke again, there was pride in his voice. "Daddy couldn't kiss it and make it better. But he handed out the tough love when he had to."

Payne smiled and ducked his head, both pleased and a little embarrassed by the praise, especially since he could just about see the hearts in Tyler's eyes.

"I swear, you two are the cutest things," James said fondly. "If I'm not invited to the collaring ceremony or the wedding or even both, I'm going to be quite put out."

"I haven't asked him yet," Payne said, darting a glance at Hunter to see how he was responding to what James had said. Hunter had only just figured out Payne was in love with him, so he might not be ready to talk about collaring or weddings yet, even though both sounded like good ideas to Payne.

Hunter darted a quick look at him, then lifted his chin. "I'd prefer to wait until I'm over my issues. Or at least most of them. I'm only just getting used to the idea that I'm not so broken and that Payne could really love me."

"When you're ready, we'll talk about it," Payne said, and he couldn't resist the temptation to skim his forefinger lightly along Hunter's throat. "You'd look so hot with black leather around your neck."

Hunter's skin grew flushed, the color creeping up his throat and into his cheeks. "Yes, well..." He cast a heated look at Payne. "Maybe we should see about a room now? Or even heading home?"

"Home, I think," Payne said.

"Maybe we could go too?" Tyler turned a beseeching gaze on James, who stroked his hair tenderly.

"I can give the leather fashion show a miss," James said.

"Sounds good to me." Hunter smiled at James and Tyler. "I hope you have as nice a time as I believe we will."

"I'm sure we will," James said, smacking Tyler's ass after Tyler slid out of the booth and stood up. Tyler let out a little whimper, his pretty face already growing flushed. "Good night, my darlings!" James called out as he exited the booth and slid his arm around Tyler's shoulders. "I hope to see you back here soon."

Payne waved as James sauntered away, Tyler in tow, then looked at Hunter. "Shall we?"

Hunter slid out of the booth. "And James called *us* cute?"

"We're very cute," Payne said as he followed. "But so are they."

"No one ever calls me cute," Hunter growled, wrapping an arm around Payne's shoulders and pulling him close.

"James thinks you're cute," Payne said, sliding one hand into the back pocket of Hunter's black fatigue pants. "So do I."

Hunter growled. "Well, if you do, I guess it's okay." He gave Payne a heated smile. "But I know who has the cutest ass, and it ain't me."

"I won't argue," Payne said with a little smirk. Hunter wasn't the first person to compliment Payne's ass, but his was the only opinion Payne cared about.

Once they were back in Hunter's SUV and headed home, Payne rested his hand on Hunter's thigh, debating how to bring up a subject he'd been thinking about for a while. In the end, he decided to be blunt rather than trying to ease into it gradually, since Hunter preferred direct communication.

"What do you think about talking to Herc soon?" he asked. "Do you think you're ready to try a new mission?"

Hunter was quiet for a few moments. "I think so. I'm certainly willing to see what's available. Were you thinking of working with me or sending me out on my own?"

"I prefer to work with you," Payne said, squeezing Hunter's thigh.

"If you'd like to go out on your own or with a different partner, that's fine, but I'd rather go with you."

Hunter put one hand over Payne's. "No, I would prefer to have you with me. I don't want another partner, and... well, I think it's best not to be on my own. Not yet. Maybe... well, maybe not ever, you know?"

"I get it," Payne said, relieved to know Hunter wanted him to go along. He wouldn't have been at all pleased if Hunter's first mission had been a solo one, but he also didn't want Hunter to feel like he was hovering or taking away Hunter's options. "I'll set up a meeting with Herc. He can find us something to do that's low stakes, but it'll help you get your head back in the game."

"Sure." Hunter drew in a deep breath. "I don't know if I'll freeze again or not. If I do... I guess I should retire."

"Don't fret about it," Payne said, using his Dom voice, and he smacked Hunter's thigh hard. "If you get on that hamster wheel, it'll be tough to get off. Either you'll freeze or you won't. You have no way of knowing until you're in the moment, so there's no point in dwelling on it. Even if you do, it's not the end of the world. You can work as a trainer. I'm sure Herc would be happy to put your skills to good use in his new training facility. Lawson and Greer might too."

Hunter frowned. "Yeah. I know you're right. It's hard to think about not being in the field anymore. But then... it wouldn't be the same without Stack anyway."

"No, it wouldn't," Payne said softly. "Whether you go back into the field or not, nothing is going to be the same."

"I know." Hunter cast a quick look at Payne. "I would imagine I might even be missed if I went back. Maybe."

"No maybe about it." Payne slid his hand down and fondled Hunter's knee, slanting a lascivious smile at Hunter. "I'd send you naughty pictures and emails every day to entice you home quicker."

Hunter chuckled. "That would probably do it," he said, then sobered. "I'd miss you, too. To be honest, going back into the field doesn't hold the same attraction it used to. I never thought I might be ready to settle down, but now..."

"Now you have an adorable badass who's madly in love with you and who is ready — eager, even — to keep you so satisfied the only explosions you'll think about are the ones that happen in our bed," Payne said, grinning as he leaned over to nuzzle Hunter's ear.

Knowing Hunter might be willing to give up the field for him — for *them* — was an ego boost, but it was also a relief. Payne wouldn't have tried to stop Hunter from returning to the field if it was what he wanted, but Payne would have dreaded the waiting game while Hunter was away.

Hunter leaned into the nuzzling. "Yeah, a total badass, who is willing to use those big blue eyes to lethal effect, I'm sure. But I admit the explosions in the bedroom are even more satisfying than the other type. Plus I feel like I have too much to lose. Now I know exactly why Stack was getting out. I just wish he'd done it as soon as Jake was born."

"I know, but he had to be ready," Payne said. "No one could make the decision for him, just like I can't make the decision for you. I can only try to heavily influence it," he added, biting down on Hunter's earlobe.

"You're definitely influencing it," Hunter growled. "And if you keep that up, I'm going to pull over and ravish you right here in the car."

Payne drew back, unable to keep from smiling smugly. "Patience," he said. "At least wait until we get home so you can bend me over the back of the couch."

"Sounds good to me," Hunter said. "I'm tempted to risk a speeding ticket, but I'd probably slug the cop, and jail isn't where I want to be right now."

Payne settled back and peered out the window to distract himself from growing arousal. He didn't know what kind of mission Herc would give them or how the mission would go, but he knew how tonight would go, and that was good enough for now.

15

Hunter pulled the limo into a VIP parking space, putting the vehicle in park and then switching off the engine. He took a moment to double check the vehicle's security system, then nodded to Payne in the seat beside him. Payne grinned as he got out of the car, and Hunter quickly followed, catching up to Payne before they reached the hotel entrance.

It was a swank place, even for Atlanta, but the production company in charge of *Dead Reckoning*, the most hotly anticipated television series of the year, could afford the luxury. Hunter hadn't bothered to keep up with the entertainment industry during his time in the field, but Payne had given him a crash course once Herc had offered them the assignment as bodyguards to the youngest cast member for the show.

Hunter had watched all three of the currently released movies in the *Dead to Rights* franchise, with Payne pointing out eight-year-old Chase Sanders, who played a younger version of Jon Baldwin's character, Duke Wyatt, in several flashback sequences. Fan reaction to Chase had been wildly positive, which had spurred the producers to develop a TV show based on Duke's youth and the events leading up to where the movies began. Chase had been signed to an initial three-year deal, which made him a hot commodity. Hot commodities, Payne said, rated protection, and since Jon Baldwin was an executive producer for the series, Hercules Security landed the primary contract for celebrity protection.

When Herc had approached them about the assignment, he'd mentioned it was only interim, which had appealed to Hunter, who still wasn't sure he was cut out to be a bodyguard. The assignment was for a month, while Gabriel "Mojo" Crowe, half of the original security team, dealt with a family emergency. Mojo's partner had elected to take a leave of absence, which left two positions open for Hunter and Payne. Hunter had hesitated briefly when he learned they'd be guarding a kid, but Payne had reminded him they weren't in the field, and unlike their last assignment, there was no imminent threat. The previous team had been in place for eight weeks with no problems at all, so likely it was only a matter of ferrying their young charge from hotel to set, and their nights would be free, since a six-man team was in place at the hotel where all the actors were being lodged.

They were already halfway through the second week of the assignment, and the tension Hunter had felt during the first several days had faded gradually. It helped that Chase was as smart as he was cute, and despite his tender years, he was an old hand at acting. Plus his mother, Barbara, was always around, leaving Hunter and Payne free to concentrate on curious and sometimes rather aggressive fans who wanted to get close enough to the location shoots to see what was going on or who wanted to get an autograph from the stars. Hunter and Payne traded off positions, one of them staying close to the filming while the other patrolled the perimeter with several other Hercules Security personnel to make sure no one got too close.

They reached the elevator, and Hunter punched the button to summon a car. "The forecast today calls for rain," he told Payne. He'd meant to mention it at breakfast, but he'd gotten sidetracked when Payne had sashayed into the small kitchen of their suite at a far less swanky hotel nearby wearing a towel low on his hips, a heated smile, and nothing else. "If they move filming indoors, we might have a few hours free this afternoon. I looked on the internet and found a club nearby, if you wanted to have a little fun."

"Missing our playroom already?" Payne glanced up at him with a teasing smile. "Maybe I should have packed a paddle and some cuffs."

Hunter gave him a wicked grin. "I *did* pack them. Sir."

Payne appeared delighted by the news, and he smacked Hunter's ass playfully. "Good! But we could visit the club if we get a chance. Hotel walls are notoriously thin."

"My thoughts exactly." Hunter cast a glance over his shoulder, making sure they weren't being observed, and then he leaned close to Payne so he could whisper in his ear. "That bed also isn't sturdy enough for what I'd like to do."

Payne shivered, and his expressive eyes went half-lidded. "In that case, I hope it rains buckets so we get some free time."

The elevator arrived, and Hunter straightened up. "Me, too, sir," he drawled, then motioned for Payne to step into the car ahead of him.

The ride up to the fourth floor was too short to do anything more than grope Payne's ass, and once they stepped out, they were on duty. Hunter stopped in front of their client's suite and knocked. Within moments, Barbara Sanders opened the door and motioned them inside.

"Sorry, it's one of those mornings!" she said. "I was up all night with Lucy throwing up. I hope Chase doesn't catch whatever she's got."

Lucy was Chase's ten-year-old sister, who had a small part in the production as well. "I'm sorry she's sick," Hunter said. "Do you think Payne should have a look at her?"

"I'm a former medic," Payne said. "I can check to make sure she's not getting dehydrated from the vomiting."

"Would you? I'd appreciate it," Barbara said, looking relieved. "I was going to ask you to take Chase on to his call, then ask the concierge to recommend an on-call medical service, but if you don't think she needs anything but rest, that would make it easier. I don't think she has a fever."

"I don't mind at all." Payne offered her a reassuring smile. "Let's go see what's going on, shall we?"

Payne determined it was likely a stomach bug, and he recommended rest and clear liquids. Barbara was relieved, and after a quick consultation with Chase — who hadn't been allowed into the sick room — Hunter and Payne agreed to take Chase on without his mother, then bring him back to the hotel when filming wrapped for the day.

"I'd tell you to behave, but I know you will," she told her son, kissing him on the top of his head of brown curls, which made Chase squirm.

"Of course I will, Mom." he said, then grinned at Payne. "Maybe if we get some time between scenes, you can show me more of those martial arts moves. Jon said he's been training with the mercs, and Duke's gonna have some great moves in the next movie."

"We wouldn't want little Duke to fall behind big Duke," Payne said, appearing amused but pleased by Chase's enthusiasm.

"Or to be late for his call," Hunter said. "Come on, you two. I'll watch them, Mrs. Sanders. You don't have to worry."

"I know he's in good hands. I'll see you later, boys," Barbara said.

Chase chattered all the way to the car about the scene he was shooting that day, where Duke had to hide a group of children from townspeople who were being driven mad by the sickness spreading among them. "I get to push one of the sick guys down a flight of steps. Of course he's a stuntman and won't get hurt. Jon said you would have made a great stuntman, Payne. Didn't you ever want to be in the movies?"

"Not really," Payne said. "I didn't want to fall out of buildings for a living."

"What about you, Hunter?" Chase asked, as Hunter opened the rear door of the limo and held it.

"Be in the movies? Nah. I'm big and scary enough in real life, don't you think?" Hunter bared his teeth in a playfully ferocious smile.

Chase laughed. "Yeah, you look more like a bodyguard than Payne does."

"Maybe you should ride with him," Hunter suggested as Chase got into the car. "Just to make sure he doesn't unfasten his seatbelt so he can check out all the buttons and gadgets in the back unsupervised."

"Good idea," Payne said, giving Chase a stern look before climbing into the back seat with him, and Chase smiled sheepishly.

Hunter chuckled, then shut the door and moved to the driver's side. The limo wasn't a stretch, but it was bigger than a standard sedan, with seating for up to six in the back. Hunter had driven personnel and equipment haulers that were larger, so he had no trouble maneuvering the big vehicle out of the parking space and getting them onto the road.

Payne had already punched the remote filming location for the day into the GPS, so Hunter followed its directions out of town. The sun would be rising before long, but the splatter of raindrops on the windshield told Hunter it was going to be a dreary day. He didn't mind it, especially if it meant filming was canceled and he and Payne got to play at the BDSM club.

The rain was light at first, but after a few minutes, it developed into a deluge which made it difficult to see in the darkness. Hunter slowed the car, not wanting to overdrive his headlights on the winding two-lane road. He'd driven in all kinds of hazardous conditions over the course of his career, so he tuned out the sound of Payne and Chase talking, his total concentration taken up with the road.

After a few minutes, the intensity of the downpour lessened a bit, and he glanced at the GPS, looking for a place in case they had to pull off the road. Unfortunately the abandoned mill town they were headed toward was in the back end of nowhere, so there wasn't much of anywhere to make a stop.

The road began to wind up the side of a hill just as the rain poured down again in buckets. Headlights flared ahead of them, and time abruptly slowed for Hunter, all the hair on the back of his neck standing up as the looming certainty of disaster flowed over him. It was like when he'd opened his helmet on that last fateful day and heard the horrible beeping of the failsafe on the last block of C4.

"*Brace for impact!*" he screamed, but he didn't have time to check if Payne understood. The oncoming lights were too close, and there was no shoulder on this side, the blacktop giving way to a deep ditch. The vehicle ahead of them was taking its lane out of the middle of the narrow roadway, so Hunter did the only thing he could. Pulling the wheel to the left, he flashed across the path of what he could now see was a semi, headed toward the gravel shoulder on the opposite side. He would have made it, too, if the driver of the semi, drunk or drowsy, hadn't suddenly jerked his own wheel to get back into his lane.

The fender of the semi struck the limo on its back passenger side, forcing the front of the car around to where the passenger side struck the truck a glancing blow. If Hunter had been going any faster, the entire car would have flipped from the energy imparted by the impact, but Hunter practically stood on the brakes as the rear of the limo came slewing back around. The semi roared past, just as the rear of the limo on the driver's side smacked into a tree, and the vehicle stopped in a crunch of metal and breaking glass.

Hunter was out of the limo before he even knew he was moving, running back toward the caved-in door. It was too dark to see inside, but he knew there was no use trying to get in that way, so he dashed around to the other side. There, the door was damaged from the initial impact, and it wouldn't open, so Hunter took out his gun. "Cover your eyes!" he yelled, not knowing if Payne or Chase could hear him, before he smashed the safety glass with the butt of his gun.

"Are you hurt?" he asked, peering into the dark interior. "Payne! Answer!"

"We're okay." Payne's voice was slurry, but audible.

Hunter wasn't even aware of his own terror until Payne spoke. He let out a sound like a sob, bracing himself against the side of the limo as his knees threatened to give way. Then he told himself to get it together. They weren't out of the woods yet.

"Chase! Are you hurt?" He was pretty sure from Payne's voice that Payne had sustained some kind of injury, probably in protecting Chase.

"No, Hunter." Chase sounded frightened, but then he moved close enough to the window that Hunter could see him. "Just scared."

"Good, because I need your help. I'm going to try to open the door again from this side, and I need you to pull the handle and push the door as hard as you can from your side, okay? Can you do that?"

"Sure." Chase nodded, and Hunter could see having something to do helped the kid to get over his fear.

"Okay, on three. One... two... three!"

Hunter pulled on the door handle as hard as he could while Chase pushed. Hunter could feel the muscles of his arms protesting, but he kept it up until with a shriek of protesting metal, the door finally gave.

"Great! You did it!" he told Chase, as he stuck his head and shoulders into the car. He reached for the overhead light, grateful when it came on, since it hadn't turned on automatically when the door opened as it normally would have. He looked over Chase quickly, assuring himself the boy was uninjured, then turned his attention to Payne.

Reaching past Chase, Hunter rested his hand against Payne's cheek, his heart thudding painfully. "Payne? Sir? Please open your eyes."

Payne's eyelids fluttered, and after what seemed to be great effort, he cracked his eyes open and peered blearily at Hunter. "You okay?"

"I'm fine," Hunter said. He gently felt over Payne's head. "Where did you hit it?"

"Right side," Payne said, and he closed his eyes again.

Hunter cursed under his breath, touching the area Payne indicated gently, feeling a bump already beginning to rise. He didn't see any other obvious signs of injury, which was a relief. "Concussion. Okay, Chase, I need you to pop your seatbelt and crawl into the middle set of seats. Can you do that?"

"Yes!" Chase scrambled to do what Hunter asked, and then Hunter slid into the seat next to Payne.

"Stay awake, Payne. You hear me? I'm going to call for help."

After calling 9-1-1 — and offering up a silent thanks they weren't out of cell phone coverage — Hunter jostled Payne again.

"You with me, Pita? Come on, you never stop talking. Why are you stopping now?"

"Is he okay? Are we going to blow up?" Chase asked. He was kneeling on the middle row of seats and facing Hunter, eyes wide.

"He'll be fine. Cars don't usually blow up except in the movies," Hunter explained. "I'm going to call your mom and the set to let them know what happened, okay?"

"I'll be fine," Payne echoed, waving one hand weakly. "Anyone else hurt?"

"We're fine," Hunter assured him. He put in calls to Chase's mother — who was frantic until Hunter passed Chase the phone and Chase told her how Payne had saved his life by shielding Chase with his own body. By the time Hunter got his phone back and called the set to tell them what had occurred, he could hear the wailing of sirens in the distance.

The ambulance crew took several minutes to check out Payne and Chase, and then Payne was placed on a gurney and loaded in the back. Chase jumped up into the vehicle and asked the EMTs questions as fast as he could get them out. Hunter had only a moment to kiss Payne on the forehead before he was loaded in, since Hunter had to stay and answer questions for the police. It killed him to watch the ambulance carrying Payne away, but the EMTs had assured him it seemed to be only a concussion and maybe some bruises, and Payne would be fine.

Doing accident reconstruction in the rain wasn't fun, but Hunter gave his statement as clearly and succinctly as he would have following a military operation. He presented his driver's license and his Hercules Security credentials and finished up with the officers about the time the tow truck arrived.

Fortunately, the cops offered him a ride to the hospital, assuring him he wasn't at fault for the accident. The truck driver had turned himself in, admitting he'd been drowsy and had fallen asleep, waking up only moments before the crash, but too late to stop it. Hunter thanked them for the ride and the information, then entered the hospital tired, damp, and bedraggled almost three hours after Payne had been taken away.

The nurse on duty at the ER was helpful, informing him Payne had been admitted and taken up to a room for observation. Hunter made his way to the right floor, then finally to Payne's room. He stepped inside, stopping as he caught sight of Payne sitting up in the bed.

"Lying down on the job?" he asked, smiling in relief. "I never knew you were a slacker."

"You caught me." Payne's answering smile was weak, and he still looked groggy, but he lifted his hand to Hunter.

Hunter didn't hesitate to cross the room, taking Payne's hand and lifting it to his lips. "You scared the shit out of me, you know," he said softly. "Don't do that again."

"Sorry." Payne turned wide eyes on him. "I'll try not to."

If Payne was trying to make Hunter melt, it worked. Hunter sighed, sinking down in the chair next to the bed. "I guess I'm going to have to stick around to make sure, right?" he asked. "They told me it was a concussion and a couple of bruises. How are you feeling?"

"I'm okay," Payne said, squeezing Hunter's fingers gently. "They want me to get a CT scan, of course, and the nurses have been in and out every two seconds to make sure I don't go to sleep. So much fun."

"Oh, yeah, I know the drill," Hunter said. He brushed a lock of Payne's hair back from his face. "You're Chase's hero, you know. He's convinced he'd be road pizza if it weren't for you."

"It wasn't just me." Payne started to shake his head, but grimaced and stopped. "Movement is bad. Anyway, it was a team effort. Me shielding him and your driving. Your reflexes kept it from being a lot worse."

"I wish they'd been better, so you wouldn't have been hurt at all," he said, his voice husky. "If I'd been going a little faster, I would have made it across before the truck got there. Time felt like it slowed down, you know? I'm sorry you ended up injured because of it."

Payne raised one eyebrow at him. "Do I need to cane the what-ifs out of you again? What happened isn't your fault. It's that dumbass trucker's fault. You and Chase are fine, and I'll be fine. It's not my first concussion."

Payne's words helped to soothe Hunter's guilt, and he smiled crookedly. "No, sir, I won't need another caning. And the trucker doesn't know how lucky he is that you aren't hurt worse. As it is, I could beat the shit out of him for ruining my rainy day plans. This is definitely not the bed I was hoping to get you into today!"

"It's not the bed I wanted to be in either," Payne said, chuckling. "I can't even get any healing cuddles until I'm released."

Hunter stroked the back of Payne's hand with his thumb. It could have been a lot worse, but he wished he could take Payne back to their hotel room and give him all the cuddles he wanted. "As soon as you're released, I'm yours to command. Cuddles, meals in bed, anything you want. I'll even serve you naked if it will help you heal. I just want you back with me where you belong."

Payne smiled, his eyes soft and warm with affection. "There's nowhere else I'd rather be," he said, squeezing Hunter's hand again. "Oh, have you reported to Herc yet?"

"Not yet. I wanted to make sure you were okay first." Hunter pulled out his cell phone. "Want me to do it now? That way you can chime in if you want."

"Sure, go ahead," Payne said, releasing Hunter's hand with obvious reluctance.

Hunter quickly dialed the Hercules security number, then put the call on speakerphone before reaching for Payne's hand again. When Herc came on the line, Hunter gave a quick, succinct report of what happened.

"I'll send a replacement team at once," Herc said. "Pita, you're on administrative leave for the next several weeks. You too, Hunter, because he'll need someone to watch over him. You'll both need a medical clearance before returning to active duty, but I don't want you to rush it. Concussions are nothing to fool around with, and Hunter, I want you to get checked out too. You're probably banged up and won't realize it until tomorrow."

"Understood, Herc," Payne said, although he scrunched his nose to show his dislike of being sidelined for weeks.

"Good. Take care, you two. I'll have the replacement team check in with you when they arrive." With that, Herc ended the call.

"Well, what are we going to do with all that time off?" Hunter asked, giving Payne a slow, heated smile. "Do you have any ideas, sir?"

"It seems my options are awfully limited," Payne said, widening his eyes as he gazed at Hunter. "You know how strict they are about what you can and can't do when you've got a concussion. I can't read or watch TV or go online. What does that leave?"

"No strenuous activity, either," Hunter said thoughtfully. "Should I ask your doctor if paddling is too strenuous? I'd think caning would be right out, and the flogger... well, it could go either way. Or you could lie back and let me lavish you with attention and serve your every whim." Actually, he rather liked the thought of taking care of all Payne's needs, spoiling him and making him happy. It was a duty he thought he might never tire of.

"I like the sound of the 'serving my every whim' thing," Payne said, rubbing his thumb along Hunter's inner wrist. Hunter shivered in reaction.

"Too bad we can't do anything at the moment," he said. "Though I'm willing to go get anything the doctor says you can have. Are you hungry? Thirsty? Do you want me to find a book and read to you?"

"I've got to stay awake a while longer, so reading to me sounds like a good idea," Payne said, giving him a grateful smile. "I was about to go crazy from boredom before you arrived."

"Reading it is. Let me go see what I can find. If it's like other hospitals I've been in, the nurses will have something to keep their patients from climbing the walls." Hunter stood, then leaned over to kiss Payne gently on the lips. "I love you, you know. I don't think I've ever been so scared in my life as I was for those few seconds when I called out to you and you didn't answer. Don't do that to me again, okay? I might not survive it."

"I love you too." Payne rested his palm against Hunter's cheek. "I promise I'll do my best not to put you in that situation again." He paused, gnawing on his bottom lip. "I've been putting out some feelers with Ghost. He might could use me at the training facility."

Hunter stared at Payne for a long moment. Maybe making a big change wouldn't be so hard if he had someone to do it with. All he knew was he wanted to be with Payne, no matter where they were. He'd finally found what Mark had with Jen, and the past few hours had proved there were no guarantees, whether he was in the field or driving down the street. But he would do whatever it took to make sure he and Payne were both as safe as they could be. No thrill in the world compared with knowing that Payne loved him.

Finally, he smiled.

"Would you mind asking if he has room for two?"

16

Payne looked around the dining area of the restaurant, pleased by the extra touches the owner had provided to make the venue more romantic. The additional candles and deep red roses on the tables were a nice addition that Payne appreciated. He'd rented out the entire restaurant — one of his and Hunter's favorites that served Cuban cuisine — for a private party to celebrate their one-year anniversary.

One year ago, he'd walked in the Hercules Security gym to meet his new partner, a man who was surly and withdrawn and so obviously hurting that Payne had wanted to hop on the back of his white steed and charge to the rescue right away. He didn't know if Hunter remembered the significance of the date because he'd avoided discussing it. He had plans for tonight involving more than just celebrating an anniversary, and he'd enlisted help from their friends to make everything come together.

For the past several months, he and Hunter had both been working at the Hercules Security training facility, which had necessitated a move from North Carolina to Virginia. Payne didn't mind because Raleigh was still close enough they could drive back and spend the weekend visiting Jen and Jake and having a playdate at Club Twist whenever they liked.

Payne had set up an extended weekend under the pretense they'd earned a mini vacation after the stressful year they'd had, especially Hunter. Herc had helped out by inventing a reason why Payne needed to go to Raleigh a day early, and Ezra Levin, Payne's former mentor who was in charge of the facility, had helped by inventing a reason why Hunter needed to stay behind that day instead of going with Payne.

Most of his plans for the party had been made long distance, such as booking the venue, choosing the menu, and inviting the guests. Jen was invited, of course, and Payne had even offered to cover the cost of babysitting to make sure she could make it since the party would run a little too late and be a little too adult for Jake, considering it was semi-formal. He'd indulged in his first tailor-made suit for the occasion — black with a crisp white dress shirt and a paisley silk vest.

He'd also invited James and their friends from Hercules Security and the training facility, and he'd invited Hunter's friends from Lawson and Greer. All the guests had arrived and were enjoying appetizers and drinks, and Payne tried to distract himself from his nervousness by visiting the different tables and standing clusters of people to chat while he waited for Hunter to arrive.

Right on time Hunter entered the dining room. He was talking to the restaurant owner, so at first, he didn't seem to realize anything out of the ordinary was going on, and Payne had a moment to admire the sight of Hunter in a suit, the dark fabric of his jacket emphasizing the breadth of his shoulders. At Payne's request, Hunter had decided to keep his hair long, and tonight, it was pulled back in a neat ponytail.

Hunter's eyes grew wide when he recognized the people filling the dining room. "Payne? Did everyone decide they couldn't live without black bean soup?"

"Surprise!" Payne rushed across the room to greet Hunter, arms outstretched. "Happy anniversary," he said as he slid his arms around Hunter's shoulders and pushed himself up on his toes for a kiss.

Hunter's strong arms engulfed him, holding him tightly as Hunter returned the kiss. Then he pulled back, his dark eyes full of warmth as he smiled at Payne. "I figured you would remember, and that's what dinner was about." He placed his lips close to Payne's ear, dropping his voice so it wouldn't be heard by anyone else, though there seemed little danger of it among the clapping, cheers, and catcalls. "Happy anniversary, sir."

"How could I forget the day I knocked the man I love on his ass?" Payne said with a mischievous grin as he drew back.

"I certainly haven't forgotten," Hunter said with a playful smile of his own. Payne hadn't seen the bitter, withdrawn man Hunter had once been in a long time. Not that Hunter's PTSD was gone. He might suffer flashbacks for a long time to come, but the frequency and severity had lessened over the last year. He'd had a few bad days, like the anniversary of Mark's death, but he was on the road to recovery. "You aren't planning to knock me on my ass today, are you? Is that why you invited everyone we know?"

"I thought it might be nice to celebrate two things with the people we care about," Payne said, his heart beating faster as he slid his hand into his jacket pocket. "The first being our anniversary, of course."

"That makes sense," Hunter said, tilting his head to one side, his eyes bright with curiosity. "What's the second?"

Payne drew in a deep, steadying breath as anxiety coiled and tightened around his stomach. He didn't think this would end badly, but there was always a small chance.

"Our engagement," he said, dropping to one knee. He drew the black ring box out of his pocket, opened it, and held it out to Hunter, hoping he didn't notice how much Payne's palms were sweating. "If you say yes, that is."

Hunter's eyes grew wide in surprise, and he drew in a breath, easily heard since the entire room had fallen silent in anticipation. He looked down at the simple white gold band, and for a moment, Payne thought there was a suspicious glitter in Hunter's eyes. "Considering the fact I'm not *totally* stupid, the answer is... yes, of course!"

Laughing with relief, Payne stood up and removed the ring from its box. "Let's make it official, then." He clasped Hunter's left hand

and slid the ring onto his fourth finger, and then he brought it to his lips for a lingering kiss.

Hunter's grin was wicked, and then Payne found himself being spun in place and dipped back over Hunter's strong arm, with Hunter's lips on his in a firm, demanding kiss. The kiss stifled Payne's startled laughter, and he parted his lips eagerly and clung to Hunter's broad shoulders.

After a time — and even more whistles and catcalls — Hunter pulled Payne back to his feet but kept an arm around his shoulders. "I love you," he murmured, his voice pitched low. "More than anything in the world."

"I love you too," Payne said, cupping Hunter's cheek in his palm. "I'm ready to start our forever together."

"Me, too. Sir." Hunter leaned into the touch. "You know, I have my collar on under my shirt..."

A little frisson of arousal rippled through Payne, and he had to remind himself this was their party and they couldn't duck out early. But he loved knowing when Hunter was wearing the collar. He'd asked months ago if Hunter was interested in having one, and when Hunter said yes, they had picked one out together, opting for a titanium eternity style collar that would look like a necklace to the unsuspecting eye.

"Keep it on for our private celebration later," he said, giving Hunter a heated smile.

"Yes, sir." Hunter leaned in to steal another quick, hard kiss, then looked at their guests. "Well, thank you all for coming to help us celebrate our anniversary." He looked at Cade Thornton, who was standing with his arm around his husband, Jude. "A special thanks to Herc for taking me on and matching me up with Payne. And to Matthew Greer and John Lawson for doing their best to get me the help I needed but sure as hell didn't want."

There was laughter, and then Hunter glanced at Jen. "And to Jen for being my friend and loving me despite everything. And finally, to Payne..." He looked at Payne, and his feelings were plain for everyone to see. "You saved me. I didn't realize it, but I was yours from the moment you kicked my ass and laid me out on the mat. Thank you for that, and for picking me up afterward and putting me back together again."

Tears stung Payne's eyes, and his lips quivered as he mustered a watery smile. "I'm glad I could help. You were worth saving."

Hunter eyes were suspiciously bright, too. "You believed in me even when I didn't. I'm yours forever."

"And I'm yours," Payne said, drawing Hunter down for a lingering kiss.

"Aw, shit, Pita. Enough with the mushy stuff!" Daryl Greer's distinctive drawl broke into the moment. "When do we get to the booze?"

Hunter drew back, glaring at Daryl before breaking into laughter at his knowing grin. "Damn it, D-Day, knowing you, I figured you'd brought your own!"

"I patted him down for contraband before we left the house," Emerson, Daryl's partner, said as he slid his arm around Daryl's waist. "He's clean for once, literally and figuratively."

Daryl snorted, then reached into his jacket to pull out a flask. "You know me better than that, Doc," he said. "I hid it in the truck before we left."

"I tried," Emerson said, and then he plucked the flask from Daryl's hand and unscrewed the cap so he could take a swig.

Chuckling, Payne clasped Hunter's hand and twined their fingers. "Let's mingle, shall we? They'll serve dinner in twenty minutes or so. I asked them to prepare your favorites, and there'll be music for dancing after dinner. Afterwards, we can probably call it a night, so we can get to our private celebration," he said, wagging his eyebrows playfully.

"Sounds good to me," Hunter said, his smile knowing. "Then I can show you the tattoo I got this morning when you thought I was doing something for Ezra."

"You got a new tattoo?" Payne drew Hunter away from the others, intrigued by this new mystery. "Where is it? What's the design?"

"It's over my heart, and it's a phrase that means a great deal to me," Hunter said.

He took Payne's right hand in his, then placed Payne's palm flat against the left side of his chest. Smiling tenderly, he leaned close.

"No Payne, no gain."

ROOM FOR ONE MORE

HERC'S MERCS #8

FOREWORD

Trigger warnings —

This book contains mentions of child abuse, child rape, human trafficking, and child sexual assault. These horrors are NOT explicitly shown, and are not gratuitous in nature. The intent in presenting these subjects is to show their impact specifically on the mental health of characters who are trying to end these vile crimes and those who commit them.

1

The old-fashioned landline rang as Joe was pouring iced tea into a glass. He carefully placed the pitcher on the counter before reaching to pick up the receiver.

"Morrissey."

"Hey, M. It's D-Day." The caller didn't have to name himself, since Joe had recognized Daryl Greer's distinctive growl on the first word. "I'm gonna be headin' out to the lake this weekend to fish, 'cause Doc has a conference in New York. You interested?"

Normally Joe would have been glad to accompany Daryl out to his camp on Jordan Lake for some quiet, peaceful relaxation away from people. It wasn't that Joe was antisocial, not exactly, but he often felt out of place in big crowds, and his taciturn nature wasn't suited to the pursuits of a social butterfly. Spending time with Daryl was different, because he was almost as quiet and reserved as Joe himself. They got along well.

"Can't," he replied. "I'm starting a mission tomorrow, but thanks for the invitation."

"Well, damn." Daryl sighed. "Guess I'll have to go alone. You gonna be out of town?"

"Yeah." A motion outside the big picture window overlooking his yard caught Joe's eye, and he watched as Brian Finnegan came around the side of the garage. Finn was dressed in nothing but a pair of cutoff denim shorts, riding low enough on his hips to give a glimpse of a dark treasure trail. His tanned torso gleamed with sweat, and his dark hair was damp, an errant curl straying over his forehead. Black grease was visible on one of his cheeks—a single streak—no doubt the product of his labors on Joe's HVAC system. As Joe watched, Finn pulled a wrench out of his back pocket and went to work on the compressor unit, loosening the bolts at the top that held the fan motor in place. His movements were precise, and the slight curve of a smile on his lips made Joe wonder what Finn was thinking about.

"Morrissey? You there?"

D-Day's voice's brought Joe out of his reverie. "Uh, yeah. Sorry."

"Am I interruptin' something?" There was an edge of amusement to Daryl's tone. "You and Finn weren't gettin' busy, were you?"

"No." *Not yet.* "He's fixing my heat pump."

Daryl snickered. "I thought you said you weren't gettin' busy," he drawled, and Joe's cheeks grew warm. It was a sign of how distracted he was that he'd unknowingly handed D-Day a perfect set up. "I'll let you get back to it. Later."

"Later," Joe replied, absently replacing the phone on its hook. Finn was wrestling the fan motor out of the compressor, and he couldn't help but watch, admiring the flex of muscles beneath Finn's smooth skin.

Finn placed the motor on the ground and bent over it, positioning himself to give Joe an unobstructed look at his firm, denim-covered ass. It had to be deliberate, but it also had the desired effect. Joe's mouth went dry, and a zing of arousal shot down his spine.

Finn straightened and rested both hands at the small of his back. He pivoted to present a three-quarters view, making Joe wonder what he was up to. With his eyes closed and lips parted, he arched his spine and let his head fall back, exposing the long, clean line of his throat.

The zing became a full-fledged thrum as Joe caught sight of the dark bruise on the side of Finn's neck. He remembered very well how it had gotten there, the way that Finn's skin had felt as he'd bitten down on it, then drawn it between his lips to suck. Finn liked being bitten, and God knew Joe loved to mark him. It was the only sign of possessiveness he dared show.

Lacing his fingers, Finn stretched his arms high over his head and twisted his torso back and forth as if working out an ache, but was that a flirty smile peeking from behind the curve of his bicep? Given it was Finn, the answer was probably *yes*.

Knowing that Finn was teasing him only increased Joe's need to do something about it, so he moved back to the table and picked up the glass of sweet tea, its sides already dripping with condensation. He headed to the back door, stepping out into the rapidly heating July morning.

He stopped a couple of feet away from Finn, not bothering to hide his admiration as he let his gaze travel over Finn's body. They were close in height, though Finn was lean and rangy, while Joe had wider shoulders and more muscle. This close, Joe could see the brilliant green of Finn's eyes—they gleamed with mischief—and spot the dimples that creased his cheeks. Joe knew he was good looking enough, but Finn was strikingly handsome, his features boyish and his mouth always curved in a ready smile.

They were opposites in so many ways, and sometimes Joe wondered what Finn saw in him, even if they were only friends with benefits. Finn was outgoing, with a warm personality that drew people in like a magnet, where Joe was quiet and reserved, often fading into the background without notice. Finn's wit was keen, his laughter bright and infectious, while Joe rarely more than chuckled. Joe was quietly methodical, his house neat and organized, while Finn's apartment always looked like a tornado had just run through it.

Strange as it was, they somehow made a natural team. They'd met at Lawson & Greer, where Finn had signed up after a couple of tours as an Army field medic. Joe had joined only a week earlier, after mustering out of the Navy Seal program, and they'd been paired together for training. Later, they'd left the company together to join Cade Thornton when he'd founded Hercules Security, and that was when the *with benefits* had been added to their friendship. In the eight years since, things hadn't progressed any further, at least on the surface. Joe was a homebody, and even if he never admitted it, there wasn't anyone else in his life—and he wasn't looking for anyone. Finn wasn't the type to be tied down. He had the occasional fling, but Joe was always there waiting when the flavor of the moment was gone. Joe would always be there for Finn, no matter what.

"You look hot," Joe said, meaning the double entendre. He held out the glass of tea. "Thirsty?"

Finn accepted the glass and pressed it against his flushed cheek, his lips curving in a tempting smile. "I'm a little heated."

Joe took a step closer. "When you're done, you could cool off with a shower," he replied. "Then, if you wanted, I could heat you up again."

"I'm just about done," Finn said, holding Joe's gaze as he ran the glass along the side of his neck, leaving a wet trail in its wake. "I need to put the motor back in and bolt it down, but I'll definitely be ready to cool down soon."

"All right." Joe took yet another step, close enough now to feel the warmth of Finn's body. He lifted a hand, trailed his fingers through the cool path left by the glass, and brought them to his lips so he could taste Finn's clean, salty sweat.

Finn's eyes darkened and a hum of approval rumbled in his chest. "It'd help if I didn't have any distractions," he said, even as he rested one hand on Joe's hip.

Joe tilted his head to one side. "Would it help if I went and got in the shower? The thought of me waiting for you wouldn't distract you, would it?"

"No, but it sure as hell would motivate me to finish up as fast as possible," Finn said, dimples flashing as he shot a mischievous grin at Joe.

Joe loved the sight of that grin, loved knowing he could please Finn and make him happy. "Motivation is good." He ran his thumb along Finn's lower lip. "And I do need to give you proper payment for your help."

Finn caught the soft pad of Joe's thumb between his teeth and bit down."Hell yeah, you do." Finn caught the soft pad of Joe's thumb between his teeth and bit down.

The tiny flare of pain only heightened Joe's desire. "I'll leave you to it." He smiled and stepped back out of Finn's reach. "Don't take too long."

"Believe me, I won't." Finn's eyes glowed with interest, but he didn't reach out to keep Joe with him. Instead, he turned his attention back to the motor, seeming ready to make good on his promise to hurry.

Joe took a moment, again, to admire Finn's ass, and then he turned and headed back into the house and through the master bedroom to the big en suite bathroom. He was a man of simple tastes, and the rest of the house was comfortable without a lot of fussy details, but for the bathroom, he'd gone all out. He'd put in a free-standing whirlpool tub big enough for two and a shower stall that was even larger, with massaging jets and a wide bench seat.

After putting on some soft mood music, he turned on the shower and set the temperature to warm. While the water heated up, he collected lube and a condom, just in case Finn was in the mood to be taken. Then, he stripped and got into the shower, standing in the warm spray while he waited for Finn to join him.

Finn entered the bathroom a few minutes later, already naked, and his cock stirred as he stood in the doorway. He raked a heated gaze up and down the length of Joe's body. "Told you I wouldn't be long," he said as he sauntered across the room to join Joe under the spray.

Joe couldn't help but admire how Finn looked, all lean muscle and attitude. Finn had a kind of self-confidence that was sexy as hell, and sometimes Joe wondered how he'd gotten lucky enough to have Finn in his bed. "You're worth the wait."

Finn slid his arms around Joe's waist and leaned in to nip at Joe's bottom lip. "So are you. Now, about that payment... what's your offer?"

The sensation of Finn's hot, wet body sliding against his was incredibly arousing, while the bite made Joe hungry for the taste and feel of Finn's lips. He ran his hands down Finn's back to cup them against the cheeks of Finn's perfect ass. "I could suck your cock until you explode, or fuck you up against the wall," he murmured. "If either or both are appealing."

"I'm greedy," Finn said as he pressed close and mouthed kisses along Joe's jawline. "I want both, especially since you're going on a mission without me. Suck me, then fuck me. Make me remember it for *days* after you're gone."

Joe tilted his head to give Finn better access, and he tightened his hands on Finn's ass, kneading it while he pressed their hips together so Finn could feel his need. "I can do that." He wanted Finn to remember him because leaving Finn behind was going to be torture.

Finn threaded his fingers in Joe's hair, and he nibbled and licked a path down Joe's throat. "Do it," he murmured against Joe's skin. "I want it. I *need* it."

The raw appeal in Finn's voice was enough to drive Joe wild. With a feral growl that would have surprised any of his friends— except for Finn—he grasped Finn by the shoulders and pushed him back against the shower wall. Then, he captured Finn's lips in a deep, demanding kiss, knowing how much Finn liked it when Joe was rough. Something about Finn brought out Joe's aggressive, dominant side like no one else ever had. Parting his lips, Finn surrendered with a throaty moan, and he tightened his arms around Joe.

Joe didn't hesitate to plunder Finn's mouth, reveling in the sweet taste of Finn on his tongue, and in the needy sounds Finn made. He rocked his hips up, wanting Finn good and hard for what he planned next. Finn arched against Joe, letting Joe feel his growing arousal.

After several moments, Joe pulled back. "Now let me give you what you want," he murmured. He began to press open-mouthed kisses against Finn's skin, working his way downward as he slowly dropped to his knees. He looked up at Finn and smiled wickedly before taking Finn's cock into his mouth with a moan.

Finn sucked in a hissing breath and threaded his fingers through Joe's hair, a flush rising in his cheeks. "You're so fucking hot like this," he said, watching Joe avidly. "I love your mouth so much."

Joe hummed his approval of the praise before sliding a hand up Finn's body so he could toy with one of his nipples. He pulled his head back and swirled his tongue around the tip of Finn's cock before taking him in deeply again. Finn groaned and tightened his fingers in Joe's hair, moving his hips in shallow little thrusts.

"It's not going to take much...," he said, his voice low and breathy.

For a moment, Joe considered drawing out the torture, but he decided to let Finn take the edge off. Finn's stamina, as far as Joe could figure, was about equal to a sixteen-year-old's, which for him was both a source of awe and, at times, consternation. He tapped Finn's hip with his free hand, giving Finn permission to fuck his mouth however he wanted. Finn accepted the invitation with a heart-felt moan and began to thrust, claiming Joe's mouth.

Joe gave himself over to it, relaxing his throat and taking Finn in as deeply as he could. He loved doing this for Finn, loved giving him pleasure. Whatever Finn needed, Joe was more than happy to give. It wasn't long before Finn's breathing grew rough and ragged, and his body grew taut as he neared the edge. He fisted his hand in Joe's hair and let out a wild cry as he let go.

Joe moaned his approval, continuing to suck Finn, not wanting to miss a drop. He leaned into Finn's tugging hand, enjoying the edge of pain, and looked up at Finn, drinking in the sight of his face. The enraptured expression Finn wore increased Joe's own arousal. He loved knowing that he could do this for Finn, that he could give him this release.

As his pleasure ebbed, Finn sagged against the wall of the shower and stroked the back of Joe's head. "Perfect," he said, gazing down at Joe with satiation gleaming in his half-lidded eyes. "Now let's take care of you."

That sounded good to Joe. He drew back, releasing Finn's cock with a little kiss, before straightening up. He ran his hands over Finn's chest, dragging his nails over Finn's skin. "All right. But first I want a kiss. Then I'll fuck your brains out."

With a sensual smile, Finn slid his arms around Joe's shoulders and leaned in to claim a deep, hungry kiss. Joe closed his eyes, returning the kiss measure for measure. No matter how many times they made love, every time was unique and wonderful. Finn filled up all the empty places in Joe's soul and made Joe feel safe in ways no one else did.

After a short time, he pulled back. "Let's get you ready," he murmured and then reached toward the shelf where he'd placed the condom and lube. He picked up the bottle, keeping it out of the water stream, and popped open the top. "Good thing this is a big shower."

"Who would've guessed you're such a hedonist?" Finn teased. He turned around, placing his forearms against the tiled wall. "How's this?" He gave Joe a flirty smile over his shoulder as he arched his back to put his ass on display.

The sight made Joe's cock throb. "Perfect," he said breathlessly. He coated his fingers with lube and put the bottle back on the shelf. "Now let's get you ready."

He slid his fingers down Finn's ass and began to circle his tight pucker. Leaning closer, he nipped at the back of Finn's neck, before starting to suck hard. Moaning, Finn dropped his head forward, offering Joe better access.

"Oh, yeah, mark me up," he murmured, a shiver running through him. "Give me something to remember you by."

Joe didn't hesitate to do as Finn requested, biting down and worrying at his skin. At the same time he pressed two fingers slowly into Finn's body, his eagerness to bury himself inside Finn making him begin to tremble. Finn rocked back as if trying to send Joe's fingers deeper.

"I'm good," he said, breathless. "Fuck me, Joe. I need you *now*."

There was no way that Joe could resist Finn's plea. He removed his fingers and held them under the water for a moment to rinse them before reaching for the condom. "I need you, too," he growled as he ripped open the packet. He rolled the condom on before picking up the lube again, wanting to make sure he didn't hurt Finn. After coating himself, he dropped the bottle, not caring where it ended up, and grasped Finn's hips. "Ready?"

"Yes!" Finn pushed back eagerly, offering himself up.

That was all the encouragement Joe needed. With a heartfelt groan he moved forward, claiming Finn's body with one smooth, slow thrust. He buried himself deeply, enjoying the sensation of Finn's body, hot and tight around him. "God, Finn. You feel so good, so perfect!"

Finn gave a soft cry as he threw his head back, his body pliant and welcoming. "Feels good to me, too," he moaned.

Joe flexed his fingers on Finn's hips. "Good. Because I don't think I can hold out for long." He pulled back slightly and then thrust in again, deep and hard. "Want you too much."

"Don't hold back." Finn looked over his shoulder, and his green eyes blazed. "Fuck me as hard as you want. As hard as you need."

With a soft moan, Joe did as Finn said, letting his need overwhelm him. He pulled back again, then rocked forward, and again, faster, harder, claiming Finn's body with rough, pounding thrusts. Only Finn could make him feel like this, drive him to the point of desperation, but Joe loved it. He loved Finn—even if he couldn't say the words out loud.

His need spiraled higher and higher, sweat slicking his skin as much as the steam of the shower. Finn made him feel primal, and he gave himself over to the moment, until with one final thrust, he came. Ecstasy coursed over him in a bright, hot wave. Finn's fair skin was flushed, and his breathing was labored as he rocked with Joe, as if Joe's pleasure was spilling over into him.

"Yes... yes... so good, Joe...."

"Yes." Joe slowly melted against Finn's back, breathing hard, and nuzzled Finn's neck. He sighed gustily. "Give me a minute. We can wash off and I'll take you to bed and get you all messy again."

Finn braced against the wall to support Joe securely, and Joe could feel as well as hear his satisfied hum. "Take your time," he said. "I'm in no hurry."

Joe wasn't, either, and he pressed a kiss to Finn's neck, closing his eyes and reveling in Finn's beloved scent. He wasn't looking forward to this mission, to being away from Finn for who knew how long. He was in for a long dry spell, but it wasn't the sex he was going to miss most. It was Finn's presence, his unquestioning loyalty, his support and acceptance. Even if Joe couldn't speak of the love he felt, it was there, and every minute he was away from Finn was going to be torture. He wished he didn't have to go, but this was a job that he needed to do, and this time Finn couldn't accompany him.

Joe could only hope that the mission would be over quickly, so that he could come back home to the arms of the one person in the world with whom he felt complete.

2

When Finn arrived at Cade "Hercules" Thornton's office, he was greeted and waved through by Lexy, Herc's personal assistant. He wasn't sure what kind of temporary assignment Herc planned to put him on, but he was eager to find out. Joe had been gone a whole week already, and Finn was getting antsy.

Part of it was nerves. He didn't remember the last time he and Joe had gone on a mission separate from each other. Unfortunately, Joe's current mission called for a translator but not a medic, and Finn didn't speak Urdu. Joe wasn't going in alone and he was capable of holding his own, but Finn was still uneasy about Joe being *out there* without him. They'd worked so many missions together that they were practically a single, well-oiled unit at this point, and Finn didn't trust anyone else to look after Joe's back as well as he would.

The other part was that he hadn't gotten laid since Joe left. That wasn't usually a problem because they weren't in a committed relationship—more like very good friends with very good benefits—and Finn could find someone to hook up with if he wanted to. No, the problem was that he didn't feel like going to the effort to find someone. He'd scrolled through the dating app on his phone and kept swiping left until he ran out of options because he hadn't see anyone worth swiping right on.

Maybe, at the ripe old age of thirty-six, he was finally ready to stop indulging in random hookups. If he was honest, the thought of being with Joe long-term was appealing, but Joe was a white-picket-fence kind of guy. Joe even got wistful every time he saw someone with their dog, but he traveled too much, often leaving the country for weeks at a time, which he didn't think would be fair to the dog. Instead, Joe had a somber-faced black and gray Maine Coon named Ezekiel, who was content to stay with the elderly couple next door while Joe was away.

As much as Finn loved Joe—and he did—he couldn't take that last step toward commitment. He might be getting tired of hookups, but he wasn't a one-man man. No, his version of an ideal relationship involved at least two men, and he didn't think that would fit in with Joe's picket fence scenario.

Pushing all thoughts of his personal life aside, Finn knocked on Herc's door before opening it. "You wanted to see me, Herc?" he asked as he stepped inside.

"Finn! Good to see you!" Cade Thornton stood up, unfurling himself from behind his desk with surprising grace for such a large man. And Herc *was* big, taller than any of the men who worked for him except for Gabriel "Mojo" Crowe. He was also broad in the shoulders, and, despite the leg injury that had ended his career as a mercenary, Herc could do anything his men could, and better than most of them. He stepped forward to shake Finn's hand. "I hope you've enjoyed having a break because I definitely need your skills now."

"You have perfect timing," Finn said as they shook hands. "I was getting restless."

"Figured you might be." Herc gestured for Finn to take a seat, and then he leaned back against his desk. "I was tempted to send you along with Morrissey, but there is no way you could have passed for Pakistani, not with those green eyes. But it turns out to be a good thing I didn't. Do you remember Joker, Blaze's XO in Bravo Company?"

The handle sounded familiar, but Finn couldn't call up a face to go with it.

"I remember hearing about him," he said, wishing he hadn't sat down so he wouldn't have to tilt his head so far to look up at Herc. "Why?"

Herc seemed to notice Finn's discomfort, and he chuckled before moving back behind his desk and sinking down into his comfortable chair. "Joker's an old salt at L&G, but age and wear and tear finally caught up on him. He mustered out. He's nursing a shoulder injury from his last deployment, and I guess it comes as no surprise that us guys well over forty don't heal as fast as we used to. I've agreed to take him on to see how he likes the security business, so I'd like you to see to his training. And also make sure he gets physical therapy for his injury. He doesn't always like to do what he's told, if you know what I mean."

"Not a problem," Finn said, unable to hold back an eager grin. This mission might not land him in the middle of a war zone with lives on the line, but it would get him out of the house and using his skills. "I've had plenty of practice dealing with ornery mercs."

Herc laughed outright at that. "I'll say. I remember how you've handled D-Day's bluster. Hopefully Joker won't be that bad!"

"No one could possibly be as bad as D-Day," Finn said, letting out a little snort.

"Yeah, but he's worth it. Usually." Herc shook his head, looking amused. "Shall we go meet your new partner? Or would you rather introduce yourself?"

A little flare of alarm shot through Finn, and he regarded Herc with growing concern. "Temporary partner, right?"

Herc raised a brow. "I was only thinking in the short term. What, are you worried I'm taking Morrissey away from you forever?"

Finn released a long, slow sigh of relief. "It's just the way you worded it—'new partner'—I wanted to make sure I understood what you meant."

A teasing gleam appeared in Herc's eyes. "Sorry, I wasn't trying to give you a heart attack, Finn. Okay, your new, temporary partner. How's that? Though I recall that Joker is quite the player, if you know what I mean. You two will make a very interesting pair, for however long it lasts."

Finn's face grew hot, and he knew his fair skin was betraying him with a blush. "We'll see what happens," he said. Given his attitude about men other than Joe lately, he wasn't going to approach this new partnership with any assumptions about what may or may not happen.

"All right." Herc stood up once more and moved to the door of his office. "Let's get started. I figure you can take a couple of days to introduce him around, assess his condition, get him familiar with the facilities here and in Richmond. When you think he's ready, I can give you a cupcake assignment to break him in. Like most of the guys coming out of the field, he's going to have an adjustment to the slower pace of the job."

Finn rose to his feet and followed Herc to the door. "Sounds good," he said. "If he gives me too much trouble, I'll call for backup and let Pita work him over with those big baby blues."

Herc chuckled. "Funny you should mention Pita," he said cryptically. He led Finn past Lexy and then on toward the big gym that took up a significant amount of the Hercules Security facility. As they stepped into the spacious room, which was occupied by many of the off-duty bodyguards, Finn caught sight of Payne Gibson, AKA Pita, which was short for *pain in the ass*. Although Pita was much smaller than most of his coworkers—including his big husband, Hunter, who trailed along in his wake—Finn had heard Hunter comment that 'kinetic energy increases mass' as an explanation for why Payne was actually much bigger than he looked. At the moment, Payne was chattering away a mile a minute as he hauled a tall, rangy, older-looking man with sandy hair around, introducing him to the gym's occupants.

"And this is Mojo. He's from Oklahoma, and he's even taller than Herc," Payne said, delivering the introductions at lightning speed.

"His spotter here is Dead-eye, our best sniper. You might have heard about how he saved Geo and his clients by taking out the guys chasing them from the top of a hotel in Kyrzbekistan. Over there is Tailor. He's a medic, and we call him 'Tailor' because he threatened to sew D-Day's mouth shut once."

Finn's mouth went dry as he took in the sight of the newcomer. Why did the guy have to have a beard? A neatly trimmed beard was one of Finn's biggest weaknesses. Before he could speak or move, however, Payne spotted him and Herc and led Joker over to them.

"There you are! I was showing Joker around like you asked," he said cheerfully.

"So I see," Herc replied drily, but his lips twitched. "If I can get a word in edgewise, I'd like to introduce Joker to Finn. Joker, this is Brian Finnegan. He's going to be overseeing your training and PT."

Joker looked at Finn, and there was no missing the gleam of interest in his blue eyes. He held out a hand. "Finn, is it?" he said, his voice deep with a distinct Texas drawl. He smiled, showing even, white teeth. "Pleased to meet you. I appreciate you agreeing to take me on."

Oh, shit.

That slow, deep voice curled Finn's toes, and when he slid his hand into Joker's, the sparks nearly seared his palm.

"Hi." His voice cracked a bit. He cleared his throat and tried again. "It's nice to meet you, too."

Joker didn't release Finn's hand. Instead, his grip tightened slightly, and he put his free hand on Finn's wrist, as though he, too, had felt the tingle. "My off-duty name is Drew, by the way. Drew Martin."

"Do you prefer Drew or Joker?" Finn gazed into Joker's sky blue eyes, feeling as if he could drown in them, and he didn't bother trying to tug his hand free. "I'm pretty much always Finn. No one calls me Brian, except my parents."

"Well, you can call me anything you'd like," Joker replied. "So long as you call."

Hunter Callahan snorted and shook his head. "You haven't

changed a bit, Joker. Just be aware that more than a few of the mercs around here are taken, and these guys could kick your ancient ass for poaching." He dropped an arm around Payne's shoulders. "Of course, I wouldn't have to kick your ass. Payne is quite capable of doing it all on his own."

"And you would know," Payne said with a wicked grin as he slid his arm around Hunter's waist.

"He's got you there," Herc said. "Okay, boys, let's leave these two to get acquainted, shall we? Pita, I wanted to talk to you about the martial arts program the Richmond police asked us to consult on. Joker... you're in good hands."

With that, Herc led Payne and Hunter back toward his office. Finn watched them go, a little disconcerted about being left on his own so soon, but he was a grown man, and he could handle training the new guy.

The tall, sexy, bearded, exactly-his-type new guy.

"So, uh... did Pita show you everything, or do we need to pick up where he left off?" Finn asked. "Or did you have any questions you didn't get to ask because he was talking a mile a minute?"

"Oh, I have all kinds of questions," Joker said. He brushed his thumb along the back of Finn's hand. "But none of them are about this place. Hunter gave me a pretty thorough briefing on the drive down from Richmond. What do you say we play hooky? We could go get something to eat, maybe get better acquainted? D-Day bragged that Raleigh has better barbecue than Texas, and I don't believe it for a minute."

The simple caress sent a shiver all the way down to Finn's toes, and while he knew he ought to remain professional, he also wanted to give in to Joker's temptation. He knew where this would lead. They'd eat, they'd talk, the flirting would get hotter and heavier, and they'd end the evening in either his bed or Joker's. For the first time in a week, Finn found the thought appealing.

"Sure," he said, giving Joker's fingers a little squeeze. "I know a good place that's not too far away."

"Perfect." Joker's smile was as slow as warm honey and just as hard to resist. "I'll follow your lead, Finn. Anywhere you want to go."

Well. *That* certainly wasn't a loaded statement rife with innuendo.

"How hungry are you?"

Oh God, now he was doing it too!

Joker's eyes grew darker, and he lowered his voice. "Starving. I've been in the field for almost two years, and even if L&G wasn't as strict as the military, my opportunities for a good meal were few and far between."

"You poor deprived man." Finn moved into Joker's personal space until he could feel the heat radiating from his body. "Maybe we should skip dinner and go straight to dessert."

"Well, my mama always did say to seize the day." Joker gave a wicked grin. "At the risk of being too forward, can I suggest your place? I haven't even checked into a hotel yet."

Under normal circumstances, Finn wouldn't have taken a hookup back to his apartment, viewing it as a potential security risk to allow a stranger access to his home. Joker wasn't a security risk unless he'd somehow fooled everyone at Lawson & Greer, Herc, and wherever he'd served before all that.

"Sure, let's go. Want me to drive, or do you want to take separate vehicles?"

"I came with Hunter and Pita," Joker replied. "So I'm all yours."

"Not yet," Finn said with a playful wink as he headed to the elevator so they could go down to the parking garage. "But you will be."

Joker chuckled as he followed along in Finn's wake. When the elevator arrived, he stepped in behind Finn, and as the door closed, Finn found himself pushed up against the wall, with Joker's lean, hard body pressing against him. Joker gave a soft groan. "God, you feel so good."

Finn tipped his head back slightly so he could see Joker's face, and he slid his arms around Joker's lean waist. "If it matters, we've got eyes on us right now."

"I don't care if you don't," Joker murmured. He paused, apparently checking to see if Finn would object, and when nothing was forthcoming, he leaned in and captured Finn's lips, kissing him firmly but with a hint of a question.

Finn parted his lips and slid his hands down to Joker's ass as he returned the kiss. Exhibitionism wasn't one of his kinks, but he didn't care about the security cameras, either. He doubted they were the first two people to make out in the elevator. Hell, if Herc and his husband Jude hadn't done a lot more than make out all over the building, he'd be shocked.

Apparently Finn had answered Joker's question satisfactorily because Joker deepened the kiss, exploring Finn's mouth hungrily. He seemed absorbed in finding out how Finn liked to be kissed, so much so that he didn't stop when the elevator chimed its arrival at the parking level.

"Well, damn," a voice interrupted them. "Don't y'all know this don't count as a room?"

Finn drew back and shot an annoyed glare at Daryl "D-Day" Greer. "Haven't you ever heard of priming the pump?"

"From the look of Joker, here, if you do any more priming, you'll have a blowout before you get home." D-Day's smile was positively evil. "Pace yourself, dude."

Joker snorted. "I knew about sex before you were born, pipsqueak," he said, but he pulled back. "We were just on our way to that room you mentioned." He glanced down at Finn. "Are you ready?"

"You bet I am." Finn gave Joker's ass one last grope before he exited the elevator and headed to his SUV.

All thoughts about chatting to pass the time during the drive fled once Joker started living up to his handle by teasing Finn mercilessly. Joker fondled Finn's knee and stroked and squeezed his thigh while stopping just short of touching Finn's cock. Finn squirmed in his seat and tried to hold back moans—and to avoid getting in a wreck. Somehow they made it to his apartment in one piece, and he practically dragged Joker up to the tenth floor.

Once they were inside with the door closed and locked behind them, Finn curled his fingers in the fabric of Joker's shirt and tugged him close. His place was a wreck as usual with empty pizza boxes on the coffee table and several days' worth of dishes stacked in the sink. He'd thought about hiring someone to come in and clean once a week, and Joe had dropped "subtle" hints about it often enough, but he'd never gotten around to setting anything up.

"I've got condoms and lube in the bedroom," he said. "I've got a few toys, too, if you're into that kind of thing. Conveniently enough, I'm such a slob that the bed is already unmade."

Joker chuckled, his eyes gleaming with desire. "Toys might be for round two. I'm wound up enough that round one might be over awfully quick. Maybe even too quick for the bedroom, if you don't hurry that perky little ass up and show me where it is."

"Right this way." Finn clasped Joker's hand and led him down the hall.

The bedroom door was standing open, revealing Finn's untidy bed and the clothes littering the floor. Finn went straight to the nightstand and yanked open the drawer, and he rummaged around until he found the open box of condoms and bottle of lube he kept stashed there. He held up both and waggled them enticingly.

"At Hercules Security, we're like the Boy Scouts," he said with a playful leer. "We believe in always being prepared."

"It makes a fellow proud to be a soldier," Joker said with a chuckle. He stalked toward Finn, his gait predatory, his hunger clear to see. "I already know you taste as good as you look, but I see a package that needs unwrapping."

Finn put the condoms and lube aside and struck a pose with his hands on his hips. "Well, I guess you'd better get to it," he said, watching Joker with a challenging stare.

"Mouthy, aren't you?" Joker asked. He stepped into Finn's space, his hands going to the hem of Finn's black T-shirt. "I'm used to mercs pushing back. I know just how to handle ones like you."

A smile tugged at the corners of Finn's mouth even though he was trying to look tough and defiant. "How's that?" he asked with a proud lift of his chin.

"Oh, that's easy."

Joker tugged at Finn's shirt, pulling it half up, then, in a lightning fast move, he spun Finn around. Wrapping Finn's arms in the shirt, he pushed at Finn's shoulders, forcing him to bend at the waist. Snugging his hips up against Finn's ass, Joker teased him with slow rolls of his hips. "Like that."

Finn moaned and pushed his ass back, loving the feel of Joker grinding against him. He was familiar with this trick—he'd used it himself a time or two—and he didn't bother fighting against his restraints. He liked them too much for that.

"Oh, you enjoy that, don't you? Why am I not surprised you like it rough?" Joker tugged at the T-shirt, tightening it as he tied a knot in the fabric. Joker reached around Finn's waist, quickly unfastening and unzipping his camouflage pants. It took only a moment for Joker to pull down Finn's pants and his boxer briefs, letting the fabric pool around Finn's boots, leaving him bare-assed. Then a hard swat landed against one firm cheek. "How about that, Finn? Do you like that, too?"

Finn let out a startled yelp, and a hot flush washed over his body in the wake of the pleasurable sting. "Yes! I like it! I want more!"

Joker laughed, landing a blow on the other cheek before scraping his nails over Finn's sensitized skin. "Such a pretty ass. Even prettier with my hand print on it. Your skin pinks up so beautifully."

Finn's answering moan was low and throaty, and he pushed his ass up as much as he could. "Oh yeah," he said, peeking over his shoulder at Joker and giving him a mischievous smile. "My skin will show your marks so well."

"Mmm." Joker ran his warm hand up Finn's spine. "I see a few other marks, too. You're a busy boy, Mr. Finnegan. But I'm here now, so you'll only think of me, right?"

Memories of Joe rose up in Finn's mind—specifically memories of how he'd gotten those fading marks in the first place. During their last night together, he'd asked Joe to bite and scratch him hard enough that the evidence would last a few days. He'd wanted to see and feel Joe's marks on his body as a reminder for as long as possible.

But Joe wasn't here. Joker was. Finn was happy to lose himself in the moment.

"Right," he said, his voice low and throaty with need. "Right now, I'm thinking only about you."

"Good." Joker scraped his nails down Finn's back. "Now, let's see, where were we? Oh yes. Your pretty ass." Joker swatted Finn again, once on each side and then soothed the sting with gentle strokes. Finn felt him lean to one side and heard the snap of the bottle of lube being opened. "I warned you this might be quick. I'd better get you ready before I get so wound up I end up humping you like a horny sixteen-year-old."

"I don't need a whole lot of prep," Finn said, thinking about all the nights he'd fucked himself with a dildo, pretending it was Joe. Besides, his entire body ached with the need to be taken and filled, and he wanted Joker in him *now*. "Just hurry up and fuck me senseless."

Joker groaned, thrusting his hips hard against Finn's ass. "You're going to drive me out of my mind," he panted. After a moment, he took a half step back, and then Finn felt hot, slick fingers pressing against his entrance. After a teasing circle, Joker slid them inside. "You seem as eager as I am."

"There's no *seeming* about it," Finn said, and he let out a deep groan at the feel of Joker's fingers sliding deep, and he rocked back, trying to push them in even further. Joker obliged by turning his hand and curving his fingers a bit as he sought Finn's sweet spot. Finn cried out when Joker found it, the electric jolts of pleasure sizzling along every nerve until his body was taut and quivering with need. "Please," he groaned, rocking more in a vain attempt to relieve the aching tension building up. "Please...."

Joker removed his fingers, leaving Finn empty. Finn couldn't see what Joker was doing, but he heard the condom packet being ripped open and a zipper being lowered. Maybe Joker had some special ability with condoms, or maybe he was as desperate as he claimed, because it seemed like only a moment before Joker was entering him, his hard, thick cock stretching Finn and filling him with heat.

"Yes!" Finn threw his head back and clenched his fingers in the fabric of his shirt, his skin growing hot and dappled with sweat as his arousal built nearly to the breaking point. "Do it! Fuck me—hard as you want. I need it!"

"So do I!" Joker gasped and then pulled almost the whole way out before surging forward again, his movement hard enough to almost knock Finn flat onto the mattress. Joker gripped one of Finn's hips and began to fuck him, hard and deep, pounding Finn just as Finn had begged him to do.

The rough fucking felt so good—*so right*—that Finn willingly let go of rational thought and gave himself over to the pleasure, his pleas for more devolving into incoherent moans and cries. Joker was giving him exactly what he needed, and he wanted more. Joker wrapped his hand around Finn's cock and began to stroke him. Joker bent partway over Finn's body without losing his rhythm, and then he bit down near the base of Finn's shoulder.

That bite was all Finn needed to send him over the edge, and he let out a wordless cry as he came hard, bucking against Joker's hand. Finn's pleasure was Joker's undoing, because he surged deep one last time, his own cry echoing Finn's. As the waves of pleasure ebbed, Finn collapsed on the bed, panting but blissfully sated.

"Mmm...." He wanted to say more and express how much he'd enjoyed such a fast and furious romp, but his brain was still jelly, and he didn't feel up to forming complete words yet.

He heard footsteps receding, a brief pause, and then approaching again. Strong, gentle hands turned him over, and a warm, damp cloth glided over his skin, cleaning him up. Next, his boots were removed, his pants and underwear stripped away, and at last the shirt binding his arms was loosened. Finally he was nudged upward toward the pillows before a warm, naked body slid into the bed beside him, and he found himself pulled against Joker's side.

"You still owe me that barbecue," Joker murmured, his lips close to Finn's ear. "I may be fast, but I'm not cheap."

With a drowsy chuckle, Finn rolled onto his side, pillowed his head on Joker's shoulder, and flung one arm across Joker's waist. "After that, I'll get you some barbecue, sides, *and* a sweet tea."

"Well, it's good to know I earned it," Joker said. "Rest first. Then dinner. And I think we need to have a little talk."

"About what?" Finn asked, nuzzling his cheek against the warm curve of Joker's shoulder.

"Later." Joker yawned, pulling Finn even closer against him. "You've worn this old man out."

Nestling against Joker's lanky body was different from cuddling up to Joe, who was broader if not taller, but Finn liked it. Something about Joker felt right. He'd never felt this comfortable and relaxed with anyone other than Joe before, especially not with someone he'd just met. He wasn't sure why he felt this way, or what it meant, but for now, he was content to rest in Joker's arms and enjoy the moment.

3

It was long past the regular dinner hour when Drew finally confessed he couldn't go another round without "fueling the furnace," and to his relief, Finn agreed. They'd spent hours in bed after the nap following their first, almost frenzied coupling, taking things slower and learning each other's wants and needs. Drew felt he knew more about Finn's body in one afternoon than he did about any lover he'd had in the last ten years. Not that he was going to complain.

Neither of them felt like going out, so Finn suggested they order in. After seeing the number of pizza boxes littering Finn's apartment, Drew wasn't at all surprised that Finn also had a drawer full of menus, and after a brief consultation, Finn had ordered fried chicken, mashed potatoes, green beans, and banana pudding from a local mom-and-pop place. The food was delivered quickly, and soon they were seated on Finn's comfortable sofa, holding loaded plates, with big glasses of sweet tea in front of them on the coffee table.

Drew didn't hesitate to dig in, closing his eyes in bliss as the hot, crispy crust of the chicken almost melted on his tongue. He chewed, swallowed, and then sighed happily. "So good," he said, giving Finn a little bump with his shoulder. "Pita's a damned good cook, but this is like sex on a plate."

Finn chuckled and nudged Drew in return. "You really *have* been deprived for a long time."

"Oh, come on," Drew said, leering at Finn playfully. "You've been deployed before, right? So you know how it is. Field food is still field food. No matter what you try to do to it, it's never home cooking. And I already admitted I've been deprived of sex. Woefully deprived, as if you couldn't tell."

Finn laughed as he leaned forward and rubbed his ass with exaggerated care. "I probably won't be able to walk right tomorrow. Not that I'm complaining."

That seemed like a good lead in for Drew to bring up something he'd been wondering about, ever since he'd walked into Finn's bathroom after their first round. "So, am I going to have to worry that someone will take exception to your sore ass?" He gave Finn a sideways glance. "I couldn't help but notice that you aren't the only one using that bathroom."

"Oh, that's Joe's stuff," Finn said as he dug into his mashed potatoes and gravy. "Joe Morrissey. He keeps some necessities here, and I keep some at his place. You don't have anything to worry about, though."

Somehow that answered Drew's question without answering it at all. "Is he your ex? Or just a friend?"

Finn poked the mashed potatoes with his fork for a few moments before setting his plate on the coffee table. "Technically, we're friends with benefits," he said, shifting to sit facing Drew.

Drew let out a breath he hadn't realized he'd been holding. "Okay. I just wanted to make sure I wasn't poaching on someone else's territory. Especially another merc. It's a way to get real dead, real fast."

Finn laughed again, but it was quieter and less natural sounding than before. "You're not poaching. Joe and I have an understanding. When he gets back, I'll tell him what happened. I always tell him when I hook up with someone else, I always use condoms, and I get tested regularly."

Drew could tell there was something bothering Finn, yet he didn't know him nearly well enough to guess what it was. Years of experience had taught him it was best just to ask and get things out in the open. It was a practice that had served him well as XO of a company of deadly killers, and he figured Finn was cut from the same material as the men Drew had led.

"But something is bothering you," he said quietly. "Do you want to talk about it?"

Finn clasped his hands in his lap and tightened his fingers until the knuckles turned white. He blew out a sharp breath. "I probably shouldn't tell you any of this. We just met, and I'm supposed to train you."

Drew shrugged. "I think we threw the normal *professional* boundaries out the window the minute I was buried balls deep in your ass, don't you? You don't have to talk to me about it, if you aren't comfortable, but you probably should talk to someone. You weren't concerned before we had sex, but something is eating at you now."

"Do you want a drink? I want a drink." Finn shot to his feet and hurried over to a small bar. He retrieved a bottle of top-shelf bourbon and poured himself two fingers. He downed that in one shot and poured himself some more before holding up the bottle and giving Drew a questioning look.

"Nah, thanks," Drew waved a hand. "I just spent the last couple of years dry. I probably can't hold it as well as I'd like."

Finn returned to the couch and set the bottle on the coffee table before sitting down again, keeping a little distance between himself and Drew this time. "Before we had sex, I thought this would be another hookup. One and done, you know?" He took a sip of bourbon and then released a quiet sigh. "I didn't expect us to click so well. That hasn't happened since.... Well, since Joe."

The little thrill Drew felt at Finn's admission was offset by the fact that Finn was obviously not jumping for joy about their chemistry. He was quiet for a moment, gathering his thoughts. He didn't want to add to Finn's turmoil, but he wasn't about to lie, either. With a sigh he put his plate down next to Finn's, steeling himself for what might be a difficult conversation.

"I haven't clicked with anyone like this either, not in years," he admitted. "It sounds to me like Joe is your anchor, right? You tomcat around, but you always go home to him in the end. Is that a fair assessment?"

"Fair and accurate." Finn tossed back the rest of his bourbon and put the glass aside. "The truth is... I love Joe. But we want fundamentally different things. He'd be perfectly happy with getting married, adopting a dog and maybe some kids, and living the white-picket-fence scenario. I've known for years that I'm not cut out for monogamy, so I pretend my feelings don't run that deep and keep our friends-with-benefits situation going until he meets someone who can give him everything he wants."

Drew contemplated Finn's revelations, but it was hard to give any advice when he had never met this Joe, and had no idea what kind of man he was outside of Finn's description. "Look, maybe it's none of my business, but I admit, I don't want whatever this is between us to be a one-and-done. But, I can tell you're pretty hung up on this guy, even if you think you want different things out of life. Are you sure that's what he really wants? And does he want that with you?"

"I don't know." Finn shrugged. "I didn't want to mess up what we have, so I haven't asked."

"Am I correct in assuming, though, that you want to see what could happen between us?" Drew reached out and touched Finn's shoulder. "I'm interested, but if this is going to eat you up, it's better just to let it go. You're a hot guy. You could go back to the way things were and just forget me."

"I don't want to let it go, and I don't want to forget you." Finn rested his hand against Drew's cheek and stroked it with his thumb. "I love Joe, but no one else has made me feel the way you do in years, and I don't want to walk away from that."

"Okay, what *do* you want?" Drew leaned into the touch. It had been so long since he'd felt the kind of desire he did for Finn, and he knew he was taking a risk. Hell, they both were, because who knew if things would burn out in a week or a month, and maybe in that time Finn would have wrecked a relationship that was important to him in a way that was more than just physical.

Finn searched Drew's face and then leaned in and brushed his lips against Drew's. "I want to see where this takes us," he murmured.

Drew closed his eyes, kissing Finn back, but after a moment he pulled away. "All right. So... what about your Joe? Have you ever brought a boyfriend home to daddy before?"

Finn shook his head. "Like I said, I tell him any time I hook up with someone else, but it's never lasted longer than a weekend at most. He knows I don't want to be monogamous, but he's never had to deal with a situation like this. I don't know how he'll react."

Drew smiled crookedly. "When does he get back? Maybe we'll spend that whole time in bed, get it out of our systems, and decide we're better as friends. Or maybe you'll find someone younger and hotter than me, and decide I was an aberration. We'll never know unless we try, right? Maybe Joe doesn't have anything to worry about, anyway."

"He should be back in another two weeks, three at most." Finn slid his hand around to cradle the back of Drew's head in his palm. "You're right. This may be a spark that burns itself out, but in the meantime, I want to fan the hell out of the flames," he said, sliding his fingers through Drew's short, light brown hair.

"I like that plan." Drew slid closer, pulling Finn into his arms. "I've had enough to eat. Now I'm hungry for dessert. And I know just what I want to devour."

Finn shifted to straddle Drew's lap and snugged his hips against Drew's. "Banana pudding?" he asked, widening his eyes with faux innocence as he rocked his hips.

"Only if I get to lick it off you," Drew replied. He reached up with both hands, framing Finn's face. "You're sweet enough without embellishment. And I'm starving for the taste of you."

With a soft moan, Finn swooped in to capture Drew's lips in a deep, hungry kiss as if he, too, hungered for something only Drew could provide.

Drew parted his lips and let the taste and heat of Finn flow over him. Maybe it had just been too long since he'd had a lover, and Finn was like every fantasy he'd had in the last two years come to life. But something was whispering to him that they could have something more. Something special, something that could last. As a man who'd lived by his senses and instincts, depending on them for survival, Drew wanted to trust his gut, but he knew he wasn't the one who would make the decision. Finn was the one with something to lose, and in the end, it might come down to whether Finn could possibly need Drew as much as he needed Joe.

Drew had no idea what Joe was like, but he had the feeling he was going to find out. He just hoped that one of them didn't end up heart-broken in the process.

4

Finn didn't expect that Drew would need much training, more like an introductory course on how working for Hercules Security differed from working for Lawson & Greer. The biggest difference, of course, was that most missions wouldn't take Drew into an active warzone, although there were always exceptions.

For example, the first mission involving their current client, Senator Ellen Paxton. Geo Kensei had been one of the Hercules Security reps assigned as her bodyguard back when she was a Congresswoman. Geo had accompanied her for what should have been a routine diplomatic visit, but civil war broke out in the host country and derailed the whole thing. Geo's partner had been killed, but Geo had gotten the senator out safely, and now she worked exclusively with Hercules Security for personal protection. In fact, Herc had picked up a fair bit of new business thanks to her recommendations.

Finn and Drew had been sent to DC to serve as her temporary bodyguards while her regulars took leave. It was an easy gig, one that would introduce Drew to what to expect during a typical security detail without much risk of anything going south.

Senator Paxton lived just over the Maryland state line. Her home was located in an upscale neighborhood attached to a small town that catered to the politicians who wanted a more quiet and remote place to settle down away from DC. Finn and Drew hadn't seen much of the area. They were pulling the night shift, which was considered the easy detail, so their view consisted of the grounds of the Paxtons' McMansion and the interior of the three-car garage from their surveillance van.

About the most exciting thing that had happened so far was the night a possum meandered onto the Paxtons' lawn, and Finn and Drew had spent a good fifteen minutes watching it and placing bets on which way it would go. But Ellen Paxton was a model client—she treated her mercs with respect—and Finn thought Drew needed an introduction to the tedium that was bodyguard work, anyway.

"Think we'll see that possum tonight?" Finn swiveled away from the monitors long enough to wink at Drew.

Drew smiled, slow and hot. "Want to make a bet about it? Winner gets to pick what we do when we get back to the hotel."

Finn leered at Drew in return. "You're on," he said, feeling a familiar ember of arousal kindling in his belly.

Any thought that they might fuck it out of their systems in a matter of days was long gone. If anything, Finn wanted Drew even more now that they had developed a familiarity with each other's likes and dislikes. No one since Joe had sparked and sustained such potent chemistry with him, and he was enjoying every minute.

"I say no," he added. "I'm willing to bet someone called an exterminator or animal control on Mr. Possum by now. I can't see folks in an area like this tolerating something as pedestrian as a possum on their property."

"Now, now, do I hear a bit of judgement in your tone, Mr. Finnegan?" Drew asked. "For shame. One of the fine people in this development could be one of D-Day's cousins. Maybe they trapped and ate Mr. Possum. Or rescued him from the dangers of a suburban lifestyle. But I'll say yeah, we'll see him. They're crafty critters, you know, and I suspect the fruit trees around here are particularly tasty, what with everyone having gardeners."

"It's a bet." Finn held out his hand and gave Drew a challenging look.

"I better get to scanning, hadn't I?" Packed as it was with electronics, the interior of the van was pretty confined. As Drew slid his hand into Finn's, he suddenly tightened his grip, pulling Finn half out of his seat. Drew leaned forward at the same time and pressed his lips against Finn's in a hard kiss.

As much as Finn wanted to part his lips and surrender, maybe even straddle Drew's lap, he couldn't. They were still on the clock, so he tried to satisfy himself with a little taste to tide him over until their shift ended.

"I reckon you better," he said, sounding breathless as he pulled back.

Drew gave Finn's hand a final squeeze and released it. "I want to win, and I have just the forfeit I want in mind, too," he said, his blue eyes gleaming. "But I'm not going to tell you what it is. You'll just have to hope I win."

"I think we'll both win whether the possum shows up or not."

Finn had never been less interested in staring at monitors, but he was a professional with a job to do, and so he focused on the video feed from the front of the house and the street view, while Drew monitored the back and sides of the house.

Time slowed to a crawl, though they kept each other awake by talking about the movies Drew wanted to see now that he had the chance to catch up on the things he'd missed while in the field. At just around two o'clock in the morning, Drew sucked in a startled breath.

"Finn... there's movement at the back, and it isn't Mr. Possum. I think we have an intruder creeping along at the property line, moving low and slow."

Finn tensed as he swiveled around and checked the monitor. Drew was right. "Call it in," he ordered, a surge of adrenaline bringing him fully alert at once. He drew his gun as he stood. "I'll check it out, see if the guy runs when he realizes he's been seen."

"On it." Drew's voice was as crisp and professional as anyone Finn had ever worked with, and Finn knew Drew had been in far more intense situations than this. He quietly opened the sliding door and stepped out into the garage.

There was a door at the rear of the big room that led out into the backyard, and he awarded Drew points when the door's alarm was silently disarmed as Finn approached, a light beside it blinking from red to green. He opened the door and nodded, knowing Drew would catch it on the monitors, before he slipped out into the dark, quiet night.

The Paxtons' yard was larger than most of the others in the neighborhood, but like them it was bordered by a high privacy wall and meticulously landscaped. The intruder had to have come over the wall where it abutted a neighbor's yard. It was possible the person was just some teenager sneaking out of their girlfriend's or boyfriend's house, but Finn had to treat the situation as one with deadly intent. The lives of the senator and her family depended on Finn's judgement.

Having trained with a former Mossad agent in stealth, Finn knew how to move across grass in virtual silence. He doubted the intruder had any night vision equipment, but he couldn't bet on it, so he kept as many of the bushes and trees between himself and his quarry as possible while he moved up behind. Whoever he was pursuing wasn't anywhere in Finn's league when it came to stalking, and Finn heard the man curse quietly as he stumbled over something.

Now that Finn's eyes had adapted, he caught the movement of the intruder no more than ten feet in front of him. He crossed the distance in three long strides and pressed his gun against the back of the man's head.

"Stop where you are and surrender, or I'll shoot," he said.

The intruder let out a startled breath and started to turn. Despite his warning, Finn didn't want to blow away some kid, but he couldn't take a chance that the guy was about to attack, either. So he flipped the safety and turned his hand, smacking the butt of his gun against the intruder's head.

As Finn had intended, the guy dropped like a rock, knocked out cold. He was just starting to bend over to check his quarry when he felt something small and cold pressed against the back of his own skull. Somehow someone had gotten the drop on him, and now the tables were turned.

"That wasn't very nice," a harsh voice said close to Finn's ear. "Knocking my partner out like that. I guess I should return the favor before I pay a little visit to the senator."

Finn froze in place, not wanting to piss the guy off and possibly take a bullet to the head. He was still trying to come up with a plan of action when the pressure of the gun was removed, and he heard a grunt and angry muttering behind him. He whirled to find that someone had yanked the intruder away and had the guy in a sleeper hold.

"He dropped his gun," Drew said, appearing untroubled by the struggles of his captive, which became weaker as the man was deprived of oxygen. "You okay?"

"I'm fine," Finn said, awash in relief. Drew had his back. Just like Joe would have. "Thanks."

"Anytime, partner." The man he was holding sank to his knees, and Finn saw a flash of white teeth as Drew grinned. "Saw this asshole come over the wall just as you passed by. Figured that it was safer to sneak up behind him than get you trapped between two opponents. Check and make sure there isn't a third, okay?"

"On it."

Finn searched the grounds for any other intruders while Drew secured the ones they'd found, but if those two had any backup, they'd done the smart thing and bailed. He finished his investigation about the time their own backup arrived, and he returned to the van to give his report.

Drew joined him a few minutes later. "The police are here. We'll have to give statements." He smiled at Finn, but there was worry in his eyes. "You were as cool as a cucumber when that guy got the drop on you. Nice job. Some guys just can't keep their heads in a situation like that, and it usually gets them killed. You okay?"

"I'm *fine*." Finn was amused but also touched by Drew's concern. "I've been in worse situations."

"Yeah, I know. You were on that nuke adventure with D-Day," Drew replied. He stepped closer, reaching out a hand to brush his fingers over Finn's cheek. "Just wanted to be sure, okay? It matters to me."

Finn's heart softened, and when it reformed, he realized part of it had given itself over to Drew's keeping. He leaned into the touch and offered a smile full of the new warmth and affection he felt. "Thanks. I do appreciate it."

"Sure."

Drew said the word softly. With a sigh he closed his eyes and leaned in to claim Finn's lips. The kiss was gentle, yet somehow full of promise. Finn rested his hands at Drew's waist, lingering over the moment of connection.

There was a sound from outside the van, and Drew released Finn, stepping back with a crooked smile. "I guess we'd better talk to the police. Once we do, we're off the clock according to Herc."

"Let's get it over with." Finn moved away, but he paused long enough to smirk over his shoulder at Drew. "Maybe once we're off the clock, I'll let you perform a hands-on examination, so you can make sure I'm okay."

Drew chuckled. "Let me? I was going to insist. It's only wise to be checked out after a physical confrontation. You're a medical man. I'm sure you know that."

"Oh, of course." Finn chuckled as he went to join the police officers, more than ready to give his statement and finish up all the paperwork so he could go home with Drew and receive the most enjoyable *physical exam* of his life.

By the time Joe stumbled off the plane at Raleigh-Durham International airport and into the car sent for him by Hercules Security, he'd been on the move for over forty-eight hours straight. He'd done worse trips in his life, but it had been a few years since he'd had anything quite as bad as the past month. Infiltrating a segment of the sex-trafficking ring that had become one of Cade Thornton's personal missions had been difficult, but it was worth it to see the scumbags who dealt in the misery of women and children brought to justice. But however good Joe felt about what he'd helped accomplish, he felt dirty. Contact with such human filth was terrible, and he couldn't wait to have a hot shower and see Finn. There had been times when the thought of coming back to Finn's arms had been the only thing that kept him going.

"Here you go, Morrissey." The driver of the big sedan was a young merc called Steel, and he looked at Joe with something akin to reverence, no doubt because of his age and longevity in the field. Joe glanced out of the window, surprised to see that they'd already arrived at his house on the outskirts of the city. "Do you need any help with your bags?"

"Nah, thanks. I've got it." Joe unfurled himself from the back of the sedan, grabbing up the small travel bag that was all he'd brought back. It held only two things of real value, both of them gifts for Finn. "Thanks for the ride."

"Any time!" Steel smiled warmly, a gleam in his dark eyes. "If you ever need a lift, I'm always available."

Joe smiled back and waved Steel off without saying anything else. It was only when he was halfway up the walk that he realized Steel had probably been hinting at something beyond just transportation from the airport. He shrugged it off. The young merc was good looking, but Joe considered himself taken. Permanently.

His house was dark, and he wondered if Finn was still out on assignment. He hadn't been able to keep in regular contact with Finn, but he'd gotten one message that Finn was training someone and had gone to DC. It was a disappointment, but Finn had his job to do, the same way Joe did—and Finn wasn't the hearth-and-home type anyway.

The front door had an electronic lock, which opened to Joe's code. The house alarm started beeping, and Joe moved to the wall, disarming it. He wished he'd called his neighbors and asked them to drop Ezekiel back off, so there would have been someone there to greet him. It was rather depressing to come home to a cold, empty house after so long an absence.

He climbed the stairs and walked down the hall to his bedroom. The door was open, and when he stepped inside he suddenly stopped short, arrested by the sight of Finn stretched out on his king-sized bed. Finn wore only a pair of gray sweatpants that left the rest of his sleek, toned body on display. He had a book in front of him, and Joe didn't miss the fact that there were condoms and lube placed at the ready on the nightstand.

"You're the best sight I've seen in my life," he said softly. "God, I missed you."

Finn's face lit up, and he tossed his book aside. He bounded off the bed and over to Joe like an eager puppy, and he flung his arms around Joe's shoulders. "I've missed you, too. Are you okay? Every-thing still in good working order?"

Joe wrapped his arms around Finn's waist, pulling him close so that he could bury his face against the side of Finn's neck. He breathed in deeply, immersing himself in Finn's beloved scent. "Yeah, 'm okay," he murmured, pressing his lips against Finn's warm skin. He pushed his hips forward, letting Finn feel his growing arousal. "I hope things still work. Not that I had a chance to use them." Or would have if even if he'd had the opportunity—not that he'd say that to Finn.

"Let me take care of you." Finn's breath was warm against Joe's ear. "Whatever you want. I picked up a couple of steaks. I can fire up the grill while you relax, or I can scrub your back in the tub. Or, if you're too tired for any of that, we can take a nap and have an X-rated celebration when we wake up."

"I'm not sleepy. Or hungry." Joe lifted his head and smiled at Finn, just happy to be in his presence. "How about a bath? I can wash off the travel grime, and we can see where it goes from there."

"I thought that might be appealing, so I put a couple of towels on the warmer bar." Finn slid one hand down and patted Joe's ass before pulling away. "I've got those sandalwood candles you like in there, too. We can dim the lights and have some atmosphere going. Are you interested in any bath salts or bubbles? If you're sore anywhere, the salts might help."

Joe smiled. Finn was so thoughtful and always seemed to be taking care of him. "Sure, the salts sound good. And maybe I can talk you into giving me one of your incredible massages afterward? I think I'm starting to feel the approach of forty—sleeping on planes isn't as easy to shrug off as it used to be."

Grinning, Finn pointed out the cinnamon massage oil waiting on the nightstand. "Way ahead of you, buddy. You're getting the royal treatment."

"Sounds great." Joe reached out to caress Finn's cheek. "You really do take good care of me. I missed that. It was cold and lonely without you."

"I missed you, too." Finn drew Joe into a warm kiss and parted his lips, inviting Joe in. Unable to resist, Joe pulled Finn close once again, kissing him deeply, exploring his mouth and reacquainting himself with Finn's taste. It seemed like a lifetime, rather than a month, since he'd felt this safe, and he held nothing back, moaning against Finn's mouth.

Finn tightened his arms around Joe as he yielded to the exploration willingly, and he pressed against Joe as if he wanted to merge their bodies.

It was tempting to just tumble Finn onto the bed and ease the growing ache of arousal, but Joe didn't want their reunion to be a fast fuck. He wanted to take time and make sure he was pleasing Finn, to indulge them both in long, leisurely lovemaking. Not that he would ever admit as much to Finn, but he wanted every time they were together to be special, because to Joe, every time truly was. Even after more than eight years, being with Finn meant the world to him, and if he could never say how much he loved Finn with words, lest it scare Finn away, at least he could do it with his hands, his body, and his mouth.

After a few long moments Joe pulled back. "Well, once I get cleaned up, I'll show you exactly how much I missed you," he said softly. He patted Finn on the ass. "So... bath?"

"As you wish." Finn's smile was sultry as he drew back, and he clasped Joe's hands and squeezed them before heading to the bathroom.

Joe watched as Finn turned, anticipating the sight of Finn's ass outlined by the fabric of the sweatpants. But as Finn's back came into view, Joe couldn't help biting down hard on his tongue to hold back a gasp.

Finn had never, ever made a secret of the fact he had other lovers. Over the years he'd had a lot of hookups, and he'd always been honest with Joe when they happened. Which was considerate and made sense, given the way STDs could spread. Finn was always scrupulous about condoms and being tested, and Joe was, too—even though he hadn't been with anyone except Finn since they'd first gotten together. But while Finn had occasionally shown up sporting a few marks here and there from rough encounters, he'd never once shown up with the array of bite and scratch marks Joe saw on his back. Either Finn had been to a really wild orgy, or he'd hooked up with someone for what looked like a hell of a lot more than a weekend fling.

While Joe had learned to simply accept that Finn only saw him as a friend with benefits and not allow himself to feel possessive or jealous over Finn's need for more than just him, the sight of those marks sent a cold chill down Joe's spine that ended up as a lump of ice in his gut. This was something different. Even though he'd been away for a month, Joe had the awful feeling that something had changed about their relationship while he was gone, but he had no idea what.

Finn glanced over his shoulder as if making certain Joe was following, but the playfulness in his expression faded, replaced by concern. "Is something wrong?" he asked as he faced Joe once more.

In all their years together, Joe had never directly lied to Finn. Not that he felt the need to confess everything he felt at any given time, but he'd never told an actual lie.

Until now.

"Of course not," he said, turning away to grab his case. "I just remembered that I got you something in Pakistan. A bowl I saw in a marketplace in Karachi. It's hand-painted and colorful, just like you like."

"Thanks, babe. I'll add it to the collection." Finn's smile returned as he watched Joe rummage around in his bag. Instead of using matching place settings, Finn bought handmade cups, bowls, and plates of various sizes and colors from the countries he visited.

Joe pulled out a blue silk bag and handed it to Finn. He'd been so pleased to find the brightly colored bowl and had spent more than a few hours contemplating the pleasure he thought Finn would get from it. It was a very unique design, the rounded curve of the ceramic forming into the shape of a tulip on one side, and the whole piece was covered in intricate patterns in every color of the rainbow. "I saw it and thought of you, and it made me happy."

Finn loosened the drawstrings and opened the bag, and he let out a delighted gasp when he pulled out the bowl. "This is amazing! I love it. Thank you!" He picked up the small white box nestled in the bowl and held it up, regarding Joe curiously. "What's this? Something of yours?"

Joe felt his stomach drop. He'd forgotten he'd put the box in with the bowl, and even though he had bought the contents for Finn as well, something about those scratches on Finn's back suddenly made it seem like a stupid, pointless gift. He should probably just lie again and say that it was his, and he knew Finn would let it go without another thought, but some part of him wanted—maybe even needed —to see how Finn reacted.

"No, it's something else for you," he said softly. "But I don't know if you'll like or want it."

Finn carefully placed the bowl on Joe's dresser and opened the box. His eyes widened when he saw the white-gold ring inside. "That's a Celtic trinity knot, isn't it?" he asked as he lifted the ring and held it up to the light. "It's gorgeous, Joe. The emerald matches my eyes."

"Yeah." Joe felt his face flushing a bit. He didn't indulge in emotional displays very often, and he was suddenly a bit embarrassed at how soppy and sentimental it probably seemed. "That's why I bought it. Things were... hard on the mission. Dark. I liked looking at the ring and the bowl because they reminded me of you and that there were good things for me to come back to."

Finn slid the band on the ring finger of his right hand, before closing the distance between them and pulling Joe into a light, lingering kiss. "I'm glad," he said when he drew back at last. "I wish I'd been there. I wish I could've gone with you. It didn't feel right staying here and not having your back."

Joe swallowed hard against a lump in his throat. He supposed it was too much to hope that Finn might put the ring on his left hand instead, but the gesture reminded him that his place in Finn's life wasn't ever going to be what he really wanted. It wasn't Finn's fault, either—it was simply the way things were between them. Joe was grateful to at least be Finn's best friend and the person he trusted most in the world. It had been enough for him for years, and it would continue to be enough. Other men might come into Finn's life, but they were gone quickly and without regret in Finn's eyes.

"I didn't wish you were there," he admitted. "I wouldn't have been there myself if Herc hadn't asked me. I've never seen such ugliness. I wouldn't have wanted you to see it."

"The mission was a success, right?" Finn rested his hand against Joe's neck and stroked Joe's jaw with his thumb. "Let's focus on that and go wash all the ugliness away."

Joe smiled crookedly. "I'd like that. Yes, the mission was a success, thank all that's holy. But I don't know if I could do it again. Even for Herc." He didn't realize until he said it that the words were true. Joe considered himself a simple man, and he could deal with evil—in his job, he'd had to—and while the adversary in this case had undoubtedly been one of the most horrible men he'd ever run across, it was the knowledge that they hadn't taken him down sooner that was like a rip in Joe's heart. There were plenty of dead bodies by the time the mission was over, but even though Joe knew saving every victim had never been more than theoretically possible, it still hurt that they couldn't. What he needed more than anything right now was the warmth of the man he loved to soothe the jagged edges of his damaged soul.

"Come on." Finn slid his hand down Joe's arm and twined their fingers. "I'll run a bath as hot as you can handle it, and I've got a loofah and lemon verbena soap with your name on them. I want you to lie back and let me take care of you," he said as he tugged Joe toward the bathroom.

Joe willingly followed along, though he couldn't help glancing at the scratches and bruises—obviously bite marks—that decorated Finn's back. Some of them were fading, while others looked fresh enough that they might have been done the previous day. Or perhaps even that morning. Not that he would ask. *He never did.*

"Wait here," Finn said, stopping Joe next to the huge whirlpool tub. "I'll undress you, but I want to get the bath started first."

Joe waited, watching as Finn started the water and added the bath salts. Finn moved with languid grace, and Joe always enjoyed observing Finn, no matter what he was doing. "I feel like I have sand driven into my skin. A nice soak will feel really good."

"I'll bet it will." Finn made a detour to the vanity to pick up a lighter. "You can soak as long as you want. We'll start the washing away process with a shampoo and scalp massage," he said as he lit the two thick, round candles on either end of the tub ledge. "How does that sound?"

"Perfect." Joe reached out, brushing a hand over Finn's soft, thick hair. "You take good care of me."

Finn's answering smile was warm and sweet as he leaned into the caress. "I try," he said. "I enjoy it."

"Thanks." The sight of Finn's smile soothed a bit of the unease Joe felt from the sight of Finn's back. Finn was here, after all, and that was what really mattered.

"Anytime. Now let's get you undressed and into the tub." Finn slid his hands beneath the collar of Joe's black leather jacket and eased it off Joe's shoulders and down his arms. Joe shrugged slightly, helping.

"Don't be surprised that I've got a few new scars. One guy went at me with a knife after I relieved him of his gun."

"Shit, seriously?" Concern flickered in Finn's expressive green eyes. "Do you need me to check anything?"

"It should be okay." Joe caressed Finn's cheek, touched by the concern. "Couple of stitches, that's all. Nothing deep. It's healing fine."

"What about the others?" Finn tugged the hem of Joe's black T-shirt and worked with him to get it up and off.

"So shallow they didn't need stitches." Joe held up his left arm so Finn could see the neat line of stitches on his forearm. He pointed to the red lines on his left pec and the upper part of his stomach. "He missed my ink, I'm glad to say."

"Thank God." Finn leaned in and pressed his lips against Joe's right shoulder where his tattoo sleeve started. "I love your ink," he murmured against Joe's skin.

Joe closed his eyes, letting the warmth of the kiss flow over him. "I'm glad. You'll have to help me decide what to get next."

"I keep telling you, it should be a four leaf clover on your ass," Finn said, flashing a mischievous grin as he started unfastening the fly of Joe's cargo pants.

Joe chuckled. "How many times do I have to tell you, I'm not getting that?" He shook his head. "I may be as much of a *son of the ould sod* as you are, but I'm not about to go *that* far!"

"Fine, so make it a leprechaun." Finn wormed his fingers beneath the waistband of Joe's boxer briefs and eased them down along with the cargo pants.

"Only if you kiss me arse," Joe said in a lilting brogue. "How about it?"

"You act like I've never done that and a hell of a lot more to your ass," Finn said, his voice laced with amusement.

Joe grinned. "Too true."

With Finn's help, he got out of the rest of his clothing—boots thudding on the tile and shedding sand. When he was finally bare Finn urged him into the tub, and he sank into the hot, scented water with a sigh of relief. "This feels great."

"It's going to feel even better once I get my hands on you," Finn said as he knelt at the end of the tub behind Joe's head. He slid his arms around Joe's shoulders and leaned forward, releasing a quiet sigh that ghosted past Joe's ear. "I'm really glad you're back," he said softly. "I missed you."

"Did you?" The question was out before Joe could stop it, but he said it softly, so he hoped Finn wouldn't take it as a criticism. "I know you were busy with the DC assignment, and your new trainee."

"I was, but that doesn't mean I didn't think about you or miss you." Finn fell silent and absently nuzzled his nose beneath Joe's ear. "Although, I wasn't celibate either," he said at last.

"I sort of figured that out." Joe closed his eyes, letting himself float a bit. No doubt Finn was going to tell him about his hook ups during the past month, just like he always did. A part of Joe never wanted to know about what Finn did with other men, so that he could pretend

Finn was his and his alone, but he always listened, to remind himself that he had no real claim on Finn's heart. Oh, Finn loved him as a best friend, but Joe knew Finn wasn't really in love with him and needed more than Joe could give.

"It's the guy I've been working with," Finn said. "Drew Martin. You might've heard him mentioned as Joker. He's from Lawson & Greer."

Another merc? Joe turned his head to look at Finn in surprise. Finn didn't hook up with guys from work because it could easily get awkward once Finn's interest waned and he moved on. Finn normally used a dating app, or stuck to people he met socially. For him to have changed his mind about someone from work was unusual. And disturbing. "Oh?"

"Yeah." Finn went quiet again, and he tightened his arms around Joe. "He started flirting as soon as we met. I thought he was a player, you know? That we'd have a good time, and that would be it."

Joe heard what Finn said, and also what he *didn't* say. His stomach twisted, because he
had an idea where this was leading. "But it wasn't."

"No, it wasn't," Finn said. "I haven't had chemistry like this with anyone since you, so I've been enjoying it."

"Oh." Joe fell silent, unsure what to say. This had never happened before. He normally didn't have a lot to say to anyone but Finn, but now words failed him completely. Did Finn want his blessing? Or was he going to tell Joe the two of them were over, he was being replaced with this new guy? What could anyone say when the person they loved met someone new?

Finn drew in a deep breath. "I was wondering if you'd be okay with me seeing him," he said, a hopeful note in his voice.

So it was a blessing Finn wanted, and probably for Joe to bow out so that this Joker could take over Joe's place—apparently former place—in Finn's life. There was a sick, jealous part of him that wanted to say no, but when it came down to it, Finn's happiness mattered. Apparently more than his own.

"You don't need my permission," he said, his voice a bit ragged.

"I've never tried to control you, and I don't own you. Do what you want, with who you want. Just like you always have, right?"

Finn went still. "I know you'd never try to control me, but yeah, I do need your permission. You've been okay with me having the occasional fling, but this is different. This would mean sharing my time and attention more than you're used to."

"I want you to do whatever makes you happy." Joe closed his eyes, again, wishing this entire thing was just a bad dream. "If that means you want him, I'm not going to stand in your way."

"That's not...." Finn blew out a sharp huff. "Look, I know it may be selfish and greedy, but I want both of you. Is there any way that can happen?"

"You already talked with him about this?" Joe felt his heart breaking. Somehow, he'd gone away for a month and his whole world had somehow tilted on its axis.

"I told him about you," Finn said. "He knows how important you are to me. We haven't made any promises or arrangements because I wanted to talk to you first."

Joe sat up, pulling away from Finn but not turning around. He wanted to get out of the bath and run, because this was not what he wanted to be hearing. How could Finn spring this on him cold? How could Finn expect him to welcome losing what bit of Finn Joe actually had? Maybe this was Finn's way of letting him down easy. Get Joe to share time, and slowly Finn would spend more and more time with the new man, and Joe would be left with nothing. All this for a guy Finn had only met a month before?

"Sounds like you've already decided what you want. Me... I don't know. I've never thought about it—not like this, but I guess a part of me always knew you'd fall in love with someone else someday."

"Does that mean you don't even want to try?" Finn asked, sounding far more subdued than Joe had ever heard him be before. "I don't want to choose, Joe. I've got enough room in my heart for both of you."

Finn didn't deny being in love with this new man, and the pieces of Joe's heart shattered completely. "If you're in love with this guy, you probably really want to be with him. I can't imagine he'd want to share you, either. Put yourself in my place, Finn. What if I had come back from Pakistan, hauling some stranger in and telling you I was in love with him, but that I still wanted to have sex with you? How would you feel?"

Finn shifted to sit on the ledge of the tub, facing Joe, and he raked his fingers through his hair. "I... can't answer that," he said. "I don't know how I'd feel. I'd want you to be happy, and I don't want to be hypocritical, but...." He spread his hands and shrugged. "I don't have an answer for that."

"But you want me to give you one." Joe couldn't look at Finn, because he didn't want Finn to see the agony he knew must be reflected in his eyes. "And I can't."

"You're right," Finn said quietly. "I'm not being fair. I don't want to push you into something you aren't ready for or worse, something you don't want, so if you need time to process, I understand."

"Thanks." Joe drew in a shuddering breath. He really didn't think that being second best in Finn's life wasn't going to be enough, and the new guy would probably do his damnedest to push Joe out, anyway. But he couldn't bear to hurt Finn, so it was better if they just gave things distance and time. Finn would have the man he loved, and Joe... well, he would know that Finn was happy.

He stood up, stepping out of the tub and reaching for a towel, wrapping it around his waist. "I guess I'm not in the mood for a bath anymore."

Finn got up as well and regarded him somberly. "You want some space?"

"Yeah." Joe ran a hand through his hair, still not meeting Finn's eyes. "Just... I'm still your friend, right? No matter what?"

"Of course you are."

At least Joe would have that, cold comfort though it would be. "Thanks."

"Okay, well, I'm going to get my stuff and head out. If you need anything.... If there's anything I can do... I'll be here." Finn leaned in and brushed a kiss against Joe's cheek, and then he left Joe alone in the bathroom.

Joe stood still, listening to the sounds of Finn in the bedroom. He heard Finn getting dressed and collecting his things, followed by the sound of Finn's footsteps going down the stairs. Finally he heard the door to the garage open, then close, and the sound of Finn's car heading away. Away from Joe and toward the man Finn loved.

Even though he'd always known this day would come, nothing could have prepared Joe for the pain of it. He slowly walked into the bedroom, seeing the mussed sheets where Finn had lain, waiting for him. The promise of shared pleasure, of holding the man he loved, was now nothing but a memory, Joe walked out of the room and down the hall. He couldn't bear to sleep in the sheets that smelled of Finn, knowing that Finn loved someone else, had *chosen* someone else to share his life with. Instead, he opened the door to his guest room, walked over to the bed, and laid down on the mattress, curling into a ball as he gave in to his misery at last.

He'd lost the only person in the world who really mattered, and while Joe had never told Finn he was in love with him, somehow that didn't make it hurt any less.

6

After he left Joe's house, Finn wasn't sure what to do with himself. He didn't want to go home because his mind was too turbulent for him to be alone with it. A good workout might help, but he didn't want to use the gym at headquarters because the chance that he might run into someone who'd ask why he wasn't with Joe was too high. At the same time, he didn't want to be alone, but the idea of hanging out in a public space, like a coffee shop or all-night diner, wasn't appealing because he felt too restless to sit still.

That left him with one viable option, which was how he ended up at Drew's apartment building, asking to be buzzed in.

"Hello?" Drew's deep voice held a note of curiosity, and Finn knew there were no cameras, only the call boxes, so Drew didn't know who was buzzing. "Are you sure you have the right apartment?"

"Pretty sure," Finn said, a wave of relief sweeping over him at the sound of Drew's voice. The way his luck was running tonight, he wouldn't have been surprised if Drew wasn't home. "It's Finn. Can I come up?"

The door buzzer sounded. "Of course."

When Finn stepped off the elevator at Drew's floor a few minutes later, he spotted Drew standing just outside his apartment door, appearing concerned, and he had a sudden, overwhelming urge to run over and throw himself at Drew. He made himself keep to his normal pace, however, and he mustered a smile when he reached Drew.

"Thanks for letting me in," he said.

"You're always welcome," Drew replied. He took Finn's arm and urged him into the apartment. Once he'd closed and locked the door, he put his arms around Finn and held him. "Something's wrong, isn't it? Did something happen to Joe?"

"Not during the mission." Finn slid his arms around Drew's waist and leaned against him, drawing comfort from Drew's warm, solid presence. "He made it home safe and sound. I waited for him at his house, and we were having a nice reunion until I told him about you." He hesitated. "About us."

Drew went still for a moment, and then he drew back so he could look down into Finn's face. "If I may ask, what did you tell him? Whatever it was, I assume he wasn't happy."

"No, he wasn't happy." All the butterflies roiling in Finn's stomach sank to the bottom to form a heavy lump that made him nauseated. "I told him the truth. That I thought we'd have a fun little fling, and that would be the end of it, but we have stronger chemistry than I expected. I asked if he'd be okay with me seeing you."

Drew sighed. "Come on, let's go into the living room, and I'll get you a drink. I think you need it. Hell, I think I need one, too."

Drew led Finn to his comfortable sofa, then went to his sideboard to pour them both glasses of bourbon. He even brought the bottle over and put it on the table in front of them before handing Finn one of the glasses and sitting down beside him. "I'm not going to push, because your relationship with Joe is something special, I know. Most of it is none of my business, but I'm here to listen, and to help, if I can. Okay?"

Finn accepted the glass and took a sip, hoping it would help calm him somewhat. "I don't even know what to say. I feel like we just broke up, even though he didn't say that in so many words."

Drew put an arm around Finn and rubbed his shoulder. "So what did he say? That he didn't want you to see me? Or that he didn't want to see *you* anymore? Somehow, this doesn't sound like the reaction of someone who's just a 'friends with benefits,' Finn."

Scrubbing his face with his free hand, Finn tried to figure out how to explain the conversation. "He said he wants me to be happy. That he needs time to process. He asked how I'd feel if he brought back a stranger and said he wanted to see both of us."

Drew was quiet for several long moments. "I wasn't there, and I don't know him, so I'm not sure what that means. It sounds like a reasonable reaction. You're asking him for a big change to your relationship, one that he wasn't expecting, and one that means he's not the only person who gets to spend time with you. Maybe it's not as bad as you think. Maybe he does just need time to process. Unless...."

"Unless what?" Finn sat up straight, alarm zinging through him.

Drew shrugged. "Look, I've never met the man, so I could be off base. But everything you've said about your relationship—the way he treats you and the fact that he doesn't see other people—has made me think his feelings for you are a lot deeper than just friendship. To me, it sounds like he's in love with you. If that's the case, he's probably feeling like his whole world just crashed down around him. I've had friends with benefits before, and we all joke and tease each other about our various flings, but no one actually gets upset if their buddy wants to fuck someone else on a regular basis."

Finn stared at Drew, stunned into silence. He wanted to deny the possibility that Joe loved him, because that would mean he hadn't managed to protect Joe at all, but Joe being in love with him would help that whole conversation make a hell of a lot more sense.

"He's never said anything about love," he said, although he wasn't sure whether he was trying to convince Drew or himself that Joe couldn't possibly be in love with him.

"Have you?" Drew asked gently. "To him, that is. *I* know how you feel about him."

"No, I didn't tell him." Finn stared into the depths of his bourbon, feeling even more confused now than when he'd left Joe's place. "I thought I could keep him safe from being disappointed because I can't be the kind of white-picket-fence guy he wants."

"Oh, Finn." Drew sighed, leaning close to brush a kiss to Finn's cheek. "You're a good man, but whether you ever told him you were in love with him or not, it wouldn't change how he feels about you. Even if he wants that white picket fence, it sounds like he wants *you* more. Otherwise he would be seeing other people, trying to find the person who could give him that dream. But he hasn't, right? You told me he only sleeps with you. That says a lot about what he feels. I don't know him, but I *have* seen pictures. A guy that hot could be fucking half the gay men in this city if he wanted. Hell, I'd do him myself, given the chance."

"So what do I do now?" Finn knocked back his drink and set the empty glass on the coffee table. "Go back there and tell him how I feel? I'm not sure how much of a difference it would make. He didn't like the idea of me seeing you very much."

"That, I don't know." Drew gave Finn's shoulders a squeeze. "I wish I had a crystal ball so I could give you the answers. You and me, Finn, we're a lot alike. We grab life and live it, but we need an anchor. For the last twenty years, Lawson & Greer has been my anchor. The company and my cadre were to me a lot of what Joe is to you. You told me Joe was your rock, and I get the feeling you're not going to be happy without him, right?" He was silent for a moment. "I almost feel like I should bow out and settle the question for you. But if I'm totally honest, I don't want to do that. You matter to me more than anyone I've met in a long time. I want to see where this goes between us— and I'm not saying you can't see other people, especially Joe. I want whatever part of you that you can give me."

Finn leaned against Drew and rested his hand on Drew's thigh. "I don't want you to bow out," he said, feeling icy tendrils coil around his heart at the mere thought. "I wish there was a way I could be with both of you without hurting either of you." He drew back and offered a wry smile. "Wishful thinking, I know."

"Not when it comes to me, at least." Drew smiled. "I don't know if there's a way to convince Joe I'm not trying to take you away from him, but I can try. To him I'm the big bad monster stealing away the man he loves."

Finn thought about the way Joe had withdrawn and how he'd spoken about Drew. "Probably," he said, inclining his head to acknowledge the point. "Okay, so if we're a lot alike, what would you do if you were me?" he asked, hoping for any kind of guidance he could latch onto. He was so far out of his depth, and he had no idea how to proceed.

"That's rough because I've never had anyone in love with me before." Drew smiled crookedly. "Nor anyone I've loved the way you love Joe. I guess it depends on if you want to keep him in your life, and how badly you want that."

"I don't want to lose him, but I don't want to lose you, either." Finn let out a shaky laugh and scrubbed his face again. "I'm greedy, I guess."

"It's not greedy, not if it's what's in your heart." Drew gave him another one-armed hug. "I'm glad I matter to you, because you matter to me, too. I think if I had a Joe in my life, I'd give him time. Maybe right now he sees this as an either-or situation. He doesn't know me. He doesn't even know how deeply you care about him, so he doesn't have the complete sitrep. He might not even be willing to accept all of it at this point, but if he loves you, he's not going to be able to stay away from you. So... I guess do what any good leader would do. Leave the door open. Tell him you care, but more importantly, *show* him. And I'll do everything I can to prove to him I'm not trying to monopolize you, that there can be room for us both in your life." He paused and looked at Finn with a raised brow. "I doubt it's likely to come up, but how would you feel if he and I unexpectedly hit it off? I mean with the same chemistry you and I have. Would that bother you?"

Finn tried to imagine Joe and Drew together, drawing on what he knew about their bodies. He imagined them both wearing nothing but black cargo pants, imagined Drew making Joe shiver by tracing the darks whorls of Joe's tattoo sleeve with his fingertips. He could visualize Joe pulling Drew in and teasing with the rasp of his lightly furred abs against Drew's skin, and a subtle dominance battle as they kissed. Tugged hair. Fingers biting into hard muscle.

"No...." Finn worked to get the word out past his dry mouth. "I can't say that it would."

Maybe if Joe or Drew were with someone else, he might feel differently, but the thought of the two of them together—of watching them, maybe getting himself off while they fucked—was far more arousing than he expected.

Drew chuckled. "Seems you like the idea. Well, who knows? Stranger things have happened. I doubt he could ever feel about me the way he feels about you, but acceptance might be enough, right?"

"Maybe," Finn said. "Hopefully." He sighed and slumped against the back of the couch. "I'll give him some space, and we'll see what happens."

"And in the meantime, I'll be here for you." Drew put his glass down and turned to face Finn fully. "That's not me trying to take Joe's place in your life. I wouldn't want to do that, even if I could. And it's not me saying he's doing anything wrong by needing time and space to figure this out, because he isn't. I'm betting he'll figure out pretty quick that you're worth anything he needs to do to be with you. He's used to being your rock, and it's going to bother him not being there for you, as much as it bothers you that he isn't."

"I hope you're right." Finn rolled his head on the back of the couch to look at Drew, and he offered a grateful smile. He had more hope now than he'd had when he first arrived. "I won't drop the L-bomb on him yet. It might seem manipulative if I do it now. I'll only detonate it if I have to."

"Sounds like a plan." Drew reached out to caress Finn's cheek. "Do you want to stay here tonight? We don't have to do anything, but if you just need someone to hold you, I'm available."

For once, Finn wasn't in the mood for sex, but he didn't want to be alone either. "I'd like that," he said with a little nod.

"Good. Would you like another drink first? Or something to eat?" In his own way, Drew was as much of a caretaker as Finn, or Joe, for that matter.

"What were you doing before I got here?" Finn asked. He wasn't hungry, and he didn't want to get drunk, but it was only a little after eight o'clock, so he didn't want to go to sleep, either.

"I was going to pop some popcorn and start on those Hobbit movies I missed while out being a badass merc," Drew said. "I'm still a couple of years behind the pop culture curve."

"That sounds perfect." Finn leaned over and took off his boots, making himself comfortable while Drew made the popcorn.

Drew returned a few minutes later with a huge plastic bowl filled with hot popcorn and a couple of sodas. Finn wasn't interested in either; instead, he stretched out on his side with his head in Drew's lap, and he let the sights and sounds of the film wash over him while Drew absently stroked his hair. Gradually, the peacefulness of the simple domestic moment relaxed him enough that his brain finally stopped its anxious tumbling. He closed his eyes and drifted off to sleep.

7

On Monday morning, Joe came in early to the main Hercules Security office to write up his report for the mission in Pakistan. After that, Herc debriefed him in person, wanting to know everything about the human traffickers Joe and his teammates had captured or killed. It wasn't something Joe especially cared to relive moment by moment, but at least it helped take his mind off the situation with Finn and the fact that Joe had lost him to someone else.

"Are you all right?" Herc interrupted Joe's account of the last day of the mission, and Joe glanced up from his notes, meeting Herc's sharp blue gaze, seeing the unmistakable concern in his boss's eyes.

"Yeah." Joe tilted his head to one side. "Why do you ask?"

"You just seem a bit off." Herc leaned closer across the table. "I know this was a tough one, Joe. You did amazing work, and you can be proud of having saved a lot of lives. It was an ugly situation, though, and there's no shame in needing to talk to one of the psychologists."

Joe liked and respected Herc, and knew Herc took the well-being of his employees seriously. "Thanks, but I'm okay. It's not the mission.

It's... something else." There was no way he could talk to Herc about Finn. Or talk to anybody else about it.

Herc continued to look at him for a few moments. "If you say so. But remember, the counselors are there for personal stuff, too—not only the fallout of hard missions."

"I know." Joe looked back down at his tablet. "This is something I have to work out for myself."

"All right."

Joe was relieved when Herc dropped the subject and returned to the debriefing. Joe had done nothing for the last two days except think about Finn. He wondered if Finn was serious about still wanting both him and this new guy, or if it was Finn's way of letting him down easy by putting the decision in Joe's hands. He knew Finn cared, and that Finn wouldn't ever want to hurt him, even if he had fallen in love with someone else. Of course, Finn had no idea Joe was in love with him, so there was no way Finn could realize just how much the situation was killing him inside. He had to find a way to act like it was really no big deal, that it had been fun while it lasted but that now they would just be buddies.

Would they still be partners?

Joe felt as though a knife had been thrust into his gut. He hadn't considered until that moment that Finn might want to be partnered up with the new guy, and the thought of losing Finn completely was almost enough to make him cry out. He closed his eyes, wondering if he could even stay with the company if that happened. Joe liked his cadre, but Finn had *always* been his partner. He didn't want anyone else.

"Joe!"

He opened his eyes as Herc spoke sharply, realizing with dismay that he'd stopped listening to Herc's questions.

"Sorry, boss," he managed to say, wondering where he'd lost track of the discussion. "I think I'm still jet-lagged. It was a horrible flight back, and my time zones are still screwed up."

Herc gave him a piercing look. "Okay, that makes sense. I thought you'd fallen asleep on me. I think you should go home and give your-self a couple of days to get back in the swing of things."

More time in his own head wasn't something Joe wanted, so he shook his head. "I'll be fine, boss, I promise. I think I just need to get back to work."

Herc didn't look convinced, but after a moment he nodded. "Okay. Let's end the debrief here. I'll go over everything and let you know if I need more info."

"Thanks, boss." Joe was relieved Herc wasn't going to push him to go to counseling again.

"Come on, let's get out of here. I have an assignment lined up for you, anyway."

Herc stood, and Joe followed along, wondering if Finn had already spoken to Herc and this was how Joe was going to find out Finn had asked for a new partner. But no... Finn wouldn't do some-thing like that. He'd tell Joe himself.

Herc pulled out his smartphone and typed something in before leading him out to the common area. The other employees were reporting for the day: getting their assignments, picking up equip-ment, or heading for the locker room to change for workouts. Herc beckoned Joe to follow him with this last group and made his way straight to the back wall where Joe and Finn had their lockers.

And there was Finn. Joe shouldn't have been surprised, but he was. He went still, gazing at Finn and hoping his fear wasn't plain to see on his face.

"Hey, Finn." Herc punched Finn playfully on the shoulder. "Ready for a new assignment? Joe says he's ready to go."

Finn gave an exaggerated wince and rubbed his shoulder, but his smile faded slightly as he studied Herc. "I'm ready. Is everything good?"

"As far as I know." Herc gave a slight shrug and glanced at Joe. "Your partner seems to be a bit jet-lagged, but I'm sure you'll watch out for him and make him get any help he needs, right?"

Finn's eyes narrowed as he peered at Joe, and he nodded. "You bet I will, Herc."

Joe would normally have protested that he was fine, but he was so relieved Finn was still his partner that he could only draw in a deep breath and pray that his knees didn't give out. He hoped that Finn couldn't tell how close he'd been to bolting from the room. It was hard to look cool and unaffected when he wanted to sag against the wall, pitifully grateful to know Finn didn't want to end their partnership. At least he would still have Finn in his life.

"Good. What I have for you shouldn't be too taxing, anyway. There's an international environmental summit that will be taking place at NC State next month, and we've been retained to provide security for the event, since there are likely to be protests on both sides of the issue. I want the two of you to take point." Herc reached into a pocket of his cargo pants and pulled out a business card, which he handed to Finn. "Here's the contact information for the coordinator at the university. I think this is perfect for the two of you. Finn, you'll know what potential medical personnel should be on call. Joe, I want you to make sure the people working security have a good smattering of different languages, just so we have a chance of picking up on potential threats in the making. Got it?"

Finn tucked the card into a pocket and nodded. "Got it, boss man."

"Okay, I'll leave you to it." Herc clapped Joe on the shoulder. "Put together a list of requirements and get them to me by Thursday." With that, Herc turned and made his way back out of the locker room, responding to greetings called out by other employees.

When Herc left, Joe was at a loss for what to say to Finn, so he turned to his locker, opening it and checking over what he'd left there a month ago. The good thing was that Joe was normally quiet at work, so Finn probably wouldn't think it was unusual for him to go about things in silence.

Finn closed his locker and leaned against the door, facing Joe. After a few seconds, he folded his arms across his chest. "What's up?" he asked, raising one eyebrow.

Joe shrugged, reaching for the shoulder rig he normally wore for concealed carry. "Not much. Had my debrief on the Pakistan mission with Herc this morning."

"I figured that much," Finn said. "I meant what's up with Herc being concerned about you?"

There was no way Joe could say that he was pretty sure Herc was picking up on his inner turmoil, so he shrugged again and deflected, not wanting to lie outright. "It's the jet lag. I've had a hard time sleeping since I got back, so I'm not as focused as usual."

"That's what you're going with? Jet lag?"

Joe delayed responding as he slipped off his blazer and got into the shoulder rig. He started on the buckles, trying to come up with an answer that would satisfy Finn. "What else could it be?"

"Golly, Joe, I don't know." Finn shot him an incredulous look. "Maybe something to do with our last conversation?"

Summoning up all his courage, Joe met Finn's eyes. "I'm fine, Finn. I told you, I want you to be happy. If this guy makes you happy, you have my blessing, if you want it." No one would ever know what those words cost him, and he was glad to have managed to get them out without a single tremble in his voice.

Finn held Joe's gaze and kept his voice low. "Sure, I want your blessing, but I want you, too. You make me happy, Joe, and what we've got is older and stronger. I'm a greedy little fuck, and I want both of you, but if I can only have one, I pick you."

A part of him wanted to jump on that offer and tell Finn to forget about this new guy, that Joe would do everything in his power to make him happy. But that was the *weak part*, the selfish part, and he knew in the long run it wouldn't work, anyway. Finn loved this other guy—Drew, he made himself think the name—and if Joe took Finn's offer, it would not only be self-centered, it would make Finn unhappy in the long run. Joe would end up losing him anyway, because Finn wasn't in love with him, not the way he was with Drew.

He shook his head, dropping his gaze to the ground. "I won't do that to you. It wouldn't be right. You're my friend. I'd never make you give up the man you love."

Finn stared at him before letting out an exasperated huff. "Come on," he said, grabbing Joe's arm and tugging. "I've got something to say, and I want witnesses."

Surprised, Joe let Finn haul him out of the locker room. "I don't understand. What is it?"

Finn dragged him all the way to the gym and didn't stop until they were standing in the middle of the room.

"Attention!" Finn raised his voice to be heard above the clank of bars and weights, and the grunts as the handful of mercs in there working out pushed their straining muscles. "Attention, everyone! I have an announcement."

Joe was bewildered by Finn's strange behavior, and he looked around at his cadre—men he had known for years. They'd worked together, fought together, bled together, and Joe trusted all of them with his life. Well, except for one man in the corner, but he ignored the stranger. This was still embarrassing, and he lowered his voice, leaning close to Finn. "What are you doing?"

"Something I should've done before now," Finn said. He clasped Joe's hands and looked him straight in the eyes. "Joseph Patrick Morrissey Junior, I am in love with you."

Over by the weight rack, Mojo picked up a couple of twenty-five-pound dumbbells and shot a sardonic look in their direction before returning to his bench. "And?"

"Old news, buddy," said Dead-eye, amused.

"Damn it, Finn, you interrupted us to tell us something we already knew?" D-Day chimed in. "What's next, you gonna tell us you're Irish and gay, too?"

Joe let the catcalls wash over him. He couldn't look away from Finn's beautiful face, his breath catching at the way Finn's green eyes met his with conviction. "You are? Really?"

"I really am," Finn said, squeezing Joe's fingers tightly. "I should've told you before, but I was scared. I thought we wanted things that were too different. But I'd rather work my ass off to find a way for us both to get what we want and need than lose you, so... fuck it. I've said it in front of witnesses, so I can't take it back now even if I wanted to."

Joe swallowed hard, feeling his throat threatening to tighten up so he couldn't speak, and that wouldn't do. He'd never expected Finn to say those words, and he forgot everything else—the men watching them, the fact that they were at work, all the doubts that had plagued him for the last few days. He returned the pressure of Finn's hands. "I'm in love with you, too," he said, his voice softer than Finn's had been. "I've loved you for years, but I didn't want you to feel like I was pressuring you, so I never said it. I love you, Brian Sean Finnegan."

With that, he pulled Finn into his arms and kissed him hard. Finn wound his arms around Joe's shoulders and pressed close as he parted his lips and kissed Joe back with eager enthusiasm.

There were more ribald comments, but Joe ignored them in favor of deepening the kiss. He needed this—needed Finn—to heal the broken parts of his soul.

After a time, however, he pulled back to look at Finn, his joy tempered by the knowledge that even though Finn loved him, there *was* someone else who also had a place in his heart. "I guess we still need to talk."

"We do." Finn paused long enough to flip off the mercs who'd been teasing them before turning his attention back to Joe. "Just the two of us?"

"Yeah." Joe stepped back, even though what he really wanted was to kiss Finn, again, and delay the difficult discussion they were going to have. "Let's go outside."

"Lead the way." Finn gestured toward the exit.

Joe nodded, taking Finn's hand and heading toward the exit. They had to walk past the stranger in the corner. As they got closer, Joe glanced at the man and remembered where he'd seen this guy before. He was in pictures Hunter had shown Joe of his old unit in Lawson & Greer. This, then, was Joker, Hunter's old XO who was now employed by Hercules Security. The other man Finn loved.

For the moment, Joe decided to ignore his existence. It was probably juvenile, but he wanted Finn to himself for just a few minutes, to revel in the knowledge that Finn loved him. The other guy could just wait.

Once they were outside, Joe pulled Finn toward one of the paths through the trees. Herc had put his headquarters in the midst of a park-like setting, one that provided the mercs a little privacy and room to get out and run if they needed to. It also helped to have a peaceful place to take refuge when the job got stressful.

They walked in silence for a few minutes, and Joe kept his hold on Finn's hand. Finally, however, he knew he had to speak. "I never suspected, you know. That you loved me as anything more than a friend."

"You weren't supposed to know." Finn slanted a wry smile at him and squeezed his hand.

"Neither were you." Joe shook his head. "Everyone else knew, though."

"I guess the only ones we were good at hiding from was each other." Finn laughed, his eyes sparkling with humor over the situation.

"You wanted to know what Herc was worried about. I can tell you now that I was worried you might not want to be my partner anymore. It caught me in the middle of the debrief, and I must have blocked Herc out completely. I don't panic under fire, but I almost did at the thought of you not wanting to be with me any longer."

"Don't be stupid." Finn shouldered him playfully. "You aren't going to get rid of me that easily."

"Well, I didn't know," Joe said. "I wasn't thinking rationally. The idea of it was so painful that I knew I'd have to leave the company."

Finn's expression grew somber. "I'm sorry you were so worried. I should've told you how I felt sooner. Maybe you wouldn't have had so much doubt about us. About me."

"It's okay. I wasn't forthcoming about my feelings, either." Joe shook his head. "We need to figure out where to go from here, though."

"Well, you know what I want." Finn cocked his head as he regarded Joe with a questioning look. "Why don't you tell me what *you* want, and we'll see about working out a compromise that works for both of us?"

Joe nodded before frowning in thought. "If you really want him, I'm not going to stop you from having him. I suppose if we just go back to the way we were, it's no different than before. You're just seeing the same guy, instead of different ones."

"Right, and I'd be seeing him more often," Finn said. "But I'll try to balance my time between the two of you. I don't want you to feel like he's taking up more than his fair share. The important thing is communication. We've put all our cards on the table, so no more secrets, right?" He fixed Joe with a pointed look. "No suffering in silence. If something's bothering you, tell me. We'll figure out how to fix it. Okay?"

Joe stopped and turned to look at Finn. "No more secrets. I'll do my best not to be jealous, but I can't promise I won't be. To me, he's an interloper. I don't know him, and I have no reason to trust him. I don't *want* to know him, okay? Maybe it's petty of me, but that's how I feel."

"Then you don't have to." Finn cupped Joe's cheek in his palm and stroked it with his thumb. "I'm not going to force you to interact with him if you don't want to. All I ask is that if you do start feeling jealous, tell me so we can figure out why and what might help."

"Okay." Joe closed his eyes and leaned into the caress. "I'll do my best."

"That's all either of us can do." Finn pressed a kiss to Joe's lips, light but lingering.

Joe returned the kiss, but after a few moments he pulled back reluctantly. "I guess so."

"Are you ready to get started on the job Herc gave us?" Finn raised one eyebrow, a mischievous smile tugging at his lips. "Or would you rather make up for our ill-fated reunion?"

Joe smiled slightly. "You don't have any other surprises for me, do you?"

"I'm fresh out." Finn spread his hands wide.

"In that case, my house happens to be right on the way to NC State," Joe said. "Maybe we need a premeeting meeting. For strategizing."

"So let's adjourn to your place and start strategizing," Finn said with a playful leer.

Joe smiled, taking Finn's hand and starting toward where he'd left his SUV in the parking lot. Maybe things weren't exactly the way he wanted them to be, but now he knew Finn loved him, and he'd put up with a lot just to hear Finn say those words again.

8

Even though Drew had already seen how messy his apartment could be, Finn spent some time tidying up after work so the place would look halfway decent—or at least less cluttered. He'd texted Drew earlier to see if he was free that evening, and when Drew said yes, Finn extended an invitation.

My place around 1900? I'll provide the pizza if you bring the beer.

Drew replied with thumbs-up and beer mug emojis, which Finn took to mean he was in favor of the plan.

Finn wanted an evening for just the two of them for a couple of reasons. For one thing, he hadn't been great company the last time they were together. He'd been too preoccupied with worrying about Joe to give Drew his undivided attention. For another, Drew had witnessed Finn's declaration of love, and Finn wanted to check in and make sure everything was okay.

The extra-large supreme meat pizza arrived a little before seven o'clock, and Finn slid the box into his preheated oven to keep it warm until Drew arrived. He busied himself with getting plates, napkins, and a bottle opener ready while he waited for the doorbell to ring.

Just after seven, the doorbell chimed as expected, and Finn opened to find Drew there, holding up a six pack of Guinness. He was dressed in jeans and a black leather jacket, and he smiled widely, the expression set off by his close-trimmed beard. "I figured Guinness for the Irishman, eh?"

"Always a good choice." Finn slid his hand around to the back of Drew's neck and drew him into a lingering kiss.

When they finally parted, Drew grinned wickedly. "Too much of that and it won't be pizza on my mind."

"Don't worry, dessert is on the menu," Finn said as he stepped aside to let Drew in. "Have a seat. The pizza's here, and I've got pint glasses if you'd rather not drink from the bottle."

"Sure, a glass would be good." Drew moved over to the sofa, sinking down on it with a sigh. "Feels good to sit down. Dead-eye has been running my ass ragged in the gym. He claims that the desert made me 'soft'. I told him it wasn't the desert, it was the ten years I've got on him."

Finn let out a derisive snort as he headed into the kitchen. "I can provide a good reference when it comes to proving you aren't soft." He glanced over his shoulder at Drew with faux coyness. "Not in any sense of the word."

Drew laughed. "You're helping to keep me young. You have the sex drive of a horny sixteen-year-old."

"I can't argue with facts." Finn got a couple of pint glasses and retrieved the pizza, setting everything up on the coffee table in front of Drew. "Eat up," he said, flipping back the lid of the box to reveal a pizza laden with sausage, pepperoni, bacon, and beef. "You're going to need the protein later."

"That sounds promising." Drew reached for a napkin and didn't hesitate to scoop up a slice of pizza. He bit into it, closing his eyes and chewing with a contented expression on his face. "God, I missed pizza. My waistline didn't, but I sure did."

Finn popped the caps off a couple of bottles of beer and poured one into a glass before offering it to Drew. "Between me and Dead-eye, you'll work off the pizza in no time."

"Let me just say, for the record, I prefer your work-out regime to Dead-eye's." Drew accepted the beer with a nod of thanks. "I think his real problem is that he was a Navy Seal and I was an Army grunt. He has to show off."

Finn laughed as he plated a slice of pizza for himself and settled on the couch next to Drew. "He survived Seal training. He's earned the right to flex. Joe's a Seal, too. They're tough motherfuckers."

"Yeah, that they are." Drew scooted closer to Finn so their shoulders touched. "Speaking of Joe... he's not going to show up at my place and murder me in my sleep, is he?"

"He'd never murder you in your sleep," Finn said, nudging Drew playfully. "He'd want you awake so you'd know who was coming for you. You're safe for now."

Drew let out a snort of amusement. "Oh, that's *so* comforting. How long do I have? Does he plan to try intimidation first? I swear when he looked at me in the gym yesterday, I got the feeling he was wishing me off the face of the earth. He's got that cold, murderous stare down to a science."

Finn had seen that expression on Joe's face countless times while they were on missions, but he'd never had it directed at him—and never wanted to.

"Joe can be... intense," he said. "I'm not going to pretend he's happy about the situation, but he's accepted it. I think telling him how I felt helped."

"Good." Drew leaned over to brush a kiss to Finn's cheek. "You seem much happier, which makes me happy."

"I'm glad he's not shutting me out anymore," Finn said, nestling against Drew's side as he took a couple of bites of pizza. "It feels good being honest with him about how I feel, too. We had a nice talk and settled some things." He glanced at Drew. "That's one reason why I wanted to see you tonight."

"I kind of figured." Drew turned slightly so he could face Finn and took a sip from his beer. "Honesty usually is best. You might have avoided the bad feelings if you'd both just fessed up years ago. As far as you and I go... I guess since I didn't get a 'Dear Drew' call, we're good?"

"We're good," Finn said softly. He put his plate aside and rested his hand on Drew's thigh, wanting the comfort of contact. "He's willing to tolerate you being my lover because he wants me to be happy. You have that in common," he added with a wry smile. "I promised I'd balance the time I spend with both of you as best I can, and we both promised not to keep secrets from each other anymore. If this is going to work, we all need to communicate honestly." He drew in a deep breath, bracing himself to take the next step. "Which leads me to the next thing I wanted to say." Finn tightened his fingers on Drew's leg and gazed at him somberly. "Maybe I'm rushing, but what we have is good and special, and I haven't felt anything like it since Joe. So I want you to know I'm falling in love with you."

Drew smiled and then leaned in to kiss Finn, sliding his hand behind Finn's head and threading his fingers into Finn's hair. When he pulled back, he rested his forehead against Finn's. "I'm falling for you, too. You're different from anyone I've ever known, and you knocked this old merc on his ass from the moment I saw you."

Finn let out a shaky laugh, relieved his confession hadn't been unwelcome, and he let all the warmth and affection he felt show in his smile. "Now I'm officially out of secrets, and we're all on the same page." He rested his hand on Drew's cheek and closed his eyes briefly. "I really want this to work," he murmured, more to himself than to Drew.

"I think it could, at least as far as I'm concerned." Drew sighed. "I think a lot will depend on your Joe, and how he ends up feeling about me. How do you want me to handle it? Should I try to make friends?"

"I think the best thing you can do right now is give him plenty of space," Finn said. Joe didn't like being pushed, and in this case, it would make him dig in his heels harder—or punch Drew in the face. "He wants to pretend you don't exist, and for now, I think we should let him. He needs time to adjust to the new normal. Maybe down the road he'll realize you aren't a threat and be more open to the idea of meeting you. But right now... hard no."

Drew rolled his eyes. "He's in denial. Got it. I don't think that's terribly healthy on his part, but I'll respect both your wishes. He's got to be aware that since we all work for the same company, he's going to have to face it sooner or later." He raised a brow at Finn. "Unless you want me to leave Hercules Security. I don't want to, but I don't want to make this harder than it has to be on you. As far as I'm concerned, Joe can just put on his big boy undies and deal with me professionally if necessary, but I don't want you to be stressing about it."

"Don't you dare leave," Finn said, scowling at the mere thought. "I'm willing to give Joe some space and time because this is all new territory for him, and he's making some major adjustments for me. You're right, it's not sustainable in the long term, and I don't want to spend the rest of my life with a big-ass elephant in the room when I'm with him. At least if you're around at work, he'll have to face reality at some point."

"Sounds good." Drew leaned in for another kiss. "Enough about Joe for one night. If he can pretend I don't exist, I feel fine with limiting the fucks I give about his tender feelings. I do have sympathy for him, but I'm not going to let him pillory me, either. So... pizza and beer, then I'll see what I can do to make you walk funny for a couple of days. How does that sound?"

"That sounds like my idea of a perfect evening," Finn said, and he leaned over to retrieve his plate, eating his pizza with far more gusto.

The situation wasn't perfect by any means, but it was a lot better. All three of them were on the same page now, and maybe... eventually... one day, Joe would move from denial to acceptance. Finn didn't dare hope the three of them would end up happy together—that was a pipe dream stemming from his deepest fantasies—but as long as he never had to choose between them, he would be happy with what he had.

9

"Hey, Morrissey! How are you doing?"

Joe glanced up from his locker to see Jason Hekili waving at him from near the door of the room. The big Hawaiian bodyguard walked over, and Joe smiled, pleasantly surprised. "Thunder! What are you doing on the East Coast? Is Pixel with you?"

Pixel was Chris Hardison, Jason's husband and the chief computer geek for all of Hercules Security. Normally the two of them worked out of Alec "Red" Davis's Los Angeles office, but Jason had spent several months in Raleigh and Joe had been one of his main trainers when he'd first started with the company.

Jason nodded. "Yeah, we're out here for the environmental summit thing. Herc requested Red to send him anyone who was between assignments to help out, and it was a bonus that Chris was free to help with coordination." Pixel was Chris Hardison, Jason's husband and the chief computer geek for all of Hercules Security. Normally the two of them worked out of Alec "Red" Davis's Los Angeles office, but Jason had spent several months in Raleigh and Joe had been one of his main trainers when he'd first started with the company.

"Great. Finn and I are in charge of the summit, but I haven't gotten the updated personnel list yet." Joe closed his locker. "I was about to work out. If you want to hit the gym with me, I can update you on the planning."

"Sounds good." Jason looked around. "Where is Finn, anyway? I swear when I first started working here, I thought the two of you were Siamese twins, since I never saw one of you without the other."

Joe barely managed to keep himself from wincing. A lot of people had begun to notice that he and Finn weren't arriving and leaving together every day the way they used to. Joe had merely shrugged off the comments, since it wasn't anyone's business. No doubt after their public exchange of declarations, people expected them to act like Herc and his husband Jude, who had been caught making out more than once in Herc's office. But both Joe and Finn had tried to act professional toward each other at work since the beginning, though in the end it hadn't fooled anyone. Joe had no idea what the gossip was going to be if and when it got out that Finn was sleeping with another merc.

"I don't think he's here yet," he replied, giving a slight shrug. "And we aren't attached at the hip, despite rumors to the contrary."

Jason laughed. "Okay, I get it. Sure, give me two minutes to change and we can hit weights. I'm definitely interested in the summit, since Hawaii is so vulnerable to the changing environment."

Joe waited, chatting with Jason about Red Davis and the other mercs in California while Jason donned shorts and a tank top. The two of them made their way to the gym, where several of their cadre were already hard at work.

Jason had just gotten set up on a bench to do presses, with Joe spotting him, when Joe heard his name called once again. Tyson Briggs, also known as Dead-eye for his crack sniper abilities, came toward him, and following along behind him was Joker. Drew. The last person in the world Joe wanted to see.

"Hey, Joe! I wanted you to meet my new partner." Dead-eye's dark face was split with a wide grin. "He's an Army grunt, but he's almost tough enough to make the cut."

Joe glanced at Drew, but immediately turned his gaze down to Jason, adjusting his grip on the bar. "Hello."

"Joe Morrissey, right? I've heard a lot about you," Drew said. "It's nice to meet you."

Joe glanced up. He narrowed his eyes as he caught the innocent expression on Drew's face. There was no way Joe could say the same; he'd choke on the words, and that would cause a lot of questions. As it would if he cut the man dead, so he decided on a comprise. "And I've heard a lot about you." Too much.

Tyson's grin faded, replaced by a look of puzzlement. "Did we catch you at a bad time?"

Joe couldn't possibly explain the situation, not even to his fellow Seal. "Sorry, Thunder and I were just about to go over our mission. Thunder and Pixel are assigned under Finn and me for the NC State environmental summit."

"So are we," Tyson said, and he smiled again, this time at Jason. "Good to see you, Thunder. This is Joker, also known as Drew Martin. Drew was XO for Bravo Company at Lawson & Greer. Drew, this is Jason Hekili, one of our West Coast brothers. He came to us via Hollywood, but don't hold that against him. He's been through a couple of shitstorms and earned his way just like the rest of us."

Drew's smile became more natural as he extended his hand to Jason. "Hollywood, eh? Were you an actor?"

"Mostly bit parts and B-grade horror," Jason replied, sitting up on the bench and shaking Drew's hand. "I had a short-lived series, but I think I've gotten more exposure from the "Men of Hercules Security" calendar we did for charity." Jason laughed. "I was certainly more *exposed*, at least."

"We were *all* exposed." Tyson punched Joe on the shoulder. "Even our quiet one here. Finn stripped down without even being asked, big surprise. I understand Joe took some convincing."

Joe felt his face heating. "But I did it. For charity."

"There's a calendar?" Drew's face lit up with interest. "Is it for this year?"

"Two years ago," Dead-eye said. "It sold out and had a second printing. I bet Herc still has copies somewhere, if you want one."

Joe looked away. He didn't care for the thought of Drew having one of the calendars. Not that he was ashamed of his picture, not at all, but it made him feel oddly vulnerable. Like Drew would be judging him. He muttered in Russian, an epithet, wishing Jason had kept his damned mouth shut.

"I may ask him about it," Drew said, giving Joe a shrewd look. "I'd like to see how you guys were posed. I bet Joe here had the *sexy innocent* thing going. Am I right?"

Joe glanced up, unable to keep himself from shooting Drew a Glare of Messy Death. Fortunately no one else caught it, and Joe looked away again, with another muttered Russian profanity calling Drew's parentage into question.

"Hey, guys!" A new voice entered the conversation, and Joe spotted Finn approaching. He was smiling, but Joe could practically see the "oh shit" thought balloon over his head. "What are we talking about?"

"The hot Herc's calendar," Drew said. "They got my curiosity up about it."

"I've still got mine, even though it's out of date," Finn said, moving to stand next to Joe. "All I'm saying is, Lee's a damned good photographer."

It was true, and Joe had a few photos of Finn—and of both he and Finn—that Lee Albright had taken. He'd even allowed a few more risqué photos to be taken of himself—at Finn's urging and solely for Finn's benefit—with the promise no one else would ever see them.

But there was no way he was going to mention that little bit of information. Once Jason had greeted Finn, Joe reached out to touch Finn's shoulder to get his attention. "Thunder and Pixel are working for us at the summit. So are Dead-eye and... his partner." For some reason Drew's name, even his merc name, got stuck in Joe's throat. "Should we get a conference room and run down what we have?"

"Joker," Drew said in a gratingly pleasant voice. "My handle is Joker. Or you can call me Drew. I'll answer to either."

"Sure," Joe said, his own voice syrupy sweet, but he looked through Drew as though he wasn't even there before turning his attention back to Finn. "Conference room?"

"I think that's a good idea," Finn said, donning the closed neutral expression Joe only saw when they were playing poker. "Let's go."

Lexy gave them one of the small meeting rooms with a table, computer hookup, and a whiteboard, and Jason called Pixel to let him know about the meeting. After Pixel arrived—he'd been paying a visit with his Raleigh counterparts in the computer security office—Finn and Joe brought everyone up to speed on their meetings with the NC State coordinators and ran over the initial security models they were looking at.

When the meeting concluded, Joe stayed at the computer as the others left the room. He wanted to see which other mercs were available for the mission, and whether or not he could judiciously request an alteration to the team.

Finn lingered as well, and once he and Joe were alone, he closed the conference room door and leaned against it. "Is this how it's going to be?" he asked quietly.

Joe looked up. "What do you mean?" he asked cautiously.

"Don't insult my intelligence, Joe," Finn said, although he appeared more weary than angry. "You know exactly what I mean. You couldn't even say his name."

"No, I couldn't." Joe ran a hand through his short hair. "I came into work figuring I'd have a peaceful day with *you* getting ready for this assignment, and instead I have Dead-eye ramming his wonderful new partner down my throat and find out he's assigned to our mission. Sorry, but I'm only human, Finn. I thought I could pretend he didn't exist, and I'm not going to be allowed to do that."

Finn bowed his head and fell silent for a long moment. "I'm sorry," he said at last, lifting his gaze to meet Joe's. "I didn't know they were assigned to us. I wouldn't have put you in that position. I hope you know that."

Joe stood up and crossed to Finn, laying his hands on Finn's shoulders. "I know. It's not your fault, and yeah, I realize this is on me.

It's my problem, not yours, okay? I'll learn to live with it, if I must. Just... I need some time, okay?" He didn't want Finn to feel guilty. It was hard enough knowing that the nights Finn wasn't with him, he was with Drew. Joe wasn't going to mention that the second night after Finn had confessed his love, Joe had gotten drunker than he had since he'd been a plebe at the Naval Academy. He had spent most of the next morning hanging over a toilet.

"I love you, and I don't want to keep hurting you." Finn covered Joe's hands with his own and watched Joe with troubled eyes. "It's bad enough that I've caused you turmoil on a personal level. I don't want it to affect you on a professional level, too. I said I'd pick you, and I meant it. I'll break it off with Drew, and it'll be just the two of us again."

Finn had made the offer before, but Joe was a realist, and as much as he wished he could accept it, he couldn't. "I won't do that," he said softly. "I appreciate it, but I know it would make you unhappy, and I'm afraid I'd lose you in the long run. You're not a one-man man, Finn. I understand that. I've always understood it. It's just... this is different. Knowing this guy means something to you. Knowing you love him. When you were just having hookups, it didn't bother me, because there was no comparison between them and me, you know? I never had to wonder what they were giving you that I couldn't. With him...." He shrugged, not knowing what to say.

"Meanwhile, I'm making you unhappy, and I'm afraid I'll lose you in the long run, too," Finn said.

"That won't happen." Joe might have some uncertainties about the situation, but wanting to be with Finn wasn't one of them. "I've stuck by you for eight years, haven't I? Yes, there's a selfish part of me that wants you all for myself, but that's on *me*, not you."

"You sound sure right now," Finn said, appearing unconvinced. "But things change. What if you can't come to terms with so much as admitting he exists? I don't want you to be miserable or to doubt yourself because of me."

Joe leaned forward, pressing his forehead to Finn's. "I can't predict the future. I wish I could. All I can say is that I'll try. And the reason I will is because I would rather have half of your heart, Brian Finnegan, than all of anyone else's in the whole world."

"You have it," Finn said, tightening his fingers around Joe's. "There's a place in my heart that's yours alone, and if I lose you, no one else could ever fill it. Not even Drew. I know it's hard for you to understand, but from my perspective, there's no comparison between the two of you. You're wondering what you lack that he doesn't, but neither of you lack anything. I'm looking at what you both *have*."

Finn's words helped to soothe a little bit of the ache in Joe's heart, but he still couldn't help but believe there was something he didn't have, or else he'd *be* everything Finn needed—the way Finn was everything *he* needed. "Thanks. It's just... it's like what I asked you before, you know? What if I came to you and said I loved someone else, a stranger you didn't know, had never met. How would it make you feel, Finn?"

"I know I'm asking a lot," Finn said. "I know this is a huge adjustment, and I want you to take all the time you need. If it turns out to be too much, tell me. Meanwhile, do you want me to talk to Herc about getting Drew off the team?"

Joe felt a little guilty that he'd been trying to do exactly that. "I don't know. Maybe it's best to let him stay. I don't want... Drew... to say I was unprofessional, but he needs to realize you and I are in charge. He may have been an XO, but he's just a junior guard on this mission, and he's still in training. If he fucks anything up, I'll bust his chops the same as I would anyone else."

Finn drew back and fixed Joe with a sardonic look. "Why do I get the feeling you'll be putting everything he says and does under the microscope to find a reason to bust his chops? If things stay like they were today, Dead-eye, Thunder, Pixel—hell, probably everybody who works here—will notice. This may be a lowkey mission, but we still need to be a functional team."

Joe released Finn's hands and stepped away with a frown. "I told you, this was dropped on me all within five minutes of you showing up, Finn. I'm sorry I had a reaction to it. To *him.* You say you don't want me to be unhappy, but you're calling me on it when I am? And you accuse me of being ready to find a reason to dump on him? Maybe I'm the one who should ask to be removed from the mission in that case, because you're saying I can't be a fair leader."

"I'm sorry." Finn rested his hand on Joe's shoulder and stroked it soothingly. "I didn't mean to sound accusatory. I know you're a fair leader. You don't have to put up with him on the team just to prove your professionalism."

"Actually, I think I do." Joe stepped away from Finn. "Maybe not to you, but to him. I've worked with people I've disliked before. Even people I hated before. Just leave it, Finn. I know you're trying to help, but there is nothing you can say or do that will make any of this easier, okay? I might as well give up on pretending he doesn't exist and learn to deal with it."

"Got it." Finn gave a brief nod. "In that case, I'll leave you to it. If you need me for anything, I'll be in the gym."

"All right." There was no way Joe could say the right thing in this situation. Finn seemed to alternate between trying to protect him from things and wanting him to face up to them, and Joe was sure part of it had to do with Finn feeling guilty. Not that Finn felt guilty for loving Drew, but for the fact that doing so was causing Joe so much self-doubt. "Just... know that I do love you, Finn. I'm making the best of this that I can. Not just for your sake, but for mine, okay?"

Finn closed the distance between them and captured Joe's lips in a kiss that was tender rather than deep. "I know, and I appreciate it," he murmured. "I love you, too."

"I'm glad." Joe whispered. He closed his eyes, letting himself soak in Finn's nearness, at least for the moment. "Let's just get this job done, okay?"

"Okay," Finn said, sliding his arms around Joe's waist.

Joe embraced Finn, pulling him close. "Come over to my place tonight?" he asked softly. He wasn't going to beg, but he needed Finn, he needed to know things were going to be all right between them.

Finn nuzzled his smooth cheek against Joe's neatly trimmed beard and hummed quietly. "I'd love to. Want me to bring anything?"

"Only you."

Finn was all Joe needed. He just wished with all his heart that Finn could say the same about him.

10

D rew watched as a group of young men jogged past his position, wearing shorts and tank tops that revealed toned muscles and skin glistening with sweat. Working as a bodyguard might not be as exciting as being in the middle of a free-fire zone, but not having to worry that everyone who approached might be a suicide bomber was a nice change. The eye candy available on a university campus wasn't bad, either. Of course, they were far too young, so he had no interest in them beyond their pleasant addition to the local scenery. It wasn't just that they were too young and innocent for him, either. The truth was that Finn was just about all Drew could handle.

He smiled as he glanced toward the entrance to the McKimmon Conference Center, where the Summit on Ecological Sustainability was being held. He could see Finn talking animatedly with one of the university staff, probably a professor judging by the tweedy appearance of the guy. At Finn's shoulder Joe hovered watchfully, as though he were present as much to guard Finn as anyone else. Not that Drew was surprised at all, given the way Joe felt about Finn. He wished he could crack through the shell of iron-clad professionalism Joe had chosen to erect around himself whenever Drew was around. Joe was the quiet sort, who rarely spoke unless he had something important to say, but he was silent whenever Drew was around. According to Finn, Joe had decided to be completely professional when it came to their interactions, and so far he had been, which was both a relief and a challenge in Drew's eyes. Not that he wanted to make Joe angry, especially since he had a pretty good idea that if Joe gave Finn an ultimatum to choose between the two of them, Drew would be on the losing end. But the real reason Drew took it as a challenge was that Joe was incredibly hot, and he really did have the *sexy innocent* aura down to a science.

Drew found himself attracted to Joe much in the same way he'd been attracted to Finn right from the start, and if he were honest, Joe pushed a lot of his buttons. He'd had more than one fantasy about seeing Joe and Finn together, and about being between the two of them in bed. He was sure the results would be explosive—although at the moment, he knew Joe would probably rather slit Drew's throat than go to bed with him.

Joe looked up, as though he felt Drew's gaze, and even at the distance of a dozen yards, Drew could see the smoldering look Joe was giving him. No doubt it was because Joe thought Drew was looking at Finn, and maybe even wondering if he should have taken Finn up on his offer to have Drew removed from the team. He wondered if Joe knew that Finn had made a similar offer to him, offering to have Drew removed without prejudice if Drew thought interacting with Joe was going to be too stressful. Yet Drew was the kind of man who enjoyed a challenge, and he thought getting Joe Morrissey to not only like him, but to consider him as a lover, might be the biggest challenge of his life.

Drew smiled at Joe before glancing away, looking across the walkway at where Tyson stood, watching over the groups of passing students, ever alert for danger. Tyson was an excellent partner, and once he got over ragging Drew for being Army instead of Navy, they'd settled into a good working relationship. Their skills meshed well. Drew was able to see the big picture in a situation, and Tyson was used to a smaller focus, which made sense for a man who was a crack sniper; he had to be aware of the most minute details in a situation. It meant that they could cover the entire gamut in surveillance, and on the two missions they'd had leading up to the current one, they'd managed to foil both an attempted robbery and a murder.

"Status check," Joe's deep voice came over the communications circuit. The earpieces they'd been issued by Chris were state-of-the-art, making Joe sound almost like he was standing right next to him.

"Baker one, check," Tyson replied. He was the lead of their two-man team, designated *Baker* for the mission.

"Baker two, check," Drew said. He listened as Jason and Tailor acknowledged as team "Charlie." Six men might not seem like a lot to many people, even with Chris occupying a van at the curb full of equipment to monitor the sensors they'd placed throughout the conference center. However, six trained killers was probably more than anyone would be comfortable with hanging around a bunch of scientists and diplomats. Normal campus security was stationed around the facility as well. Their job was to police the badges of attendees and deal with the more mundane matters like people who were lost or who had misplaced their cellphones. It was up to Drew and his teammates to make sure no one smuggled in bombs or guns, and that none of the protesters already ringing the building did anything stupid. That was why the team wasn't attired in business suits or casual clothing that would help them blend in with the students. All of them were outfitted in black tactical gear complete with bulletproof vests emblazoned with SECURITY, and while their guns weren't full-on assault rifles—those had been rejected by the conference organizers as being a bit too much for the situation—each man carried a fully loaded semiautomatic pistol and extra magazines, along with a taser. There were assault rifles in the van with Chris, as well as tranquilizer guns, tear gas grenades, and a small trauma rig in case things got nasty.

Tyson walked over to join him. "Heads up, looks like the boss men are coming over."

Drew glanced over to see Finn and Joe approaching. "Probably last minute orders. I bet the conference delegates are on their way from the hotel."

"Curtain's about to go up," Finn said when he reached them. Although he retained a professional demeanor, his expression grew softer when he looked at Drew. "Campus security is standing by, and Pixel's running an automated scan for any threats that pop up online."

"Sounds good," Tyson said.

Drew couldn't help but smile a bit at Finn. "We're ready, boss." He looked over Finn's shoulder at Joe. "I mean, bosses."

Joe gave no reaction whatsoever to Drew's slight jibe, and Drew figured he didn't want to face Joe at poker. About the only tell Joe had shown was a tendency to mutter in Russian when he was annoyed—and it probably would have pissed him off to know Drew spoke the language and had understood every time Joe had called him a "bastard" under his breath.

"Thunder and Tailor are monitoring the protestors," Finn said. "I want you two to keep an eye on the arrivals. Make sure no unauthorized personnel approaches the delegates' cars."

"On it," Drew said. "We've got this. Right, Dead-eye?"

"Easy peasy," Tyson replied, giving a thumbs up. "Come on, partner. Between the two of us I bet we'll scare off everyone, including the delegates."

With a last, lingering look at Finn, Drew followed in Tyson's wake. It was going to be a long and tiring day, but at least at the end of it he could look forward to an evening with Finn. That alone made any tedium worth it.

11

Finn swept his gaze around the area as he patrolled outside the conference center near the rear exits, keeping his pace slow and steady. The conference was on its third day, and so far, everything had gone smoothly. There had been a couple of times when they'd checked out alleged suspicious activity. In fact, Joe had left Finn to patrol alone for a few minutes while he joined Tailor and Jason to investigate a report. But every incident had turned out to be nothing of note, and Finn expected this one to be the same.

A small part of Finn wished Joe would be held up until their shift ended, which he knew was unkind, but things had been tense between them lately. Finn was trying to balance his schedule fairly between Joe and Drew by planning two nights per week each, which gave them an equal amount of time and gave him some downtime as well. He loved them both, but sometimes, he needed to decompress and spend an evening doing nothing but catching up on the magazines he subscribed to or playing *Red Dead Redemption 2* by himself.

Last night, he was supposed to hang out with Joe. Rarely did he make concrete plans with either of them. Like him, Drew preferred to be spontaneous and do whatever they were in the mood for, whether that was going out to eat or to a movie, binging a show on Netflix, or tumbling into bed. Joe was also easy-going, although he preferred activities that allowed them to stay in. But last night, Joe had asked if they could postpone their night together, which was unexpected.

Finn agreed without asking any questions. Poking Joe about something tended to make him close up even tighter. Joe would talk about it if and when he was ready, and while part of Finn was afraid it meant Joe was starting to pull away from him, he reminded himself that Joe had stuck by Finn for eight years and would continue to do so. Joe always said what he meant and meant what he said. Finn was counting on that now.

He also suspected the situation with Drew wasn't the only factor behind Joe's behavior. The recent mission to Pakistan had affected Joe in ways Finn hadn't seen before, and he was starting to think Joe was dealing with PTSD in the aftermath of whatever he'd experienced. After the conference was over, Finn was going to suggest that they hold off on taking another mission and that Joe talk to one of the company therapists. Chris had vouched for Dr. Matthews, giving him credit for helping Chris through the grieving process when he lost everything he owned in a fire and was stuck in a safe house.

Finn was also considering whether he ought to put his relationship with Drew on hold for a while. He didn't want to break up—that thought was too painful—but having to accept the presence of another man in Finn's life might be a complication Joe didn't need right now. The problem was, he didn't know how Drew might react to that. Drew might see it as a sign that Joe was Finn's priority and opt out of the relationship because he didn't want to feel like he was always in the back seat.

Blowing out a frustrated huff, Finn tried to push aside the tumultuous thoughts roiling around in his head. He needed to focus on the task at hand, not on his screwed-up love life. In theory, having two men was exactly what he'd always wanted, but the reality was far more complicated than he'd imagined it would be. He never realized how conflicted he'd feel about being in the middle, for one thing. It would probably be easier if all three of them took the same approach to relationships, but no, Finn had to fall in love with Mr. White Picket Fence.

Maybe he ought to give monogamy a try. He'd been with Joe for eight years, after all. Surely that meant something. Would it be so bad if he couldn't roam once in a while? That level of commitment would make Joe happy.

But his heart wrenched at the thought of never feeling Drew's arms around him, of never again experiencing their easy connection and explosive chemistry. Giving up Drew would hurt on levels Finn didn't want to think about, and he knew he'd risk growing to resent Joe even if he broke up with Drew voluntarily.

He didn't know what the right thing to do was, and that was driving him crazy.

"Excuse me? You're one of the Hercules Security people?"

Finn turned around to find a young man looking at him hopefully, and he was almost grateful for the distraction from his thoughts.

"Can I help you?"

The young man smiled and stepped closer, holding up a piece of paper. "I have a message for you."

"From who?" Finn asked as he took the paper. No one on the team would send a written message, and he couldn't think of why anyone would need to pass him a note. Frowning, he glanced down at the paper, but the words weren't English, and his spidey senses started tingling. "What is this?"

The young man was still smiling, and Finn didn't notice anyone else until another man—this one much bigger—was suddenly behind him. He felt a quick, sharp sting against his neck, and as he drew in a breath, a wave of dizziness washed over him.

"This is what you Americans call payback," a harsh, deep voice murmured close to his ear.

Finn tried to fight back, to shout—anything that would give him some time and maybe get his teammates' attention—but his arms were weak and unresponsive, and he couldn't get any words out.

"Oh, you are feeling ill!" The big man put an arm around Finn's waist, while the younger man came to his other side. "Here, let us help you to your friends. They are outside, we saw them."

Somehow the tone of the man's voice wasn't at all reassuring, but Finn couldn't even turn his head to get a good look at the big man. They started walking him toward the rear exit of the building—which was *not* where Chris was with the Hercules Security van. He struggled to shrug them off, but his muscles grew weaker with every passing moment, and he could barely pick his feet off the ground as he shambled along between them.

Maybe Joe would return, he thought with a little flare of hope. If Joe showed up in time, he'd take care of these two assholes.

There was a man waiting by the rear exit, but he was with Finn's captors, because he smiled nastily and opened the door for the others.

"You got one. I thought they'd never split their teams," he said. "Let's get him into the van."

Finn could see a big black van parked in the loading dock, and as he watched, yet another man slid the door open from the inside. The two guys supporting him hurried faster now, letting Finn's feet drag on the pavement.

Just before they reached the van, there was a shout from behind them, and Finn recognized Joe's voice.

"Stop or I'll shoot!"

The younger man glanced behind them, but Finn's captors didn't halt. There were cracks of gunfire, and the big guy on Finn's right let out a cry of pain as at least one of the bullets impacted on him. But it was too late; the man inside the van grabbed his injured teammate, while the younger guy and the man who had been at the door pushed Finn into the van. Finn could hear footsteps pounding toward the van, which had to be Joe in pursuit.

Finn found himself dropped onto the cold metal floor of the van, his head bouncing painfully. But he was turned in the right way to catch sight of Joe running toward him, a look of desperate determination on his face. Joe had his gun up, and as the door to the van closed and the driver took off with a squeal of tires, Finn heard the impact of more bullets, shattering the windows of the van. The vehicle didn't stop, but over the roar of the engine he heard Joe bellowing in rage, a sound of pure, visceral fury unlike anything Finn had heard from his lover before.

Finn's last thought before darkness overwhelmed him was, *you guys are so fucked*.

12

"Morrissey! Holy fuck, what's happening?"

Jason's voice reached Joe through his earpiece, but he ignored the question as he stared after the van, unable to believe someone had snatched Finn away right in front of his eyes. It was impossible that anyone could have gotten the drop on him, and yet it had happened. All Joe could think about was getting Finn back.

"Pixel! Call 911 and report that Brian Finnegan has been kidnapped. We need an APB put out on a black van, Maryland plates M as in Mike 302443. Call Herc. Tell him four guys snatched Finn from the summit. We need a quick response team on the double. Everyone else, inside the conference center. Tailor, you get with campus security for any of their internal camera recordings. Thunder, Dead-eye, Joker—we scour every inch of this fucking place to see what we can find to help us figure out who took Finn."

"On it," Chris acknowledged at once.

"Shouldn't we give chase?" Jason asked, breathing hard into his mike as he was obviously running flat out.

Joe was already heading back toward the rear of the conference center, and he could hear sirens approaching. He flipped the safety on his gun as he neared the door, not wanting to shoot any campus police who came through. He was as icily calm and yet more furious than he could ever remember being. That was good—he had to keep it together to find Finn.

"By the time we got to our cars, they'd be long gone. Better to let the cops chase and Herc to get a specialist on it," he replied. "In the meantime, I want the evidence before it's picked up by the campus cops. They can't handle this, and the Raleigh police will have to call in the FBI. By the time they figure out jurisdiction, Finn could be dead. We're not going to let that happen."

"Hell, no, we aren't." Drew's voice was a low, angry growl.

Joe opened the rear door again, and he saw campus police approaching. "Dead-eye, get here on the double. You and Joker both. I'm going to be stuck talking to the police, and I need you to lock this area down. Finn may have tried to leave us a clue, and if so, we need to find it."

Within five minutes the entire Hercules team was there, except for Chris, who was monitoring the feeds in the van. Joe had enough time to brief them on what he saw and set them to looking for evidence before he had to give a statement to the police. The conference organizers also wanted a report, but by the time the cops cut Joe loose, Herc had arrived. He shooed Joe toward his team before taking over the political duties, much to Joe's relief.

Joe hurried over to Jason, Tyson, and Drew, who were standing around something on the ground, not letting the cops at it yet. Joe was glad—screw jurisdiction. This mission was about *Finn*, and as far as he was concerned, Hercules Security had jurisdiction. "What have you got?"

"A note," Drew said, his expression troubled as he looked at Joe. "It's written in Urdu."

Joe felt all the blood leaving his face. Urdu was the official language of Pakistan, and he was far too familiar with certain very bad elements who were based in that country. He crouched down, pulling a pen out of his pocket so that he could lift the folded portion of the note.

We know you killed our friends, the note read. *Now you will pay.*

Joe stood up, balling his hands into fists so tight that the pen he was holding shattered. "I know who did this. They were coming for me." The ice in the pit of his stomach churned, threatening to make him throw up, but he clamped his jaw down on it. Now was not the time for panic. Not if he was going to save Finn.

"What does this have to do with you?" Tyson asked, appearing puzzled. "Are you sure this isn't a diversion? Do we need to clear the convention center?"

"It's the mission I was on in Pakistan. We were going after another part of that human trafficking ring Pixel found a few years ago. The damned cockroaches just kept coming back, and we thought if we could kill the leader, we could kill it once and for all." Joe grimaced. "I guess we didn't do as good a job as we thought, and somehow they must have found out who I work for. And they fucking took Finn!"

"*Fuck.*" Drew raked his fingers through his short hair and grimaced. "If this is revenge, the clock is ticking. No way Finn is getting out of this alive unless we find him."

"Don't you think I know that?" Joe turned on Drew, scowling. "I'm going after them. I won't let them kill Finn, especially since it's me they want."

"I'm going with you," Drew said in a tone that brooked no argument. "You'll need backup, and I know the language."

The last thing Joe wanted was this interloper tagging along when he had a job to do. "I don't want you. I want D-Day. He's better at this shit than anyone else."

"Unfortunately, Daryl is in French Guiana with Emerson." Herc's voice came from behind them, and Joe turned to see his boss approaching. "Joe, you do need backup."

"I'll go," Jason spoke up. "I went up against these guys before, remember?"

There was a squawk of protest from Chris, but before he could speak, Herc shook his head. "I need you here to help Pixel. You've gotten almost as good at the electronics end as Pita, and unfortunately Pita is tied up at the moment. I can't spring him for at least two days. Joker is right—he speaks the language, and he's had more recent combat experience than anyone else. This is definitely a combat situation, so it's the two of you. Dead-eye, you're going to be auxiliary; we may need a sniper, so I want to hold you out of the thick of things. I have Pixel running Finn's GPS tags now, so I want you two ready to go. Am I clear?"

"Clear, Herc," Joe said, taking a deep breath. He didn't want to work with Drew—he didn't *trust* Drew to have his back if things fell into the crapper. At the end of the day, though, Joe also knew he couldn't go into this without the resources of Hercules Security, so he had to play by Herc's rules. For now.

"Clear, sir," Drew said, appearing grimly satisfied.

Joe put on his best poker face; he couldn't let Drew see how pissed off he was. Finn came first, and finding him was all that mattered. "I want one of the executive protection SUVs, full auto weapons, and every kind of nonlethal load we have available. If we have to frag a whole location, I want to make sure we don't get Finn by accident. I'd just as soon tranq these assholes and kill them later rather than risk anything happening to Finn."

"You can have anything you need," Herc replied.

"Pixel, do you have a fix on Finn's GPS yet?" Joe asked. He turned and started walking toward the front of the building, not caring if Drew came along. He was going to head after Finn, and damn anyone who got in his way, and that included Drew Martin.

"I'm pretty sure they're jamming the signal," Chris said, an exasperated edge in his voice. "I'm working on it, but these guys are pros. I can't get a lock on them. I'll keep you updated."

"Shit." Joe thought quickly, turning over options. "What about traffic cams? Have the cops had any luck with that plate?"

"No love on that front," Chris said. "The number you gave is from plates reported stolen two days ago. The cops haven't spotted the van —or at least not a van with those plates or a busted window. My guess is they've ditched it. Either they had a backup vehicle already prepped or they've stolen one. My money is on the backup."

These people had kidnapping down to a science. It was how they made their money. However, they'd want to avoid detection, too, and that meant one thing.

"South. They'd go south, I'm sure of it. Running for the empty areas past I-40. There are lots of places where there's nothing but farms and woods for miles, all the way down to the Cape Fear River. Can you listen for any reports of suspicious activity? Maybe we'll get lucky and they'll break in, or a bunch of foreigners will scare the crap out of some local paranoid."

"On it," Chris said.

Joe stepped out of the convention center, heading for his car. Drew was right on his heels, but there wasn't anything he could do about that. When he reached the vehicle he unlocked it and then got in and fastened his seatbelt. Drew slid into the passenger seat. He glanced at Joe as he buckled up.

"What's our first move?" he asked.

Joe wished he could ignore the question, but he couldn't. At the moment he really didn't give a damn about professionalism, but he had his orders.

"I'm going back to HQ." He started the car, putting action to words. "I'm picking up one of our executive protection vehicles, which all have GPS locators and trackers. I'm going to load up every damned weapon I can find and hope that Pixel gets something. Until he does, I'm following my gut. You may know Urdu, but I know Raleigh, and I've gone up against these guys before. They don't want prying eyes for what they're going to do. They want something, or they would have just killed him outright. They're either going to sweat him for info, or they're going to try to set up an exchange. They must know they can't get him out of the country, not from here. Not unless they have a private plane, but I don't think that's what they want. I'm betting what they want is me. They just don't know who I am. Yet."

"They sure as hell won't find out from Finn," Drew said. "He'd rather die than give you up."

"Yeah, which is stupid." Joe grimaced. "He should tell them what they want. I'll go with them. Anything I have to do to save him. Even if it kills me."

Drew let out an amused snort. "That's probably what he's thinking right about now, too. He'll do anything to save you, even if it kills him."

"I won't let that happen." Joe said the words with utter conviction. He *would* save Finn. Anything else was unthinkable. "Just don't get in my way."

"I'm not planning on it," Drew said, his voice quiet but determined. "I want to get Finn back, no matter what it takes."

Joe tightened his grip on the steering wheel. "Yeah, I get it. I don't trust you to have my back, but I don't care as long as you get Finn out. That's all that matters to me."

"You may not trust me, but I've got your back. For Finn's sake, if nothing else."

"Don't ask me to believe that." Joe growled in disgust. "I know what you want, and I know that if I'm not in the picture, you get it. So spare me any insincere words of support."

Drew regarded Joe with disbelief. "You think Finn would miraculously become a fan of monogamy just because you're not around? *Please.* Finn isn't the type who can give everything to one man. If it wasn't you, it would be someone else. He loves you, and you're important to him, so by extension, I've got your back because I don't want him to be hurt."

"Yeah? Well he loves you, too, so I'm sure you know he'd be just fine eventually." Joe shook his head. "Then you'd have him because you wouldn't have to share him with anyone else he loved. The hookups meant nothing. That's why I could live with them. I'm sure you'd live with them, too."

Drew studied Joe, his eyes narrowed shrewdly. "You're throwing the word 'love' around, but I'm not sure you understand how deep it runs with Finn. Just because he's not monogamous doesn't mean he doesn't care deeply. Losing you would cause him a lot of damage."

"I understand more than you think." Joe glared straight ahead. He should probably just cut Drew off, but if anything did happen to him, he didn't want Drew telling Finn how awful Joe was. Maybe, just maybe, he needed to get some of this off his chest. "Finn has been my lover, my partner, my heart... my *everything* for the last eight years. My reason to get up in the morning. I never tied him down because that would have killed his spirit. You've been around him what, six weeks? I know losing me would hurt him. I know it hurts him to know he's hurting me by being with you. I know he wishes he could be just with me and be satisfied, but he can't. And I won't ask that of him, even if it means sharing him with you. Don't presume to think you know what I understand. You don't know me. You know nothing about me."

"If you understand so much, why do you keep saying he'll be fine if something happens to you?" Drew asked, frowning at Joe. "Why are you implying we'll have a perfect life with you out of the picture, as you put it? Either you don't really know how much Finn values you or you're seriously undervaluing yourself. Which is it?"

The question pulled Joe up short, but he didn't want to think about it. He didn't want to let Drew inside his head. "I'm not implying you'll have a perfect life, just the one *you* probably want. Anything else is none of your fucking business," he snapped.

"Don't presume to think you know what I want," Drew said, lobbing Joe's own words back at him. "You don't know anything about me, either."

"Yeah? I know you want Finn." Joe laughed, but there wasn't any humor in the sound. "I know that you want him enough to stick around when you see that he's conflicted about you and how being with you makes me feel. He even offered to give you up if that's what *I* wanted, but I'm not that selfish. As far as I'm concerned, you're hurting him, but if he wants you, I'm not going to stand in his way."

"Oh, you think I haven't seen how this is tearing Finn up?" Drew's eyebrows climbed to his hairline as he fixed Joe with an incredulous look. "You think I haven't offered to bow out? You think I'm enough of an asshole that I can stand by and watch him hurt and do fuck all about it, unlike Saint Joe? Is that what you think?"

"I don't think I'm a fucking saint," Joe snapped. "But yeah, I think you're a selfish prick."

"It takes one to know one, then, because you're still with him too," Drew shot back.

"Yeah, and when *I* offered to bow out, he fucking announced to the whole company that he was in love with me." Joe's dislike of Drew only grew the longer they talked, but he was damned now if he was going to let Drew make him feel like shit. He could do that well enough on his own. He didn't need this fucker piling on him. "I'd kill for him. I'd die for him. Can you say the same, Mr. Johnny Come Lately? He'd get over you a hell of a lot easier than he'd get over me. So if you think I'm selfish, *fuck you.*"

"I don't think you're selfish," Drew said with a little shrug. "I think you're being hypocritical, but more than that, I think you've got something eating at you that's bigger than what's going on between the three of us, and it's coloring everything else."

"Yeah, well, you know what? I don't give a fuck what you think." Joe steered the car into the Hercules Security parking lot, pulling into a space and stopping. He turned off the ignition and looked at Drew. "If I were a hypocrite, I'd've taken Finn up on his offer to dump you. If I didn't love him, I'd leave him and this fucked up mess of a relationship that apparently isn't making anyone happy. So what's your angle, Joker? Because I may love Finn, but I don't give a shit about you personally, and it won't hurt my delicate feelings if you say the same."

Drew studied Joe in silence, and then he gave a little "what the hell" shrug. "We don't give a shit about each other for different reasons. I don't know you well enough, so the only reason I give a shit about you is because Finn loves you. You're important to him, so by extension, you matter to me. You, however, see me as competition. I'm an intruder, and you've got up some pretty thick walls against me even though you don't need to. I don't want to take Finn from you. I couldn't even if I wanted to. I don't want to fuck up your relationship either. It's older and stronger than mine. I know that. What I'd like is peaceful coexistence so we aren't all in a fucked-up mess."

"So tell me this, Mr. All I Want Is Peace, why *don't* you just bow out? If you aren't really competition, why don't you go away?" Joe snorted. "If my relationship with Finn is older and stronger, why are you sticking your cock into it?"

"I could bow out." Drew inclined his head to acknowledge the point. "Finn and I talked about it. He didn't want me to. I get what you're saying, Morrissey. The newcomer ducking out is the more honorable move to make. I could still take a powder. It'd hurt a hell of a lot worse now than it would've a few weeks ago, but I could do it. So I do the honorable thing and break up with Finn... and then what? He goes back to hooking up with strangers? What if he finds someone else who strikes the same kind of sparks I did? Are you going to run that guy off too?"

Joe shook his head, feeling defeated. "It's too fucking late for you to bow out now, and you damned well know it. Yeah, you could have done the honorable thing, but that time came and went, so now you're stuck. I'll be damned if I'm going to have you tell Finn I ran you off. I'm not doing that to him, and neither are you, do you understand me? Especially since I get the feeling there's a price on my head. Someone has to be there for him, you asshole. And you got yourself elected."

"I accept," Drew said, a sardonic edge in his voice. "Now are you going to sit here and jaw at me some more, or are we going to go find Finn?"

A cold wave of pure rage flowed over Joe, and he was glad he'd left his gun back with the cops. If he'd had it now, he'd've been awfully tempted to shoot Drew and damn the consequences.

"Fuck you, Martin," he said and then unfastened his seatbelt and got out of the car. All he knew at the moment was that he had to save Finn, no matter what. Though it was starting to look like dying in the process might be a hell of a lot less painful than living.

13

W hen Finn returned to consciousness, he was aware of little things first. The chafe of restraints—real metal handcuffs, not zip ties—against his wrists. A dull ache in his shoulders said his arms had been cuffed behind the metal chair he was in for a while. A blindfold tied a little too tight around his head. He had no idea how long he was out, but he thought it was a pretty good sign that they were no longer traveling. Chances were good that they were holed up somewhere relatively close to Raleigh.

Not that it mattered if they hauled Finn all the way to Timbuktu. Joe would find him. Between Joe's unrelenting determination and all the resources Hercules Security had at its disposal, the question wasn't *if* but *when* the extraction team would arrive. All Finn had to do was stay alive long enough for them to get there. Whoever had taken him was fucked, but they'd be fucked even harder if Joe shifted from rescue to revenge.

Finn strained to hear any faint sounds that might give him a clue about where he was and if any of the people who'd kidnapped him were in the room.

"I see you are awake." The voice came from in front of him. Male, deep pitched, with a melodious accent. The man had a tone to his voice that was both mature and used to command. "We have some questions for you."

Finn's mouth was dry, probably due to whatever they'd stuck him with, but he sat up straight and turned his head in the direction of the voice. "You can ask. Doesn't mean I'll answer."

The man chuckled. "Ah, but it is in your best interest to do so, fully and completely. We don't have any real desire to kill you, but we also cannot sell you. You're far too dangerous, and we know your associates are coming after you even as we speak. But we are also patient, and have ways to... compel you. Unpleasant ways. Your friends will not find you before we could do something very, very bad, so your cooperation is only to your benefit. Besides, all we desire is a name. One little name, and we will leave you here and let your associates know where to find you. Alive, even."

"The carrot and the stick," Finn said, nodding as if in approval. "A classic opening gambit. But hey, if it ain't broke, don't fix it."

"We are reasonable men," the interrogator replied, and Finn heard him as he shifted closer. From the height of his voice, he was sitting across from Finn, and he leaned closer. "Since you fully appreciate the stakes, let's get to the question. A man from your organization caused a great deal of trouble for my employers. He would have recently returned from Pakistan, and he speaks the language. Tall, dark haired, bearded, and muscular. That is all we know about him, but I suspect you can tell me at once who this man is."

Fuck.

Joe. They wanted Joe.

Finn would go through the hell of being tortured for anyone at Hercules Security. They were his family, and he'd do just about anything to protect them. But he'd die before he ever gave up Joe.

"You think tall, dark, and muscular narrows it down any?" Finn let out a sharp bark of laughter. "Have you seen the guys who work at my organization?"

"Which is why we had to risk taking you," the man said. "You understand the difficulty of our position, I'm sure. We could risk kidnapping one of you and get the name, or we could blow up the entire Hercules Security facility and hope we got the right man. This is a... personal issue for my employer, however. He doesn't want to chance the guilty party getting away. He wants this one man in particular. I'm certain you know who it is, since there can't be many of you who just returned from my country. But if you prefer, we will blow up your company and kill a number of your companions. We would still have you, of course, and maybe afterward you could verify that we got the right man. It is your decision."

"Yeah, because blowing up a building in the heart of a major metropolitan area won't bring *any* unwanted attention down on *your* organization," Finn said, almost insulted by the empty threat. The least they could do was make their threats plausible. "Possibly on an international level. But sure, indulge me. Are you going to use internal or external methods? The building's pretty big, so one bazooka isn't going to cut it if you're going the external route. You'd need some heavy firepower from multiple sources if you want to take down the whole building. Planting explosives inside the building would be even trickier. I mean, security is in the *name*."

This time the man laughed. "You Americans. So smug. So righteous. And you never learn. Bazooka, you say? How quaint an idea! But no...." The man leaned in again, and this time his voice was filled with soft menace. "We have a small, private jet at the Raleigh-Durham airport. The pilot will take off with the jet loaded with fuel, and other hazardous cargo. The pilot will radio that he has mechanical troubles and bail out of the plane, which will crash into your headquarters. Crude, perhaps, but effective—and it will appear to be a tragic accident."

"Sure, sure, because our West Coast branch would never think to use all of their resources to investigate and make sure it really was an accident. Uh-huh." Finn nodded, forcing himself to sound casual. He was probably pushing the limits of this guy's tolerance, and once that happened, other elements would be introduced into their little chat. Finn knew he couldn't delay being tortured forever, but with every minute that passed, the team was that much closer to getting him out.

"I'm sorry, I can't see any way this isn't going to end badly for you, either in the long or short term."

"Ah, I see the problem. You are laboring under the mistaken assumption that we care what your people, your company, or even your government could do to us. We do not. Our business is risky. We lose groups all the time. There are always new ones to take their place. It is simply the way things work in our world. If your coworker had destroyed a cell of our organization, we would not care. The weak *should* be culled from the herd. But your coworker killed my employer's son—his only son, just eighteen years old. My employer desires this man, and he will stop at nothing to get him. He has left the issue of collateral damage at *my* discretion, however, and I am a man who abhors waste. So the price of this information, you see, is in your hands. While you still *have* hands, at least."

Joe was in deep shit. If it was personal, this guy's claim about going after Joe carried a lot more weight, which gave Finn even more incentive to resist whatever they subjected him to. He'd rather die himself than turn Joe over to some sadistic asshole out for revenge.

"I'm sorry about your employer's son, but I can't help you, buddy," Finn said, shrugging as much as his bonds would allow. "You can threaten to blow up buildings and remove body parts all you want, but that's not going to dig up information I don't have. Operational security is a thing in our business. The only missions I know about are my own, and I wasn't in Pakistan."

"I would say your loyalty is admirable, but it is nothing but foolishness. You may practice 'operational security,' but I know men talk. They *brag*. I have no doubt you know exactly of whom I am speaking. I will ask you nicely just one more time. The name."

Shit. This was it. The talking was over, and the hurting would begin. Whatever pain Finn endured would be nothing compared to what they inflicted on Joe if they got their hands on him.

"I don't know." Those three words were the only thing Finn intended to say from here on out.

"Such an unfortunate decision, but so be it." There were a few moments of quiet, though Finn heard slight movements. Then the door to the room opened. "Our guest has refused our hospitality. Therefore, it is time to begin. I would tell you this won't hurt, but I would be lying. Such a pity, Mr. Finnegan. I hope your coworker is worth the pain."

He is. Finn closed his eyes and focused inward as he braced himself for whatever lay ahead.

14

Drew stood out of the way and watched silently while Joe stockpiled an increasingly larger selection of weaponry and equipment to take on their extraction mission. He thought the C-4 and antiaircraft missile were verging on overkill, but he didn't say anything. Joe seemed to need them along with everything else, maybe to reassure himself that he had every tool he could possibly need to free Finn from his captors.

On one level, Drew understood. He was scared shitless about what Finn was going through, about the condition they'd find him in, about whether they'd find him before it was too late, about whether they'd be able to find him *at all*.

On another level, however, the word "obsessive" was starting to pop up in Drew's mind more often, and he didn't think concern about Finn was the only factor behind Joe's behavior. But at least Joe's fury was cold, focused, and calculated, so Drew wasn't worried about him falling apart during the mission. After the mission ended... well, that was a different story. Maybe he didn't know Joe well enough to make such assessments, but he'd seen similar behavior in men under his command at Lawson & Greer, and he thought he knew the signs of someone on the verge of cracking well enough.

If Joe trusted him—if Joe even liked him a little—Drew might have said something, might have suggested getting some professional help for whatever was eating him alive, but Joe neither trusted nor liked him. Drew figured Joe would interpret anything he said along those lines as an attack or an attempt at sabotaging him.

Drew had no desire to undermine Joe on a professional or personal level. On the contrary, he wished he knew how to bridge the gulf yawning between them, and not just for Finn's sake. Had they met under different circumstances, he thought they could have been friends, maybe more.

"Just about done?" he asked, watching as Joe stacked several boxes of ammo on the plain metal table set up in the middle of the Hercules Security weapons vault, which would have put any bank vault to shame in terms of both size and security.

Joe paused, looking over his stockpile with a critical eye. "Almost," he said as he reached for a tranquilizer gun and a clip of darts. "That should do it. Now we have to head south and hope Pixel picks up something that will give us a location."

Finn's captors must have figured he was tagged with GPS locators, since Chris hadn't picked up so much as a blip out of them. Either they were being jammed, or they had been removed and destroyed. Either way, it was bad news when it came to getting a fix on Finn.

"I'm sure he will," Drew said, to reassure himself as much as Joe. Chris seemed like the kind of brilliant tech expert Drew had seen in movies. In fact, he'd heard Chris was even scouting with drones, and he hoped Chris had as much success in overcoming the obstacles as his fictional counterparts did. Unfortunately, real life was usually more difficult. "Want some help loading this stuff up?"

Joe glanced over at him, his expression unreadable—at least to Drew. Joe had a hell of a poker face. "All right. I also recommend you get some body armor. There are plate carriers and such in the locker over there, if you haven't had a custom set made yet."

"I've got my set from Lawson & Greer. I'll pick it up before we leave."

Needing body armor was a clue that Joe wasn't ruling out the possibility of a fire fight. He might be hoping for one, given his state of mind.

"All right." Joe picked up several of the gun cases. "I had Lexy sign out an executive protection SUV for me. It's got armor, run flat tires, and a reinforced front. We can plow through a house if necessary."

"Good to know." Drew picked up as much of the equipment as he could carry and followed Joe out. "I take it this is a no-holds-barred mission?"

Joe smiled grimly. "I want at least one of them alive, if we can arrange it. Personally, I have no stomach for torture, but D-Day...."

Drew had worked with the infamous merc on enough missions that Joe didn't need to elaborate. D-Day was a tough, ruthless son-of-a-bitch whose personal line in the sand was carved out several feet away from most people's. If Joe intended to turn over their captive to Daryl for interrogation, Drew almost felt sorry for the poor bastard.

Almost.

"I'll keep that in mind," Drew said. "Anything else I should know before going in?"

Joe stopped at the entrance to the company's garage and turned to look at Drew. "Finn comes out alive. That's all that matters. Anyone and anything that gets in my way is history. And if I have to play Horatius at the bridge for you to get Finn out, I'll do it."

"I hope it doesn't come to that," Drew said, regarding Joe somberly. This wasn't the first time Joe had mentioned being willing to die for Finn, and while he admired the sentiment and the intensity of emotion behind it, he also had to wonder if Joe was developing a death wish. "I plan to do my best to make sure we *all* get out alive."

Joe simply shrugged and hit the powered opener for the door. He headed toward one side of the huge garage, which was filled with vans, limousines, sedans, motorcycles, and even a couple of boats on trailers. They passed most of the smaller vehicles. Joe stopped beside a massive, old-school Hummer that could probably have taken on a freight train and held its own. "Here's our ride. I would have gotten us a Bradley, but apparently D-Day took both of them to South America."

Drew shook his head, amused despite the seriousness of the situation. Of course Daryl would take military-grade fighting vehicles
that were maybe one step below a tank to protect his husband.

"Sometimes I'm not sure if 'go big or go home' was inspired by D-
Day or if he heard it once and adopted it as his life's motto."

"It could go either way," Joe acknowledged, something that wasn't
quite a smile curving his lips. It was barely there, but it was still the
least grim he'd looked since Finn was taken. Probably having a plan
of action and getting into a mission mindset was helping to settle
him, which was good. True professionals in any area functioned
better when they had a task and purpose. It was true even if their
purpose was killing.

They loaded their cargo into the Hummer, but before they
headed back inside for more, Drew stopped Joe with a hand on his
shoulder.

"Look, Morrissey... Joe," he said, watching Joe's face intently. "I get
you have no reason to trust me, but I'm telling you anyway. I've got
your back. I'm on team Burn It To The Ground And Salt The Earth
when it comes to getting Finn back, so however you want to do this,
I'm with you. No questions asked."

Joe went very, very still beneath Drew's hand, but Drew could feel
the tension in Joe's muscles, the instinctive coiling as though Joe were
expecting an attack and was prepared to strike back without thought.
There was a flash of something on Joe's face, there and gone so
quickly Drew couldn't be sure what he was seeing, before Joe's
expression settled once again into the nonexpression Drew usually
got. "For Finn's sake, I'll accept that. Now let's finish loading and get
on the road."

"You got it." Drew nodded as he withdrew his hand, satisfied with
the response.

This was as close to a truce as he was going to get with Joe. For
now, it was enough.

15

Christ, Finn... where are *you?*

The words repeated over and over in Joe's head as he steered the big SUV southward along Wake County back roads. They were on the way to check out the fifth potential site Chris had found in the last two hours, but Joe was starting to wonder if his instincts had been wrong about where the kidnappers would have taken Finn. They'd gambled everything on this one shot, yet even with Chris and Jason flying a half dozen drones in aircover looking for potential places, even with Tailor scanning the police bands listening for something to indicate suspicious activity, nothing had panned out. It was as though the kidnappers had disappeared into thin air, leaving no clues as to where they'd gone or what they'd done with Finn.

The repetition was annoying, but at least it was better than the litany that had been playing at the beginning of their hunt. That one had been, *My fault, my fucking fault,* and it had been a lot more difficult to bear. Yet as time passed and the other's hopes for finding Finn started to fade, Joe refused to give up. He would keep at it until they found Finn, no matter what. Finn had to be alive—the alternative was unacceptable.

"Hey, Morrissey... there's a report that just came in of suspicious activity at a house on Lake Wheeler off View Water Drive in an area called Lakewood Farms. A neighbor was out in their boat and noticed a man in the woods behind a house that was closed up for the season."

Joe's heart leapt, and he clenched his fists on the steering wheel. "Got it, Tailor. Pixel?"

"On it," Chris replied, his voice tense with concentration. "I have one drone ten minutes out of that area. I'll keep it over the lake, so it doesn't look like I'm looking."

"Good." Joe glanced over at Drew. "Can you contact the police for Wake County? Give them your Hercules Security ID number. Let them know we are investigating."

"On it." Drew grabbed the cell phone assigned to their vehicle and made the call.

While Drew focused on the authorities, Joe punched up the address on the GPS as Tailor read it out. They were almost fifteen minutes away from the spot in question, which Joe was determined to get down to ten. He wanted to be there when the drone made its pass; if it was the kidnappers and they spotted the drone, Joe didn't want them to have any kind of a head start.

Fortunately the summer season for tourists had ended and those who came for the fall leaves hadn't yet started, so traffic was light. This section of Wake County had some very affluent homes, since it was far enough from Raleigh to avoid city taxes while close enough for commuting into the capitol.

Drew returned the phone to its place and glanced over at Joe. "What's the plan when we get there?"

Joe considered. Something about this appeared far more promising that their other leads. "We can give Pixel's drone a few minutes to scan. He'll get photos, and maybe he can sync one up with one of the suspects from the surveillance video from the conference. If he does, we go in hot. If he doesn't... we go in, but with at least one set of nonlethal loads. There's probable cause for a crime, at least trespassing, but I don't want to kill anyone who isn't one of our targets, if it can be helped."

"Solid," Drew said with a brief nod, and he sat up straighter as he peered out the window as if adrenaline was making him restless.

"Our best bet for a live capture might be a guard, if that's who was spotted on the outside," Joe said, hoping to distract Drew from any thoughts that could impact the mission. "How are your take-down skills? Had much experience with silent infiltration?"

"It's not my strong suit," Drew said. "I can try, but you don't want me taking the lead."

Joe considered for a moment. "I'll locate and take out the first guard I see. You back me up. Then we'll head for the house. Let's go for silenced loads. If someone with Finn hears shots, they might have orders to kill him."

Drew breathed in deep and released the breath slowly as if to ground himself. "We got this."

Joe nodded, more to himself than Drew. "There's a public boat dock about half a mile away. Let's park there, just in case they have lookouts up at the road. There's no way to mistake this thing for anything other than bad news coming to call."

Five minutes later they were at the dock, and Joe pulled the Hummer to the far end of the public parking area. There weren't many cars in sight, which was a good thing for helping them keep a low profile.

"Let's load up," he said as he unfastened his seatbelt. "Pixel! Anything on the drone?"

"I've got movement in the trees at the house in question, but I can't get a fix on anyone," Chris replied tensely. "A glimpse of a man, possibly armed, but I only got dark hair and dark clothes. Want me to go in for a closer look?"

Joe hesitated. "No, Pixel. Hang tight." He glanced at Drew. "This could be a shitstorm. Last chance to hang back."

Drew shot Joe an incredulous look. "Fuck that," he said, a growl underlying his voice. "Let's nail these motherfuckers and get Finn out of there."

"Okay." It probably was a good thing Drew was along, as little as Joe wanted to admit it. If nothing else, someone would be there for Finn if Joe bought the farm. "Give me a two minute lead, since I want to go in silent. Let's go."

They left the Hummer after gearing up, with Joe slipping into the woods as quietly as a cat. He didn't pay any attention to Drew; if he was spotted, there wouldn't be anything Joe could do for him, so Joe chose to focus on the way ahead.

Joe wasn't quite as good as Ghost or Pita at silent movement, but he was good enough for this job. He was able to get into sight of the house they were targeting without any challenge, and he stopped for a moment behind a large tree to report, keeping his voice low. "Joker. I'm in sight of objective. No guard in sight."

"Copy that," Drew said, keeping his voice low as well. "Ready for company?"

"Negative. Let me proceed first. Stay back at least fifty meters in case someone slips in behind me." He glanced over his shoulder to where Drew was stationed behind a tree several yards behind him. Drew gave a thumbs up, and Joe nodded.

Well, this was it. Drew claimed to have his back, and Joe got the feeling he was about to discover if Drew was telling the truth or not. Drawing in a deep breath, Joe started forward toward the house.

It was still daylight, so Joe kept to the trees as much as possible. He was still alert for an outside guard, and it turned out to be a good thing he was. As he neared the rear porch of the house, a man in camouflage rounded the nearer corner of the building. Any thought that he might be a noncombatant were given lie by the HK433 compact assault rifle he held close to his chest. Unless people in the area had taken to mowing down deer instead of hunting them, this had to be the Pakistanis who had kidnapped Finn.

The confirmation caused a wave of icy calm to flow over Joe as all uncertainties were laid to rest. Almost without thinking, he spent two seconds switching the tranq gun out for his suppressor-equipped Glock 17. He would have preferred to take the guard alive, but it was too dangerous with the guy armed the way he was. Joe would rather have a quick, quiet kill and hope they could take alive one of the others inside.

The guard was about to pass in front of Joe's position at a range of about twenty-five meters. Joe lifted his gun and sighted the kidnapper. He drew a breath. Without hesitation, he released it and fired.

The suppressed weapon made a sound barely louder than a cough, and the guard spun in place, shot cleanly through the head. He dropped to the ground, and Joe moved immediately, wasting no time to double-check the kill. That was Drew's job now, and Joe had to get inside and find Finn as fast as possible.

The house had no basement, only a crawlspace as evidenced by the low access door Joe could see, which meant he had to mount the porch to gain entry. It also meant that Finn was likely being held in a central area of the building, since it was only a single-story in height. There might be a guard at the windows, but Joe's instincts told him this was supposed to be a fast assault with minimal operators to lower the likelihood of detection. Joe had now killed or incapacitated at least two of their personnel, which meant there were two or possibly three still in play. If they had one person working on Finn while another stood guard, then there was likely only one other guard in the house. Or at least, that's what he hoped.

The porch steps were concrete, and Joe crossed to them easily, pressing against the brick of the house as he mounted them. When he reached the top, he tested the porch door, which was fortunately unlocked, saving him several moments. He opened the door slowly to minimize any sounds and then slipped onto the porch, easing the door shut on its springs.

There was a nice seating group facing the trees and lake, behind which a long wall of glass offered a view into the house. There was no one in sight, but Joe could see only a single room, which appeared to be a lavish kitchen. He tested the knob of the nearest door, finding it also unlocked. Before opening it, he said a brief prayer. If the place had a newer alarm system that alerted every time a door was opened, he was about to announce his presence.

He turned the knob slowly and then pushed the door inward,

relieved not to hear the telltale beep of an alarm. It took him only a moment to slip inside, but he left the door open to facilitate Drew's entry—or his own sudden exit, if it became necessary. Now that he was inside he could hear voices, followed by a sharp cry of pain that had to have come from Finn.

Time slowed down as it always did on ops, and Joe felt like he was moving in slow motion even as he made as much haste as he could toward the voices, gun raised to deal with any threat. He didn't see any other guards as he cleared each room on his way forward, and he wondered if there was another outside whom they'd somehow missed. As it was, he reached the open door of what appeared to be an office, and as he peered cautiously around the jamb he spotted another guard cradling an HK, who appeared to be watching avidly as an older man in a suit and tie used a metal baton on one of Finn's knees.

Joe didn't even think about what he was going to do. Instinct took over. He raised his gun and put a bullet in the head of the guard before he stepped into the doorway, turning his gun on the torturer.

"Stop right there. Drop the baton, or I swear I'll put a bullet in each of your kneecaps before I start to get really nasty."

The man had frozen when the guard began to topple over, dead where he stood. He turned to face Joe, a strange smile curving his lips. "Ah, I see reinforcements have arrived. Excellent. This one is most uncooperative. Perhaps you'll be a better subject for inter-rogation."

The pronouncement made Joe frown, but he didn't lower his weapon. Instead he glanced at Finn, clamping down hard on a surge of rage at the sight of Finn's injuries. Instead he kept his voice light. "Hey, partner... sorry I'm late."

Finn was blindfolded, but he lifted his head and turned in the direction of Joe's voice. "It's okay," he said, his tone suffused with relief. "I knew you'd turn up sooner or later, but I was getting kind of bored with waiting."

The smart-ass reply made Joe's tension ease just a bit. If Finn could still joke, he hadn't been broken. Injuries to the body, as Joe well knew, could heal a lot faster than having your spirit flayed into nothingness. Plus it meant that Finn hadn't doubted Joe would come for him.

"Yeah, I figured you'd had enough of a vacation and came to haul your ass back to work," he replied. He refocused on the guy in the suit. He was older than the guards and had the distinct air of someone in charge. "Sorry to put an end to your fun, but you'll be coming with us, and I promise that you'll be paid back for your hospitality. In spades."

"Maybe." The guy smiled again, but it held no warmth. "Then again... maybe not."

Joe hadn't heard a thing, but he felt the barrel of a gun pressed against the back of his head.

"Don't move."

Joe cursed himself for not clearing the entire house before making his presence known. He could have sworn there was no one else inside. Maybe this guy had come in through the front after Joe had already headed for this room, but it was sloppy. It might be a mistake that was going to cost him and Finn their lives.

Before he could frame a reply, he heard the guy behind him gasp, and he instinctively ducked his head away from the gun even as he felt an impact against the body armor on his back. In that moment of distraction, the man who had been torturing Finn suddenly bolted toward the room's front window, crashing through it and out into the yard.

"Shit!" Joe turned enough to see Drew standing behind him, gun in hand. "Take care of Finn!" With that, he ran for the window as well, launching himself out of it in the torturer's wake and taking off after him.

He'd acted on instinct, not wanting the bastard to get away, and he was hot on the man's heels as the guy streaked away. He fired his gun over the man's head, not wanting to kill him outright because they still needed answers about what was happening. To his surprise, the man didn't stop.

Joe was a big man, and while he could run for long distances, he wasn't as fast as Finn or Dead-eye over short distances. The torturer was either a former track-and-field athlete, or else pure terror was giving him speed, because he actually began to pull away from Joe, leaving Joe with the choice of shooting him in the back—something the police would frown far more upon than his killing of the guards —or allowing him to escape.

There was also a third alternative.

"Pixel! Lock in on my GPS beacon! I'm in pursuit of one of the kidnappers, but he's faster than I am. I need you to get a drone on this guy before I lose him!"

"On it!"

A moment later, a dark drone swooped down and homed in on the torturer, keeping pace with him far more easily than Joe could.

Joe slowed down, watching until he was sure Chris had locked on and then he turned and headed back toward the house. "I'm going to secure the location, but it's time for backup to roll," he said to Chris. "Also notify Wake County PD and get the helicopter up to evac Finn. He's conscious but injured."

"Roger that," Chris said with brisk efficiency. "I'll give you an ETA for the helicopter as soon as I have one."

"Thanks. I'm returning to the house now."

Joe made it back, heading through the front door and returning immediately to the study. He saw that Drew had removed the blind-fold and was now behind the chair, dealing with Finn's restraints. All he wanted to do was pull Finn into his arms, but he settled for dropping next to the chair on his knees, afraid to touch Finn in case he caused him any more pain.

"Hey. How bad is it?" he asked, bracing himself for the answer. Finn was a medic, so he'd know damned well how badly he was injured.

"Could be worse. Could be better, too," Finn said with a wry smile, his eyes warming with affection as he gazed at Joe. "Ribs—cracked and possibly broken. Left leg—multiple fractures. Lower abdomen—blunt force trauma with possible internal bleeding. Pretty face, mercifully unscathed."

Joe lifted one hand, surprised to see it was shaking, and laid his palm against Finn's cheek. "I'm sorry it took us so long. I'm sorry they took you at all. It should have been me. This is all my fault."

Drew finished freeing Finn's arms, and Finn let out a sigh of relief as he rubbed his wrists, which showed signs of chafing and bruising.

"It's *not* your fault," Finn said, reaching out to Joe in return. "They're the bad guys, remember? You saved lives. You saved innocent *kids*. They didn't have to retaliate. It was their choice. I don't blame you. I blame them."

Joe wasn't going to add to Finn's misery by arguing with him, but he knew the truth. This *was* his fault, and he'd do anything to make it up to Finn. "I'll get them, I promise. I'm going to make them all pay for doing this to you. I'm going to make them *suffer*."

"I don't give a fuck about making them suffer." Finn clasped Joe's hand tightly and brought it to his lips. "I just want you to stay safe."

Joe knew the chances of that were pretty low. "They wanted me, didn't they?" he asked, holding onto Finn's hand like a lifeline. He could feel his eyes stinging, emotions rushing in to replace the adrenaline he'd been riding for too many hours. "They could have killed you, and it would have killed me, too."

Finn gnawed on his bottom lip, his inner battle showing in his expressive eyes, and he nodded slowly. "Yeah, they were looking for you. They don't have a name, and I sure as hell didn't give it to them, but it wasn't hard to figure out they meant you. They said you killed some head honcho's son, and he's out for blood."

A lump of ice formed in the pit of Joe's stomach. He wouldn't call any of the kills on his recent mission anything but justifiable, but he had the sinking feeling he knew exactly which of them was the one they were after him for. It was the one that had sickened him most because the man he had shot had been barely an adult, and yet he'd been brutalizing a child.

Joe closed his eyes. "If they want me, they'll never stop," he said softly. "And they won't care who they have to hurt to get to me. I'm going to have to end this, or we'll never be safe."

"Wait," Finn said, a flare of alarm visible in his eyes. "The guy who got away mentioned a private plane at RDU that was loaded up and waiting. Even though the guy threatened it as a means of taking out our headquarters, maybe it's really his escape plan. All we have to do is catch the guy, figure out who he's working for, then let Herc handle it. He'll figure out a plan and throw a ton of resources behind it. Problem solved."

Drew had remained quiet, seeming more focused on freeing Finn's injured leg as carefully as possible than on their conversation, but he spoke up now. "I think that's a good idea," he said without looking up at either of them. "Use what you've got available."

For a moment Joe thought about arguing, but he decided that nothing he could say would change Finn's mind. But he wasn't going to risk any of his cadre for this. It was a personal matter, and it was his fight, not theirs.

"We can discuss it later," he said. He squeezed Finn's hand and then moved back, rising to his feet and looking down at Drew. "Thank you for having my back... and saving my life. I owe you one."

Drew glanced up at last, a slight smile curving his lips. "Any time."

Joe nodded in acknowledgement, feeling a little awkward. He knew he was guilty of letting his personal feelings interfere with his professional conduct, and he'd misjudged Drew. If Drew had wanted to get Joe out of the picture, he'd had the perfect opportunity to do so. Instead, he'd saved both Finn and Joe.

"Well, I'll go check to see if our evac is close," he said, moving toward the door. He owed Drew the opportunity to be with Finn and talk to him, but he wasn't quite ready to witness it. Not yet. Maybe not ever, but definitely not now.

"I'll go." Drew stood up and skirted around the chair. "You can stay here and look after Finn."

It was tempting to take the offer, but Joe had to stop denying what was between Drew and Finn just because he didn't want it to be happening.

Reaching out, he put a hand on Drew's arm. "No, you stay," he said. "He needs you, too."

Drew's eyebrows climbed at that, but he inclined his head in acknowledgment or thanks or perhaps both. He squatted beside Finn's chair and touched Finn's arm gingerly. Finn smiled slightly, but his features were taut with pain, and his breathing was growing labored.

"If they aren't here, tell them to hurry up," Finn said. "I'm ready for some good drugs."

"On it," Joe said and left the room. They needed to get Finn to the hospital, needed to find the man who'd tortured him, and Joe had some hard decisions to make.

The rescue was over. The mission, however, was just beginning.

16

The steady beep of the heart monitor provided background noise, something Finn could tether himself to as he floated in a twilight state between asleep and awake. The antiseptic tang in the air grounded him as well, letting him know he was safe, not still trapped and blindfolded in that torturer's room. If he opened his eyes, he would see the bland decor of a private hospital room, where he'd been moved once the ER doctors were satisfied that he was stable. He'd need surgery on his leg, but the gamut of tests they'd subjected him to had shown none of his injuries were life-threatening.

Currently, he was alone, but that would change once word got out that the tests were finished and he was settled in a room. No doubt Joe was in the nearest waiting room, sitting as still as a statue and not speaking to anyone unless he had to. Drew was probably with him.

The door opened, letting in the noise from the hallway. Finn rolled his head on the pillow and cracked his eyes open, hoping his visitor wasn't a nurse coming to check his vitals or shove a bedpan under his ass.

But instead of medical staff, he saw Joe standing in the doorway, looking concerned and oddly hesitant. "Hey."

"Get in here!" Finn beckoned to Joe with the arm that wasn't hooked up to the IV and monitors, and he let the happiness he felt at seeing Joe show in his welcoming smile.

Joe hurried over to the bed, taking Finn's hand in his and squeezing it. Finn could feel an actual tremor in Joe's fingers. "How are you doing? Do you need anything?"

"Nope, I'm good." Finn squeezed Joe's hand in return, wanting to offer as much reassurance as he could. "The damage wasn't nearly as bad as it could've been."

With a sigh, Joe lowered himself into the chair next to the bed. "There shouldn't have been any damage at all, Finn. I still feel like this is my fault. I wish they'd taken me instead. I never want you to suffer because of me. Never."

Finn paused, having to work a little harder than usual to pull his thoughts together. He understood Joe's perspective; he would have felt the same way had their positions been reversed. Hell, he felt guilty over falling for Drew because it had caused Joe pain and doubt.

"It's easy for me to say you shouldn't blame yourself," he said at last. "But I don't blame you for what happened. Not at all. It's not about you, personally. Those assholes would've come after whoever was on that mission. If it'd been Jason, Chris might be lying here instead of me. Someone would've had to pay no matter what."

"But it should have been me." Joe leaned close. He was a big enough man that even seated he could lean over to kiss Finn on the forehead. "I wish I had kept you safe."

"In that case, you and I are both in the wrong line of work," Finn said with a little chuckle.

Although he might be looking for different options, depending on how the surgery on his leg went. The guy who'd worked him over knew what he was doing, and he'd tried to injure Finn's leg in ways that would keep him out of the field for good. Not that Finn intended to tell Joe that, especially since he wouldn't know anything for sure until after the operation and rehab.

Joe tightened his grip on Finn's hand, his eyes straying down to the bandaging on Finn's leg as though he suspected the direction of

Finn's thoughts. "Maybe we are. Or I am. But... you understand that I have to deal with this, don't you? So you'll be safe."

"I understand," Finn said, and he meant it. He didn't want to convince Joe not to follow up, just that he shouldn't do it alone. "But I want you to take backup. Charging after these guys alone is a suicide mission, and I don't want to lose you."

Rather than agreeing, Joe smiled crookedly. "I wish I could be here for you while you heal, but I need to move on this while the trail is fresh. Are you good with that? Would you feel like I was abandoning you?"

"Playing nurse would bore you to death, and if I want someone to hover and fret over me, I'll call Payne," Finn said. "He'd do a better job than you, anyway."

"You're right about that," Joe murmured, though he seemed to relax slightly. "You'll have Drew, too. I think... I think I may have been wrong to resent him so much. I'm glad he makes you happy. You deserve to be happy."

Joe's admission made hope bloom within Finn, especially given he knew how difficult it was for Joe to make it. Knowing Joe wasn't stewing in resentment helped ease a little of Finn's own guilt, and he squeezed Joe's hand again.

"So do you," he said. "When you get home and I'm healed up enough to handle it, I'm going to make you *very* happy."

"I'm looking forward to it." Again, Joe lifted Finn's hand, pressing a kiss to his palm before releasing it He rose to his feet and leaned over the bed. "I love you, Finn. I'll always love you."

"I love you too, Joe Morrissey, and I always will," Finn said, reaching up for Joe with his free arm. "Now give me a kiss and get the fuck out. You've got bad guys to catch."

"Yeah, I do." With that, Joe leaned down and tenderly pressed his lips to Finn's, kissing him as though he was afraid Finn might break.

But while Finn was injured, he wasn't made of glass, and if they were going to be separated again, he wanted a memory they could both carry with them. He snaked his arm around Joe's neck and urged him closer, and he parted his lips with a soft moan, demanding more. With a chuckle, Joe gave in, answering Finn's demand with passion he rarely showed outside of the bedroom—or whichever room they were in when they got naked and desperate.

Finally, Joe pulled back. "Too much of that and I won't be able to bring myself to leave."

"Too much of that and we'll have a swarm of nurses in here, wondering why my heart monitor is going wild," Finn said with an unrepentant grin.

"Glad I can still make your heart race after all these years." Joe laid one hand against Finn's cheek. "I'd tell you to be good while I'm gone, but I know you."

Finn laughed, even though it made his ribs ache, and he leaned into the touch. "That's fair." He gazed up at Joe, his expression growing somber. "Be careful. I want you to come home to me."

"Don't worry about me. Focus on getting better." With that, Joe leaned in for another swift kiss and then stepped back from the bed. "I'll send Drew in."

"He's here?" Finn was pleased by that news, not only because he did want to see Drew, but also because it made getting Operation: Backup Whether Stubborn-Ass Joe Morrissey Likes It or Not underway easier. "Please do."

"He's right outside." Joe hesitated for a moment, looking at Finn. "Just remember I love you." He turned and opened the door, stepping out into the hallway. Finn heard a low exchange, and then the door opened wider and Drew entered. He looked Finn over quickly before crossing to the bed with an expression of happy relief.

"I thought I told you having sex while jumping out of a moving car was a bad idea," Drew teased him. "But no, you always have to push the limits, don't you?"

"You know me," Finn said lightly, holding out his hand to Drew. "I'll try anything once."

Drew took the offered hand, raising it to his lips and kissing it gently. "Twice if you like it, and three times just to make sure, right? My mama warned me about boys like you."

"Your mama was right," Finn said, warmed by the tender kiss.

"She generally is." Drew leaned in and kissed Finn's forehead, pushing Finn's hair back and combing his fingers through it. "How are you doing? I imagine you're not on your deathbed or Joe wouldn't have walked out the door."

"Not much else would've kept him here." Finn tightened his fingers around Drew's, drawing strength and comfort from the contact. "I need to talk to Herc."

Drew nodded. "Joe's going off on his own, isn't he? I figured from what he said that he was planning to go it alone."

"He is, because he's a stubborn dumbass who takes too fucking much onto his own shoulders," Finn said, his concern coming out as causticness. "I told him to let Herc help, but no, he's got to save the world alone. I'll be damned if I'm going to sit by while he hares off on a suicide mission."

"The Irish do have a strain of stubborn, I've noticed," Drew replied, his tone dry as dust. "And he may be a dumbass, but he's our dumbass, right? So both of us will be damned if we'll let him kill himself out of some misguided sense of honor."

Finn knew the smile spreading across his face was goofy and besotted, but he didn't care. Hearing Drew speak so possessively of Joe didn't bother him. Instead, it filled him with hope that the future would be far better than he thought it could be—assuming they got Joe back home in one piece.

"Damned right," he said, gripping Drew's hand as tightly as he could. "Our dumbass has no idea what he's up against with the two of us working together."

Drew chuckled. "Yeah, he doesn't stand a chance." He grew more serious, squeezing Finn's hand in return. "I take it you want me to go after him."

"All I had in mind was asking Herc to organize a team to follow Joe and be there to pull his nuts out of the fire if necessary," Finn said. "But if you're volunteering.... Well, there's no one I'd trust more to take care of Joe."

Drew nodded. "He would see a whole team coming, even if it's Herc's guys. But he won't expect me. He told me to take care of you."

"Which would you rather do?" Finn asked, suspecting he knew the answer already. "Sit around the hospital and watch my bruises fade, or go after Joe?"

"It's probably safer for me to remove my tempting person from your presence so you can concentrate on healing." Drew grinned wickedly. "I know you wouldn't be able to resist being naughty. So I'd best go after Joe and save both of you from yourselves."

Finn didn't try to argue. He couldn't, really. No doubt he'd be tempted to push himself a bit when he felt better if either Joe or Drew were around, but if they were both gone, he could—and would —wait and focus on healing.

"It might be the best thing for all three of us," he said. "Be careful, okay?"

"Always." This time Drew's kiss was on Finn's lips and he didn't hesitate to deepen it, as though aching to savor Finn's taste.

Moaning, Finn yielded and slid his arm around Drew's broad shoulders, holding him close while he could. Drew took his time, but after several long moments he drew back, smiling ruefully. "I accuse you of not behaving, but if it weren't for this hospital bed, I'd be the one pushing the limits. I should go before Joe gets too much of a head start on me. I have no doubt I'll be able to track him, but I don't want to make it harder than it has to be."

"Good idea," Finn said, releasing Drew with reluctance. He wasn't thrilled about both of the men he loved running headlong into a dangerous situation without him there to help, and waiting to hear from them would be excruciating, but he wasn't in any shape to do more than that.

Drew picked up Finn's hand again. "I love you, you know. And I like Joe, believe it or not. I'm not just doing this for you, but for all of us. Maybe if I save his ass again, he'll finally believe I'm on his side, too."

Finn twined his fingers with Drew's and squeezed gently. "I love you too," he said. "He's thawing a little. I can tell. Just go easy on him. That mission in Pakistan shook him in ways I haven't seen before. He needs help—more than you or I can give him. But we've got to get him home in one piece before he can get it."

"Yeah, I got the idea he's dealing with some heavy shit, but I won't promise to go easy on him. Joe strikes me as the kind to refuse gentle efforts at persuasion. It's gonna take some tough love to make him face up to whatever is eating at him."

Finn's eyebrows climbed as he listened to Drew, and he had to acknowledge the point even as he was surprised by Drew's insight. "You're probably right, so I'll amend my statement to do what you need to do. I trust you."

Drew smiled, the wry expression reminiscent of Joe's crooked smile. "Now if I can just get Joe to trust me, maybe we'll get somewhere." He squeezed Finn's hand and then released it. "You take care of yourself, and I promise I'll take care of Joe, whether he wants me to or not."

"That's the spirit." Finn gave a little fist pump as he watched Drew move away from his bedside. A small part of him wanted at least one of them to stay with him while he faced the arduous path ahead, but he couldn't ask that of either man under the circumstances. "Hurry up every chance you get."

"I will." Drew stopped at the doorway, giving Finn a heated look. "You concentrate on getting better so we can celebrate when I bring our dumbass home, okay?"

Finn couldn't help but smile, pleased by the promise he saw in Drew's eyes. "I'm looking forward to it already."

Drew blew Finn a kiss before heading off, letting the door close softly in his wake. Finn watched him go, worried about both Joe and Drew, and what they were walking into, but he was determined to channel his worry into productive action.

He reached for the phone on the bedside table and dialed a number.

"Hey, Lexy, it's Finn. I need to speak to Herc right away."

17

Less than five minutes after leaving Finn's bedside, Joe was in his SUV. He sat, staring out the window, collecting himself for what he knew he had to do. It wasn't just that he had to bring down Finn's torturer; that was only a beginning. To keep Finn safe, to make sure that Finn and Drew had any kind of a chance to live their lives without constantly looking over their shoulders, he had to take this all the way to the top. He had to go back to Pakistan, the country he'd promised himself he'd never set foot in again.

Taking a deep breath, he keyed on his earpiece. "Talk to me, Pixel. Tell me you have a track and ID on the guy we're chasing."

"Copy, Morrissey," Chris's voice came back over the channel. "I managed to get a clear picture of him before he slipped drone coverage. There's no record of him entering the country, at least not under his real name, but an alert from Interpol says that he's Jalal Emani, a Pakistani national who trained with al-Qaeda. His last known whereabouts were in Pakistan, and he's associated with the human trafficking ring that you and I both have had run-ins with."

The information came as no surprise to Joe. He started the SUV. "Good. Send a picture of him to my phone, would you? Where did you lose him?"

"Just north of Lake Wheeler. There was a report of a stolen car in that area about ten minutes after I lost him. Police put out an APB for it, even though they weren't sure it was him, but it was found ditched just south of Cary."

"Got it."

And suddenly Joe did have it. He knew where the guy was headed, knew what his plan must be. He didn't tell Chris, and he was sure Finn hadn't reported in to Herc yet. Right now he and Drew were the only ones who had the information, and Drew was safely back with Finn. That meant only Joe still had a slim chance of catching the guy before he escaped.

Without hesitation, Joe steered the SUV out onto the road and pushed the accelerator to the floor.

DREW DIDN'T LIKE LEAVING Finn, but he knew that Finn wouldn't be able to concentrate on recovering from his injuries if he was worrying about Joe. Whatever the big merc was planning, Drew had to figure it out and try hard to get there in time.

He left the hospital, annoyed but unsurprised that Joe had already taken off. Since Drew had ridden with him to the hospital from where they'd found Finn, that left him without transport, at least temporarily. He tried hailing Joe on comms, but Joe didn't answer. It was time for a backup plan.

"Pixel! Joker here. Can you have someone bring a vehicle to the hospital for me? And tell me where Morrissey is?"

There was a moment of silence before Chris spoke up hesitantly. "Herc is en route, but the GPS in Joe's earpiece says he's still there. He's maybe fifty yards north of your present position."

Drew glanced north, where the parking lot stretched out, almost wall to wall with cars, despite the lateness of the hour. "Hang on."

He hurried northward, covering the distance quickly. "Pixel, I don't see him or his SUV. Are you sure you have the right location?"

"I'm positive," Chris said. "Look a couple of yards east."

A suspicion formed in Drew's mind, one that was confirmed a couple of minutes later when he found what he was expecting. Bending down, he picked up Joe's discarded earpiece. "Pixel, Joe ditched his comms. Do you have GPS on the SUV?"

"Negative. It's been turned off." Chris sounded puzzled. "Why would he toss his earpiece? Do you think he was carjacked?"

"No, I think he did it on purpose." Drew frowned down at the device in his hand. "What was the last communication you had from him?"

"About fifteen minutes ago. He asked for an update on the fugitive, and I gave him the ID of Jalal Emani, who probably stole a car and abandoned it near Cary. He acknowledged the info, and that's the last I heard from him."

Shit. Obviously Joe had figured something out, or at least thought he had, and he was headed to where he thought Jalal Emani was going—and Joe didn't want company.

"Joker, this is Herc."

The voice in his earbug was much deeper than Chris's and held a ring of command that had even a seasoned officer like Drew straightening his spine in response. "Copy, Herc. Are you almost to the hospital?"

"Two minutes out. Stay where you are. Pixel sent me your location, and I'm headed to you."

Drew chafed a bit at the delay, but mostly it was because he needed to be moving, even if he didn't know where he was going. He didn't know the Raleigh area as well as Joe did, so he wracked his brain trying to figure out what must be driving Joe on.

Almost precisely two minutes later Cade Thornton pulled up in one of the big SUVs that was virtually identical to the one Joe was in. Drew opened the passenger door and got in.

"What's the status?" Cade asked, as he headed back toward the hospital entrance. "Finn said he thought Joe was planning to bug out, and it looks like he was right. But where could he have gone? We lost the guy."

"I don't know." Drew frowned in thought. "Pixel said he told Joe about the abandoned car and that's when he must have ditched his GPS. South of Cary, he said. What's up that way?"

"A bunch of high tech firms, a lot of very expensive houses. Maybe they've got some kind of safe house," Cade replied.

"Finn didn't say anything about another location being mentioned, at least not to me." Drew ground his teeth. "What else?"

"North of that is the Umstead State Park, then the airport."

Suddenly a light dawned. "That's it! The airport! Finn said the guy claimed they had a private plane at the airport, and threatened to ditch it right on top of Hercules Security HQ. What if that was a lie, but the plane is real? Maybe that's how these guys got into the country to begin with, or at least got to Raleigh."

Cade nodded. "I think you're right." He stopped the SUV at the front of the hospital and unfastened his seatbelt. He reached into a pocket and tossed Drew a key fob. "You go, I'll send reinforcements. I need to debrief Finn and see what other information he has that might be critical."

"Got it." Drew took the fob and then released his seatbelt as well. "Have the reinforcements keep back, okay? I'd prefer to handle Joe myself. I have a better idea about his headspace than the rest of you do." He paused, drawing in a breath. "He's skirting the edges of going dinky dau, Herc. You know what that means."

Cade raised a brow at Drew's use of the old military slang term for someone on the verge of losing it. "Joe's the last person I would expect that from. He's a rock."

Drew shrugged. "With enough pressure, even rocks can shatter, and he's had a lot of pressure, believe me. I don't know about all of it, but I can guess. He's carrying guilt and anger and jealousy and pain, and I think he's close to the breaking point. So let me handle him, at least for the moment. If I can't talk him down, I'll conk him on the head and we'll get him back that way."

Cade nodded slowly. "All right, Joker. You've had a hell of a lot of experience with PTSD, so I'll defer to your judgment in this. Just... take care of him, okay? Finn's not the only one who values him."

"Yeah." Drew wasn't sure of how much Cade knew about the

triangle of him, Joe, and Finn, and what it was costing all of them, but he didn't feel the need to elaborate. Not yet, at least. "Don't worry, Herc. I'll keep him safe. I promised Finn."

"You do that."

Cade got out of the SUV. A minute later Drew was heading out of the parking lot and toward the airport, hoping that he'd get there before Joe did something drastic. Not that Drew gave a damn if Joe shredded Jalal Emani into microscopic bits if it made him feel better. The torturer deserved whatever he got. Drew wasn't going to try to save Emani's life—he was going to try to save Joe's. Because there was no way Drew wanted to face Finn again without Joe safe and sound beside him.

18

It took Joe twenty minutes to reach the airport, five of which he spent on a brief diversion to retrieve a couple of items from his house, which fortunately was on the way. He also changed from the Hercules Security SUV into his own private vehicle, because taking an armored car loaded with weaponry onto the airport property was a sure way to get stopped and questioned, even with his company license and identification. Besides, for what he planned, he didn't need a lot of firepower. He had his concealed carry weapons and two extra magazines. If he ended up using that much ammo to deal with Jalal Emani, he was probably a dead man anyway.

His credentials got him into the general aviation section of the airport, where private planes were loaded and serviced. He'd been through the area many times, since he had a pilot's license and was even qualified on the two helicopters Herc had bought for the company.

At the gate to the private aviation hangars, Joe showed the guard the picture of his quarry. "Have you seen this guy? He's meeting with my clients and isn't answering his phone."

The guard squinted at the picture. "Yeah, he came through about fifteen minutes ago. Headed for the G.A. terminal."

"Thanks, I appreciate it." Joe set off toward the terminal. He parked the SUV and reached for the laptop he'd picked up during his brief stop at home. Within sixty seconds he was looking at the flight plans filed by the pilots of the small private aircraft based out of the terminal. If Jalal Emani was making an escape, there would have to be a flight plan filed, and it would likely have been done in the last fifteen minutes.

"Where are you, you son of a bitch?" he muttered as he scrolled through the flight lists. For a small airport, RDU was generally quite busy due to the presence of large corporations like SAS and the other players in the Research Triangle area. There were several listings, but a new one popped up in the queue for an Eclipse 550 private jet, bound for Ottawa. "Gotcha!"

It was only a few hundred meters to the hangar listed in the queue, and Joe left the SUV, hurrying toward it on foot. He had to be cautious, since he wasn't sure if Jalal had any other allies still in play. He doubted it, but he was too close to his goal to risk getting careless now.

As he approached the hangar, he kept close to the wall to avoid being spotted. When he reached the big doorway of the hangar, he peered around the corner, immediately spotting the Eclipse. The door of the plane was open, and he could see movement inside. He slipped into the hangar, drawing one of his guns and circling around so he could approach the plane out of sight of the door. Since he wasn't sure how many adversaries he faced, he needed to get a closer look before rushing on board.

Through the front windshield he could see only one person, and the guy definitely looked like Emani. He was wearing a headset and holding a clipboard, probably preflighting the plane as quickly as he could. But if Emani was the pilot, that was a good sign he was alone. Joe took a deep breath and made his move.

Running fast and silent, he crossed the hangar floor out of Emani's sightline and ducked under the wing. Moving more slowly, he mounted the steps into the plane, keeping as silent as possible. Emani was muttering under his breath in Urdu, obviously annoyed at the list of checks to be performed before takeoff, but not yet desperate enough to avoid the safety protocols. That meant he wasn't expecting Joe's presence, and that gave Joe the element of surprise.

He moved up behind the pilot's seat and then pressed the barrel of his gun to the back of Emani's head. "I don't think you're going anywhere, Jalal," he said softly in Urdu. "So put up your hands and get out of the seat, nice and slow, so we can have a talk."

Emani froze in place. He lifted his hands and slowly rose from the seat. Joe backed up, and Emani turned, his eyes widening as he caught sight of Joe.

"You must be the one we were looking for. How nice of you to turn yourself in to me so I can take you back to Pakistan."

It was all bravado, Joe knew, but the guy had balls. "I might be going to Pakistan, but you aren't," Joe replied.

"What, are you going to take me to jail?" Emani asked. "Tie me up and haul me in to face justice? You Americans are so weak on your own soil."

"Are we?" Joe smiled nastily and lowered the barrel of his gun slightly. "No, I'm not taking you in to face justice, I'm going to dispense it myself." He squeezed the trigger, shooting Emani in the leg.

The man cried out, his leg buckling, sending him toppling to the floor. The shot had made little sound because of Joe's suppressor, so he wasn't worried about attracting too much attention.

"That's for what you did to Finn's leg," he said. "Now, we can have a conversation about your employer. I'm told you are after me because I killed your head honcho's son. I want the name, and I want it now. Or so help me, my next shot will be between your eyes."

"Go to hell!" Emani clutched his thigh, trying to staunch the bleeding.

"I see you need some more persuasion." Joe stepped closer. "Let's see if you can take it as well as you dish it out." Joe drew back his foot and then kicked Emani in the ribs as hard as he could. He felt the snap as ribs broke. "How about now? Want to tell me?"

Emani's face was twisted in pain. Joe felt nothing—no satisfaction, no hatred, *nothing at all*. He needed information, and he was prepared to do whatever it took to get it.

"No!" Emani gasped, glaring at Joe in defiance.

Joe shrugged and pressed his foot against the ribs he'd just broken. Emani squirmed, cursing at Joe in Urdu, but Joe didn't relent. He pressed harder, knowing he was probably causing internal damage, but not much caring. "How about now?"

Apparently Emani's ability to handle pain wasn't as great as his ability to inflict it. "Stop! Stop! I'll tell you!"

Joe eased his foot back, but kept his gun pointed at Emani's head. "I'm listening."

"Ismail Abbasi is my employer. You killed his son Farrokh, and he wants you dead in return." Recovering a bit of his bravado, Emani sneered. "He won't stop, you know. I may have failed, but he will send others, again and again."

"Not if I put an end to it." Joe didn't feel victorious, just a slight sense of satisfaction that he now had a name. "And speaking of endings, I think it's time to put some closure on this and make sure that you never hurt anyone I love ever again."

With that, he began to squeeze the trigger.

"Joe! Stop!" A familiar voice made him pause, and he glanced back to see Drew rushing up from behind.

Joe frowned, annoyed at the unexpected interruption. Why did it have to be Drew, of all people? "You shouldn't be here. Go back to Finn. You need to take care of him while I'm gone."

"Finn is just fine." Drew stood beside Joe and rested one hand on his shoulder. "We're more concerned about you."

"I'm fine, too." Joe didn't lower the gun. "You should go. You don't want to be a witness to what I have to do."

"You don't have to do it," Drew said, his voice low and gentle, and he squeezed Joe's shoulder. "I'm sure this asshole has enough on his record to get sent away for life. He's not worth killing."

Joe hadn't thought beyond getting rid of Emani to eliminate the threat to Finn, but maybe Drew had a point. "I can't stick around for the cops. I need to get to Pakistan." He glanced at Drew. "I'm not going to let you stop me. I have to make sure no one comes after Finn."

"Then let's truss him up and call Herc," Drew said. "Let him handle it. We'll head on to Pakistan."

"What do you mean, we?" Joe shrugged off Drew's hand. "This is my problem. Not yours. I'll handle it. Trust me, you don't want to be involved. This whole situation takes fucked up to a new level."

Drew moved to face Joe and fixed him with a relentless stare. "After you left, Finn and I had a talk. We agreed that you're a stubborn dumbass, but you're *our* stubborn dumbass, so one of us needed to go with you to make sure you don't do anything stupid. Finn couldn't, so here I am, and this is definitely my problem, too. I want *both* of you to be safe."

While Joe no longer thought that Drew had it in for him, and had even started to trust him a little, he had no doubt Drew was there only because Finn requested it. Unfortunately, there didn't seem to be much Joe could do about it at the moment, so he'd have to let Drew ride along. But Joe had a plan, and it didn't involve taking anyone with him, so he'd just have to lose Drew as soon as he could. "Fine. I don't have time to argue the point with you right now. This plane has a takeoff window in about ten minutes, and I intend to use it."

"Then let's get him secured and be on our way," Drew said, appearing satisfied.

"You want him secured, you do it." Joe holstered his gun and stepped over Emani. He slid into the pilot's seat. "I have to finish preflighting the plane."

"On it," Drew said. "Won't take but a couple minutes."

Joe shrugged and picked up the headset, putting it on before reaching for the clipboard. If Drew wanted the guy alive, it was now his problem. If he didn't make it back to the plane in time, Joe was leaving, no matter what. Dismissing Emani from his mind, he turned his attention to readying the plane for takeoff.

Less than five minutes later, Drew dropped into the copilot's seat. "Package is secured in the hangar and ready for pick up. The delivery service will be here shortly."

Joe didn't acknowledge the comment, instead turning his attention to the telltales and seeing that Drew had secured the door. "Fasten your seatbelt. We're cleared to head to the runway."

The next phase of Joe's plan was underway. Ismail Abbasi was already a dead man. He just didn't know it yet.

19

Drew emerged from the bathroom with a towel secured around his waist, his skin still rosy from the heat of his shower. He rubbed his short hair dry with a hand towel as he sauntered over to the king-sized bed he'd claimed. Joe was stretched out on the other king bed, focused on his laptop and not paying attention to Drew, which wasn't unusual. Joe behaved as if he wanted to ignore Drew out of existence—or at least out of his and Finn's lives. But for now, Joe was stuck with Drew because he wasn't about to let Joe go to Pakistan alone.

Joe had flown them to Dulles while Drew contacted Herc about getting them on the first available flight to Pakistan. He didn't bother hiding that he was asking Herc for help; they had the resources, so they might as well use them. If anyone could pull strings on their behalf, it would be Herc, but the earliest they could leave was on a nine o'clock flight the next morning, so Drew arranged for a hotel room as well.

Fortunately, there were plenty of shops in and around the hotel, so Drew could buy clothes, toiletries, a carry-on, and a charger for his phone. Joe had stopped by his house and picked up everything he needed on his way to find Emani, but Drew only had his wallet, passport, and the clothes on his back, and while he was no stranger to roughing it, he felt like he'd done his fair share already during all the years he'd spent deployed in the desert. These days, he intended to enjoy the comforts of air conditioning, clean clothes, and regular showers.

"Bathroom's all yours if you want it." Drew loosened the towel around his waist and let it drop as he reached for a pair of black boxer briefs on the bed, not thinking twice about flashing his ass. He'd left body modesty behind in boot camp, and besides, if Joe saw anything he'd never seen before, he could throw his hat at it.

Joe glanced up, though if he was surprised to find Drew naked he didn't show it. Instead he perused Drew's body in an almost clinical fashion, one brow raised. "Thanks. I'll shower in a few minutes."

Drew wasn't sure whether to be amused or offended by the dispassionate appraisal, but he settled on amused. "Like what you see?" he asked, unable to resist teasing Joe just to see if he could get a reaction.

Joe frowned. "You have a good body, and you know it," he said. "I was a little curious, that's all."

"Not bad for forty-four, eh?" Drew smiled wryly as he got dressed in the boxer briefs, a pair of gray sweatpants, and a Museum of Air and Space T-shirt. "Of course, I have to work a lot harder at it now than I did a few years ago."

Joe sighed quietly and looked back at his computer screen. "Finn seems to like it. I guess that's all that matters."

"He hasn't voiced any complaints so far. I don't have any complaints about his either." Drew tossed his damp towels back into the bathroom and then went back to stretch out on his bed. "I haven't gotten to see yours yet, though, so I can't venture an opinion."

Joe looked up again, and there was a flash of something in his eyes. Drew wasn't sure if it was pride, or temper, or maybe even challenge, but it wasn't as cold as the expression Joe normally showed him. "Why would you even care?" he asked. He closed his laptop and then put it aside and rose to his feet. "I don't have anything I'm ashamed of."

"I care about as much as any gay man cares when looking at a hot guy," Drew said with a little shrug. "You're an attractive man when you're not glaring at me like you wish you could kill me with your brain."

Joe grimaced as he ran a hand through his hair and muttered something under his breath in Russian about not losing his temper. "Look, I'm trying to make the best of things, okay? I realize you aren't out to sabotage me with Finn, and you proved you can be trusted. I don't want you dead, because yeah, that would hurt Finn, and Finn has suffered enough because of me. But this isn't easy. I don't know you. I don't know what you really want. I don't even understand why you're here. I don't need a babysitter, and I'm not even sure I need your help."

"I'm here because Finn and I agreed we don't want you going on this mission alone," Drew said in the patient tone he usually reserved for small children—or grown men who acted like small children. "What I want.... Well, there are layers to that." He leaned against the plump pillows and stacked his hands behind his head. "In the short term, I want to eliminate the threat to you and Finn. I'm here as your partner, not your babysitter, and while you may not think you need help, Finn and I do. As for not knowing me, that could change on this little road trip. I wouldn't mind getting to know you better."

There was no mistaking the look of cold anger on Joe's face. "Don't patronize me. You may have been an XO at Lawson & Greer, but you sure as hell aren't my boss."

"No, I'm not your boss, but I know a brat when I see one," Drew said. Given that Joe already hated him for existing, he didn't see how he could make things worse by being blunt. Hell, maybe Joe would come to respect his straightforward approach. Stranger things had happened.

Instead of giving Drew a glare or an icy reply, Joe's head rocked back as if Drew had slapped him. His face turned white, and he abruptly spun away, walking quickly toward the bathroom as though he couldn't tolerate being in Drew's presence for another moment—

or maybe because he was trying to hide something he didn't want Drew to see.

Drew watched him go, deciding not to say anything for now. He got the sense that he'd stepped on something painful, and he intended to apologize, but Joe might be more receptive after a little time and space. Instead, he picked up a book from the stack on the nightstand. They had a long trip ahead of them, so he'd bought several books to keep him occupied on the flights.

After a couple of minutes of silence, Drew heard water running in the shower. It ended a short time later. After another short pause, Joe walked out of the bathroom completely naked.

Drew knew Joe was a big man, but naked he somehow looked even larger. His shoulders were broad, his waist narrow, emphasizing his washboard abs and the defined bands of muscle on his arms and legs. He had a full sleeve of tattoos on his right arm, a design made up of stylized flames and flowers, which terminated in a mandala-like sun on his wrist.

Seeming as unconcerned about his nudity as Drew had been, Joe crossed to where he'd left his small travel case on a chair. He took out a pair of black briefs and donned them, not rushing but apparently not trying to put on a show, either.

Drew let out a low wolf whistle, hoping to ease some of the earlier tension with a little levity. "Nice ink. Nice lots of things, actually."

"Thanks." Joe continued to dress, pulling out a black tank top and a pair of black sleep shorts. "Your ink is nice, too."

"Thanks." Drew watched Joe get dressed, enjoying the play of hard muscle beneath skin. "If you ever want a closer look, just let me know."

"You'll need to keep them covered in Pakistan," Joe replied. "Tattooing is a sin. To some, a major one. I have a waterproof pigment I use to cover mine."

"I should be okay as long as I wear long sleeves and pants in public, right?" Drew closed his book and put it aside. "Or do I need to get something to cover up mine as well?"

Joe glanced in Drew's direction. "You should be fine, just don't roll up your sleeves if you get hot. For all the time you were in the Middle East, did you go out away from camp much?"

"Nah, too dangerous," Drew said. "We didn't stray far from camp even in small groups, much less alone."

"Mmm." For a moment Joe looked thoughtful. "I'm going to be honest. I'm not sure what in the hell to do with you when we get to Islamabad. I can pass as a native, since I speak the language fluently. I was going to try to get back in along the same channels I used in my previous mission, but you won't be able to go with me. They don't trust foreigners."

"We've got a long flight to figure it out." Drew sat up and swung his legs over the side of the bed, facing Joe directly. "Meanwhile, don't think I haven't noticed you deflecting any personal stuff like you're Neo in *The Matrix*."

Joe sat down on his bed. "Yeah, so? Don't I have a right to privacy?"

"Sure, you do," Drew said, spreading his hands. "But you're saying you don't know me while avoiding getting to know me, or letting me get to know you. I'm aware you'd be thrilled if a sinkhole opened up right here and took me under, but until something happens, you and I are connected through Finn. I don't see any need to be at odds, if only to keep from stressing him out."

Joe scowled. "Look, you keep making me out to be the villain here, you know that? I told you, I accept you for Finn's sake. I even trust that you aren't going to knife me in the back to get rid of *me*. So stop saying I want something bad to happen to you, like I'm some evil piece of shit. Sounds like you don't trust me!"

"I don't think you're evil or a villain," Drew said. "I think you've got a lot of thick walls up, and that's not healthy." He paused and studied Joe, wondering how much he could nudge. "I'm sorry about what I said earlier. It looked like I hit a nerve, and I didn't mean to."

"So being a private person isn't healthy? Not wanting to divulge my life story to someone just because they want it is bad?" Joe shook his head, obviously agitated. "Why would I tell you a damned thing when every other word out of your mouth is you 'knowing' that I want you dead? Why would I give you that power over me?"

"I don't think you want me dead." Drew leaned back on his hands and watched Joe intently. "I think you wish Finn and I had never met. That Finn didn't love me and I didn't love him. That I'd break up with him, or he'd break up with me. I think you want things to be like they used to be because it was easier dealing with Finn having occasional hookups than it is to deal with sharing. But I don't think you wish me any *real* harm."

"I don't waste time wishing for something that won't happen," Joe stated flatly. "I learned a long time ago that action is the only thing that causes change. Finn's happiness matters more to me than my own, and it's not like he would have suddenly discovered monogamy was his thing, whether you had showed up or not. So don't think I'm spending any time worrying about it, because I've accepted that you're here to stay. I've accepted that I have less time with Finn because of it. I've accepted that you somehow make him happy, and that apparently you give him something I don't. Sounds like you're the one obsessing, Martin, not me."

Drew mulled over Joe's response, not entirely sure he believed every word of it. Joe was talking a good game, and maybe he thought he'd accepted the situation, but acceptance on an emotional level could be a whole different thing. Or maybe Joe meant every word and something else was eating at him. Finn suspected as much, and Drew was starting to as well.

"Great!" he said, and he beamed at Joe, deciding to take a different tactic. "If that's the case, maybe we can get to know each other better. I mean, if you and I get along well, maybe end up friends, we could spend time with Finn together. Hell, I wouldn't mind if we became more than friends, and I'm pretty sure Finn wouldn't have any objections, either."

Joe's mouth dropped open, and there was obvious shock written on his face. After a moment he shook his head. "Quit being an asshole, Martin. You don't want me, and I don't want you. You think that just because you're fucking Finn, it means I'm going to fall into bed with you too? In this case, I don't give a fuck what Finn wants. Who I sleep with is *my* choice."

"Absolutely," Drew agreed with a firm nod. "Neither Finn nor I would ever want you to feel coerced but don't make assumptions about what I do or don't want. You're smart and hot, and we've probably got enough in common to get along. I'd fuck you with or without Finn in the same bed. He'd probably at least want to watch, though."

"God." Joe ran a hand through his hair again, mussing the short strands. "That's... wrong. On so many levels. For you to say you believe I wish you'd disappear in one breath and then say you want to sleep with me in the next? Even taking Finn out of the picture, sex isn't casual to me, not the way it is to you and Finn. And before you get on your high horse again, that's not a judgement. You said you wanted to know me? Fine. Know this. I have to have an emotional connection to someone before I'd ever consider going to bed with them, and polite antagonism isn't the right connection. And for the record? I haven't slept with anyone but Finn since we got together eight years ago."

"I admire your loyalty," Drew said. "And I don't just mean sexually. It seems to be one of your core values."

"Yeah, well, it's just who I am." Joe shrugged. "Finn is all I've wanted or needed. We've been through a lot of shit together. Maybe I don't love easily, but I damn sure love forever."

A little pang shot through Drew, and he envied Finn. He'd never had anyone love him so deeply and fiercely as Joe loved Finn. "He's a lucky man," he said softly.

Joe's brows shot up. "I think I'm the lucky one that Finn loves me. He's the only one who ever made me believe I was worth loving."

Drew tried not to let the surprise he felt at Joe's admission show on his face, but he wasn't sure how well he masked it. He'd never guessed Joe harbored a deep-seated insecurity, given how confident he seemed. Maybe that had something to do with Joe's reaction earlier when Drew called him a brat.

"Then you must have known a lot of dumbasses," he said, gazing at Joe steadily. "You're definitely worth loving."

"You don't know that." Joe turned his face away. "You don't know me. You don't have any reason to even like me. You seem to think I'm immature and selfish and closed off."

"I also think you're loyal, brave, and a good leader who knows how to focus and get shit done," Drew said. "You're a good man, and anyone who doesn't think you're worth loving is a dumbass."

Rather than appearing flattered, Joe's expression seemed troubled. "How can you think I'm a good man when you think I'm selfish and immature? I'm starting to wonder what your game is here."

"I said I think you wish things would go back to the way they used to be," Drew said, still watching Joe closely. Joe seemed to be stuck in an either-or mindset, which could be due to jealousy, or a sign of whatever deeper issue Joe was wrestling with. "I didn't say that's selfish. It's understandable, given the upheaval your relationship with Finn has gone through lately. Being upset over a huge, unexpected change doesn't make you a bad person."

"No, you think it makes me a dumbass." Joe sighed, closing his eyes and laying back against the pillows. "You insult me one minute, flatter me the next, say you would sleep with me when you don't even seem to like me. I don't know you, and I sure as hell don't understand you, Martin. Just talking to you makes me dizzy."

"Well, maybe it wouldn't if you'd stop looking at everything as a binary issue," Drew pointed out. "Just because I recognize your flaws doesn't mean I can't recognize your virtues as well. Besides, you keep putting words in my mouth. I didn't call you selfish, and I didn't say being upset makes you a dumbass. I did call you a brat, which was out of line, and I meant my apology."

"Sure. Whatever." Joe kept his eyes closed. "I only have your words to go by, so yeah, everything seems pretty binary to me. You keep pushing me to give you more than I'm comfortable with and then tell me it's my fault for having walls. You don't know my life, don't know what I've been through, and I doubt you care. Maybe this is your way of trying to get me to accept you and Finn, but I told you, I've accepted it. I can't change it, and if you make Finn happy, fine.

But if you ever hurt him, Martin, you won't think I'm a good man anymore. You'll think I'm your worst fucking nightmare."

"Noted." Drew stretched out on the bed again and reached for his book. He'd gotten about as far as he was going to with Joe for now, and pushing harder would only make Joe barricade the walls even more than they already were.

Baby steps, he reminded himself. He could get through to Joe eventually. He just hoped he succeeded before whatever was eating at Joe caused him to blow up or burn out.

20

A fter the long flight to Pakistan, their arrival, in Joe's opinion, was almost anticlimactic.

Stepping from the cool of the plane into the sweltering heat of Islamabad almost stole Joe's breath, but he'd experienced it before. He followed along behind Drew, keeping a certain amount of distance and not speaking. It was part of the roles they'd come up with on the flight from Dulles to Dubai. Drew was pretending to be an American businessman looking for new markets for his software company, while Joe was his Urdu-speaking assistant.

The thirteen hour layover they'd had in Dubai enabled them to purchase clothing and luggage suitable to their cover story, and to even have a small stack of business cards printed up at a shipping center in the airport. Drew had to use his real name, since he didn't have the fake IDs that Joe had kept from his previous mission, but the cover should be sound enough to stand up to casual scrutiny for a couple of weeks. Herc had even arranged for a voice-mail drop that was listed on the business card, and Chris had hacked together a "Martin Associates" website, just in case.

It was probably overkill, but Joe knew from previous undercover missions that *not* having your cover story backstopped was asking for trouble. Drew had been right that having Herc's help in setting up the logistics made things much easier. Not that Joe would have needed anything like this if he'd been alone. Even if he didn't really want Drew there, he knew it was better to include him rather than have Drew blundering along in his wake, possibly blowing Joe's cover and getting them both killed. *Or worse.*

Part of Herc's assistance was arranging for a driver and a hotel, for which Joe was grateful. He hadn't slept much in the past seventy-two hours since Finn's abduction, and he knew that finding their quarry was going to require them both to be at the top of their games. Now that they'd made it to their destination, it was time to slow down, look, and listen, and not make any mistakes that might end up blowing the mission.

They were booked into a two-bedroom suite at the Islamabad Marriott, which despite being a chain was a quite luxurious hotel. After claiming their baggage and locating their driver, they went to the hotel, and once Joe had tipped the bellman and the door was shut, he almost sagged in relief.

"We made it," he said as he headed toward the minibar. "I definitely need a drink."

"Have a seat." Drew waved him toward the plush sofa and headed to the bar as well. "I'll pour one for us both."

Joe hesitated, his knee-jerk reaction being to say that he could take care of himself, but he stopped the impulse and simply nodded, moving to the sofa and sinking down onto it. "Bourbon, if they have it, please. Neat."

"You got it."

Drew poured two drinks with a generous hand and carried them back to Joe. He handed over one glass before dropping onto the sofa as well, and he let out a soft sigh. "Feels good to be out of an airplane seat."

"Yeah." Joe accepted the glass and drank deeply, feeling the burn of the alcohol as it went down, warming him in a way that the heat outside hadn't. "It's a long damned flight."

He still wasn't sure how he felt about Drew or how to treat him. Drew confused him, and he couldn't get a good feel for the kind of person Drew truly was. Logically, he knew Drew had to be okay, not only because Herc had hired him, but because Finn loved him. It was, however, hard to get past his initial feelings of Drew being an interloper who was taking something precious from him.

There was also the matter of him not really knowing Drew and the reserved, suspicious part of Joe's own nature that viewed Drew as a threat. It didn't help that Drew had triggered some bad memories, however unintentionally. Maybe things would have been different if Joe had met Drew before Finn had, if he could have had the opportunity to get to know him without the associated bad feelings before Finn had fallen in love with him, but no amount of wishing would change the situation. Joe was left feeling like he was walking down a slippery slope without any support.

"It damned sure is, and I'm creeping into *getting too old for this shit* territory," Drew said, leaning his head on the back of the sofa.

It was on the tip of Joe's tongue to snap back that no one had asked Drew to come along, but it suddenly didn't seem worth the effort. Maybe it was exhaustion catching up with him, but Joe was suddenly tired of the verbal sparring.

"Happens to everyone eventually," he replied with a shrug. He thought about Mark Hansen, a merc known as Stack, who had worked for Drew at Lawson & Greer, and whom Finn and Joe had known fairly well. Stack had been the partner of Hunter Callahan, who now worked for Hercules Security. Stack had died in the field while saving Hunter's life when the removal of an explosives-filled vest from a kid wired as a suicide bomber went wrong. "Or it does if we live that long."

"Ain't that the truth," Drew said softly, his expression turning pensive as he lifted his head and stared into his glass.

This was the first time Drew had displayed any uncertainty that Joe had seen. "Feeling your mortality, I take it? Working for Herc might not involve IEDs and suicide bombers like we had at L&G, but there's still danger, or at least there is for anyone in the field and not just managing or teaching."

"Oh, I've been feeling my mortality for about eighteen months," Drew said, one corner of his mouth quirking up in a wry smile.

Apparently Drew was thinking along the same directions Joe had been, which wasn't surprising. "I get it. It hit all of us who knew Mark. Hunter was a walking disaster until Payne took him in hand."

"Oh, man. Hunter...." Drew put his glass aside and scrubbed his face with both hands, looking weary. "Me and Blaze cleared the camp, but I went back. What if that poor kid wasn't the only surprise those assholes had planned for us, you know? I kept my distance, but I had a clear view. I saw it happen. And Hunter.... It took me a long time to stop hearing those screams."

Joe couldn't help the sympathy he felt for Drew, not after hearing the stories from Hunter about what had happened. Drew had been the XO for Bravo Company, which meant he had been, at least in part, responsible for Mark and for what had happened. Not that he was to blame, since he hadn't strapped bricks of C-4 to a little kid and sent him in to blow up the camp, but officers were always responsible for the men under their command. It was hard enough for Finn, Joe, and D-Day, who had worked with Mark and Hunter before, to deal with. It had to have been worse for Drew having one of the men under his charge blown to bits in the line of duty.

"I can't imagine." Joe shook his head. "I always thought D-Day would be the one to get his ass wasted, not Stack."

"You'd think." Drew gave a little snort. "Stack had a family. He was mustering out. He'd been playing it safer than usual, but something about that kid triggered his inner white knight. Maybe dad instincts. I don't know. It happened so fast, he probably didn't think about it at all. Just did it. We got Hunter the hell out of there as soon as possible, and I wouldn't have been surprised to hear he'd eaten a bullet. I'm glad Payne was able to help him."

"Me too." Joe took another sip from his glass, the alcohol allowing him to finally relax. He knew he wouldn't be able to completely let his guard down until Abbasi was in custody—*or dead*—but he wasn't going to let anything happen to Finn. No matter the cost. "Just goes to show why you shouldn't take anything for granted, I guess."

"Definitely not." Drew retrieved his glass and downed the drink in one swallow. "I wanted to get out of there myself," he said in a low voice. "But we were down two men, and Blaze needed me to help get shit back to normal. So I worked my ass off to wear myself out, but I had nightmares, anyway. Sometimes I was watching Stack die again. Sometimes it was me on that C-4." He glanced sidelong at Joe with a small, rueful smile. "I've been saying it was age that drove me out of the desert, but it wasn't just that. Not even mostly that. I was ready to be stateside, and I pulled my time on the therapist's couch as soon as I got home."

Joe wasn't sure why Drew was telling him this, but he couldn't bring himself to tell him to stop. There was a part of him that didn't want to listen to Drew's pain because it made him harder to ignore, harder to treat as just another merc he didn't much like. Another part of Joe understood what Drew had gone through in a way that anyone who hadn't been in the military, and had their ass on the line, couldn't. He knew what it was like to have friends and teammates die, to have to stand by while it happened because there wasn't anything you could do to stop it. He knew what it was like to have not only his own life, but the lives of everyone he cared about, in jeopardy.

"I think I need another drink," he said and then drained his glass. He stood up and held out a hand for Drew's glass. "What about you?"

"I wouldn't say no." Drew handed over his glass without hesitation.

Joe took it, crossing to the minibar and got them refills. Two drinks wouldn't be enough to get him even tipsy, but maybe they would help him sleep. He returned to the couch and handed Drew his drink before settling back in his former spot. He wasn't sure what to say, but somehow he felt he had to acknowledge Drew's admission of what many might consider a weakness.

"Did therapy help?" he asked quietly. "I know Hunter said conventional methods didn't work for him. I'm not exactly sure what he and Pita used that *did* work, but I have my suspicions."

"It helped, yeah," Drew said, sipping his drink this time. "But I was on board with it. I couldn't keep walking around in that headspace. I didn't *want* to." He shifted to face Joe, his expression alight with curiosity. "Mind if I ask what you suspect?"

Joe hesitated, not sure he should reveal his suspicions, but he doubted Drew would be judgmental about it, given his casual attitude toward sex. "Payne is a lot more... um, *forceful* than you might think. I overheard a few things between him and Hunter in the locker room. I wasn't eavesdropping, but people seem to forget I'm around, so they say things in front of me. I think Payne took Hunter in hand in a very dominating fashion, if you know what I mean."

Drew's eyebrows climbed, but he didn't seem shocked or offended. "Huh. I never would've guessed. I can see how that could have therapeutic value, though."

"Maybe for some." Joe grimaced before taking another swallow from his glass. "I couldn't do it."

"What, BDSM in general, or being dominated?"

For a moment Joe thought about refusing to answer, thinking it might be too revealing, but then he shrugged, realizing it probably wouldn't come as any big surprise. "Being dominated. At least not in that way. I can follow orders and take direction at work, but otherwise? No."

"Bet you'd be good at giving the orders, though." Some of the weariness faded from Drew's expression as he glanced at Joe with a small but mischievous smile.

Joe snorted. "Maybe, maybe not. It's not Finn's thing, so it's a moot point."

"I've tried it a time or two." Drew watched Joe closely, as if gauging his reaction. "I liked it enough to do it again."

"You'd damn sure better ask Finn if he's okay with it, before you go tomcatting around," Joe replied, frowning at Drew. "And me, too, for that matter. I'm not going to have mine or Finn's health put in jeopardy if you engage in a lot of risky behavior. I'll put my damned foot down about that, you better believe it!"

"Hah! I was right." Drew gave him a playful wink. "You'd be good at it. But don't worry. I haven't been with anyone but Finn since the first time we hooked up, and I don't plan to be. I don't *need* to be," he added with a little snort. "That boy's a handful."

Joe looked away. He didn't want to hear about Finn and Drew having sex. It made him unhappy to think about. "I don't want to know," he snapped and then slammed back the rest of his drink.

"Sorry, I wasn't trying to poke at a sore spot," Drew said. "I wanted to reassure you that I'm not going to do anything that could hurt you or Finn, that's all."

"That's all you needed to say." Joe rose to his feet, suddenly needing to escape. He'd let his guard down too much, apparently. "I have no interest in what you and Finn do together, do you understand me? I never wanted to know with his hookups, and I sure as hell don't want to know with *you*. It's enough that I have to *see* marks on him that you put there. It's enough that I have to put up with you being a part of his life. I sure as fuck don't have to listen to what you like to do with him."

Drew released a long sigh. "Understood. If you'd rather I didn't leave any marks for you to see, I won't. I'm not trying to edge you out or make you miserable, and I don't want to make this harder on you than it already is."

Joe ran a hand through his hair. He was suddenly agitated, and he wasn't even certain why. He didn't want to hear about Finn and Drew's sex life, but it wasn't entirely jealousy, either. He wasn't sure what it meant, but he was too tired and stressed to think about it deeply. Maybe it was just the long trip and lack of sleep getting to him, or the fact that he'd let Drew in more than he'd intended.

"It is what it is," he replied dully. "Look, I'm tired, and you struck a nerve, okay? Do whatever you want with Finn, it's not my business. Don't make him unhappy, and I'll put up with whatever I have to put up with."

"Noted." Drew set aside his glass and stood up. "We're both tired. I think the best thing either of us can do right now is get some rest. We can figure out a plan when we wake up."

"Yeah." Joe turned away, heading toward the nearest bedroom. He had the feeling he wasn't going to get much sleep, despite his fatigue and the alcohol. Sleeping pills were out of the question, of course, but maybe he could try to meditate, try to find some tiny amount of inner peace. If he couldn't, he wasn't going to be of much use to anyone. Not even himself.

21

D rew woke up groggy and disoriented, and he didn't open his eyes. He thought he was home, and he stretched out his arm to see if Finn was there, but the other side of the bed was cold. The pillow didn't smell like the detergent he used, either.

Finally he opened his eyes, and reality came flooding back. He was in Pakistan, and Finn was in a hospital room on the other side of the world. With a grumbling sigh, he pushed back the covers and rolled out of bed. He needed to see if Joe was up so they could make a plan for going after Abassi—and see what frame of mind Joe was in. He'd thought they were making some progress. Joe had seemed to relax a little in response to Drew opening up. Or maybe it was the bourbon. Either way, things had been going well until Drew made the mistake of bringing up Finn.

Finn trusted him to look after Joe, and he *wanted* to. The fragility he sensed behind all of Joe's bluster was mashing all of his protective hot buttons, but sometimes he couldn't tell if he was doing more harm than good.

Scrubbing his fingers through his short hair, he made his way out of the bedroom and into the spacious living area of their suite, which was more like an apartment than a hotel room. Everything was quiet, and the door of Joe's bedroom stood open. Drew approached and knocked as he peeked inside.

"Joe?"

The room was empty, and Drew didn't hear any sounds coming from the adjoining bathroom. A flare of panic shot through him, and he entered the bedroom and looked around as if that would somehow make Joe materialize out of thin air.

"Joe!"

But there wasn't an answer, and the stillness in the suite let him know he was, indeed, alone.

"Motherfucker...." Drew blew out a sharp breath, his mind racing. Had Joe gone after Abassi alone? Of course he had. What other reason would he have for sneaking out while Drew was asleep? It wasn't like he had family and friends in the area to pay a friendly visit.

He strode back into his bedroom to grab his phone and call Herc. Maybe there was a way Chris could track down Joe before he got in over his head with Abassi.

While he was dialing, he heard the door to the suite open and close, followed by Joe's voice. "Hey, are you up? I got breakfast."

Drew canceled the call and hurried out of the bedroom, a mix of relief and irritation washing over him when he saw Joe. "Where were you? I thought you'd gone off and left me."

Joe looked up from where he'd been unloading the contents of a tray onto the table. "Why would you think that? I left you a note next to the coffee pot. Go check if you don't believe me."

Drew glanced over at the coffee maker on the little kitchenette counter, and sure enough, he spotted a piece of paper propped up against it.

"Sorry," he said with a sheepish smile. "I didn't think to look for a note."

Joe gave a grunt, continuing to offload the tray. There were two covered plates, as well as a cloth-covered basket and a bowl of fruit, along with two glasses of orange juice. "Of course you didn't." He glanced up at Joe, his expression wary. "I know you don't trust me, but if you don't mind, I'm hungry. Can we at least eat before arguing again?"

"I was worried about you, that's all." Drew released a long breath. Last night had definitely been the product of alcohol, not progress.

Joe sighed, dropping into one of the chairs. He scrubbed his face with his hands and then looked at Drew again.

"You don't have to worry. I'm not going to do anything stupid." He picked up a fork, toying with it. "Thanks for giving a damn. I didn't sleep much last night, so I did a lot of thinking. I'm tired of being at odds with you. I accept you and Finn are together, okay? I don't want anything bad to happen to you, and I'm willing to try to be friends. It's just going to take time. You seem to be a decent guy, and maybe if we'd met before you got involved with Finn, I'd've been better about it. But I couldn't help feeling like you were taking away what bit of Finn I actually had. You don't know what it's like to love someone for years and know they'll never be yours. Not really. Not fully."

Drew sat down across from Joe and leaned forward on his elbows. "No, I don't," he said. "I can only guess how difficult it is. How much it hurts. But I don't want to be at odds with you, either." He paused and then decided to take a risk. He stretched his hand across the table and touched Joe's arm lightly. "I want to help. In whatever ways you'll let me."

Joe didn't flinch, but he wouldn't meet Drew's eyes, either. "I don't know what you can do to help. I just have to learn to be more accepting, I guess."

"Take your time," Drew said, keeping his hand in place. "This is a big change, and you've had a lot to deal with lately on top of your relationship with Finn. I've got your back with Abassi, and I'm willing to listen if there's anything you want to talk about. No judgment."

"Sure. Thanks." Joe drew in a deep breath and then lifted the lid off his plate. "Let's eat, and we can discuss what to do about Abassi. I didn't know how you liked your eggs, so I went for scrambled. Plus bacon and sausage. Do you want coffee?"

"Scrambled eggs are fine, and bacon's even better." Drew

squeezed Joe's arm lightly, and then he pushed back his chair and stood up. "You got breakfast, so I'll make the coffee. I hope you like it strong."

"Strong is good with me," Joe replied. He glanced up, and for the first time he offered Drew a slight smile—small and rather sad, but a smile nonetheless.

Heartened by the sight, Drew grinned. "You got it," he said as he headed over to the coffeemaker. "So did you have any ideas about how to get to Abassi?" he asked, deciding it might be easier if they focused on less emotionally fraught topics for now.

"First we have to find the right one. There are at least seven of them here in Islamabad. What makes it harder is that Abassi wasn't one of the names on the list of targets from my previous mission, but he would have to be pretty high up to have the authority to order the kind of attack we faced—especially stateside. There are another ten men with that name in Karachi, but Pixel had tracked Emani back to Islamabad, so we're probably safe starting here. If we rule out men under thirty, who wouldn't be old enough to have an eighteen-year-old son, that leaves five men we need to find. Two of them run family-owned markets, one is a retired businessman, one is a taxi driver, and the last works for a tech firm. My bet is on the retired businessman or the tech, but we can't rule any of them out immediately."

"So step one is gathering information." Drew retrieved two coffee cups from the cabinet and started looking around for sugar. "Can we get Pixel to help with that?" he asked, glancing over his shoulder at Joe.

"He's done all the preliminary legwork. He's even looked on the dark web for information." Joe grimaced. "These guys are tricky. We thought we'd gotten to the upper levels and eliminated them, but apparently there are more layers than we knew about. They're like roaches—hard to kill, always coming out of the woodwork, and they reproduce so fast it's hard to be sure you've gotten them all. At this point, I think we need to check out each of these guys, see which one of them lost a son recently, and go from there."

"Works for me." Once the coffee finished brewing, he poured two cups. "Any particular one you'd like to start with?" he asked as he handed Joe a cup.

"Thanks." Joe said. "I think maybe the retired guy. From what Pixel said, he's pretty well-off. Sounds like he'd have the time to be a criminal mastermind."

"Okay, we'll start with him." Drew watched Joe over the rim of his cup, debating whether to ask the question that was poised on his tongue. He risked alienating or pissing off Joe by asking, but he suspected the answer factored into what was bothering Joe above and beyond his relationship issues. "Do you remember shooting the son?" he asked in as gentle a tone as he could muster.

He deliberately avoiding using language that alluded to the son's age. Abassi's son might have been only eighteen, but that was old enough to know the difference between right and wrong. He was no seven-year-old loaded down with C-4 and ordered to walk into a mercenary camp.

"Yeah." Joe put down the coffee cup, his lips twisting into a pained grimace. His face seemed to go paler, too, as though the memory was deeply disturbing. "I didn't know he was barely more than a kid himself. I came upon him beating the shit out of a little girl who couldn't have been more than eight or nine, and I have my suspicions he'd been raping her, too, because she was naked and covered in blood. I didn't ask questions, I didn't even *think*. I just shot him, one burst right through the head. I don't know if he was armed, and he probably never even saw me coming. I didn't give him a chance to surrender. I just saw that he was about to kill the little girl, and I shot him."

"Jesus...." Drew had assumed the son had been with a group of men who'd fired on Joe's squad, and Joe had doubts about whether he'd done the right thing because maybe the son had been at the wrong place, at the wrong time. But no, the situation seemed pretty clear-cut to Drew. "I'd have done the same thing. Is the girl okay?"

"She's alive, last I heard." Joe scrubbed his face with his hands again. "As far as okay, who the fuck can say if she'll ever be okay? Or any of the other victims, for that matter. And there are always more victims, because there are always more of the monsters who prey on the weak and innocent just because they can. This goes on all over the world. All we can do is fight it—we'll never be able to stop it, no matter what we do."

"Yeah, but fighting it is better than letting it happen," Drew said. "You saved those people—those *kids*—from a fate I wouldn't wish on my worst enemy. That's not pointless or useless. I'm pretty sure they'd agree."

"Yeah. But it'll break your heart. It almost broke me." Joe shuddered. "You can only fight shit like that for so long before you start to lose yourself. I was in the thick of it for a month, in the filth and slime, and I sometimes I feel like I'll never be clean again."

Every caretaker instinct Drew possessed was screaming, and he wanted to do nothing more than hold Joe close and offer comfort, but he doubted Joe would accept it. Joe had probably come home in need of that comfort from Finn, only to experience another nasty shock. No wonder Joe had been wound up so tightly. He'd been denied a release valve when he needed it most.

"You don't have any reason to feel dirty or stained," Drew said, leaning forward. "You're a good man, and you did the right thing. He was beating a child. Do you think he would've surrendered peacefully if you'd given him the chance? Do you think he would've felt an ounce of remorse? Hell, no. He was old enough to know what he was doing and how fucked up it was."

"I know that, and that's not what bothers me most." Joe glanced at Drew. "He should have known better, but what was he taught, growing up in an environment like that? If you think about it, he was abused, being taught that he had the right and the power to victimize people. Did he ever have a chance to know right from wrong, when he was brought up to believe that the most heinous of wrongs was right and normal?"

Drew inclined his head to acknowledge the point. "Probably not, but you can't beat yourself up over speculation. You saw a threat and eliminated it. That's what you were there to do."

"I did what I did. Right from my perspective, wrong from that of that boy and his father. We could argue semantics all day, but what it comes down to is that now this man wants to kill me and the people I love. So he has to be stopped by any means necessary." Joe drew in a deep breath. "I will do this because it has to be done, but after that, I never want to set foot in this country again. Being here makes me feel like my own demons are too close to the surface."

No doubt Joe was concerned about his killer instincts turning him into what he hated most about the traffickers, but Drew thought perhaps bad memories had something to do with it, too.

"I get it," he said quietly. "I never want to go back to Iraq."

"Something like that, yeah." Joe shuddered. "I just want to get this done. All I care about is keeping Finn safe, no matter what I have to do to make sure he is."

"I'll do whatever it takes to help you," Drew said, although at this point, he meant far more than just protecting Finn, even if Joe didn't realize it yet.

"Thanks." Joe picked up his fork again, grimacing in distaste at his plate, as though his appetite was gone. Even so, he shoveled up a forkful of eggs. "And if we're going to do that, we'd better eat. Guys like us need to eat. Going up against killers while your blood sugar is fucked up isn't good."

Drew picked up a piece of bacon, his resolve to help Joe, and see him safely through this, growing even stronger. He'd be damned if he returned to Finn without Joe. Finn needed Joe, and Joe.... Well, Drew was becoming more and more convinced that Joe needed *him*.

22

"Shit. This is a dead end."

Joe glanced away from the house they'd been surveilling, not bothering to hide his frustration. They'd spent the majority of the last two days watching the retired businessman whom Joe had thought was their leading suspect, but it was becoming increasingly obvious that he couldn't be the Ismail Abassi who was leading a human trafficking ring. The guy was in his sixties, and while that didn't preclude him being their suspect, his behavior did. He spent a lot of time at a coffee house playing Ludo with a group of men close to his own age. Joe had gone into the coffee house and listened to their conversations, all of which seemed to revolve around the typical subjects—their children and grandchildren, politics, and soccer. Chris's check of the man's phone records had been equally fruitless, so unless he used a series of burner phones constantly, he wasn't in contact with anyone in the network Joe had taken on. They'd watched his house, just in case it was all an elaborate cover, but after seeing the man come and go, watching all his visitors and deliveries, Joe was ready to admit he wasn't their guy.

"Agreed," Drew said. "Want to move on to the next one on the list?"

"Yeah. That would be the businessman." Joe took out his phone, checking the time before pulling up the address and giving it to their driver. "Do you think we're going about this the right way? I could get back inside with the traffickers. It might make it easier."

"No fucking way." Drew shook his head vehemently. "This may be a slower process, but we're getting the job done."

Joe nodded, chewing on his lower lip for a moment as he considered the options. He didn't want to go back undercover, not after the shit he'd witnessed, but there was the possibility that none of their leads would pan out. Still, this was just the first one, and he told himself that Finn and the rest of Hercules Security were on alert for anything Abassi might try. Joe felt he and Drew were safer being in country, since Joe doubted Abassi would expect someone to bring the fight to his doorstep so quickly. He didn't want to be complacent, but he thought they had a good chance of catching Abassi unaware, as long as they could find him quickly enough.

The thing that surprised him most was that he and Drew made a good team. Their skills meshed well, and following their first morning in Islamabad, things between them had been far less strained. As Joe relaxed and became more accepting, Drew did as well. They weren't anything like friends, but Joe had decided that treating Drew as he would any other coworker he didn't know very well was the best thing for both them and the mission.

They arrived at the businessman's office address. "We should probably case the building. I'll have Pixel schedule an appointment with the guy as soon as he can get one. Are you good with your corporate tech manager cover?"

"I'm good," Drew said, his tone matter-of-fact rather than cocky. One good thing Joe could say about Drew—if he had to—was that he was honest about both his abilities and his limitations. Whether due to age and wisdom, or an innate characteristic, he didn't seem to need to prove himself.

"Okay. Shall we take a look around this building? I'd say split up, but since you don't speak the language, if you ran into problems, you might not be able to get out of them."

"Yeah, I'd feel better with my interpreter close by," Drew said dryly.

Joe snorted. For some reason Drew seemed to think Joe was bossy or dominant, when Joe had never really seen himself that way. "Come on, this shouldn't take long. I want to be prepared for tomorrow. What's rule number one?"

"Always know your escape route." Drew gave him a thumbs-up. "We got this."

Joe told the driver to wait as they got out of the car, making their way to the office building. Drew could read a certain amount of Urdu even if he didn't speak it, so Joe didn't have to translate the directory for him. The office they wanted was on the tenth floor of the twenty story building. Joe suggested they take the elevator to the top floor and then go down via the stairs, checking each floor for anything unusual.

They made short work of the reconnaissance, which didn't reveal anything of concern. Joe was almost disappointed because an anomaly would at least given him some hope they were on the right track. The lack of one didn't mean they *weren't*, but Joe found himself eager to get through this mission so he could get back home. To Finn.

They finished up just about the time most of the offices were closing for the day, so it took them a few minutes to get through the press of people and to the car. Once they were in the rear seat, Joe turned to Drew. "Back to the hotel, I guess. Unless there's anything else you think we need to do."

Drew gazed at him speculatively. "Any chance I could talk you into some sightseeing? I've never been to this area before, and I probably won't be back, so I wouldn't mind looking around a bit. Maybe we could find a good local restaurant for dinner while we're out, too."

Joe was surprised at the suggestion, but another evening in the hotel didn't appeal much, either. Nor had he had much of an opportunity to take in the culture of Islamabad on his previous mission, and it would probably do him some good to have some positive associations with Pakistan, rather than all the horrible ones he'd accumulated. "Sure. What kind of things would you like to see?"

Drew pulled out his phone and opened an app. "Let's see what landmarks they've got around here.... Oh, hey, we aren't that far from the Pakistan Monument. We could check that out. The Bari Imam Shrine looks interesting, too."

"Sure." Joe gave the driver directions, and they set off through the increasing traffic. After about twenty minutes they arrived at their destination. The Monument was interesting, shaped like a blooming flower with four open petals around a star-shaped central courtyard. There was a museum of history attached to the monument, and as they wandered among the exhibits, which detailed ancient civilizations in the country as well as Pakistan's battle for independence, Joe found himself relaxing for the first time in weeks.

"This was a good idea," he told Drew, after they'd spent almost two hours looking at everything. "Thanks for suggesting it."

Drew offered an easy smile. "I thought a little down time might do us both some good." The smile turned into a mischievous grin as he pulled out his phone and waved it. "Let's take a selfie and send it to Finn. We can do the whole wish you were here thing."

Two days before, Joe would have automatically protested, not wanting to do anything that seemed to show any sort of connection between he and Drew. But, as he thought about it, he knew that a picture of the two of them would probably please Finn a lot, and it didn't cost Joe anything. "Okay," he said with a shrug. "Where do you want to do it?"

"Somewhere with a good view of the city in the background." Drew glanced around, and then he grasped Joe's arm and led him over to a particular spot. "Right here," he said, guiding Joe where he wanted him. He slid one arm around Joe's shoulders and leaned in as he held up the phone at an angle that captured them both, plus the scenic background. "Ready?"

"Sure," Joe replied. He smiled slightly at the phone, hoping this would make Finn happy and reassure him that everything was okay.

Drew took a couple of pictures. "This one is good," he said, holding out the phone so Joe could see the one he'd selected.

The photo showed the two of them looking like typical tourists, and the view behind them was beautiful. Drew's smile was wider and seemed more genuine than Joe's. In fact, he didn't look at all awkward or stiff about being so close to Joe.

"Fine with me," Joe replied. He didn't like having his picture taken, and he hoped that Finn wouldn't see his awkwardness. "Finn should like it."

"He'll love it." Drew remained standing close to Joe while he sent the text.

"I'm sure he'll see it soon." Joe calculated quickly. "It's ten o'clock in the morning there. He should be awake."

Sure enough, Drew's phone pinged no more than a minute later, and Drew chuckled as he read Finn's response. "He says we're hot together, and it's not fair we can set off his heart monitor from thousands of miles away."

Joe shook his head. Finn had to be teasing, since Joe highly doubted Finn had any interest in Joe and Drew hooking up, despite what Drew claimed. "That's Finn. Never serious."

"At least he's in good spirits," Drew said, tucking his phone away again. "He must be doing well postsurgery."

"That's what he told me yesterday." Joe had been quite anxious about Finn's leg, but the break had been repaired, and while Finn was in for a long bout of physical therapy, the prognosis was for him to make a full recovery. "Thank God he's not expected to be left with a limp. It doesn't make me feel less guilty about what happened, but at least he won't have to live with a reminder for the rest of his life."

"He doesn't blame you," Drew said, keeping his voice low and gentle. "You shouldn't blame yourself."

Something inside Joe twisted painfully. "Easier said than done. I may have saved that little girl, but it almost cost me Finn."

"But it didn't. We got him out, and he's going to be fine. All's well that ends well, right?"

Drew was trying to be comforting, but Joe shook his head. "I can't look at it that way. At least not yet. Maybe someday, if I'm lucky."

"Finn and I will help if we can." Drew clapped Joe's shoulder and offered a reassuring smile. "Meanwhile, how about dinner? I'll treat, since I'm supposed to be the high-rolling executive."

"Sure." Joe was happy enough to leave the subject of guilt behind. He had stared down that particular dark hole far too much in the last few days, and he needed to keep focus. "How about something Kashmiri? They go in for a lot of meat."

Drew's face lit up with interest. "You're talking my language. Do you know a good place?"

"I do." Joe beckoned Drew to follow him. They'd have a good meal, and hopefully Joe would be able to sleep. Today's investigation had been a disappointment, but he was hopeful for tomorrow. Ismail Abassi's days were numbered. Joe was going to make sure of it.

23

A case of the late evening munchies had driven Drew out of his bedroom and into the kitchenette, and now he stood in front of the fridge with the door open, debating whether he wanted to make a sandwich or heat up the takeout he'd brought home from the restaurant. Dinner had been so good that he'd ordered another entrée to go and had encouraged Joe to do the same so they'd have a meal ready and waiting, but he couldn't stop thinking about the curry.

The sound of laughter distracted him from his indecision, and he glanced toward Joe's room. The door stood open, and he could hear other voices, although they weren't loud enough for him to make out what they were saying.

Joe laughed again—a full, rich sound unlike anything Drew had heard from him before. Hell, Drew didn't even know Joe *could* laugh. But *something* had lifted the weight of guilt and depression from Joe's shoulders, even if it was only temporary, and Drew had to know what it was.

He closed the fridge door and headed over to Joe's room, and he paused outside to knock on the doorframe.

"What's up?" he asked, peering inside.

Joe glanced up from his laptop, and to Drew's amazement, he seemed to squirm, like a small boy caught doing something naughty. "Oh... um, I was just watching a couple of guys make a vlog."

"What vlog?" Drew asked. "I could use something new, especially if it's funny."

"I doubt it's something you'd be interested in," Joe replied, a flush rising on his cheeks as he closed the laptop.

Joe's embarrassment only spurred Drew's curiosity, and he went to sit down on the edge of the bed where Joe was reclining against the pillows, his long legs stretched out and crossed at the ankle.

"We won't know unless you tell me what it is," Drew said, giving Joe's hard bicep a playful poke. "Come on, I promise I won't laugh."

Joe's lips hardened into what promised to develop into a stubborn line, but then he sighed. "If you laugh, I'll beat the shit out of you."

Drew held up one hand as if he was being sworn in and drew a large X over his heart with the other. "I will not laugh. Do you want me to pinky swear, too?"

That made Joe snort and roll his eyes. "No, you don't have to go *that* far." He hesitated before finally seeming to make up his mind. "Look, I read a lot, okay? It can get pretty boring on missions sometimes, and when Finn goes out without... well. When I'm alone. I read all kinds of things. Survival magazines. Thrillers. Science fiction, fantasy, mysteries. And romances." He dropped his gaze to the closed top of the computer, not meeting Drew's eyes.

Drew blinked, taken aback by that new tidbit of information. Joe was one of the last people he'd ever peg as a romance reader. "Gay or straight romance?"

"Gay. Sometimes it's... nice, you know? To be able to identify with the characters and their situations." Joe lifted his chin. "I'm not ashamed of it. I just hate having people tease me for enjoying romances sometimes. It pisses me off."

But Drew had no intention of teasing Joe. With a delighted smile, he climbed on the bed and sat cross-legged, facing Joe. "Who's your favorite author? I finished binging R.K. Epson's contemporary

Western series last month, and it was *really* good. Lots of cowboys in tight jeans rolling in the hay together."

Joe finally looked at him again, his mouth dropping open. He seemed incapable of speech for at least thirty seconds, and there was no mistaking his expression of stunned surprise. "Wait... are you telling me you read gay romance, too? *Really*?"

"Yep, really," Drew said, both pleased and amused he'd managed to surprise Joe in a good way. "Like you said, it's nice being able to relate."

"Huh." Joe seemed off-balance, and he shook his head. "I never would have thought you'd be the type to enjoy romances, but I guess people would think the same thing about me. Big scary mercs aren't supposed to be mushy inside."

"We're big, scary mercs, but that's not all we are." Drew debated whether to say what he was thinking, but then he decided he might as well. He'd already made himself vulnerable to Joe once in talking about what happened in Iraq. "It's nice to read about happy endings," he said at last. "About the kind of life I'll probably never have. You know, coming home to a husband and a dog, living out the white-picket-fence scenario."

Joe gave him a sudden, sharp glance, eyes narrowed. He seemed about to say something, but instead he dropped his gaze again, letting out what appeared to be a deliberate breath. "I enjoy romantic suspense and urban fantasies the most," he admitted. "I read a lot of Angie Leonard and Sandra Crane. Oh, and Jim Walker. He's one of the guys on the vlog, actually. Him and his husband Bill."

"What's the vlog?" Drew asked, hoping to keep Joe distracted. "I don't think I've heard it."

"The Fabulous Gay Romance Review." Joe opened his laptop again, turning it so that Drew could see the screen. "They cover a big variety of things, not just romance books, but movies, audiobooks, and even plays. They interview authors and have guest reviewers, too. What I really enjoy is watching their recordings of them making a show. The flubs and asides and commentary are great. They're funny guys, and Bill has a variety of facial expressions that crack me up. Especially the way he uses his eyebrows."

"Strong eyebrow game, huh?" Drew chuckled. "Mind if I watch it with you?"

"You really want to?" Joe seemed hesitant, as if not entirely sure Drew wasn't having him on.

Instead of replying, Drew shifted so he could lean against the headboard and stretched out beside Joe. Even though he didn't nestle close—Joe probably would've kicked him out if he'd tried—he could still feel the warmth radiating from Joe's body, and he became acutely aware that he was in bed with a hot, buff, sexy, growly man. Too bad Joe wasn't the slightest bit interested in him, he thought ruefully. He wouldn't have minded acting out some of the sex scenes in their favorite books.

"Start it up," he said, forcing himself to focus on the laptop instead.

Joe didn't protest Drew's nearness. He shifted the laptop around, balancing it between them. "I'll go back to the beginning. You heard me laughing because Jim kept trying to say 'prestidigitation' and screwing it up, and every time he did Bill's eyebrows would twitch."

Drew settled in to watch, grateful for the respite—and for the moment of rapport with Joe. Maybe the more Joe learned about him, the less Joe would see him as a threat. At the very least, he hoped he and Joe could develop a decent relationship without any lingering jealousy or resentment marring it. Anything more than that.... Well, that was probably a pipe dream best suited for the pages of the romance novels they both liked.

24

"That's suspicious," Joe murmured.

He and Drew were sitting at an open-air café on one of Islamabad's busy main streets, sipping drinks and pretending to enjoy the relative coolness of the morning. The café just happened to be across from a shop that sold rugs and fabrics in native Pakistani patterns, and also happened to be owned by one Ismail Abassi, who was forty-six years old and had run the shop since the death of his father. That was all the information Chris had been able to dig up on the man; despite the high-tech nature of Islamabad, there were still plenty of people who didn't have significant online presences. Added to the fact that many of the government records were incomplete, it made ferreting out information far more difficult than normal for Hercules Security's cyber guru.

After their meeting with the businessman and almost a week of surveillance, Joe was convinced the guy wasn't their target. They'd been forced to proceed down their list of suspects and had spent a couple of days watching the first shopkeeper on their list, who ran a café across town, but not only was he only thirty-eight and therefore pretty young to have an eighteen-year-old son, the guy's wife and a virtual herd of small daughters worked in the café with him. They seemed like a happy, prosperous family, and that Ismail Abassi worked the café from early in the morning until late in the evening. Joe had learned to trust his instincts about people, and the personable shopkeeper wasn't the type to be the mastermind of a human trafficking operation.

Which brought them to their current target—the second shopkeeper, who was not only older, but also a much harder man than the café owner. Joe had seen him yelling at a customer, gesticulating angrily until the cowed woman had walked away. It seemed odd to Joe for a shopkeeper to drive off a customer, unless the shop in question was a front for something else. Perhaps something sinister.

"He could just be an asshole," Drew said.

"No, not that." Joe took a sip of his coffee, pretending to have no interest in the shop. "A woman just came out, but when she went in about ten minutes ago, she had a child with her."

"Oh shit...." Drew covered his surprise by focusing on his coffee and leaning forward as if listening intently to Joe. "That merits a closer look, I think."

"Yeah. I suppose it could be a daughter bringing a kid to visit the grandparents, but the woman barely acknowledged Abassi on her way past." Joe bit his lip. "You know, rugs have been used to smuggle people and bodies before. This guy certainly would have the means to transport captives all over the city, and even to other cities."

"True, but that seems pretty blatant," Drew said. "If Abassi has enough people coming in with kids, but not leaving with them, someone's going to notice. You'd think the operation would be more inconspicuous than that, you know?"

"Yeah. But maybe the fact that no one would think that people would be that overconfident is a cover in and of itself. If enough customers come in with kids and leave with them, the occasional drop-off might go completely unnoticed."

"You want to watch a while longer or go check it out?"

Joe considered as he finished his coffee. "Let's check it out. I'll head into the shop. You circle around back. Check for a loading dock, see if you see anything suspicious. I'll try to figure out what happened to that kid. That work?"

Drew nodded as he pushed back his chair and stood up. "Let's do it."

"Text me if you find anything, and I'll do the same."

As Drew walked off, Joe took out his cellphone, pretending to consult it to give Drew time to get to the back of the building. After a minute, he rose from his seat, before moving casually toward the street corner. He crossed with at least a dozen other people when the traffic light changed and spent his time glancing in other shop windows while actually keeping a close watch on his goal.

Foot traffic had picked up, and Joe saw another woman exit, one he was certain had entered with two children. Abassi was haggling with another customer, and while his attention was diverted, Joe took the opportunity to slip past him and into the shop.

The space was almost claustrophobic, stacked high with rolled-up rugs on one side, and bolts of fabric on the other. There were a couple of customers inside the shop, women who were at a counter talking with a younger woman who was measuring out fabric. There were a couple of children inside as well, but they were close to their mothers. Of the children who had entered and not left, Joe saw no sign.

He headed toward the rear of the shop, wondering if the kids had been taken into a storage room. That's when he happened upon a wooden staircase, almost hidden behind a hanging rug. Looking upward, he realized the shop had a second level, but it didn't appear to be meant for access by customers. That seemed like a perfectly good reason for Joe to head upstairs, to see if anything suspicious was going on.

Despite his size and the rickety nature of the staircase, he was able to head upward in virtual silence, testing each step carefully just to make sure it would take his weight. As he climbed, he became aware of sounds above him, running feet and shouts from children. His heart began to pound, and he hurried now, not caring about being detected. If there were kids in danger, he had to save them.

There was a door at the top of the stairs, and he opened it a crack, surprised to peer in at a brightly lit space. Several children were running around, laughing as they played a game of chase, while a young woman clapped her hands and tried to call them to order. After a moment they obeyed, moving out of Joe's sight toward what must be the back of the room.

He opened the door wider, needing to see what he was up against in the realm of opposition. Surprised, he stared in a at several tables where at least twenty children were seated, some of them with toys, others with crayons, seeming engrossed in their tasks. As well as the young woman who had crossed his line of sight, there were three other women, one of them older than the others. Some instinct must have alerted her because she glanced toward the open door.

"Hello!" She called out in Urdu. "May I help you?"

Given that he'd been expecting to be greeted with shouts and possibly even gunfire, Joe froze for a moment and then smiled at her. "Um, I thought there might be more rugs up here."

The older woman shook her head. "This is a daycare. My husband runs the rug shop. You should go down and ask for Ismail— he'll help you find whatever you're looking for."

"Thanks." Joe watched for a few more moments, long enough to convince himself the woman wasn't lying. The children seemed happy, not frightened like those he'd seen before. The atmosphere was pleasant and welcoming, and he realized that he'd misread the situation. A daycare... how could he have known?

Chagrined, he headed back down the stairs, pulling out his phone. He texted Drew.

There's a daycare upstairs. Unless you've found bodies in rugs, I think we got it wrong.

No bodies, just rugs, Drew texted back. *What now?*

Regroup, Joe replied. *Let's meet back at the hotel and consider our options.*

It took nearly half an hour to get back to the hotel, since they'd decided to walk rather than use the driver Herc provided. As he took the elevator up to their floor, Joe's phone buzzed with a text. Pulling it out, he read it quickly, and his heart began to pound.

Call me ASAP! Chris had texted both him and Drew. *Important!!!*

Was something wrong with Finn? That was, of course, Joe's greatest fear, but he forced himself not to hit the speed dial for Chris. He returned to their room instead, not surprised Drew had beaten him back.

"I hope this isn't bad news," he said, holding up his phone. "Nothing better have happened to Finn!"

"I think we'd be hearing from Herc if that was the case," Drew said, placing a steadying hand on Joe's shoulder. "My guess is Pixel found something."

The nature of Joe's relationship with Drew had been slowly changing over the course of the last week, since they'd bonded a bit over their shared interest in gay romances. Joe had found himself starting to relax in Drew's presence, and oddly enough, the warm weight of Drew's hand gave Joe comfort.

"I hope you're right." He dialed Chris's number, putting the call on speaker so Drew could hear.

The phone barely had time to ring before Chris answered, his words tumbling out in high-pitched excitement. "I *think* I found your dude!"

Joe glanced at Drew. "Which one, Chris?"

"The cab driver," Chris said. "I hacked into the local camera system, and I've been tracking him for the last couple of days. He dropped different people off in the same area—not conclusive, right? But get this—dude picked up a known trafficker and took him to the same place. They got there maybe five minutes ago, and dude parked the cab and got out with the trafficker."

Joe's heart began to hammer. "That has to be him! Drew, we have to get out there right now. This could be our chance!"

Drew's eyes were alight with anticipation. "Get the stealth radios, and we'll go."

"On it." Joe hurried to his room, retrieving his radio, taking a few moments to double check his weapons and pick up extra magazines.

The weather was too hot to get away with wearing a jacket to conceal the clips, but he, like Drew, was wearing pants with specially designed hidden pockets. Just as their ballistic armor was made to be conformal and virtually undetectable under their T-shirts, so the pants let them carry a good deal of equipment without appearing scary enough to spook civilians.

Drew called for their driver, since the location Pixel had given them was across town. They were dropped off a couple of blocks from the actual location, and Joe gave the driver instructions to take a break and wait for their call. Sending him away was a calculated risk, since it removed one avenue of a hasty departure, but if they had to get away quickly, it wasn't going to involve taking a chauffeured sedan.

Chris let them know the locations of the cameras he'd hacked, so they avoided them as much as possible as they moved closer to their target. Joe doubted Abassi's people were using them to monitor their surroundings, but they couldn't take the chance.

The area was industrial, but there was an odd lack of vehicular traffic, almost as though it was a weekend instead of a normal work-day. That in and of itself was suspicious, but considering how much money the trafficking ring and their handlers controlled, it was likely they'd rented out several of the surrounding buildings as a buffer against having their activities detected. As Joe and Drew moved closer, they began to hug the sides of buildings, taking care to watch for guards.

They finally drew into sight of their destination, and Joe grimaced, noticing the fence around the area. "I only see the cab, no other vehicles. That doesn't mean it's just Abassi and his passenger inside. Do we storm the building, or wait for them to come out?"

"If we wait, we won't catch them in the act," Drew said. "We don't want another daycare situation. Let's get inside and look around before we move on Abassi."

"Right." Drew had a good point, and there was also the possibility that if they were in the building and they had the wrong man, they could wait until he left before departing themselves. But Joe's gut was telling him this was their guy and there was a chance he could put an end to the threat to Finn and himself once and for all.

The fence was at least ten feet high, which ruled out being able to climb over it without being noticed. A quick look around the area, however, revealed that there was one building close enough to it that they could jump over and down from its roof. After making sure that they were unobserved, Joe and Drew gained the roof and quickly jumped down, moving to the side of the building they wanted and hugging the wall.

The building was made of cinderblock, and the windows were of glass brick that was both thick and unbreakable. It was two-stories, with two access doors, as well as a tall metal roll-up door that would allow a truck inside. This didn't seem like a place where the traffickers could hold people for long periods, but it did have all the signs of being a transshipment point, where human cargo was transferred between vehicles.

The doors were, of course, locked, but from what Joe could see they weren't alarmed. He removed a lock-pick set from one of his pockets and made quick work of the lock.

"All set?" he asked softly, pulling his gun.

Drew gave a curt nod, holding his gun at the ready. Joe opened the door, and they stepped into the building.

Inside it was dark. Only faint, red emergency lights providing illumination, but there were several vehicles visible in the dimness. Joe closed the door quietly. He gestured for Drew to fan out so they could clear the area before determining their next move. Joe crept up one side of a line of trucks that filled the loading area, checking the space between each. He could see Drew doing the same thing from the other side. They met up again at the end of the row.

"Nothing." Joe pointed upward. There was a stairwell close by their position, leading to whatever was on the second floor.

"You're the stealthy one," Drew whispered, giving Joe a teasing smile. "Lead on."

Joe rolled his eyes, but he made his way to the staircase. He kept his gun at the ready as he mounted the steps. The second floor didn't cover the whole of the building. Instead, it extended over half, almost like an oversized loft, with windows overlooking the floor below. Fortunately for them, the windows had either blinds or curtains obscuring them, though now that his eyes were fully adjusted to the low light, Joe could see illumination around the edges, indicating there were lights on. He kept his attention on the door at the landing, trusting Drew to keep watch for anyone who might enter behind them.

When he finally gained the landing, he waited for Drew to join him, using the time to press his ear to the door. He could hear the voices of two men beyond the door, both raised as though arguing, but he couldn't make out the words. It was anyone's guess about how many other people might be inside, but Joe knew they were going to find out soon.

By the time Drew was in place, the voices had receded, as though the men had moved deeper into the room. That was fine with Joe, since it meant their attention might not be on the door. Drawing in a deep breath, Joe gripped the doorknob, turning it slowly to make sure it wasn't locked.

Amazingly, it wasn't. Joe glanced at Drew, giving him a nod and a silent three count. On the final number, he pushed the door open. They slipped into the room, trying to be silent.

Unfortunately, there was a guard by the door, and he turned with a shout of surprise, his hand going to his gun. Time seemed to slow down as Drew stepped in to deal with the guard, clubbing him on the head with his gun. Even as the guard fell, Joe was striding deeper into the room, looking for Abassi.

The human trafficker was at the far end of the room with two other men, one of whom seemed to be a guard because he was drawing a weapon. Joe lifted his gun, barking out a command in Urdu.

"Drop it!"

The guard paid no attention, pulling his gun and firing a shot in Joe's direction. It went wide. Joe returned fire, hitting the man in his gun arm, forcing him to drop the weapon.

Abassi and the buyer seemed to have good survival instincts, since they dove for cover behind some of the beds that lined the room. For the first time Joe became aware of what he was seeing, and his stomach flipped over in horrified repulsion.

Metal beds almost filled the room, although only a few at the far end seemed to be occupied. There were wrist and ankle restraints dangling from chains on each, used to restrain the captives who were brought here. Even as he noticed these things, Joe was rushing toward the far end of the room, determined to catch Abassi. There was a chance Abassi or the other man were armed, but Joe couldn't risk there being another exit by which Abassi could escape.

"Ismail Abassi!" He called out. "We have something to discuss!"

There was no reply, but Joe hadn't expected one. When he reached the downed guard, he stopped long enough to kick the man's weapon away. The guard cursed at him in Urdu, using his good hand to grip the arm Joe had shot. Blood seeped between his fingers. The guy would probably bleed out without medical attention, but Joe didn't care.

"Be quiet or I'll shoot you again," he said, pointing his gun at the guard, unsurprised when the man glared at him but fell silent.

Joe turned his attention back to locating Abassi. He saw movement behind one of the beds, and he reached out quickly, capturing Abassi by his jacket, yanking him to his feet.

"Who are you?" Abassi spat. He was a small man, perhaps five feet, four inches in height, slightly built with plenty of silver in his dark hair. He was physically unimpressive, but Joe had no doubt this was the snake he'd come halfway around the world to find.

"My name is Joe Morrissey," he replied. "You sent a bunch of men after me. They tortured the man I love. That was a big mistake."

Abassi's eyes widened. "You! You killed my son! My only son!" he spat, beginning to struggle in Joe's grip. "You deserve to die! I wish they'd killed all of you!"

Joe brought his gun up, pressing it against Abassi's head. "Too bad for you, they didn't."

"Look out!"

Joe heard Drew's shout, and he whipped his head around, seeing the apparent buyer rising from behind another bed with a gun. There was no way Joe could move out of the way, and he couldn't move his own weapon fast enough to shoot back. But even as the buyer fired, Drew fired a shot that caught the man in the chest.

Abassi lunged in Joe's grip, trying to get away, but he timed things all wrong. His compatriot's shot went wide, and Abassi got in the way, taking the bullet in the shoulder.

"No!" Joe didn't release his captive, even as the small man cried out and fell to his knees. "You're not getting away! Look at me! I want my face to be the last thing you see before I send you to *Jahannam!*" Abassi squirmed, but Joe pressed his gun against the man's head again. "Time to get what you deserve."

"Joe, don't." Drew's voice was a calm, quiet counterpoint to the roiling tension in the room, and he approached slowly, holding his gun off to the side. "I know you think it'll feel good to blow his head off, but you'll regret it later."

"No, I won't." Joe's voice was hoarse, and he felt rage coursing over him. "It's the only way to make sure Finn is safe!"

"No, it's not." Drew moved close enough to touch Joe, but he didn't reach out. "I can call Herc. He's got the task force you worked with standing by. They'll be here in minutes. Let them handle it. They might get information out of him that could save even more victims, and you won't have his blood on your hands. He's not worth it."

Part of Joe wanted to ignore Drew's words. He wanted so badly to end Abassi's life that he was shaking, as close to the edge of giving into pure rage as he had ever been in his life. But the rational part of him knew Drew was right. As much as he wanted Abassi dead for what happened to Finn, there was still a right and a wrong in this situation. Killing Abassi in cold blood, as much as it would ease his rage, would be the wrong thing to do.

Joe released his captive before holstering his weapon. "Tie him up," he said in a hollow voice. He looked away, and that was when he noticed the occupants of the beds for the first time.

Half a dozen young boys and girls were strapped to the beds, all of them unconscious. Joe's gut twisted. They were chained up like animals ready for the slaughter. They were probably considered special "merchandise" by the traffickers, and no doubt that was why Abassi had brought the buyer here: to purchase one or more of them for resale in the sex trade.

"Oh God," he said, covering his eyes. "Call the task force, get them here. This... I can't do this. Not again."

Drew grabbed Abassi's arm and wrenched it behind his back, purposely cold to Abassi's yelp of pain. "Sit down, Joe," he said, a hint of command in his voice. "Take some deep breaths. I'll handle this."

Joe wasn't aware of obeying, but he found himself sitting on the floor. He put his head in his hands, shutting out the sight, and sank into his own private despair.

25

After a debriefing conversation with Herc, Drew glanced over at Joe's bedroom. The door stood open, and the interior was dark and still. He would have bet anything that Joe hadn't moved since they returned to the hotel and Drew helped him into bed.

As expected, the task force had arrived quickly, and Drew turned Abassi over to them without a qualm, too concerned by Joe's thousand-yard stare to give any fucks about Abassi's fate. The bad guy was in captivity and his victims in that warehouse were getting help. Drew had done what he could for the task force, but now his focus was entirely on Joe. The day wasn't saved yet.

The whole way back to the hotel, Joe had seemed catatonic. His eyes were open, and he obeyed Drew's instructions, but he hadn't said a word since he'd sat down on the cold floor of that holding area. Drew had guided him into his bedroom and helped him out of his boots and body armor, and now he was curled up under the covers, unmoving and still silent. Drew wanted to climb into bed with him and nestle close in hopes that having a warm, solid presence nearby would offer some comfort, but he'd had to report to Herc first.

He'd let Herc know he wasn't sure when they'd be able to leave the country, since Joe was in no state to travel. Herc had assured him they could remain in the suite on the company's dime for as long as necessary and offered whatever type of help or resources Drew might need. Herc even suggested sending of the company psychiatrists, but Drew didn't think Joe was in any shape to talk to a shrink yet.

He looked down at his phone, debating whether to call Finn, but he didn't want to field a bunch of questions that he didn't know the answers to, so he decided to send a text instead.

Mission accomplished. I'll fill you in later. Our dumbass needs attention right now.

Then he turned off his phone, left it on the coffee table, and headed into Joe's room. As expected, Joe hadn't moved. Drew sat down on the bed and reached over to rub Joe's shoulder.

"I talked to Herc," he said. He knew Joe could at least hear him even if he wasn't processing the words on a conscious level. "He's coordinating with the task force to mop up. We can stay here as long as you want. There's no rush."

He paused just in case Joe decided to respond, but Joe didn't, and so he took off his boots and got under the covers.

"I'm gonna be right here." He snuggled up against Joe's back and draped one arm across Joe's waist. "I'm not going anywhere."

Joe didn't move, and at some point things must have caught up to Drew, because he drifted off to sleep. Sometime later he was woken up by movement, and he realized Joe was thrashing, in the grip of a nightmare.

"No! No! Please don't! Don't hit me! I'll be good, I promise! Just don't hit me anymore!"

"Joe?" Drew sat up and grabbed Joe's shoulder to shake him awake. "Joe, wake up! It's just a nightmare. No one is going to hit you."

There wasn't much light in the room, but Drew's eyes were dark adapted, so he was able to see Joe's eyes open and the expression of confusion on his face. "Drew? Where are we?"

"We're back at the hotel." Drew settled down behind Joe again, and this time, he wrapped his arm around Joe and held him tight. "Everything's fine. Abassi's in custody. Herc's handling the cleanup details. Finn knows we're okay."

Surprisingly, Joe didn't pull away. He was quiet for a long moment before Drew felt as much as heard his sigh. "It's over?"

"It's over." Drew offered a reassuring squeeze. "You did good."

A shudder ran through Joe. He pulled away, getting out of the bed and rising somewhat unsteadily to his feet. "I need the bathroom."

Drew threw back the covers and climbed out of bed as well. "You okay?" he asked, watching Joe with growing concern.

Joe nodded jerkily and headed toward the bathroom. He walked like a man who'd had a few too many, but he made it, turning on the light and closing the door behind him. After a few minutes Drew heard the toilet flush and water running. The water was turned off, but Joe still didn't come out.

"Joe?" Drew knocked on the door and waited, but when he hadn't gotten any kind of response after about a minute, he opened the door, deciding the risk of pissing off Joe was worth it to make sure he was all right.

He found Joe leaning on the sink, staring into the mirror with the kind of blank, hollow-eyed expression that Drew had seen before on the faces of men who were close to the edge, and his stomach knotted up at the sight.

"Joe, whatever you're seeing right now, it's not real," he said, resting his hand on Joe's shoulder and rubbing it gently. "You're here with me in a bathroom. A really nice one, but still a bathroom."

Joe didn't react to the touch, and he didn't look away from the mirror. "It never ends, does it?" he asked, but Drew wasn't sure if Joe was speaking to him, or to his own reflection. "Never."

"No." Drew hated saying it, but they both knew the truth. "But we do what we can to mitigate the horror. That's all we can do."

Joe dropped his head. "I'm so tired. I don't want to fight anymore."

Drew was probably the last person Joe wanted comfort from—the last person he'd choose to turn to—but Drew was all he had, and

Drew wasn't going anywhere. His heart ached at seeing Joe's pain, and he understood it all too well. He'd felt the same way after Stack died.

"Then don't." Drew slid both arms around Joe's waist and held him close. "You don't have to fight if you don't want to. If you need to rest, rest. I've got you."

To Drew's surprise, Joe nodded. "Okay. I want to go back to sleep. For a long, long time."

"Let's get you back to bed, baby," Drew murmured, guiding Joe away from the mirror. "You sleep as long as you want. I'll be right here if you need anything."

"Thanks." Joe leaned on Drew, letting Drew help him back to the bed. Joe sat down on the edge, then fell over, his head hitting the pillow with a thud.

Drew got Joe's legs onto the bed and pulled the covers up. "I'm going to get some water in case you wake up thirsty, and I'll be right back, okay?"

"Okay." Joe's voice was muffled, but at least he was answering. He hadn't checked out again, and he wasn't protesting anything Drew wanted.

Seeing Joe so docile was new and a little alarming, and it made Drew want to help him all the more. He went to get a couple of bottles of water from the fridge and returned quickly. He left the bottles on the nightstand in easy reach, and then he got back into bed and gathered Joe in his arms again.

"You're safe," he said, hoping the words helped on some level. "I'm here. I'm not leaving you alone."

"I'm always alone," Joe murmured. "Alone in the dark."

"Not anymore," Drew said, tightening his arms around Joe. All of his protective instincts were surging to the forefront, and now his heart was getting in on the action. If Drew wasn't careful, *Finn* might be the one who had to share. "I'm with you."

Joe said something unintelligible, but his breathing slowed down and grew even, so Drew knew he had fallen asleep. He relaxed in

Drew's arms, as though allowing himself to take the comfort in slumber that he probably would have rejected if fully conscious. Drew remained awake to watch over Joe while he slept, hoping that holding Joe close and stroking his back would keep the nightmares at bay.

26

He was lost.

It was dark.

A sea of screams roiled in the blackness.

Hard to see.

Cries for help pierced clearly into his mind.

Despair crowded in on him from the people around him, trapped in their private hells. He wanted to help. Get them out.

Set them free.

Red lights flared, and the screams grew louder. Someone was coming, and a lump of dread formed in his stomach, weighing him down. He couldn't move, and he felt the walls closing in around him, the ceiling dropping down. Lower and lower, tighter and tighter, until he felt he was being crushed. The pain was unbearable, and he opened his mouth and began to scream.

"Joe!" The sound of his name broke through the haze of dream-pain, and he was jostled awake by someone shaking his shoulders. "Wake up! It's just a dream. You're okay."

"No!" Joe flailed his arms and he found himself sitting up, feeling disoriented. He didn't know where he was, and his heart was pounding so hard he thought it might burst from his chest. He glanced over at the man next to him, feeling confused when it wasn't the tormentor he had expected to see. It took a while for it to register, but he finally sighed out the name. "Drew?"

"Yeah, baby, it's me." Drew slid his arms around Joe and rubbed his back soothingly. "You were having a nightmare. It wasn't real."

"No. Not real." Not this time, at least. Joe scrubbed at his face, trying to push away the images his mind kept plaguing him with. He didn't know how long it had been going on, but it seemed like forever. He knew he'd awakened at various points, and Drew was always there, either next to him in the bed or sitting in a chair nearby. Joe vaguely recalled Drew bringing him food and water, helping him to the bathroom, but mostly letting him sleep. Even now Joe was tired, his body heavy and lethargic, but for once he was firmly in the present. He remembered the mission, but he shied away from thinking about it. He didn't want to, not yet. Not when he felt so raw that it was like all the skin had been scraped from his body. Or maybe all the scabs were torn off his soul.

He began to shiver. "So cold. Why is it so cold?"

"You kicked off the covers." Drew pulled the disheveled blankets back up and smoothed them around Joe. "You can stay close to me, too, if you're still cold."

Joe curled against Drew, seeking his warmth. He was grateful for Drew's calm, steady presence. "I know this will sound weird, but I'm glad you're here, and not Finn."

Drew settled down beside Joe, holding him close and tight. "Why is that?" he asked, his tone laced with surprise.

"I don't want him to see me like this," Joe said. "I'm the one who is strong for him. The one he can go to when he's hurting. He sees a lot of pain, being a medic. He doesn't need mine, too."

Drew remained silent for a minute or so, then nuzzled his cheek against the top of Joe's head. "Who's strong for you?" he asked softly.

The gesture was comforting, and Joe was surprised that Drew touching him and cuddling him felt so good. Joe wasn't used to clinging to anyone, not even Finn, but he felt the urge to hold fast to Drew, to let Drew help take away the pain he was feeling. It was a bit disturbing, because there were things about his past Joe hadn't shared with anyone, not even Finn. Somehow, telling Drew didn't seem as terrifying.

"I've been strong for myself." He shuddered. "I don't feel strong now, though, and it's a little frightening."

"Yeah, I know." Drew's tone was matter-of-fact. "It's going to be scary until you feel steady on your feet again. That's normal. But you've got me to be strong for you, if you want me to."

Joe closed his eyes. "Why would you do that for me? I've been... well, I guess *not friendly* would be the kindest way to describe it." Now that he was able to take a small step back from his misery, he was aware of how much Drew had done for him—how much Drew had been doing from the beginning, even in the face of Joe's hostility. It made him feel ashamed, so much so that his eyes began to burn. "I'm sorry I was a dick to you."

"You were, yeah." Drew's chuckle rumbled and vibrated against Joe's ear. "But you had multiple good reasons to be. I'm not holding it against you."

"That's generous." Joe drew in a shuddering breath. "Thanks. It's... it's been hard. I felt like all I had was Finn, and when I needed him most, you'd stepped in and taken him from me. I hated you for it."

"I get it." Drew gave him a little squeeze. "It would've been hard enough adjusting to having me around under normal circumstances, but Finn figured out something else was going on, and once we started working together, I saw it too because I've been there, done that. I wanted to help."

For once Joe's embarrassment was greater than the pain. "I don't know why. Is it for Finn? Because I feel like I don't deserve it, the way I've been."

Drew fell silent again, and when he spoke at last, his voice was quiet and gentle. "Would you feel like you deserved it even if you hadn't been a dick to me?"

The question caught Joe by surprise. He hadn't thought of it that way, and he wanted to shy away from the difficult thoughts. But the way he'd treated Drew before, and the support Drew had given him, meant the least Joe could do was be honest. He needed to open up, at least a little, in repayment, since all he'd done was shut Drew out.

"Not really," he admitted, his heart constricting. "I guess there's a part of me that's broken. I just hide it well."

"I figured." Drew squeezed Joe again as if wanting to comfort and reassure him. "You make so much about Finn and what he wants and needs. I haven't heard you talk a lot about what you want or need. You lashed out because you were in pain. That doesn't make you less deserving of help. It means you need it more than ever."

"Maybe." Joe was glad he couldn't see Drew's eyes. It was easier this way, somehow. "I... I don't know. Maybe there are things that can't be fixed. You learn to live with them."

"Getting help doesn't always mean fixing the problem. It means getting the tools you need to learn how to live with it in a way that it doesn't fuck up the rest of your life." Drew gave a wry little snort. "My therapist had to say that a lot before I finally believed it."

"That was about Stack?" Joe hesitated before giving Drew a little squeeze in return. "It must have been hard."

"It was." Drew released a long sigh that Joe felt rather than heard. "I'd seen men die before, but not like that. Plus he was one of mine, you know? I felt responsible even though there wasn't a damned thing I could've done. Explosives were Stack and Hunter's specialty, not mine. If I'd been closer, maybe I could've done something. Taken his place. I didn't know. I just felt like I'd failed him, or it should've been me because I was the XO."

"I can understand that." And Joe did. He would have felt the same way. "I'm sorry you had to go through that. It sucks."

"I'm sorry for what you went through here the first time," Drew said, caressing Joe's back with long, soothing strokes of his hand. "It did some damage. But it's not what broke you, is it?"

Joe felt the twisting sensation he always did when he thought about his past. Normally he didn't dwell on it, preferring to look forward, not back. He'd never told anyone—not D-Day, not Herc, not even Finn—about what he'd gone through. He didn't want them to look at him as damaged, to see him as somehow being less than what he was now. But Drew had seen him at his worst, at his weakest, so it seemed stupid to deny it.

Yet talking about it was hard, so hard, and he was silent for several minutes, trying to find the words. "I speak nine languages. Did you know that? Fluently. And I'm familiar enough with a dozen more to get by if I have to."

"I knew you were good with languages. I didn't know you were *that* good," Drew said, a strong note of respect in his voice.

"Yeah. Not many people do." Joe swallowed hard. "But what no one knows is that I was scared to talk for a long time. I barely said a word until I was in school."

Drew pulled away just enough so that he could see Joe's face. "Why?"

It was difficult for Joe to speak of his past, despite it having been over twenty years since it had been an issue. "I had a stutter. A bad one. My father used to hit me every time I stumbled over a word."

"Jesus." Drew's expression darkened with anger, and he tightened his arms around Joe. "What the fuck was wrong with him?"

Despite the remembered pain, now that he started, Joe knew he had to get it out. "My mother died when I was still a baby. Cancer. My father.... He started drinking. When I started talking, and it wasn't perfect, I think it set him off. Or gave him an excuse. I don't know. He hit me when I spoke, and when I stopped talking, he would lock me in a closet. He called me a stubborn brat and told me he wished I'd never been born."

"Mother*fucker*." Drew's voice thrummed with anger as he held Joe tight, almost tight enough to steal his breath. "That was abuse. You know that, right? He was an abusive asshole, and you didn't deserve any of that."

"I know. And so did the teachers at school. That's why I was taken away and put in foster care." Joe shuddered, remembering what it felt like. "I remember being almost more frightened at being taken away than I was when I was with him. Strangers... how would they treat me, if my own father did such things?"

"But it got better?" Drew asked, an edge of trepidation in his voice.

"Eventually. I was sent to therapy, and it helped. But after my father went to rehab, they gave me back to him." He shifted restlessly. "That was a mistake. I was with him for six months before he started drinking again. It was another three before they got me out. Three months of hell. That's why seeing those kids... it just about killed me. I *know* what they must be going through. I know how helpless they feel. Because I felt that way, too."

"You're not helpless anymore." Drew's voice sounded thick, and he clung to Joe tightly. "You aren't alone either, and you deserve a lot more than you let yourself have."

Joe swallowed again past the painful tightness of his throat. For Drew to be so generous, after everything, was more than he felt he deserved. "Mostly, I don't think about it. It's been years since it really bothered me. It was just... this whole thing. The kids, the evil scumbags hitting them, raping them. Then I go home and my anchor was gone. After that... all this again. I don't know what I deserve. I feel like I don't know much of anything, anymore."

"We had shitty timing, and I'm sorry for that," Drew said. "But Finn doesn't have to be your only anchor. You could have two."

"You must be crazy," Joe murmured. It wasn't the first time Drew had said something like this, but that was before Joe had confided in him about these issues. "You can't want to take on someone as fucked up as I am right now. I think the best thing I could do for you and Finn both is just... go away for a while. It would be easier with just the two of you. Uncomplicated."

"Oh, fuck *that*." Drew fixed Joe with a stern look that brooked no argument. "Finn loves you, and as crazy as it sounds, I care about you, too. You leaving wouldn't be the best thing for either of us. In fact, how about you stop thinking about us and think about what *you* want? Would walking away from Finn make you feel any better?"

The thought of losing Finn hurt like hell, but Joe only shrugged, weariness suddenly catching him, making him feel defeated. "It's not all about me." Releasing a shuddering breath, he closed his eyes. "But if you don't mind, I don't want to talk about it anymore. I'm tired."

"Okay," Drew said, stroking Joe's short hair with gentle fingers. "Go back to sleep if you want to. Would it bother you if I watched something for a while? I've been binging on that gay fiction review show while you were out, but if the noise would disturb you, I'll read instead."

"No, it's fine." Joe sighed, leaning instinctively into Drew's touch.

Drew reached for the laptop sitting on the nightstand on his side of the bed, and he balanced it on his lap and set up the show. He kept the volume low, but Joe could hear the familiar sound of Jim and Bill's voices as they discussed the books of the week. It was soothing, being snuggled up to Drew's solid warmth, his head pillowed on Drew's chest. He could hear the vlog, hear the sound of Drew's steady breathing, and it helped ground him. Hopefully it would be enough to keep the nightmares away, at least for a while. He gave in to the drowsiness that was falling over him, but he did have one final thing to say. Rubbing his cheek against Drew's chest, he sighed.

"Thanks for caring."

27

D rew was startled out of sleep by the sound of moans, and his first conscious thought was that Joe was having another nightmare. Joe hadn't had nightmares every night, but it happened often enough that Drew didn't bother sleeping in his own room of their suite anymore. He wanted to help rouse Joe out of his bad dreams as quickly as possible and offer solace in the aftermath. The bed was king-sized, so even though they were both big men, they had enough space to sleep comfortably. Both of them were accustomed to sleeping in far worse conditions in the field, anyway.

But as he reached full wakefulness, he felt a warm, solid presence plastered against his back and the heavy weight of an arm draped across his waist, and he realized the timbre of Joe's moans was... different. He became acutely aware of Joe's hard cock pressed against his ass, and he lay still, wondering what the hell he should do.

If he woke up Joe now, Joe might be embarrassed, or even angry, that Drew knew about his erotic dreams, especially since Joe was probably dreaming about Finn. *There was no way in hell he was dreaming about Drew!* Drew didn't want to risk losing any ground after the slow, tenuous progress they'd made in their relationship lately. On the other hand, if Joe somehow found out Drew knew about the dreams and hadn't told him, that might cause problems down the road. *Shit!*

He didn't know what to do, and so he opted to do nothing. He let out a quiet, shallow huff of amusement that finding himself in Joe's arms for the first time made him wish for the simplicity of a trauma-induced nightmare instead.

Joe was breathing hard, and then suddenly he gasped and went still. Drew could feel a tremor in Joe's arm as he slowly lifted it and started to pull away.

Drew considered pretending to be asleep and letting Joe withdraw, but his caretaker instincts wouldn't let him.

"You okay?" he asked. He tried to keep his voice quiet, but in the still, dark room, he felt like he was yelling.

Joe swallowed hard enough to be heard. "Sorry. I didn't mean to wake you. Or invade your space."

"It's okay. I haven't been the little spoon in a while. It was nice," Drew said, realizing he meant it.

Joe was quiet for a moment and then there was a sound suspiciously like a sniffle. "I guess so."

Drew rolled over to lie facing Joe, peering at him with concern. His eyes had adjusted to the faint light filtering through the curtains enough that he could see Joe, but not enough to let him read Joe's expression.

"What's up?" he asked softly.

He felt more than saw Joe's slight shrug. "I guess... I'm feeling lonely," he admitted, his voice raspy. "Feeling like things will never be right again."

Drew shifted closer, his heart aching for Joe, and he rested his palm against Joe's stubbled cheek. "Right in what way?"

Joe didn't answer immediately, but Drew could almost feel the weight of his gaze, as though Joe was looking for something specific. He must have found it, since he finally answered. "Like I'll never feel normal things again. Like I can never look at Finn without feeling guilty, never be with him again because I'll always wonder if somehow he'll blame me."

"Blame you for what?" Drew frowned slightly, puzzled. "You don't have anything to feel guilty about."

But Joe shook his head. "For him getting hurt. His leg... what if it doesn't heal right? What if he has to give up his career, like Herc did? What happened was because of me, whether I intended it or not. What if... he doesn't really want me anymore?"

"What happened was because of those traffickers, not you," Drew said firmly. "You don't need to worry about Finn's leg, either. He told us the surgery went great, remember? With some rehab, he'll be good as new." He stroked Joe's cheek gently with his thumb, hoping Joe believed him, and took some comfort from the reassurance. "He misses you. He's worried about you. He still loves you."

Joe's breathing hitched again. "I'm afraid I'm going to lose him. That things won't ever be the same."

Drew slid his arm around Joe to stroke his back soothingly. "Well, no, they won't be," he said. "The last two missions affected you in ways you're still working through, and you're not going to be the same man on the other side of that. I'm not the man I was before Stack died. It's not good or bad. It just is. You've also got me in the picture now, but I don't want to edge you out." He gnawed on his bottom lip, debating how much he wanted to reveal. "I care about you a lot," he said at last, hedging a little. Joe probably wasn't ready to hear the full truth.

Joe gave a shuddering sigh. "I couldn't have gotten through these last few days without you. I probably would have curled up and died. I know you didn't have to be here for me, but I appreciate it. I guess... I guess I care about you, too."

"You guess?" Drew teased, giving Joe a playful nudge.

"Fine. I care about you." Joe sniffled again. "Even if you can be an ass."

"It's part of my charm," Drew said with a quiet chuckle. He stroked Joe's back in silence for a moment, wondering how much he could test the walls before Joe fortified them again. "Okay, we care about each other. What do you want to do with that?"

Again he felt the weight of Joe's gaze. "I don't know. I feel adrift, I suppose. Lost. I've always been the steady one, the one who was sure. Now... it's like I'm a ship without an anchor." There was a wealth of hurt and loss in Joe's voice. "I feel like I'm that little boy again, never sure when the closet door finally opened if I'd find myself in heaven or hell."

"Do you trust me?" Drew held his breath as he waited for Joe's response.

The silence stretched out between them for an eternity, and when Joe answered, his voice barely more than a whisper.

"Yes."

"Then you have an anchor," Drew said, tightening his arm around Joe. "I'm here, and I'm not going anywhere."

With a low groan, Joe moved closer and slid his arms around Drew in return. He rested his head on Drew's shoulder, the biggest sign of acceptance and trust Joe had ever given. Drew felt the way Joe trembled, as though he was finally releasing something long pent-up and hurtful. "Thanks."

Drew gathered Joe close and tight, wishing he could somehow alleviate all of Joe's fears and doubts, but Joe had to overcome them himself. All Drew could do was offer support and solace when needed.

"You don't have to thank me, baby," he said, pressing a kiss against Joe's hair. "I want to be here."

Drew felt the damp warmth of tears against his shoulder. "I'm so cold inside. Numb. Like I'm a hollow shell."

"Then let me help you feel again." The words were out before Drew even realized he was thinking them, paired with an urge to kiss Joe that was too strong to resist. He might end up getting his ass kicked, but he didn't care. Joe needed him.

Before Joe could respond, Drew leaned in and brushed his lips against Joe's—offering, questioning, but not taking. Joe had been through too much, had too much taken from him lately.

To his surprise, Joe moaned softly, and began to kiss Drew back. He tightened his arms around Drew, pulling him closer, as if Joe did want and need him as an anchor, as something to help fill up the emptiness. Echoing Joe's moan, Drew parted his lips in a silent invitation and pressed against Joe, aligning their bodies so Joe could feel his warm, solid presence.

Joe didn't hesitate to accept what Drew offered, deepening the kiss, exploring Drew's mouth with an almost desperate need. He hooked one leg over Drew's legs and moved against him, as though he wanted to wrap himself around Drew as tightly as possible. Drew yielded to Joe's exploration, wanting to give Joe whatever he needed to feel warm, to feel whole.

Kiss flowed into kiss, and after a time Joe's desperation subsided, becoming something else, less frenzied and more curious. Drew felt Joe's big, warm hands on his back, pushing up under his T-shirt as Joe began to caress him almost tentatively, as though Joe wasn't completely certain Drew would welcome the touch. Drew hummed his pleasure into the kiss and arched against Joe's hands as he matched Joe's curiosity, wanting to taste and explore as well. He reached for the hem of Joe's T-shirt and slid it up, eager to feel more of Joe's warm, bare skin against his own.

Drew's response seemed to be the right one, because Joe's caresses became more certain. He put his hands against Drew's shoulders, and scratched his nails down Drew's back, not hard enough to break the skin, but sufficient that Drew would have marks. Drew sucked in a sharp breath, heat pooling in his belly.

"You want to mark me up?" he asked, nipping at Joe's bottom lip. "I'm good with that, but I want to return the favor, and we both need to be more naked for that."

Joe's eyes were dark with need. "All right," he said softly. He grasped the hem of Drew's T-shirt, tugging it upward. "Off."

Drew sat up and swiftly stripped off his shirt. He tossed it over the side of the bed. "Your turn," he said, voice low and husky. He'd hoped Joe would let him behind the walls enough for this, but he'd thought it was a longshot. Now that it was happening, he felt like an overeager teenager.

It only took a moment for Joe to strip off his own T-shirt, then he pushed Drew back against the mattress, rolling him onto his back and moving to straddle his hips. Lowering himself down, Joe pressed his mouth against the side of Drew's neck, nipping at the area just beneath his ear. After a moment, he began to suck. The sting of the nip followed by Joe's hot mouth on his skin was enough to make Drew's eyes roll back in his head, and he didn't bother to silence the moans that rose in his throat. He clamped his hands on Joe's shoulders and dug his fingernails into Joe's flesh, wanting to leave marks of his own.

Joe growled low in his throat, arching against Drew's hands. He moved his mouth lower, kissing his way down Drew's neck. When he reached the junction of Drew's neck and shoulder he bit down again, harder this time, enough that Drew knew he was going to have a livid bruise.

"Yes!" Drew threw his head back on the pillow, offering better access. He dragged his nails down Joe's spine in return.

Joe lifted his mouth away, giving a hiss as Drew scored his skin. "You like it rough?" It wasn't a question, and Joe didn't wait for an answer. Instead he lowered his head again, shifting his body downward at the same time, and he captured one of Drew's nipples between his lips, sucking it into a taut peak.

"Fuck yeah, I do." Drew answered anyway, wanting Joe to know that what he was doing was welcome. Joe was harboring enough concern about too many other aspects of his life, and Drew wanted this experience to be both connecting and healing.

Joe continued to play with Drew's nipple before moving his attention to the other. At the same time he pushed one hand beneath the waistbands of Drew's sweatpants and boxer briefs, cupping Drew's cock in his big, warm hand. He squeezed.

Drew sucked in a hissing breath, his half-firm cock growing even harder in response to the touch, and he clutched Joe's shoulders. "Feels good," he murmured, not hiding his desire as he gazed down at Joe. "It'd feel even better if we were both naked."

"If that's what you want." Joe moved away, but before Drew could do anything, Joe was tugging at Drew's sweatpants. "Lift your hips, this will only take a second."

Drew snapped his hips up, and he reached down to help Joe strip off his sweats and boxer briefs. Once they joined his shirt on the floor, he bent one knee and struck what he hoped was an enticing pose. "All yours," he said, making a sweeping gesture to encompass the length of his body. "I don't suppose you've got any condoms in your bag, do you?"

With a snort of amusement, Joe shook his head, but his gaze was riveted on Drew's body. "No. Never occurred to me I'd need any." He reached out a hand, scraping his nails down the fur on Drew's stomach.

Drew's abdominal muscles quivered in response, and he arched up, seeking more. "Too bad," he said, sifting his fingers through Joe's hair before tugging experimentally to see how Joe responded. "I'm starting to have fantasies about you pinning my wrists and growling in my ear while you fuck me through the mattress, but I reckon we can make do with hands and mouths this time."

Joe gave a small growl of pleasure at the tugging, but even in the darkness, Drew could see the way Joe's eyebrows shot up at his comment. "And here I was thinking you were no more of a bottom than I am."

Drew flashed a playful grin as he tugged Joe's hair again, harder this time. "I'm flexible. Depends on who I'm with, and what kind of mood I'm in."

Joe knelt on the mattress and grabbed both of Drew's wrists. Using one hand, he pinned them to the pillow above Drew's head. With his other hand he stroked Drew's abdomen, combing his fingers down along Drew's treasure trail. His teeth flashed in the low light as he gave a feral grin and wrapped his fingers around Drew's cock. "I guess since I can't pin you and fuck you, you'll have to settle for the next best thing."

White-hot need zinged along Drew's nerve endings, and his breathing grew short and shallow as he bucked his hips against Joe's hand. "It'll do for now," he said, sounding breathless even to himself.

"Good." Joe stroked Drew's cock, moving at a torturously slow pace. "Let's see how long you can hold out."

"Asshole," Drew groaned, but there wasn't any heat in it. He tugged at his wrists, wanting to feel Joe's strength, and he rocked his hips, trying to ease the ache of arousal that Joe was stoking, but not relieving.

"Now that's no way to get what you want." Joe stilled his hand, staring down at Drew with a frown. "Begging is more likely to make me go faster. Can you beg, Drew?"

Oh, Joe wanted to play that game, did he? Maybe he didn't think Drew could do it—or *would* do it. Maybe he thought Drew's pride wouldn't let him beg Joe, of all people, for anything, or maybe he intended it as a challenge. But Joe didn't realize how accommodating Drew could be under the right circumstances or the extent of what he'd do to get what he wanted.

He relaxed his body and went pliant and yielding beneath Joe, and he gazed up at Joe with wide eyes and parted lips. "Please," he said, following up with a soft whimper for good measure. "Please, Joe, I need more. I need *you*."

Joe's eyes grew wide, as though Drew had managed to surprise him, but then he growled again and swooped down to press his lips against Drew's in a rough, demanding kiss. At the same time he stroked Drew's cock again, quickening the pace of his hand to one that would soon push Drew toward the edge. Drew returned the kiss with greedy hunger, letting it drive his need even higher. Joe's fingers were strong and sure, and Drew couldn't help but respond as each caress made arousal coil tighter and tighter within him.

As if sensing Drew's growing need, Joe sped up the pace more. Then all at once, when Drew was fast approaching the brink, Joe stopped, pulling back from the kiss and looking down at Drew hungrily.

"Come for me."

Drew recognized the note of command in Joe's voice, and his instincts urged him to obey. He *wanted* to obey—wanted to belong to Joe the way Finn did—and so he let go, holding back nothing as ecstasy washed over him.

Joe began to stroke him again through his release, heightening and prolonging the pleasure. "Yes, that's it," he murmured, his eyes riveted on Drew's face, watching every nuance. "Good."

Drew's skin was flushed and dappled with sweat as he moved sinuously beneath Joe, gasping for air as the pleasure slowly ebbed, leaving him sated. "So good," he murmured, gazing at Joe with half-lidded eyes. "Kiss me again, Joe."

With a soft moan Joe did as Drew asked, claiming Drew's lips with his. There was a slightly different feel to the kiss this time, something that might almost be confused with tenderness, if Drew thought Joe was capable of feeling any such thing for him. Joe released Drew's wrists, and Drew slid his arms around Joe's shoulders to draw him close and tight as the kiss continued, slow and deep. Drew poured his own growing affection for Joe into it, hoping to strengthen their connection and prove Joe had his full acceptance.

After a while Joe drew back. "Let me go get a washcloth and clean you up."

"Okay." Drew stretched leisurely, a satisfied purr rumbling in his chest, and a small half smile curved his lips as he watched Joe walk away.

A minute or so later Joe was back, holding a washcloth in one hand and a hand towel in the other. He sat down on the edge of the bed and gently cleaned Drew up.

"There," he said when he'd finished. He dropped the used cloths on the floor.

"Thanks." Drew held out both arms and beckoned to Joe. "Now get naked and come here. It's your turn."

For someone who had seemed so dominant only a few minutes before, Joe now appeared to hesitate. "You don't have to," he said slowly. "I'm okay."

"No, I don't have to, but I want to," Drew said. He sat up and scooted over to sit behind Joe, plastering himself against Joe's back. He left a trail of little nipping kisses along Joe's shoulder as he slid his arms around Joe's waist and stroked his bare stomach. "I want to see how fast I can get you hard. I want to watch your face and listen to the sounds you make when you come."

Joe turned his head to look at Drew over his shoulder. "I... I don't know." He dropped his gaze. "What do I tell Finn?"

"The truth," Drew said simply. He rested his chin on Joe's shoulder and hooked his legs over Joe's thighs to make sure Joe couldn't get up and walk away. "You needed someone, and I was here for you. Maybe even admit you're a little attracted to me," he teased. "Finn isn't going to be angry or upset, especially not if you feel better as a result of it."

"It's not the sex." Joe drew in a deep breath and let it out in a sigh. "I know he wouldn't care about that, he's not a hypocrite. It's... you being here for me, instead of him. And me allowing it. You giving me something he couldn't. How do you think that would make him feel? I know how it made *me* feel, and I don't want to cause him pain."

"Do you want my honest opinion?" Drew asked, stroking Joe's chest in a way that was intended to soothe rather than arouse.

"Sure." Joe tensed slightly beneath Drew's hands, as though steeling himself to hear something unpleasant. "It's not like he and I discussed anything like this happening, and the one time I asked him how he might feel about me finding someone else, he was at a loss."

"So here's the thing," Drew said, choosing his words with care. He wanted to reassure Joe, not make him feel guilty or defensive. "Finn and I have a pretty similar outlook when it comes to relationships, and that outlook boils down to 'it's not pie.' Finn loves you. He wants you to be healthy and happy. He also loves me, so I think this is the best case scenario as far as he's concerned. If he can't be here for you, then at least you have someone he knows and trusts, and you're not dealing with this alone. I know if I was in Finn's position, I wouldn't begrudge you a damned thing because your mental and emotional health are more important."

Silence stretched out after Drew finished speaking, but Drew had gotten to know Joe well enough to realize he was considering what Drew had said seriously. After a few minutes he relaxed against Drew. "I guess you're right. I can't judge his feelings based on my own. I just... I don't want him to feel like sleeping with you is something I'm doing to get back at him. You see... things weren't that great between us just before Finn was kidnapped. I was trying, but I know he could tell it was hurting me to do it. I'd even been thinking about just... going away." Joe shrugged somewhat awkwardly. "I even broke our last date before he was taken. It was getting harder and harder to be with him, because I knew the tighter I wanted to cling, the faster I'd lose him."

Drew nuzzled Joe's shoulder affectionately, aching for all the turmoil Joe had experienced. "I seriously doubt the thought would even cross his mind. Hell, *I* know you'd never do anything like that, and he's known you years longer than I have. Your conscience and sense of honor wouldn't let you."

Joe sighed again. "Yeah." He hesitated before turning to look back at Drew again. "And what about you? Why are *you* doing this? Is it just for Finn, so he doesn't lose me?"

Drew met Joe's gaze and held it while he debated about how to respond. He wasn't sure Joe was ready to hear the truth—hell, he wasn't sure he was ready to admit it aloud—but Joe needed reassurance, and Drew didn't see the point in hiding how he felt. All three of them needed to be honest with each other or else the hurt and resentment would pile up fast.

"Maybe it started out that way," he said at last. "But I haven't been doing this for Finn for a while now. I've been doing it because you need me, and I want to help." He drew in a deep breath and released it slowly, bracing himself for what he was about to say. "I've been doing it because I fell in love with you."

Joe stared at him, his eyes growing wide with surprise. He was at a loss for words for at least a minute, and when he finally spoke, it was hesitant. "You... love me? Really? How can you, after the horrible way I've treated you?"

"Because I'm a sucker for an honorable man who needs me as much as you do," Drew said, offering a wry smile. "Besides, Finn and I both knew there was something bigger going on. I figured out pretty quick not to take it personally."

Joe was quiet again for a moment. "I don't feel like I deserve it, but... thank you. I wish I could say the words back to you, but I can't.

Not now, at least. But I meant it when I said I cared about you, Drew. You've done something for me that no one else, not even Finn, ever has. It means a lot to me."

Drew felt a twinge of disappointment that Joe didn't return his feelings, but only a twinge, and he wasn't surprised. Joe had pretty much hated him at first, so the fact that Joe cared about him *at all* now was a huge improvement.

"When we get home, Finn and I are going to work on rewiring your thinking about what you deserve," he said, giving Joe a gentle squeeze. "It's okay that you can't say the words. There's no rush. Not for that or for this," he added, stroking Joe's inner thigh. "I want to give you what you need, not force you to give me something you're not ready for."

Joe shivered at the caress and then reached back to comb his fingers through Drew's hair. "I do need you," he said softly. "I just had an attack of conscience, thinking about Finn. But I'm not worried about that anymore. If you want me... I'm yours."

"Not yet," Drew said, grinning wickedly as he wormed his hand beneath the waistband of Joe's sweatpants. "But you will be...."

28

Finn stared intently at his TV screen, his fingers dancing over the control console as he worked through a difficult level of his new Super Mario Brothers game. Making his way past the game's obstacles was enough of a mental challenge to help him forget his limited mobility thanks to the cast on his leg, but it didn't wear him out. He'd learned the hard way that his stamina wasn't up to normal levels yet postsurgery when he'd tried to make what he thought would be a quick run to the convenience store down the block. He'd hobbled on his crutches for maybe ten or so meters beyond the entrance of his building before he realized he'd never make it to the store and back, so he'd returned to his apartment and called Herc to take him up on the offer to arrange some useful services.

He'd thought Herc would set up a grocery delivery, but instead, he now had a housekeeper and a personal chef. The housekeeper had spent the better part of a week deep cleaning his apartment, and Finn had never felt more shame for his negligent attitude toward housework than when she pointedly stared at him while carrying the second garbage bag she'd filled out of his bedroom. Now she only came three mornings per week for routine cleaning, and in the

interim, Finn made more of an effort to tidy up after himself, especially since he liked how clean and organized his apartment looked.

After the first day with his housekeeper, he'd felt apprehensive about
meeting his personal chef, and he was relieved when Ezra "Ghost" Levin
arrived with canvas bags of groceries in hand. Ezra had gone to culinary
school with the intentions of being a chef after he retired from Hercules
Security, but that plan hadn't worked out as intended, so now he headed
the training facility Herc had set up outside of DC. Ezra was an excellent
cook, and he made sure Finn ate well—and far more healthily than the
pizza Finn routinely had delivered when he was on his own.

At first, Finn loitered around the kitchen when Ezra was in there
in hopes of getting a taste of whatever Ezra was preparing, but he
became so fascinated by the process that Ezra started giving him
cooking lessons so he could stop relying so much on takeout.

Ezra wasn't the only merc to visit Finn, either. Finn got calls and
texts asking if he was up for visitors almost every day, and he had
company whenever he wanted it. Payne was one of the regulars,
which wasn't surprising since Payne was also a medic and had strong
caretaker instincts. When he needed distraction from worrying about
Joe and Drew, or when he felt himself chafing against the restrictions
of his recuperation process, Finn called on the mercs. They always
came through.

But at night, he was left alone with his thoughts, which constantly
strayed to Pakistan. He was relieved when Drew texted to let him
know the mission was finished, but his relief was tempered by
concern over Joe. Rather than coming straight home, Joe and Drew
were staying in Pakistan for an undetermined amount of time, and
while Drew was keeping him updated and it sounded like Joe was
doing better, Finn was ready to see for himself. He hated not being
there when Joe needed him most, and he wasn't sure how he could
ever repay Drew for helping Joe in his stead.

He finally finished the level and paused the game, debating
whether he wanted to keep playing, or see if anyone was available to
come over. The last time they'd talked, Drew had been evasive about

when he and Joe might be returning home, which was disappointing and discouraging. His friends had rallied around him, but that didn't take the place of being able to snuggle up with his lovers and reassure himself they were both okay.

Before he could make up his mind, the doorbell rang, and he grabbed his crutches, hauled himself upright, and hobbled over to answer the door.

To his surprise, Joe stood on the welcome mat, with Drew right behind him. Drew had a hand on Joe's shoulder, as though offering support or encouragement, and Joe wore a pensive expression, as though uncertain of his welcome. He also looked paler and thinner than he had three weeks before, and there were lines beside his mouth that Finn had never seen.

"Surprise," Joe said softly, his lips quirking up in a lopsided attempt at a smile. "We're home."

Instinct and emotion took over. Finn dropped his crutches and threw his arms around Joe. His throat closed up, and his eyes stung with tears as he clung to Joe, relief and joy roiling through him.

"You're home," he echoed, pressing his nose against Joe's neck so he could breathe in Joe's warm, familiar scent.

Finn felt Joe's strong arms around him, holding him close and tight. Joe gave a shuddering sigh and then pressed his lips against Finn's temple. "I missed you."

"I missed you, too." Finn closed his eyes and leaned against Joe, grateful to have Joe in his arms safe and sound at last. "I was worried about you."

"I was worried about you, too." Joe's voice was deep and ragged. "And Drew, poor bastard, was worried about both of us."

Finn pulled back enough that he could smile at Drew, feeling torn. He wanted to embrace Drew as well, but he didn't want to hurt Joe. From what little he'd heard over the past couple of weeks, it sounded like they had at least struck a truce, so maybe it would be okay under the circumstances.

"I missed you, too," he said as he hopped over to Drew, who

reached out immediately to steady him. "I'm glad you're both home safe."

"It's good to be home," Drew said, pulling him into a tight embrace. "But maybe we can continue this reunion inside? You need to sit down."

"Definitely," Joe agreed. He swiped away what might have been tears from his eyes and smiled more naturally. "We're going to have to keep an eye on him, Drew. Finn is a great medic and a lousy patient, trust me."

Finn shot a startled look at Joe, surprised by his inclusive wording. Maybe things had gone even better between them than he thought? He didn't want to get his hopes up too high, though, so he decided not to comment. Instead, he stuck out his tongue at Joe.

"I've been good," he said. "Mostly."

"Uh-huh." Drew raised a dubious eyebrow as he released Finn and bent to pick up the crutches.

"Come on, you." Joe wrapped an arm around Finn's waist. "I'll help you to the couch, then we can talk."

Finn let Joe assist him while Drew followed with the crutches. He claimed the middle spot and patted the cushions on either side to make sure they both sat beside him and no one retreated to the nearby recliner chairs.

Joe sat down on the left, sighing as he relaxed back against the sofa cushions, putting one hand gently on Finn's thigh above the cast. "How are you doing, really?" he asked, his brown eyes full of concern. "Are you having much pain? Are you getting around okay?"

Finn covered Joe's hand with his own and offered a reassuring smile. "I'm doing good. The pain isn't as bad as it was right after surgery, and I can get around the apartment just fine. Herc arranged for a housekeeper to come a few times per week, Ghost's been making sure I eat healthy, and the guys have kept me company when I needed it."

"You haven't been pushing too hard, have you?" Drew asked as he settled in on Finn's other side after propping the crutches against an end table.

"No, I figured out my limits pretty quick," Finn said wryly.

"Good. You need to rest up and heal." Joe squeezed Finn's thigh lightly, as though afraid of hurting him with too much pressure. "I'm sorry I... we... haven't been here to help you. I'm sorry you've had to go through this without us."

"It's okay," Finn said, heartened anew by Joe's use of the plural. "I don't blame you. For anything," he added with a pointed look. "I know you would've stayed if I'd asked you to, but you would've been miserable, too. You felt like you needed to go after these guys. I get it. I'm just glad Drew was there for you since I couldn't be."

"I'm sorry any of this happened at all." Joe sighed, again. "But it's over now. Really over, I promise. We're all safe. And I'm telling Herc I'm done with undercover assignments. Not that I think he'll try to talk me out of it, but I can't do this anymore."

Finn felt as if a huge weight he hadn't been aware he was carrying had been lifted. "Thank God!" He blurted out the words before he could think better of it.

Drew laughed. "Thank God, indeed. I'm getting too old to be running after stubborn young'uns all the time."

Joe smiled ruefully. "You kept up all right, old man," he said to Drew. "But I never want danger to follow me home again." He looked at Finn, and his smile faded. "I could have lost you, and that would have killed me."

"But you didn't." Finn curled his fingers around Joe's and squeezed gently. He watched Joe in silence, thinking about things Drew had mentioned in recent texts and calls. "I'm sorry," he said quietly. "I wasn't there when you needed me after that first mission. Instead, I made things worse. I have a lot of regrets about that."

"It's not your fault." Joe shifted to face Finn more directly, and he returned the pressure of Finn's fingers. "You didn't know. You couldn't have. I didn't even know how much it was going to affect me, or I wouldn't have gone in the first place. It just happened, okay?" Joe drew in a breath. "Besides, it's not like I was honest with you about how I felt about you. Maybe that would have changed things. Maybe not, but it's not like you had any reason to think I'd feel so... jealous."

Finn gazed down at their joined hands and rubbed the back of Joe's with his thumb. Joe's absolution helped, but he still felt remorse over not providing the support Joe had needed. "We both have to try to communicate better, but I think we've learned from it. I have, at least. I know you're still having a rough time, and I'm going to help you get through it. I promise."

"Thanks. That means a lot," Joe said quietly. He looked past Finn at Drew and smiled crookedly. "Speaking of communicating better, I guess that's our cue?"

"Sounds reasonable." Drew gave a little huff of amusement. "Do you want to tell him, or should I?"

"Tell me what?" Finn looked back and forth between them, a little flutter of hope in his belly. He didn't want to hurt either of them, and he didn't want to go back to feeling torn and guilty about loving both of them, either.

"I guess I should start." Joe looked back at Finn, his expression growing serious. "I'm going to be completely honest here. I know I'm still messed up, and I'm going to need some therapy to help me get past the issues I still have. Things that have been around since I was a kid and led to all the stuff that messed me up when I went to Pakistan on that first mission. Drew... well, he helped me put a lot of things in perspective. He's been there for me, and it's changed the way I look at things between the three of us. Before you were kidnapped, I was seriously thinking about leaving and letting the two of you be together. I'm not saying that to hurt you, but I want you to understand where my head was."

"Do you still feel that way?" Finn asked, tightening his grip on Joe's hand. "I know we have different perspectives on love, but I do love you, and I don't want to lose you."

"Like I said, my viewpoint has changed a bit," Joe replied. "Drew has been a rock, which I didn't expect, to be honest, and I've come to trust him. We talked a lot."

"We did." Drew agreed. "I could understand a lot of what he was going through, because of what I went through when Stack died. I could see how much he was hurting."

Finn offered Drew a grateful smile. "I'm glad you were there," he said, and then he turned back to Joe. "And I'm glad you let him be there."

"I almost didn't let him, but he's a persistent bastard." Joe shook his head. "He's helped me get past the first hurdle or two in dealing with my issues. But...." He looked at Drew again. "I think this part is on you."

Drew rolled his eyes. "I keep telling you, you don't have to worry about it. Finn, what Joe is being so cagey about is that I've come to feel that he really is *our* dumbass. God knows why, but I've fallen for the big lug."

"There's just something about him," Finn said, unable to hold back a wide smile. "What can you do, right?" He gave an exaggerated shrug.

"Yeah, well, he pressed all my buttons," Drew grumbled, but there was a gleam of amusement in his eyes. "Go on, Joe, tell him the rest."

"I needed Drew, and he was there," Joe admitted. "We slept together."

"Wait...." Finn closed his eyes as he tried to process what he'd just heard. Given Joe's perspective on love and sex, Finn never dreamed Joe might have actually slept with Drew already. "My mind is officially blown," he said as he opened his eyes so he could stare at Joe. "Does that mean you've fallen for him, too? *Please* don't tell me you're wallowing in guilt over it, because I'll kick your ass if you are, cast or no cast."

Joe looked a little uncomfortable. "I can't honestly say I'm in love with him, no. But I do care about him. He's not... he's not what I thought he would be. It took me a long time to accept that he wasn't trying to come between us, and that he really does love you."

"I'm not entirely sure he's accepted that I love *him*, too," Drew said, looking at Finn. "We're going to have to work on him, you and I. I think he's only accepted that you love him because you've been there for him for so many years. But I'm going to do my best to convince him he deserves to be loved."

"He does." Finn nodded and swallowed hard, scarcely able to

believe Joe and Drew had come so far. He didn't want to celebrate prematurely, but he finally had some hope for a future that wasn't divided and compartmentalized. "We'll prove it to him," he added, no longer feeling reticent about reaching for Drew's hand as well and squeezing it tight.

Drew squeezed back. "We will. See, Joe? I told you it would be okay. He was worried you'd be hurt, Finn. Not about us sleeping together, but about me loving him and him caring about me."

"Yeah, well...." Joe shrugged uncomfortably. "I guess I've got a sort of blind spot when it comes to Finn. But there are a couple of other things we need to discuss. All three of us."

"Whatever you want to talk about, I'm open," Finn said, trying not to sound overeager. The last thing he wanted to do was make Joe feel rushed or pressured into something he wasn't ready for. "We'll go at your pace. You know that, right?"

"I know." This time Joe nodded. "Drew and I talked on the plane home. If you want, we're willing to work out a way for the three of us to be together. Maybe share a house or apartment, something where we can each have our own space if we want. Everything will be out in the open, so there are no misunderstandings. If we're all honest with each other, even about feelings like jealousy or neglect, then we might can make it work. Are you interested in that?"

"Yes!" The word burst out of Finn, verging on an excited shout, and he squeezed Joe and Drew's hands hard and tight. "Yes, I'm interested. I love you both so much, and if the three of us could be together...." His voice caught in his throat, and his eyes stung as he looked back and forth between them with a watery smile. "It would be a dream come true."

"There's a condition," Drew warned. "And this matters to Joe a lot. Like, deal-breaker important."

"What is it?"

Joe's expression was pensive. "I'm willing to work on this if it's the three of us, but I can't deal with you having hookups, too. I'm sorry, and if you can't accept that, I'll understand. It's going to be complicated enough trying to find a dynamic that works for all of three of us, especially with me in therapy and you still recovering from your injuries and having to undergo physical therapy for months. Neither Drew nor I are interested in any outside action, so to speak. If we're going to settle down, it's got to be all of us."

Finn sagged with relief. "No, that's fair, and I'm willing to forego outside action. In fact...."

He released their hands and leaned forward to grab his phone off the coffee table. He opened his dating app and went to the settings. Holding out his phone so they could both see the screen, he went through the steps to delete his account, before closing the app and deleting that as well.

"Done," he said as he tossed his phone back on the coffee table. "The two of you are worth it."

Joe's shoulders slumped, and it was only then Finn noticed how tense he'd been, and how hard it must have been for Joe to make that condition. Joe had never given Finn any kind of limits before, and he had probably been dreading Finn's reaction. "Thank you."

"Damn right we're worth it," Drew said. "Wise choice."

"I think it'll go down as the best decision I ever made." Finn's smile was wide and happy as he rested one hand on Joe's leg and the other on Drew's. "Anything else? Any other ground rules or conditions?"

"Just that we all be honest." Joe smiled slightly. "I know I'll have to work on my communication skills, but I'm going to try."

"So will I," Drew nodded. "I'm sure it's going to take some adjustment, but I love you both. I want this to work. I'm sure it will, if we're all on the same page. But what about you, Finn? Any requests or rules you want to toss into the pot?"

"I can't think of anything right now," Finn said, shaking his head. "But this'll be an ongoing process. Let's start with honesty and open communication as the foundation and go from there."

"That sounds reasonable." Now that everything had been settled, Joe seemed to relax. He slid an arm around Finn's shoulders and hugged him. "So now you'll have the two of us to take care of you. Think you can stand both of us hovering over you?"

"You hover, I *supervise*," Drew corrected him. "I was an XO, after all."

At that, Joe stuck out his tongue at Drew. "Yeah, yeah. Keep telling yourself that!"

Finn nestled between them, far happier and more content than he had ever thought possible. Drew was exactly what he and Joe needed to complete their little circle, and to Finn, a white-picket-fence scenario for three sounded just right.

29

"There. That's perfect."

Joe surveyed his handiwork with satisfaction. The table was set, the candles were lit, and in the kitchen, a big pot of jambalaya simmered in a crock pot. He'd already made cornbread to go with it, and all he had to do was pop it back in the oven to warm it. Beer, wine, and iced tea were available, and for dessert he'd picked up a positively sinful chocolate cake from a bakery in the French Quarter. Now all he needed was for Finn and Drew to get home, and they could celebrate the first night in their new home.

There had been a lot of changes in the last six months, but they were good ones, for the most part. Joe had started therapy with a psychologist associated with Hercules Security, and talking about his problems honestly to someone was helping him deal with both his past trauma and his more recent ones. It hadn't been easy, but Joe had forced himself to go to every appointment and be as open as he could. The work had definitely helped him make peace with a lot of the things he'd been through, to put them behind him and move on.

It had also helped to have the support of both Finn and Drew. Either one or both of them had always been there after the therapy sessions to help Joe decompress, and Joe had learned quickly that having two lovers for support and comfort really was better than just one. In fact, it hadn't taken long for the three of them to all end up having sex together, and while there had been moments of doubt and jealousy, they had settled into a relationship that was both warm and comfortable for all of them. Drew and Finn had been careful to move at Joe's pace, but they'd never made him feel that they were impatient with his naturally cautious approach to things, and the result, he thought, had been worth the wait.

The biggest change, however, had been when Herc had approached the three of them about leaving field work behind and starting up a branch of Hercules Security in New Orleans. With the enormous number of tourists and conventioneers that rolled into town on a regular basis, as well as the work available in the rest of the southeastern states, having a satellite office to coordinate things with the main office in Raleigh was not only logical, it had become necessary. It hadn't taken much to convince them to do it, either. Drew and Joe were more than ready to leave field work behind to handle administration, and Finn's caretaker tendencies and charm made him a natural to handle clients and agents alike.

So they'd left Raleigh behind, and with the money of the three of them pooled together, they had been able to afford to build a house on a lovely piece of land outside the city, surrounded with live oaks dripping with Spanish moss. Everything about the house was scaled for three large men, including a huge bathtub and shower in the master bedroom, and a custom-made bed that would hold all three of them. There were also separate, smaller bedrooms, so they each had their own space and privacy when needed. They'd gone to settlement that very morning, the house being in all their names, and afterward Finn and Drew had gone into the office to deal with business while Joe had come home to finish the last of the unpacking and make dinner. He'd also had an errand to run, though he hadn't mentioned that to the others—it was a surprise that he hoped they would welcome.

The front door opened, and the sound of Drew's deep voice

followed by Finn's hearty laughter drifted down the hall, punctuated by their footsteps on the hardwood floor.

"Honey, we're home!" Finn called out.

"Something smells awful good," Drew added.

"Come on back to the kitchen!" Joe called out as he picked up a towel to wipe his hands. He couldn't help the wide smile that curved his lips, and his heartbeat sped up in anticipation.

"Dinner's almost ready!"

"What about dessert?" Finn asked as he entered the kitchen and made a beeline for Joe. "Got anything hot and sweet for us?" He grinned playfully and slid his arms around Joe's waist.

Joe enveloped Finn in a bear hug. "That's second dessert." He kissed Finn's smiling lips, then lifted his head to leer at Drew. "First dessert is chocolate."

Drew came up behind and sandwiched Joe between the two of them, stretching out his arms so he could reach Finn as well as Joe in the embrace. "I don't know about you guys, but I'm tempted to skip straight to *second dessert*," he said, nuzzling the back of Joe's neck.

With a happy hum, Joe leaned into the nuzzling. He'd quickly come to enjoy being in the middle of Finn and Drew, to feel himself enveloped in their warmth and strength. There had been more than one night when he'd come back from therapy completely raw and aching, and the two of them hadn't hesitated to sandwich him in a supportive, comforting embrace.

"I could be persuaded, since the food can wait." He raised a brow at Finn. "What's your vote?"

"You know what they say. Life's short. Eat dessert first." Finn leaned in and nibbled Joe's earlobe.

Chuckling, Joe slid his hands down to Finn's ass and squeezed it. "All right! Second dessert first, since we do have something to celebrate. Maybe a couple of somethings, actually."

Finn wriggled happily against Joe's hands. "New house... and what else?"

Joe turned to look over his shoulder at Drew. "Why don't we adjourn to the bedroom? I have something to ask you both."

Drew's eyebrows climbed almost to his hairline, but he didn't ask any questions, only nodded. "Sure, let's go."

"Nothing's wrong, is it?" Finn asked, a flash of concern in his eyes.

"No, not at all!" Joe hastened to reassure Finn, smiling and shaking his head. "It's a surprise." He glanced back at Drew again. "One I hope you both will like."

"If it involves you and the bedroom, I'm sure we will." Drew's answering smile was wicked, and he rocked his hips against Joe's ass.

"Definitely," Finn said, relief suffusing his expression.

Laughing, Joe pressed back against Drew's crotch, wriggled, and then released Finn. "Okay, let's head to the bedroom."

Once they were in the big master suite, Joe directed Finn and Drew to sit down on the bed. He crossed to the dresser and picked up a long, flat black box. Holding his breath, he took his place between the two of them. His heart hammered in anticipation, but he thought —hoped—that this was something they would both be happy about.

"Since we've started a new life here together, I wanted to do something to begin it in a special way." He looked at Finn, gazing into his familiar, beloved green eyes. "I love you, Finn. You're my first love, my joy, and my light. You know that, don't you?"

"Yeah, I know, you big smooshball," Finn said, but his eyes were warm with affection, and he slid his arm around Joe's waist and squeezed him tight.

"Good." Joe leaned in to kiss Finn on the forehead. "I wanted to make sure." He turned his gaze to Drew, taking a moment to admire the strength he always saw in Drew, the steady, unwavering support. "Drew, it's taken me far too long to say this, but I love you, too. I fell in love with your determination, your compassion, your commitment. You've become my rock, my shelter, and my source of strength when my own seems lost. Thank you."

Drew's surprised expression swiftly softened into quiet joy, and he gazed at Joe with a wavery smile. "My pleasure," he said, cupping Joe's cheek in his palm. "I love you, too."

Joe leaned in to kiss Drew gently. "I'm the luckiest man in the world, to have the two of you love me. And to love each other. That's why I wanted to start off our lives here with something to show our bond. Finn always said I was the white-picket-fence type, the marrying kind, and I guess that's still true. Maybe the three of us can't have a legal marriage, but... well, that's just details, right? What matters is what the three of us feel."

With that Joe opened the box, holding it so both Finn and Drew could see the contents. Nestled on black velvet were three identical rings, their surfaces pure, gleaming platinum. "I had them inscribed on the inside with today's date, our three initials, and *Love Knows No Bounds.*" He looked between the two of them. "What do you think?"

Finn wrapped both arms around Joe and squeezed hard enough almost to take Joe's breath away. Drew stared at the rings as if he couldn't believe what he was seeing.

"I think," Drew said slowly as he reached out to stroke one of the rings as if testing to make sure it was real, "you should put that ring on my finger because I'm ready to say 'I do'."

"I do, too," Finn said, still clinging tightly to Joe.

Happiness greater than anything Joe had ever felt before washed over him in a warm wave, and his eyes prickled. "Thank you. Both of you," he murmured. "I hoped that's how you would feel, but hearing you both say it... I feel like my heart could burst."

"I should be thanking you," Drew said, swiping at his eyes. "I wasn't sure what the rest of my life was going to look like after I left Lawson & Greer. But somehow I found the two of you. You're my family. My home. I love you both more than I ever thought possible."

Joe picked Drew's ring out of the box—slightly smaller than his, but larger than Finn's—and held it up. "We love you, too. Come on, Finn, let's hogtie this one before he comes to his senses and tries to get away."

"Definitely," Finn said, his smile wide and joyful as he clasped Drew's left hand. He brought it to his lips and then held it out so Joe could place the ring while Drew watched and started to sniffle.

His heart full, Joe smiled and slid the ring onto Drew's finger. "And Finn called *me* a smooshball." When the ring was in place, he leaned down so he could also kiss Drew's hand. "There. You're ours now, forever."

Drew gazed down at the ring with wonderment in his eyes, and then he looked up at them and nodded. "Forever," he said, reaching for Finn's hand. He lifted it and brushed a kiss against his knuckles. "Time to show the world this one's off the market for good. Can you believe it?" He grinned at Joe as he offered Finn's hand.

"I'm sure there are broken hearts all over Raleigh," Joe agreed. He picked up Finn's ring, gazing into Finn's eyes as he slid it on to his finger. "I've waited for this for a long time. Now you belong to me and Drew, and we'll do our best to make you happy." With that, he kissed Finn's hand.

"I'm yours," Finn said, glancing back and forth between Joe and Drew as he squeezed Joe's fingers tight. " And I've never been happier." He released Joe's hand and retrieved the third ring from the box. "Now it's your turn."

"You're ours." Drew clasped Joe's hand and pressed a kiss to his palm. "We're yours. You'll always have a safe haven with us."

With that, Finn slid the ring onto Joe's finger.

Despite his teasing of Drew, Joe felt his own eyes prickling as Drew and Finn claimed him as theirs. He gripped their hands tightly. "Thank you. Both of you. This is... everything I ever wanted, even if it wasn't anything I'd ever imagined. And now none of us ever has to feel alone, ever again."

"Never again." Finn wound his arms around Joe's shoulders and leaned in to claim a kiss while Drew shifted closer and slid one arm around Joe's waist.

Joe returned Finn's kiss, parting his lips and deepening it with a moan. Here, between the two men who loved him, he'd finally found the acceptance and safety he'd always wanted. He'd never imagined it would take two men to fully complete him, but it had—and together the three of them were stronger than they ever could have been as only two.

When he pulled back from the kiss, he smiled at Finn tenderly before looking back at Drew with a wicked smirk. "I think it's time for something else, too. Something I've been thinking about quite a bit lately."

"A honeymoon at a clothing optional beach resort?" Finn asked with a cheeky grin, and Drew let out a loud snort.

"That does sound good," Joe admitted. He lifted one hand to lay it against Drew's cheek. "But I was thinking of something a little closer to home. Namely... I think it's time for Drew to make me his in every sense of the word."

Joe had never let anyone top him before. It wasn't Finn's preference, so he'd never suggested it, but now he wanted Drew to be the one to do it. He wanted to let Drew care for him in every way possible.

Drew's eyebrows drew together in a puzzled frown. "I don't follow. Isn't that what the ring is for?"

"Yes and no," Joe said. "The ring is definitely a symbol, but I wanted to give you something special. I want you to fuck me. No one else has ever done that before."

Drew sucked in a startled breath, and Finn's eyes grew wide.

"Seriously?" Finn asked, his tone incredulous.

Drew covered Joe's hand with his own, his expression softening. "You don't have to. I know you're mine."

"I know I don't have to. I want to." Joe had been expecting Drew to be doubtful, and he smiled reassuringly. "I've seen how you are with Finn. How you take care of him, the way you look at him. I want that, too." He glanced at Finn once more, needing to make sure this was something that wouldn't make Finn feel jealous or uncomfortable. "Are you okay with it? It's not something I ever offered you, I know, but you never seemed to want to top anyway."

"You could offer on my birthday, at least," Finn teased. "But no, I'm pretty much the bottomiest bottom who ever bottomed. I'm fine with you letting Drew top when you're in the mood." He leaned in and nuzzled Joe's ear. "You're right, he takes good care of me, and he'll take good care of you, too."

"Thank you." Joe pressed a kiss to Finn's cheek. "So that's settled.

All that remains is if you want me that way, Drew. If you don't, that's fine. I know I caught you by surprise."

"No, I do!" Drew said quickly with a vehement nod. "I'd love to. I wanted to make sure this wasn't stemming from some weird sense of obligation or fairness, that's all."

Joe laughed. "Finn can tell you, I'm not one to offer something like *that* just out of a sense of obligation or fairness!" He gazed into Drew's eyes, not holding back the love he felt. "I want it. I want you. Not for any other reason than I want it and want it to be something for us."

Drew's answering smile was warm, and his eyes were full of affection. "I like that idea."

"Thank you." Joe felt a sense of rightness, of anticipation. Not that he'd expected Drew to refuse, but knowing Drew did want him that way was satisfying. "So what are you waiting for?"

"We have to get you naked first." Finn wormed his hands beneath Joe's T-shirt and tugged it up, his face alight with eagerness.

"That would definitely help," Drew said as he reached out to help Finn get the shirt off.

Laughing, Joe raised his arms to aid in their efforts. "Naked is good." Once his shirt was tossed aside, he reached out to help Finn with his tie. "And the two of you are wearing a lot more than I am!"

Drew slanted a coy smile at Joe. "Wanna watch while we rectify that?"

"Oh yes." Joe pulled Finn's tie from around his neck, holding it up and waggling his eyebrows at Drew. "Put on a good enough show, and maybe I'll let you two tie me up for a change."

"Oh, hell, yeah!" Finn's grin grew even wider as he shifted to face Drew and rose up on his knees. "We can do that, can't we?"

"Damned right we can." Drew rested his forefinger just under Finn's chin. "Let's start with your jacket," he said as he trailed his finger along the length of Finn's throat, and Finn tilted his chin up, his eyes going half-lidded in response.

"You got it." Finn leaned in to keep in contact with Drew's

stroking finger as he shrugged his jacket off his shoulders and down his arms.

Joe licked his lips, his arousal mounting in a slow burn as he watched the two of them together. The first time he'd done it, it had felt awkward, even a little embarrassing, like being caught watching porn. But that had been swiftly overcome by a sensation of fascination, as he'd been able to see both their expressions, watch the heat and pleasure building between them. And he'd seen the love, too, and that had somehow made everything so much better. After that, it was the most natural thing in the world to join in, for the three of them to be together and let their passions go wherever they pleased.

He scooted back on the mattress, out of the way, so that they could reach each other more easily. "So far so good."

Once Finn tossed his jacket to the floor, Drew slid his finger into Finn's collar and tugged, and Finn obediently scooted closer, a flush of arousal already rising in his cheeks. Drew sat back on his heels, giving Finn an exaggerated look of appraisal, as if he was considering his options, and finally, he shrugged.

"You've got other shirts," he said, and then he grasped the front of Finn's shirt with both hands and yanked hard enough to send the buttons flying.

Joe chuckled, though the display made his arousal flare hotter. He'd found that he liked seeing Drew's displays of strength. "My, my, someone's eager."

Drew flashed a hungry grin at Joe. "Do you blame me? I've got him here in front of me and you lying there like a waiting banquet."

"I know. The two of us are simply too much hotness to resist. Aren't we, Finn?" Joe grinned wickedly.

"Hell, yeah, we are," Finn said, arching his back as he stripped off his shirt.

"Shoes and socks next." Drew licked his lips as he gazed at Finn's bare chest. "After that, I think you should take off your own pants and underwear. Slowly."

"Definitely. Strip for us." Joe leaned forward, watching avidly. Finn was sexy as hell, and he was a natural tease. He'd stripped for them in the past, and every time it made both Drew and Joe crazy with desire.

Finn scooted to the edge of the bed and removed his shoes and socks, then he stood up and struck a pose in front of the mirrored closet door. He cocked his hip, putting his ass on display in the mirror while he slid his flattened palms slowly down his chest to the waistband of his pants.

"Is this what you want?" Finn darted his tongue out to wet his lips, his eyes glowing with banked heat as he looked at the two of them on the bed. "To shamelessly ogle me?"

"Yeah, that's what we want." Joe moved again, shifting to sit next to Drew, threading one hand into Drew's hair. He leaned down to nip at Drew's throat before slanting a glance at Finn. "It makes us hot, doesn't it, Drew?"

Drew closed his eyes briefly, his lips curving in a soft smile while Joe stroked his hair, and when he opened his eyes again and spoke, his voice was husky. "Fuck yeah."

"Well, I guess I should give you what you want." Finn ducked his head and peeked at them from beneath his lashes in a show of coyness, but he was already unfastening his fly. He slid his fingers beneath the waistband of his boxer briefs and shimmied his hips as he eased his pants and underwear down at the same time.

"Now that's what we wanted to see." Joe drew in a breath, admiring the sight of Finn's body as he revealed it inch by torturous inch. No matter how often Joe got to see Finn naked, he couldn't help but be turned on by it. "God, you're gorgeous."

Finn gave them a playful wink as he turned and bent over just enough to give them an unobstructed view as he slid the fabric over the curve of his ass and down to his firm thighs. Finally, he stripped off his pants and boxer briefs and tossed them aside. He stood unabashedly naked in front of them, his fists on his hips and his cock already half hard.

"Now what?" he asked.

"Now you get that pert little ass over here and undress me," Drew said, a growl underlying his voice.

Joe released Drew's hair with a final caress and moved back a bit. "Yeah, take his clothes off, and let's see how crazy you can drive him in the process. You're good at that, Finn."

"You want me to get him primed for you?" Finn sauntered back to the bed, smirking at Joe with every step. "I can do that."

He climbed onto the bed and straddled Drew's lap, and Drew caressed his bare back until he was arching into each stroke like a greedy cat.

"Just who is priming whom?" Joe asked, reaching out to stroke Finn's arm. "And Drew isn't getting any more naked." Despite his words, he was enjoying the show. He'd discovered that he liked seeing Finn being pleasured, no matter whether it was Drew or himself doing it.

"Mmm... sorry." But Finn's languid smile said he didn't regret anything. "You heard the taskmaster," he said, sliding the length of Drew's silk tie between his fingers. "I have to do my duty."

Drew leaned back on his hands, fixing Finn with a challenging stare. "So you'd better get busy."

Finn unknotted Drew's tie and whipped it out from beneath Drew's collar. When he was done, he looped it around his own neck. "I'm not going to indulge in showy displays," he said with a haughty sniff, and he stuck his nose in the air as he unfastened the top button of Drew's shirt. "Unlike some people."

"I think someone needs to be spanked," Joe commented to Drew. "What do you think?"

"I think we could spank him every day and it wouldn't do a lick of good," Drew said even as he swatted Finn's ass.

Finn laughed and wriggled his hips against Drew's hand. "I'm in favor of daily spankings."

"See?" Drew smacked Finn's ass again, harder this time, and a flush spread from Finn's face down his neck and bloomed on his chest in response.

"Do you want me to undress you or not?" Finn's voice had a breathless edge as he continued unbuttoning Drew's shirt.

"If you want a spanking, you have to earn it," Drew said, sliding his hands down to rest on Finn's hips.

"Yeah, so far you're not doing much in that regard," Joe observed. He leaned back on his elbows and raised an imperious brow. "If you want to tie me up, you're going to have to do a lot better."

Drew glanced over at Joe and chuckled. "You're going to be the toppiest bottom ever."

"I sense a power bottom in the making," Finn said as he slid his fingers beneath the folds of Drew's shirt and eased it over his shoulders and down his arms, caressing Drew's skin every inch of the way.

Joe watched avidly, loving the way Drew shivered beneath Finn's touch, the way his skin began to flush as his arousal grew. "You two look so hot together."

"Of course we do," Drew replied. He leaned in to nuzzle Finn's neck and then bit down at the junction of Finn's neck and shoulder.

Finn let out a soft cry and clutched Drew's shoulders as a shudder rippled through him. "Keep that up, and I'll be done before you're undressed," he said, sounding breathless.

"Drew, behave. I know it's hard, but...." Joe warned teasingly. "Besides, maybe we can both put our marks on him later."

"Oh, all right." Drew grumbled and raised his head. "It's not helping me get any more naked, anyway."

Smirking, Finn slithered his way along Drew's body and off the bed, where he knelt in front of Drew. "We need these off before we can get to any of the fun parts," he said as he began removing Drew's shoes and socks.

Drew obligingly lifted first one foot, then the other, while Joe scooted forward enough to caress Drew's back. He leaned in and put his chin on Drew's shoulder so he could watch Finn. "You're not the only one who likes to bite," he murmured, his lips close to Drew's ear. "I fully intend to mark you up tonight."

Drew's breathing hitched. "I'm good with that. Very good."

Finn's smirk grew wider as he rose up on his knees and slid his hands along Drew's thighs from knee to hip. "I can't wait to see that," he said.

Joe drew back and pushed at Drew's shoulder. "Neither can I. Go on, let him get those pants off you. I'm anxious for you to fuck me."

"Probably no more so than I am to do it," Drew replied, caressing Finn's hair. He rose to his feet. "The boss has spoken."

Finn licked his lips, his eyes alight with desire, as he began unfastening the fly of Drew's pants, and he didn't waste any time in helping Drew out of both pants and boxer briefs at the same time.

"Your wish, etcetera, etcetera," he said, gesturing to Drew with an elaborate flourish. "He's all yours."

Drew turned, and the smile he was wearing was positively predatory. "And Joe is all ours," he said to Finn. He rubbed his hands together. "Where are those ties? We're going to get those sweatpants off him, then tie his hands to the bedposts."

Joe licked his lips, his arousal doubling as he watched the two of them. The look in Drew's eyes was hungry, and seeing that directed at him was a heady feeling. "I guess you've earned it."

Finn grasped the ends of Drew's tie that was still draped around his neck and slid it back and forth as he mirrored the predatory smile. "What'd you do with the other one?" he asked.

Joe looked back over his shoulder. "Ah, there it is," he said, grabbing it and holding it up. "Is this what you want, Finn my boy? What'll you do for it?"

"Now who's the greedy one?" Finn climbed back onto the bed and knelt beside Joe, still playing with the tie. "I already earned it."

Joe reached out to caress Finn's chest. Unlike he and Drew, Finn had little body hair, and Joe loved to touch his silken skin. "You did. Can I add a kiss for tax, though?"

"That's fair." Finn cupped Joe's cheek in his palm and leaned in to offer a kiss that was slow and deep.

Joe closed his eyes, returning the kiss. He held back nothing of his love or desire for Finn, and when they finally moved apart, he was breathless. "That'll do," he said, and handed Finn the tie.

Drew, not to be outdone, leaned in for a kiss of his own, and Joe reached out to twine his fingers in Drew's hair as he kissed Drew back, giving a little growl of need. He felt Finn's hands at his hips, tugging at the waistband of his sweatpants, and he obligingly lifted his hips so that Finn could strip them away.

Drew broke the kiss with a little nip of Joe's lower lip. "Now that you're naked, we're going to tie you up and pleasure you until you scream. Right, Finn?"

Finn's only response was a wicked grin as he grasped Joe's left arm and swiftly secured his wrist to the bedpost. "How does that feel?" he asked, running his forefinger along the tender underside of Joe's arm. "Too tight or just right?"

Joe sucked in a breath, goosebumps breaking out over his arm at the light touch. "Just right," he said. He tested the bond, surprised at how secure the silk tie was holding him. "That should work."

"Good." Drew took Joe's right arm and bound it to the other top bedpost and then mirrored Finn's caress down his arm. "Oh, you look amazing like this."

"Gorgeous," Finn said, his eyes alight with hunger. He leaned over and left a trail of nipping kisses along the same path he'd traced with his finger, pausing to tease the soft, sensitive crease of Joe's inner elbow. "You've marked me up so much. Maybe I should return the favor."

"Maybe you should." Drew rested his flattened palm on Joe's chest, an anticipatory smile curving his lips. "You start there. I'll start here," he said, and without warning, he swooped down and captured Joe's nipple in his teeth.

Joe cried out, arching up from the mattress. He clutched at the bonds, the pleasure with an edge of pain making arousal coil tightly inside him. "Yes! More!"

Drew's chuckle vibrated against Joe's skin, intensifying the sensation of his sharp teeth teasing and tugging Joe's nipple. On Joe's other side, Finn continued kissing his way along Joe's body until he reached Joe's other nipple, which he fastened onto with eager glee.

This wasn't like anything Joe had ever imagined, being unable to move his arms while his two lovers tormented him together. It felt amazing, and he was breathing hard, sweat beading on his skin as he grew hotter, need rising up right along with it. "Oh God... that feels so good!"

"We're just getting started," Drew said. "You're going to be begging long before we're finished with you."

Although they couldn't have possibly planned their strategy, Drew and Finn seemed to have choreographed their assault on Joe's body, both of them seeking out Joe's most sensitive spots to be stroked and licked and kissed from his neck to his navel. Within minutes, as Drew had predicted, Joe was so wound up and so strung out that he was begging, feeling on the verge of exploding even though neither of them had yet touched his hard, aching cock.

"Please...." he moaned, looking up at Drew. "Please... I need you now."

"What do you think?" Finn raised his head and gave Drew a questioning look. "Has he earned it?"

Drew pretended to consider the question even as he stroked his way down to Joe's inner thigh. "I don't think so, but maybe he will by the time you finish prepping him for me. You do that, and I'll be up here," he said, and he stretched out on his side and nestled close enough that he could bite down on Joe's neck.

Finn scrambled over to the nightstand to get the lube. He nudged Joe's legs apart so he could kneel between them. While Drew sucked and bit Joe's throat, Finn met Joe's eyes and made a show of slowly opening the bottle of lube and coating his fingers.

Joe had been in Finn's position so many times—it felt odd but exciting to be the one who was about to be prepped. He smiled at Finn, even as he leaned his head to the side to give Drew better access to his throat. "Do it. I want it."

Finn's lips were parted as he drew in shallow breaths, and the flush on his cheeks deepened as he reached between Joe's legs to circle his tight pucker before easing one finger in, pressing deep.

"Doing okay?" Drew lifted his head and nuzzled Joe's cheek. "If anything hurts, say so, and if you change your mind at any point, it's fine. You're still in control here."

It had felt a bit odd at first, but it didn't hurt. "I'm good," Joe said softly, leaning into the nuzzling. "I trust you both. I know you won't hurt me."

"We wouldn't hurt you *on purpose*," Finn said with an evil smirk. "But that doesn't mean we won't make you suffer." As if to emphasize his point, he began stroking Joe's prostate, sending electric jolts zinging through him.

Even though Joe had done the same thing to Finn—and more recently, to Drew—he'd never experienced it for himself. The sensation made him gasp, and he arched, pressing down against Finn's finger to send it deeper as pleasure coursed over him. "Yes! There! Right there!"

"Look at you," Drew crooned, sliding his hand down to caress Joe's taut, quivering abdomen. "It's so hot watching you let go like this."

Finn murmured his agreement as he added a second finger and stretched Joe by twisting and scissoring his fingers carefully.

Joe forced himself not to hold his breath, not to tense up at the sensation of Finn preparing him. He looked at Drew, giving him a crooked smile. "Yeah, I guess I'm kind of a control freak most of the time, huh?"

"Little bit—"

"—yeah, you are."

Finn and Drew spoke at the same time, and then Drew laughed.

"Not that we mind, but it's good to see you relax for once," he said.

Joe laughed as well, though the sound was rather breathless even to his own ears. "I put myself in your hands. Both of you," he said, looking between them with a smile. He felt safe with Finn and Drew. He knew they would take care of him, not matter what, and so he gave himself over completely to the pleasure they were giving him. "I'm yours."

"Does that mean you're ready for me?" Drew sat up and watched Joe with an anticipatory gleam in his eyes. "Or do you need more prep?"

"I can keep going." Finn widened his eyes in faux innocence even as he finger-fucked Joe harder and deeper.

Joe gasped. "I think... I'm ready," he said. Finn's fingers found that sweet spot again and sent electric tingles along every nerve in his body. "Now, Drew!"

"What did I tell you?" Finn chuckled as he moved out of the way and grabbed some tissues to wipe off his hands. "Power bottom."

But Drew's attention was focused on Joe, and he seemed to tune out the rest of the world as he took Finn's place between Joe's legs. "You have no idea how bad I want this," he said, his voice low and thrumming with a growl as he reached for the bottle of lube. "How much I want you."

"I want you, too." Need rolled over him, making Joe almost vibrate with the power of it. "Please, Drew... I need you so much!"

Drew wasted no time in coating his hard cock with lube and positioning himself over Joe. "We're gonna take it slow at first," he said, meeting and holding Joe's gaze. "Keep breathing, and if it hurts or you want to stop, tell me."

"It may hurt a little because you aren't used to it," Finn said as he settled down beside Joe, and he slid one hand down Joe's body and curled his fingers around Joe's cock. "But then it'll feel so good. I love the way you and Drew fill me up."

Joe yanked against the ties holding his hands, wishing that he could reach out and touch Finn, caress his cheek or bury his fingers his Finn's hair. Instead he smiled and then looked up at Drew, feeling his need spiral even higher as he saw his own desire reflected in Drew's eyes. "Slow is fine... so long as I feel you inside me."

Instead of responding aloud, Drew began easing into Joe, watching Joe's face intently as he did.

As Drew slowly claimed him, filling him, Joe felt more than pleasure, more than lust, even more than even love. There was a sense of rightness, of belonging, of something that he'd been missing his whole life suddenly locking into place, filling a void inside him that he'd always sensed but never been able to name. In giving himself to Drew, in having Finn there, holding him, something was made complete, something that it took *three* of them to make. No two of them would have known this—Joe had never known it himself, had never even suspected that love, that desire, was so much more than just the resonance between two people. Here, with both Finn and Drew, Joe felt complete for the first time in his life, felt the wounds of the past healing at long last. He looked up at Drew, his vision suddenly blurred, but with a smile of welcome so wide he felt it might split open his face. "Yes," he said, the word soft. "Perfect. The three of us... it's perfect."

"Perfect," Drew echoed, before he bent his head and claimed Joe's lips in a deep kiss.

"Perfect," Finn agreed as he sat up and reached over the two of them to unfasten the silk ties around Joe's wrists.

Joe returned the kiss, pouring everything he felt into it, holding back nothing of himself, not even the pieces that were broken and imperfect. As he felt his hands released, he wrapped one arm around Drew and then reached out with his other hand to grasp one of Finn's, twining their fingers together and holding on tightly. As Drew pulled back from the kiss, Joe brought Finn's hand to his lips and pressed a reverent kiss to the back of it. "Thank you. Both of you."

"Such a smooshball," Finn said, but he was smiling, and he kept hold of Joe's hand as he stretched out beside them again.

"Love you," Drew murmured against Joe's lips—and then he began to move, claiming Joe with smooth, deep thrusts.

Joe gasped, brought back to an awareness of his body and of the pleasure still there, still pulsing through him, layered with so much emotion that he could hardly contain it. "So good," he breathed, giving himself over to being claimed, to the feeling of Drew possessing him, and of Finn's hand on him, stroking him in counterpoint. His arousal burned higher, sending him toward a shining peak.

"That's it," Drew said, watching Joe's face avidly. "Let go. We've got you."

It was easy for once to do what Drew said, and Joe did, letting himself ride the spiral up and up, until ecstasy exploded through him. He cried out as he shattered, pleasure more intense than anything he could remember pulsing over him in irresistible waves. Finn stroked him until the pulses began to ebb, as if wanting to prolong his pleasure, and Drew rocked his hips in a steady rhythm to match.

"So fucking gorgeous." Drew bent to kiss Joe lightly and brushed a stray lock of hair back from his sweaty brow.

Joe opened his eyes, feeling boneless and sated, and smiled. "Mmm... yes. Both of you are fucking gorgeous. And amazing."

"And you both look gorgeous fucking," Finn said, reaching out to smack Drew's ass.

Chuckling, Joe stroked his hand down Drew's damp back. "Your turn, now. Go on, Drew... I want to see you lose yourself in me."

With a low growl, Drew began to move again, gradually increasing his tempo until he was claiming Joe with hard, powerful thrusts. Finn caught his breath and then released it on a moan as he clung to Joe.

"Yes!" Joe began to move with Drew, meeting his thrusts, sending him surging even deeper. "Now you let go. Let go for me, Drew!"

Drew thrust deep one last time, and he cried out as he obeyed. Joe saw the depths of both Drew's pleasure and love shining in his eyes.

Joe continued to move, coaxing every last bit of pleasure from Drew's body. He craned up to capture Drew's lips, kissing him gently. "Thank you."

Drew returned the kiss with equal tenderness. "Love you." He glanced over at Finn. "And you," he added as he drew back at last.

"I love you both, too." Finn rested his head on Joe's shoulder, appearing quite smug.

Chuckling, Joe turned his head to kiss Finn on the nose. "And what about you, Brian my boyo? Why do you look like the cat who ate the canary?"

"Why shouldn't I?" Finn snuggled closer while Drew got up and headed to the bathroom. "I'm in love with two sexy men who are in love with me. We're committed, and I have my own private sex show whenever I want it."

Joe shook his head even as he wrapped his arms around Finn and held him close. He knew how lucky he was, having both Finn and Drew, and it horrified him now at how close he'd come to throwing it all away before he'd even given it—given them—a chance. He shuddered, thinking about how alone he would be at this very moment if he'd done that, if both Finn and Drew hadn't been so persistent in caring for him despite his efforts to push them away.

But he didn't want to focus on that, he wanted to focus on the present, and the future. "*Nevynosimyy otrod'ye*," he muttered in Russian, just as Drew walked back into the room.

Drew laughed as he sat down on the edge of the bed and started tenderly cleaning up Joe with a warm bath cloth, and Finn glanced back and forth between them with a puzzled frown.

"What's so funny?"

"He just called you an insufferable brat," Drew said, and then he blinked innocently at Joe. "Oh, did I forget to tell you I speak Russian, and I understood you every time you called me an unwashed bastard back in the day?"

"Oh. My. God." Joe put a hand over his eyes, torn between amusement and embarrassment. He'd had no clue that Drew had understood him, and somehow he couldn't meet Drew's eyes now. "I'm sorry. I didn't know. You must think I'm a total jackass."

"Would I be wearing your ring if I thought that?" Grinning unrepentantly, Drew climbed back into bed and cuddled up on Joe's other side. "But I figured it was time for me to come clean and let you know you need to pick another language if you don't want either of us to understand your grumbling from now on."

Shaking his head, Joe chuckled. "You two. Good thing I love you both madly." He looked at Drew, raising a brow. "Speaking of coming clean, as it were, we owe Finn a little lovin', don't you think?"

Drew propped himself up on his elbow, eyeing Finn speculatively. "We could tie him up and see how long it takes to make him beg."

"Oh no. Please. Not that. Anything but that," Finn said, his voice and expression deadpan.

Laughing, Joe nodded. "Your ties are already wrecked, we might as well put them to good use," he said and then turned toward Finn and kissed him hard. He felt Drew beside him, felt Drew's lips on his neck, and reveled in the sensation of being between them, being surrounded completely in a cocoon of warmth and love.

This might not have been the relationship he would have wished for a year ago, but he had learned, however long it had taken, that three was not a crowd. Three, in fact, was exactly right.

AFTERWORD

We'd like to thank everyone who has joined us and the mercs on this literary adventure! While we aren't ruling out the possibility of additional books in the future, we're taking a break from this series for a while to concentrate on other endeavors. We hope you've enjoyed reading about Cade and his men as much as we've enjoyed writing them!

Made in the USA
Middletown, DE
19 September 2022

10754336R00245